RUTHLESS WOMEN

MELANIE BLAKE's first novel, *The Thunder Girls*, was a top-ten bestseller before being adapted into a successful stage play. She regularly writes columns for national newspapers and has co-created over 40 hours of syndicated television, but is best-known within the entertainment industry as the 'Queen of Soaps'. Her London-based talent agency represents more award-winning actresses from major UK dramas than any other, and her current client list includes stars of *Coronation Street*, *EastEnders*, *Emmerdale* and *Hollyoaks* as well as legendary US drama *Dynasty*. A true insider, Melanie has seen everything that goes on behind the velvet rope of showbiz. And now, through her writing, she's sharing those secrets...

Also by Melanie Blake

The Thunder Girls

RUTHLESS WOMEN

MELANIE BLAKE

First published in the UK in 2021 by Head of Zeus Ltd
This paperback edition first published in 2021 by Head of Zeus Ltd

ISBN (PB): 9781800243040
ISBN (E): 9781800243057

Typeset by Adrian McLaughlin

Printed and bound in Great Britain by
CPI Group (UK) Ltd, Croydon CR0 4YY

Head of Zeus Ltd
First Floor East
5–8 Hardwick Street
London EC1R 4RG

WWW.HEADOFZEUS.COM

This book is dedicated to all the ruthless women I've met along the way...

The fabulous, the feisty and the foul, in one way or another you inspired me to write this.

Meet the Players

Jake Monroe – Head of drama and sole showrunner of *Falcon Bay*, once the world's most popular soap opera, now sinking in the ratings. A sexist, ageist serial cheat.

Amanda King – Kind-hearted, well-liked executive producer. She used to share the showrunner role with Jake, but was demoted while on maternity leave.

Madeline Kane – Stunningly beautiful new owner of *Falcon Bay*'s network. Visiting from the states to oversee the show's reboot and get it back into the top slot again.

Chad Kane – Billionaire husband of Madeline. The rugged and deeply likeable son of a Baptist from America's Deep South.

Helen Gold – Head of casting and acting press officer on *Falcon Bay*. A determined, sensual woman.

Catherine Belle – *Falcon Bay*'s leading actress, seventy-years-old and fabulous. She's won every award across the globe for her portrayal of Lucy Dean, *Falcon Bay*'s lovable beach bar owner.

Farrah Adams – Ambitious writer and occasional director on *Falcon Bay*. She's worked her way up in a male-dominated field.

Stacey Stonebrook – Out-of-work primetime actress who spends her days dropping Xanax and reminiscing about her glory days.

Lydia Chambers – Former soap bitch icon, now relegated to daytime TV chat-show appearances and embarrassing PAs.

Sheena McQueen – Agent to Catherine Belle, Stacey Stonebrook and Lydia Chambers, and CEO of the McQueen Agency. Sexy, sassy and tough, she has every network by the balls.

Honey Hunter – Reclusive Oscar-winning actress who's been in hiding for decades. Still a sex bomb at fifty-six, thanks to spending multiple divorce settlements on plastic surgery.

Aiden Anderson – *Falcon Bay*'s lead director. Upper-class and charming – if you like that sort of thing.

Dan Cochran – The new Head of Finance. Surprisingly sexy for a man with a calculator.

Ross Owen – Unscrupulous showbiz hack, editor of the *Herald* and social influencer. If it's bad and in the news, he's probably behind it.

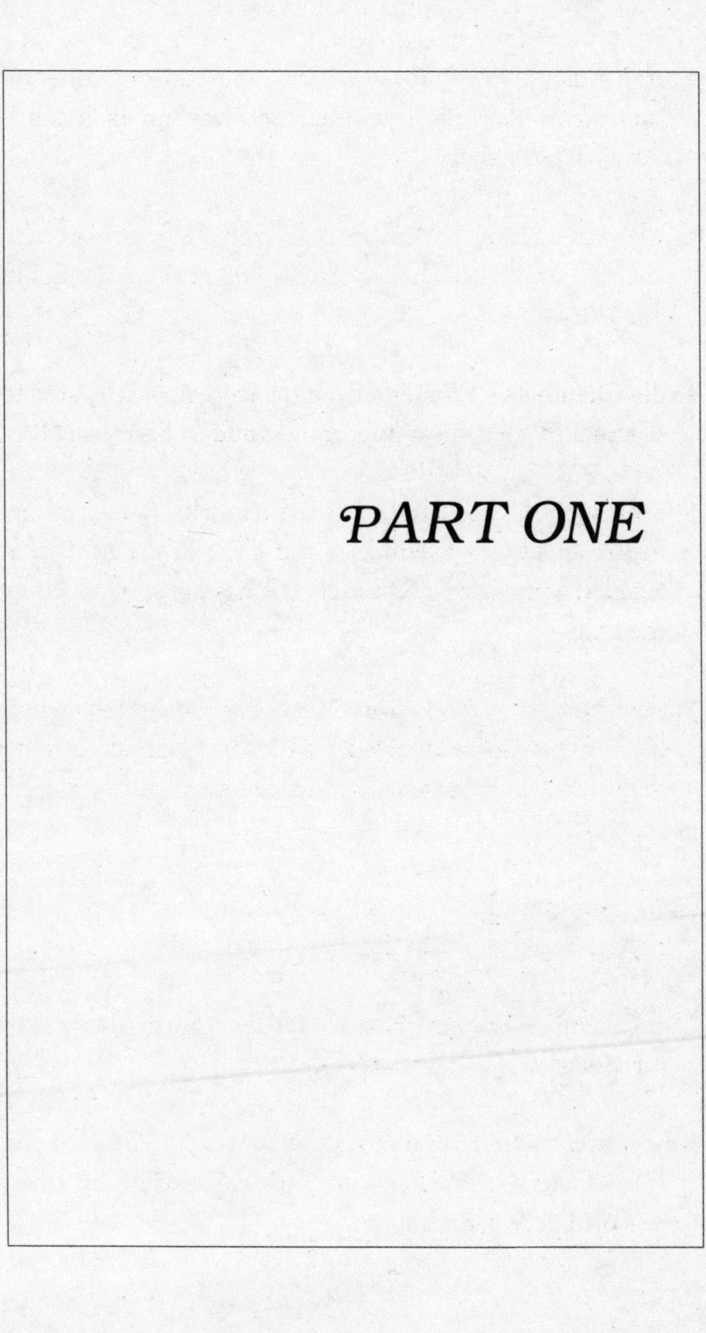

PART ONE

1

Meeting Room 6 was so bright that on sunny days the sunshine flooded through the floor-to-ceiling windows with such intensity that scripts or notes on the table would visibly fade during a long session. On cloudier days it showcased the postcard-perfect bay opposite. Little candy-coloured sea cottages, built into the rock, were dotted around as far as the eye could see and just beyond the last was a hidden beach, where, if you knew the way in, you could listen to the waves crashing and pretend you were anywhere in the world, not mere feet away from the hustle-bustle of the cast and crew working on one of the most famous location sets in the world.

The bay was the lifeblood of this meeting room. Without the bay, there would be no meeting room. For this was the production office of internationally renowned, globally syndicated soap opera *Falcon Bay*. And it was in Meeting Room 6 that the producers, writers and executives met daily to create and manage the stories designed to keep their millions of viewers tuned in. The secondary purpose of so much glass was to show the teams outside the building that the creative minds behind *Falcon Bay* were always working and always watching.

A huge white oval table surrounded by neon-pink chairs that were neither too hard nor too comfortable was central. A variety of people occupied the seats and the gentle hum of conversation filled the air, mixed with the sounds of notes being flicked through, laptops being typed on and phone messages pinging. The two walls that bookended the view of the bay were white. One had floating shelves stacked with awards of every shape and size, from traditional golden Emmys to ornate crystal domes and the classic gold-faced BAFTA.

The opposite wall held photos of *Falcon Bay*'s current cast, each pinned to a large-scale poster of the set and flecked with Post-it Notes which gently flapped in the breeze from the air-con. The room was subtly lit as most of the time the natural light was sufficient. But when storm clouds gathered, the automatic lights faded up so gradually that those in the room never noticed the change.

Meeting Room 6 was, without question, where the magic happened.

The door swung open and all eyes were on Jake Monroe as he strode into the room, ignored the packed table and silently walked towards the storyboard, which was on the wall just by the entrance. He stood frozen, staring at the scant words written there. With his muscular legs clad in tight jeans and his broad shoulders encased in a black leather jacket, he looked much younger than his sixty years. Jake's presence had always been formidable, but having recently been promoted to controller of drama by the network's new owners, whom nobody else in the room had yet met, he'd acquired an air of even greater untouchability and arrogance. He was at the very top of the food chain and he made sure everyone knew it.

After what felt like hours but was actually less than two minutes, he half turned towards the others. 'Is this it?' he asked, pointing at the board and meeting every person's eyes one by one, sending shivers down their backs as his gravelly voice echoed around the pin-droppingly quiet space.

The last face his gaze rested on was a mousey woman – hair in a bun, thick glasses and a figure that unkind people would say was dumpy. Her chair was directly under the air-conditioner and she was feeling the chill. Or maybe it was the ice emanating from her boss. Whatever the reason, she pulled a beige wrap around her shoulders. The sight of its tassels jiggling infuriated Jake.

'What's the matter with you?' he growled.

The woman's face went pale as she shuffled in her seat, causing the tassels to jiggle even faster. 'I… I was cold… so I—'

Before she could finish stuttering her reply, he closed in on her and was now right next to her chair.

'Damn right you are,' he snarled, then looked over at the rest of the table. 'And you're not the only one.'

Earlier that day, Jake had sent a 'Drop everything – emergency meeting' summons to all writers, producers and casting execs, ordering them to gather in Room 6, and signing it off with the word 'pronto'. Three hours later, here he was, surveying what were supposedly the country's finest creative minds. But all Jake could see were blank stares and a shivering mouse in cashmere. He glanced out at the angry sea. Waves were thrashing the shoreline boulders. A flash storm was approaching, both outside in the real world and right here in the world of make-believe. Someone was going to drown.

Falcon Bay was approaching its fortieth anniversary, but where once it had won every accolade and award under the sun, now it had lost more than half its viewers. Not only was it being ripped apart on home soil, where they could usually expect a bit of support, but the international press had started hammering the show too, and once they had you in their sights, it was usually the beginning of the end. The network, which made several popular and cheaply put-together reality shows but only one soap opera, had been forced to sell out to an American investment group, and the new owners had promoted Jake with just one thing on the to-do list: get *Falcon Bay* back to the number one spot.

It was a task he intended to deliver on, and he didn't care if he had to sack the whole room and start again to achieve it. But having been in the business for a long time, he knew axing one person was usually enough to shock the rest into action. It could have been any of them that day. Unfortunately for her, the Mouse had chosen the wrong moment to catch his attention.

'You're all fucking cold!' he roared.

The room bristled. The sea churned and spat foam and spray high into the sky. Nobody dared to look out the window, but nobody dared to look directly at Jake either.

They knew what was coming, and they knew how to survive. Do not meet his gaze, do not let him single you out.

He shook his head contemptuously. 'Look at the storyboard – there's not one decent idea up there, not even one! You truly are a pathetic bunch.'

Mousey girl, who was new and hadn't been told that stillness was required when Jake's mood turned, was trembling, clearly feeling even colder now she'd been shouted at. With shaking hands she slowly started tucking the wrap around herself, almost like a comfort blanket. This caught Jake's eye as he raged on, his handsome face now almost pink with anger.

'This is supposed to be the "creative zone", people,' he yelled, using his fingers to make inverted commas in the air. 'And none of you lazy fuckers are creating shit. No, actually, that's not true. All of you are creating shit – shit that no one is watching.'

As Mouse began tucking the last edge of the wrap under her leg, Jake could stand it no longer. He clicked his fingers and pointed at her. 'Get out! You're fired.'

The room gasped.

With one hand still pointing at Mouse, Jake pulled the door wide open, then stood perfectly still. He knew that in reality he couldn't just fire her like this. HR would have a field day reminding him he needed written warnings and boring stuff like that. But later he would sit Mousey in his office and lay it out for her: she was new, and she was no longer welcome, so she could either take the nice little payoff he'd offer her to go quietly or spend months fighting for it.

'But, Mr Monroe—' she began, her quiet voice squeaking.

'Save it and get the fuck out.'

Jake was no longer looking at her. He was scanning the

rest of the room, making sure they understood what was happening here. She was the sacrifice that would galvanize their collective creativity, or they'd be joining her.

While she gathered up her things in total silence, a single tear dropped down her cheek. Nobody defended her; no one even looked at her. When the Mouse reached the door, she looked back just once to see if anyone was going to step in, but nobody said a word. Another tear ran down her face as Jake slammed the door behind her. Then she was gone.

Outside, the waves had settled a little – still frothing, but not quite so furiously. The dark clouds parted and a sliver of sun spread across the beach and illuminated the meeting room.

Jake had slammed the door with such force that two cast pictures had fallen off the wall. As the creatives processed what had just happened, he crossed the room and picked up the photos, the leather on his brown Cuban-heeled boots crackling with every step.

One picture was of Jude Roscoe, who was fairly new to the show but incredibly popular with the mainly female audience demographic. He played a handyman who seemed to end up with his top off during every job he did.

The other cast card was Catherine Belle's. Catherine was undisputedly the show's leading lady, having been on *Falcon Bay* since its very first episode in 1980. Her portrayal of Lucy Dean, the owner of the *Bay*'s world-famous beachside bar and focal point, had won the show several much-coveted best actress awards over the years and against stiff international competition. Somehow, her British accent had captivated audiences from Malibu to Mumbai, the latter network even paying her the rare honour of subtitling the show rather than dubbing it, as was usual for imported dramas in that terrain.

Jake stared at the photo of Catherine, which he reckoned was at least twenty-years-old, from when she was still in what he considered the last of her glory days. Momentarily, his face softened as he recalled how fun it used to be sitting round a table at award ceremonies, the cast and crew downing endless glasses of champagne, celebrating early as they were so confident *Falcon Bay* would be called out as a winner, which it had been, time and time again. The speeches, the love from the press, the photos in the entertainment pages, the pats on the back from the network and the fat bonuses. Jake's faint smile disappeared when he realized those times were about as old as Catherine Belle's airbrushed headshot. He missed that popularity, the power it had brought the network, and he wanted it back.

Helen Gold remembered those days too. An attractive woman in her early sixties, in red glasses, a lemon-coloured Escada suit and with her flame-red hair cut in a stylish bob, she stood out from the others more casually dressed around the table. As head of casting, Helen had been responsible for employing the best actresses and actors on *Falcon Bay*. From villain to vamp, she'd found them all. Including Catherine Belle. Maybe it was because of her age, or her experience, but Helen had never been intimidated by Jake Monroe. Not one little bit. She remembered when he'd been a mere production assistant, bringing everybody's morning coffees and getting them so wrong that he'd have to go back for more. And he hated that she remembered.

'You know she can sue us for that, right?' Helen said of

the Mouse as she casually leaned back in her chair, which creaked under her. Not because she was heavy but because the chair was getting old, was no longer shiny and new. Which was how Helen sometimes felt, although she certainly didn't look it.

Jake locked eyes with her and hesitated. He would have loved to have told her to follow the Mouse right out of the door, but that would have been a step too far. He paused for a moment longer than was comfortable, allowing the drone of the air-con to be the only noise in the room, and then spoke. 'Thank you, Helen,' he replied sarcastically. 'I might not be able to rely on you creatively, but you've got my back when it comes to the dull legalese.'

Helen smarted at this but didn't show it. She liked to think she was very creative, but she was rarely given airtime by the men in power at the network, who all figured her job was as easy as pointing at an actress and saying, 'She'll do.'

'Right then,' Jake continued. 'I'm going to explain this one last time because you don't seem to understand how much trouble our show is in. Our current ratings are the worst in our thirty-nine-year history. Last week we were beaten by every other soap—'

'Continuing drama,' Helen said, cutting in. She wasn't sure exactly when 'soap' had become a bad word in the industry, but she'd become aware that the very shows that had once revelled in their 'Soap Awards' were now calling themselves 'continuing dramas', as if that elevated them above some imaginary threshold. She didn't like to use the term herself but enjoyed correcting Jake. Any chance to catch Jake in an error was worth taking, just for the fun of it.

He rolled his eyes but let it go. 'So, as well as having our arses kicked by all the other rivals, we were also beaten by *The Real Housewives of Beverly Hills* reunion show – which was a rerun.'

He let that land and watched as the embarrassment made them squirm. Then he softened a little, put a manicured hand on the table and leaned on it, to show that he was flexible, human.

'The network owners are considering cutting an episode or two. Lessening the output, lessening your burden.'

Now he'd got their attention. If that happened, advertising revenue would be down, meaning everyone's wages would be cut drastically and, with episodes axed, the media vultures would be out for them in ever greater numbers. Next stop: cancelled. He didn't have to say any of this. It was the unspoken threat that followed the mere mention of reduced production.

He stayed in that position, with one hand leaning on the table, the other tucked behind him. It was killing his back, but he knew it made him look powerful. He'd read all about that in his pile of management books: how to stand, how to use his body for subliminal messaging.

He definitely had their attention. He casually ran his hand through his hair and began to speak again.

'But I assured them that wouldn't be necessary. I said, "I've got the best writers, the best producers, the best everybody that a soap"' – he corrected himself before Helen could – '"that a continuing drama could want. *Falcon Bay* will return to the number one spot." I gave them my solemn vow.'

He met their eyes once more and spread his arms in a

benevolent gesture that also came straight out of a book and was intended to say 'over to you'. It was met with silence.

He watched and waited.

Finally, one of the writers, a newbie who actually had a pen behind her ear, leaned forward as if about to speak. Before a sound came out of her mouth, Jake halted her with a pausing finger gesture. 'And I don't want to hear the words "cancer", "pregnancy" or "Alzheimer's".'

The newbie shrank back down into her chair, cheeks red, silent, no further ideas to share.

A deafening quiet filled the room once more before somebody else finally piped up, 'How about a siege?'

Jake rolled his eyes, taking in the man's spectacularly long and full blonde beard, ripped jeans and formal waistcoat. Was this idiot a writer or a Viking? 'We did that five years ago,' he said with a sneer. 'Next!'

'Death in childbirth?' someone else shouted, loudly, as if it was such a great idea, she wanted to be certain he knew it had come from her. Her face fell soon enough, when he failed to even meet her eye.

Jake's shoulders sagged. 'We've already had a stillbirth and twins this year alone, so I think we can avoid ovary-related storylines, thank you.'

'A crash?' chipped in a lad wearing geeky glasses and dungarees.

Dunga-fucking-rees! This was *Falcon Bay*, not a hardware store. Jake fleetingly considered bringing in a dress code, but when he realized he'd be asking all the women to wear little black numbers, he was momentarily self-aware enough to let it go.

'Been done to death. Including by us for the millennium special. Have you even looked through the archive, you lazy moron?'

His blood was boiling now. If he didn't get out of the room soon, he would really lose it, and somebody would get hurt. He'd been given a written warning from HR for throwing a chair at a runner once and hadn't enjoyed the ticking-off one bit. He didn't want to show them how intense his rage was, it would make him look weak, so he'd use his voice instead of his body.

'Is that it?' he shouted. 'Where's the blue-sky thinking?'

'A shooting?' Viking Beard tried a second time.

'1999 and 2015,' Jake replied.

'A jilting at the altar?' a redhead in glasses tentatively offered.

Helen could see that Jake was close to furniture-related explosiveness. She'd had enough of his tantrums for one day and didn't want anyone to get injured, so even though storyline was not her department, she decided to throw the old Rottweiler a bone.

'I know exactly what *Falcon Bay* needs,' she said, leaning across the table enticingly, enough to get everybody's attention.

'Well, do tell us, Helen.' Jake smirked, ready to rip apart whatever pathetic idea she'd dredged up.

After a short pause – long enough to create tension but not so long as to give Jake the chance to say something else – Helen poured herself some sparkling water from the bottle in front of her, enjoying the sound of the bubbles popping in the glass. Then, spoke slowly and deliberately.

'*Falcon Bay* needs a Grade A, evil-to-the-core, would-do-anything, will-hurt-anyone-to-get-what-she-wants… bitch.' She stretched out the word 'bitch' for maximum effect.

The whole room looked at Jake expectantly.

He was surprised by Helen's quite good suggestion. The show's female characters tended to be kind-hearted rather than backstabbing; it was *Falcon Bay*'s male stars who'd always been the villains. He suddenly had a *Killing Eve* vibe floating around his head and as much as it pained him to admit it, and he certainly didn't want to show it, he was interested. 'I'm listening,' he said casually, gesturing for her to continue.

All eyes were on Helen now. She knew he was on the hook, so she took her time.

'But not just your average bitch who comes in to stir things up with one or two characters,' she continued. 'This bitch wants to take on everybody in *Falcon Bay*. Which she'll do, one by one. Unbeknownst to them, she'll have a backstory that connects her to all our characters' histories, so she'll have scores to settle with everybody. And we'll cast someone who's instantly recognizable but who hasn't been seen for a while, so viewers will come flocking back just to see what she looks like now and what she's going to do to the residents of *Falcon Bay*.'

Fuck! thought Jake, and then double-checked he hadn't said that out loud. He was both furious and excited. Why hadn't he come up with this instead of Helen? He was temporarily lost for words.

'Well?' Helen said, and smiled. She knew she'd landed a bullseye because Jake was never quiet. But then her heart sank as she realized her victory would last no longer than those few seconds. She wouldn't be able to own the idea. They'd talk about it some more in the room, it would go from writer to writer, exec to controller and finally it would come back to her to cast as if she'd never even known about it in the first place.

Eventually Jake responded, pulling Helen from her spiralling thoughts.

'I like it,' he said lightly.

'Oh, I am pleased.' Helen raised an eyebrow, deciding to at least relish this moment – it was all she'd get. She wanted to add, *You're welcome to it – which is handy, because in an hour you'll be claiming it was yours anyway.* But she liked her job, so she said nothing.

Jake looked across at the board, scanning the cast's faces. 'So, she's hot? Like, twenty-one? A fresh face? Finally we can win a sexiest female award. No more losing out because all our women are so past it—'

'No.' Helen shook her head. 'It will only work if she's at least fifty.'

Jake laughed. 'In her fifties! Don't be ridiculous. Who the hell is going to want to watch some old mutton tramping her way around the bay? What we need is a lamb.'

Undeterred, Helen continued calmly. 'If she's too young, she won't have the gravitas. This is the only way it will work. Lucy Dean was fifty when her wedding episode gave us our highest ever ratings.'

'That was twenty years ago, Helen. Youth is where it's at, these days.'

She ignored him. 'The fact that people still talk about the

wedding ep tells you how effective it was. Fifty is an incredibly powerful age for a woman nowadays, Jake. Our bitch has to be a woman, not a girl, and of course she'll be attractive.'

Despite being sixty himself, Jake found it hard to conceive of women of a similar age being considered attractive. But after many years of working in soap, he'd come to understand that he wasn't the *Bay*'s target audience, so perhaps Helen had a point.

'She'd better have had work done. If she's that age, she better not look it.' He eyed Helen knowingly. She was a living, breathing example that Botox and fillers could disguise the birth date on a woman's passport. And he knew her date, he'd looked it up when he took over, just so he could bring it up every now and then, which he knew fucked her off.

His mind flashed back to when Joan Collins was brought into an ailing *Dynasty* in the eighties. She had both helped the show stay on the air and ensured it was the world's number one syndicated series for nearly a decade, and she must have been about fifty at the time. *So, yes*, he mused, *this could work*.

He cracked his knuckles and faked a yawn, trying not to look as excited as he felt.

'As this is the only idea to come out of today, and if we're to rely on one woman being so watchable that every lost member of our audience returns, she better be one damn fine actress.'

'Oh, she will be. And they will return. It's what I do. Casting,' Helen said, signalling to Jake that she already knew he would claim her idea as his own. And then, mirroring what he'd said to the new owners, she added, 'I give you my solemn vow.'

He smiled. She'd cornered him verbally. But actually she'd cornered herself too. If he failed the new owners, it would be his neck on the line, his job, and now the same would also be true for Helen. If she cast this bitch perfectly and the show won back its lost plaudits, audience numbers and awards, that would be a win for him too. But if Helen got it wrong, he'd finally be able to show the door to 'the sack of silicone', as he liked to refer to her whenever she wasn't present.

Slowly he nodded, liking the odds. 'Okay, Helen. You work your magic. Cast us the best bitch you can find. But you better get a move on, 'cos I want her revealed in the Christmas special.'

'What?' Helen's brain whirred as she tried to figure out how long that gave her to see all the best actresses, screen-test them, pick one and get the contracts sorted.

'That's right,' Jake said. 'It's the first of September today, so you've got just under four months. Chop, chop.'

Relishing the panic that he was leaving behind in the room, Jake figured he could enjoy one more little surprise before the even bigger one. He held up the cast cards that had fallen to the floor earlier. The cards' faces were turned towards him, so the rest of the room could only see the back of them.

'As you all know, I'm a big believer in fate,' he said, flipping them and holding the faces of Catherine and Jude up high for all to see. 'So, to pave the way and help pay for our new arrival, Helen, we'll be axing one of these two cast members from the show.'

Helen's face went white.

Jake put the photos behind his back. 'I'll let you choose. Left or right?'

'Don't be so ridiculous.' Helen got out of her seat and walked towards him. 'Catherine *is Falcon Bay* and Jude is our most popular actor.'

Jake smiled. 'Left or right? It's got to be one of them.'

Helen stared at him in disbelief. He'd always been a prick, but this was insane.

'So indecisive, Helen. Tut, tut. Okay, I'll choose for you. Catherine gets to remain as our current leading lady – for now – which means Topless Wonder here can get the chop.'

He placed Jude's photo in her hand and walked away. 'I'll leave you to work on his exit as well as our incomer's new entrance – while I'm with the new owners.'

He swaggered towards the door. When he reached it, he looked back. Now he would drop the big bomb. If Helen thought playing Russian roulette with a cast photo was bad, she should wait for this beauty. 'Oh, and one final thing. Our Christmas ep… As it falls on our fortieth anniversary, we're going to go live.'

There was a collective sharp intake of breath from each place around the table.

Helen stood clutching Jude's photo. 'On Christmas Day? An actual live episode? With just months to prepare for it and all these changes?' She was almost breathless.

Jake was loving the sense of shock in the air. But most of all, he was loving the fact he'd just wiped that smug smile off Helen Gold's face.

'That's right! Ho, ho, ho,' he boomed and left the room.

2

It was not unusual for fans of one of the world's most famous soap operas to spend hours on Google Earth zooming in on *Falcon Bay*'s location, circling the glorious sandy beaches of St Augustine's island in search of the show's legendary sets. Some even hired fishing boats to get closer to the secret cove where the *Bay* was filmed, hoping to spot something they weren't meant to see and perhaps even one of the stars off-duty. But security was tight so no one had got past the *Bay*'s burly coastguards in decades.

Located in Jersey's English Channel, the picture-postcard-sized island of St Augustine's was nineteen miles off the French coast and a hundred miles off the south coast of England and truly felt like a tiny piece of paradise in the middle of nowhere. Press drones often caught glimpses of the cast and crew hard at work filming one of TV's longest-running shows, but it was a good job they couldn't hear the conversations inside the glass-fronted production offices, because if they could, they'd have quickly realized that the action off screen was way more dramatic than anything its millions of viewers ever got to see.

Meeting Room 6 – where Jake Monroe, just moments ago, had decreed that their Christmas episode would be filmed live – was positioned on the outer edge of the studios. These were comprised of several aircraft-hangar-sized buildings which were home to everything required to make a global hit show that was aired six times a week. Just down the corridor was a big open-plan production office where directors, PAs, script editors and most of the show's crew had their own spaces. This was the central hub of the building; it was Space Command, it was where people shouted across desks, conversations merged and fizzed with the electricity of gossip and new ideas. It was these conversations that the *Bay*'s diehard fans would have loved to eavesdrop on – the snap decisions that affected the soap they adored. A mere five minutes spent in this production office and any visitor would be bitten by the TV bug forever. It was sexy, exciting and buzzing with life, but, like many bugs, it could also be venomous, career-ending and deadly.

A left turn out of the production office led to the internal studio sets. This was where the interiors of the characters' homes were located: fake houses, with movable walls and no ceilings, designed to make the pretend residences look real. There were over 200,000 square feet of sets here, with each set carefully decorated to reflect the character that inhabited it – an impressive world of make-believe.

A right turn out of the production office took you into a long corridor with doors all the way down it. These were for the heads of departments. Behind one of them was Helen

Gold's office. Her room was bigger than many, because she needed to meet actors in there, sometimes several at a time. So many famous people had been through her office, not to mention the dozens of people who weren't yet famous but because of Helen would go on to become superstars. This room was where the ordinary joe could become the face of the future.

A sturdy leather-topped desk stood by the window, overlooking the beach. Helen had shagged many a wannabe actor on it. She'd chosen it for that very reason. As well as the desk, there was the obligatory couch, leaning against the wall, underneath a giant framed poster of *Falcon Bay*'s entire cast taken on their thirtieth anniversary.

To the back of the office there was a sort of acting space. Not exactly a stage but a carpeted area where an actor could stand casually and read a script. There was a camera set up so they could record it when needed. Helen wasn't averse to doing a bit of home filming there too. Just her and an actor, steaming up the room, writhing and clawing, making the kind of movie she kept for herself, for those busy nights when she didn't have time for company but still needed a quick orgasm.

She never felt guilty about her extracurricular activities. She never took advantage of anyone and she never lied – unlike the male casting directors she knew. She never let anyone think sleeping with her was a way to the top; she simply fucked whoever she fancied who also happened to fancy her, after she'd made it clear they were not getting the part. Knowing this in advance seemed to make them want to impress her with their sex skills even more, but even if they were the best lay in the world, and some wooden actors were still in her all-time top-five fucks list, no trick in the sack could impact on her casting choices. Professionally, Helen was as straight as a die.

Her tidy office space was a reflection of her organized mind. There were shelves of scripts and books about TV and film, and a few personal photos framed on the wall, mostly of her on nights out with friends and stars, who were often both. She'd always been a good-time girl who liked to have fun. A teacher had written exactly that on her school report once and Helen's mum had lambasted her for it, but Helen considered it a compliment.

On that couch, a naked Helen was currently writhing in ecstasy as she straddled a naked Jude Roscoe.

'Oh God, oh God, oh God!' she screamed as his cock plunged deeper into her.

It was a good job her office was soundproofed. She'd told the execs she needed that to keep her conversations with actors confidential and it had certainly come in handy for keeping her own activities private over the years.

Sunlight was streaming through the window, temporarily blinding her, but she didn't need to see anything right now because this felt so good. The weather had turned and the warmth of the sun's rays on her body were like an extra caress down her back. Having post-creative-meeting sex with a sea view was always a pleasure, and as much as Jude Roscoe irritated her, he was a surprisingly good lay.

She loved having sex on that casting couch and liked to think she was doing her bit to reverse history: the female casting director dominating the male actor. Jude put his big hands on her breasts and squeezed them, teasing her nipples between his thumb and forefingers as she pressed the palms of her own hands against his face. She pushed her fingers into his mouth as she moved faster, relishing every inch of his rock-hard length, letting it work for her, pressing strongly against her clit, as she slid up and down its thick shaft.

He looked up at her face as he throbbed inside her. Feeling she was close, he grabbed her hips and ground her body down, making her ride harder, faster, driving himself deeper and deeper until she let out a scream.

Her eyes were closed as the colours bloomed in her mind; the orgasm shuddered through her body and the wet release drenched him beneath her.

She waited. He was still hard; he hadn't come. He'd saved himself for her. She left it inside her. Waited. Let the flush drain from her cheeks. As she lifted his hands to her skin, she was vibrating, tingling, and now his touch was like a million feathers, making goosebumps on her body. Her breathing evened out. The cold breeze from the air-con felt electric on her sweaty back. She was still. The last remnants of her orgasm were just sidling away from her when she went at him all over again.

Twenty minutes later, Helen was touching up her make-up at her desk. She'd changed into a new dress. Jude had put dirty thumb prints on her Escada suit and ripped her cami when he'd tried to be forceful; she made a mental note to send him the bill. Important to do it before he got the news of his sacking. She could hear him in the shower, finishing himself off. Poor guy: she came multiple times but hadn't bothered to return the favour.

They'd been having sex for four months now. And that's all it was – sex. He was happily married and she was happily single. They'd had an attraction at the summer party; the alcohol had unleashed it. She'd let him go down on her by the beach, on his knees in the sand, her dress pulled up, his tongue making her knees weak. It had been dangerous and exciting. The next day at work, she thought he'd come to apologize, but he said he'd come to finish what they started, so they did it on her desk. Thank God she had a shower in the office. She hated going to meetings smelling of sex, but she loved going to meetings having just had sex. She never felt more chilled. More at peace.

She had told herself that once Jude left her office today, that would be it, the last time. She'd always had a personal rule that she didn't sleep with *Falcon Bay*'s actors. She could have them before they signed on the dotted line, she could have them after they'd left (not that she did; they had the stench of used goods), but while they were on the same show as her, it was a total no-go. It was just too goddamn messy, which was why she'd always stayed away from the current *Falcon Bay* cast. Luckily, she had no shortage of alternative offers. She mostly slept with actors because she found them so obliging. It was like they were auditioning there and then. It was such a cliché, but one she was enjoying most days.

Jude was the first time she'd broken her 'no current cast' rule. And while the sex was amazing, she wouldn't miss him when he was gone. That was probably what had made today's session extra special, because Jude Roscoe – thanks to a door slam and his cast photo falling on the floor – was about to get sacked. Given that Jude was done for, she reasoned that technically she was no longer breaking her own vow.

With Jude now in the shower, Helen had returned to her desk, the sea dancing behind her. She'd needed a good seeing to after that fractious creative meeting with Jake; she certainly felt she was due a bit of pleasure after the pain of being stuck in a room with him.

Slipping her heels back on, a pain stabbed her Achilles' heel and her thoughts turned to Dr Kirk, another know-it-all man full of his own ego. She'd gone to see him complaining of foot pain and his response had been to tell her that there came an age for every woman when she needed to hang up her high heels and slip into some flats. She'd wanted to slap him but instead took it as a challenge and underwent two painful surgeries so that she could still don six-inch stilettos as and when she pleased. She'd then sashayed into his surgery in her tightest skirt and highest heels to parade her victory. She could see, as she walked away, how much he desired her, which made her win all the sweeter.

Recalling that victory stirred her loins again; stress and confrontation always seemed to activate her libido. Now that Jude wouldn't be around for much longer, and with all the changes coming to the show, Helen knew she probably wouldn't find the time to strike up a new liaison, so she was already mentally flicking through her contacts list, wondering which uncomplicated stud would be filling his place in her sex diary. Her mind stalled at the number for Peter the plumber, whom she'd hired to redo one of her guest bathrooms. He'd given her multiple orgasms during the two weeks he was there, and on the few occasions she'd seen him since, he'd never failed to make her tremble.

She was lost in erotic thoughts when the door handle turned. Finding it locked, her visitor rapped on the door with a melodic tapping. Helen knew that knock. She walked over to the bathroom and opened the door. A naked Jude stood there in all his glory, looking excited that Helen was about to join in for round two. His cock was already springing to life again, but her words soon shut that idea down.

'There's someone at the door,' she said in a hushed tone. 'Stay in here and be quiet!' She pressed her finger to her lips.

Jude gave a 'no worries' shrug and went back to drying off his impressive body.

Damn, she thought, as she headed for the door. Seeing him glistening wet like that had put her in the mood for another round, but first she needed to deal with her visitor.

The moment she slid the lock, the door swung open and Farrah Adams walked in.

'Oh my God, the hunt for a super bitch is a brilliant idea.' She glided past Helen and plonked herself on the very couch where just ten minutes earlier Helen had been riding Jude for all his worth.

Farrah never bothered with pleasantries, always launching into whatever was on her mind.

'Why was it locked?'

'Oh, I was in the shower,' Helen said as nonchalantly as a woman who'd just had multiple orgasms could manage.

Farrah raised an eyebrow. 'I'm not surprised. I always feel like I need a deep clean after I've been in Meeting Room 6 with that dickhead.'

Helen shrugged as she took in the sight of her friend. The memories of how they'd met, although now years in the past, always seemed fresh in her mind.

At almost six foot tall, with deep chocolate skin and green eyes, Farrah had a figure like Grace Jones in her Bond Girl days and could easily have held her own on any fashion runway. She kept her hair short because, working in a man's world, she liked to present androgynously to throw off her male colleagues (all of whom fancied her like crazy). Despite her preference for dressing in manly clothes, she couldn't hide what was a truly gorgeous body: a slim physique, long, smooth legs, toned arms and tummy, and high, pert breasts. When Farrah was there, she was all the art a room needed.

Although nearly a decade apart in age, Farrah and Helen had known each other for nearly forty years. Helen had been a junior casting assistant when they met, new to *Falcon Bay* and under the watchful charge of her mentor, the formidable Caroline St James. The show was looking for a fourteen-year-old to play Lucy Dean's long-lost love child. As was often the way, one of the senior execs had lined up his daughter for the role, but to give the illusion that they'd cast the net far and wide rather than automatically going for the nepotistic choice who stood waiting in the wings, there was an audition process, which the ingénue Helen had been put in charge of. The poor hopefuls didn't stand a chance, no matter how talented they were. That sort of behaviour was rife in the studio system and it made the young Helen sick.

Back then, Helen had a tiny, windowless office which also doubled as a store cupboard. It had less air than a flat tyre and its flickering strip light was bringing on a headache, so

Helen was considering cancelling the remaining auditions. After all, what was the point? But then Farrah walked in and Helen was transfixed. She had something of Marilyn Monroe about her – not in looks, but in the way that as soon as the camera was on her, she glowed. Helen knew that Farrah would be a million times better than the dodgy shoo-in already doing hair and make-up tests. Plus the fact that Farrah was biracial would mean they'd be bringing some much-needed diversity into the show. And it would tell the world something about Lucy's taste in men, a relatively taboo subject at the time. Helen was certain that casting Farrah would be a win-win.

However, Helen was the new girl. Which meant: get the coffees, staple the scripts and look pretty – in the corner. One thing the new girl didn't do was offer her opinions. But Helen never did what she was supposed to. She lobbied everybody from her boss to the series producer, including the writers and the camera crew. She played them all Farrah's audition scene. Most agreed Farrah was something special, but no one wanted to be seen to challenge the network's decision to hire the exec's daughter. Helen had watched that audition tape in horror; the girl was more wooden than Pinocchio. So she did the unthinkable. She decided to approach the talent. It was a huge risk, but there was something so magical about Farrah that Helen just had to try. Off she strode, her heels clacking down the corridor towards the dressing rooms.

Catherine Belle was the genius behind Lucy Dean, the matriarchal beating heart of the show. As the physical embodiment of the lead character, she was therefore at the top of *Falcon Bay*'s pyramid of talent. At that time, Catherine was thirty, but she seemed so much older. Not in looks but in gravitas and a self-belief that allowed her to remain calm in any storm.

As the twenty-one-year-old Helen finally reached her dressing room and knocked gently on the door, she prayed that Catherine would remain true to her Zen-like personality and would not mind the intrusion or the break in professional protocol.

In the TV studio there weren't many places cast members could go to be alone. The green room, with its pale lime walls and neutral carpet, was always crammed full of cast learning their lines or watching rival TV shows and bitching, and was rarely the sanctuary it was meant to be, so an actor's dressing room was the only real haven they had. This was usually a small, plain room with a single window – somewhere to get changed, somewhere to take a last look at your lines before a runner came and led you out to the chaos of the set. Often these tiny rooms were shared by three or four actors, but Catherine Belle had her own dressing room, and small and plain it was not. She had three windows, a balcony overlooking the sea, and several paintings by up-and-coming Jersey artists, whom Catherine liked to think she was nurturing by purchasing their abstract work. There were a couple of Claude Cahun photos as well, to show she had class too. Nobody knocked on Catherine's door unless they were a senior producer with important information. Or a dear friend.

Nowadays, Helen could knock on Catherine's door any time of the day, but back then she was definitely not on the approved list.

'Miss Belle, do you have a minute?'

'I have plenty of minutes,' Catherine had said as Helen opened the door to find her resplendent in full Lucy Dean attire, eyes closed and sitting in a yoga position, 'and they're all mine, darling. Which is why I don't want disturbing until I'm called to set.'

Helen heard the tone and knew it wasn't good. Catherine could easily have her job terminated just for the intrusion. The sensible thing to do would have been to politely apologize for disturbing her, close the door and walk away. But Helen didn't do that.

'You won't know me,' Helen ventured. 'I work for Caroline in casting—'

'Then it's Caroline I shall call if you don't go away immediately,' Catherine interrupted, the curtness dialled up a notch.

Shit, thought Helen. This wasn't how she'd seen it going. If Catherine did call her boss, she wouldn't even make it past her trial period. This was her last chance to walk away and hope Catherine couldn't recognize her in a line-up. Which, as Catherine hadn't looked at her yet, was a real possibility. But Helen wasn't the kind to give up on what she believed in. She felt strongly that she needed to grab this opportunity – it was sink or swim.

'Please give me just one of your precious minutes and I promise you won't regret it. If I'm wrong, you can get me fired for overstepping the line and I won't fight it. But one thing I know is that if you don't watch this video, your new onscreen daughter will ruin the whole storyline for you. It'll be like acting with quicksand, and she'll pull you into it.'

She said this as fast as she could, hoping to get all her words out before she was silenced.

After a few seconds' pause, which felt like an hour, Catherine finally opened her eyes and began to cast them over Helen. She remained perfectly still in her yoga pose. Helen slowly stepped further into the room, taking Catherine's silence not exactly as acquiescence but also not as a no. Before Catherine could interrupt her, she pushed the VCR into the machine in the corner. They both watched silently as Farrah's audition sizzled on screen. It was clear from Catherine's expression that she was persuaded.

But Helen wanted to seal the deal.

'That's your daughter, right there. You act with her and the chemistry will bring you an international soap award.'

Catherine continued to stare at the tiny portable TV, the picture fuzzy on a VCR pause, and Helen watched her intently. It was obvious that, like Helen, Catherine had never seen a kid so raw, so believable or so damn exciting. And the fact that she wasn't white clearly hadn't gone over her head either. It was no secret that Catherine had been wanting to give Lucy Dean a bit of edge, and if Farrah was revealed to be the daughter she'd given away, well, that would be revolutionary in *Falcon Bay* terms in the 1980s.

Helen was wrong about one thing though: Catherine didn't just win an international soap award, she also landed her first Emmy and Golden Globe awards. And, eight years later, Farrah's last episode on the show, in which Catherine dragged her dead daughter's body from the sea, secured her first BAFTA. How could it not? Their pairing truly was TV gold. Audiences around the globe were distraught to see the partnership come to an end as Lucy Dean carried her daughter's corpse across the golden sands before collapsing to her knees and begging God to take her life instead. Sirens wailed, seagulls screamed and the stormy waves heaved as more than 200 million people cried to see Lucy Dean mourn the death of a daughter she'd never truly accepted. The pain of realizing she would never have the chance to correct her tragic mistakes touched audiences like never before and won Lucy Dean a place in their hearts forever.

Catherine became a global phenomenon, the biggest soap star in the world, and Helen's career was pretty much made off the back of her audacious move that day she'd barged in on the show's biggest star. Taking that tape to Catherine, who'd then backed Helen on pushing for Farrah over the exec's daughter, resulted in the show winning its first round of serious accolades, making Helen as golden as her surname.

When it was time for Caroline St James to retire, Helen became head of casting and was given the big office where Helen and Farrah were sitting right now. After deciding to move behind the camera, Farrah went on to become the show's head writer and nearly thirty years later had started to move into directing episodes. Despite their age differences, the three women had been friends for almost as long as the sun had risen over Falcon Bay, and they had every intention of staying friends until it set. Cast and crew alike knew the trio as the Titans of *Falcon Bay*.

As Farrah curled up on the corner of Helen's casting couch, her lips twisted into a sardonic smile and her puppy-dog eyes alive with mischief. 'So, Jake told me the idea came to him like lightning from above,' she said, flicking through a copy of *Variety* magazine that had been lying on Helen's low table.

Helen rolled her eyes. *That was a record, even for him*, she thought. 'So long as that lightning looked and sounded a lot like me, then yeah,' she replied, with a little snip in her tone.

'I knew it had to be yours. Men!' Farrah sighed, flinging the magazine to one side. 'All I need is unlimited ammo, one night and total immunity.'

Helen laughed at the outrageously tempting idea. Then, aware that she needed to get Farrah out of her office before Jude made his presence known, probably by clumsily dropping something, she held up a hand, signalling for Farrah to be quiet. She was currently doubling as the show's temporary press officer – their last one had been sacked for leaks, and Jake had been too cheap to hire a new one. She picked up her phone, her red fingernails clicking the buttons as she dialled Ross Owen, editor of the *Herald*. Most people could only get through to his harassed PA, but the number Helen dialled was his direct line. They'd had a thing or two in the past, which meant that whenever she needed press coverage she could get him on speed dial. A mutually beneficial deal, even without the added sex, which as it happened was rather good and bizarrely kinky for a man who spent his days shaming others for being anything other than virtuous.

'Helen? Everything okay?' Ross asked. Despite being rugged, handsome and physically fit, he had a little bit of a baby voice on the phone.

'I've got missed calls from you,' Helen lied, winking at Farrah, who was looking intrigued.

'From me?' he asked, genuinely confused.

'Stop ringing! You know I always tell you what I can, but I just can't tell you this.'

Farrah's face broke into a smile as realization dawned.

'Listen, I love you – you're my favourite hack.' Helen knew the word 'hack' made Ross's blood boil, which was why she always called him that. 'But this time I can't give you an exclusive. Not until it's all signed, sealed and delivered.'

'Until what's signed, sealed and delivered?'

Her fish was snagged. She could hear it in his baby voice. He smelled an exclusive and he wanted it.

'As soon as I can confirm anything, you'll be the first name on my call list. I promise. Gotta dash, it's gone crazy round here.'

She hung up the phone and twirled her silky hair around her index finger, which she did whenever she was pleased with herself.

They both glanced through the window at the peaceful scene outside. Just the lapping of the waves and the occasional screech of a seabird.

'So much for "crazy round here"!' Farrah laughed, having cottoned on to the plan before Helen had even hung up. 'How long before he calls Amanda?'

'I'd say he's already on hold. I warned her not to answer any press calls today. By tomorrow, everyone will want to know what *Falcon Bay* is cooking up.'

Farrah looked at her dear friend and gave her a wide, approving smile.

It was easy to be impressed by actresses like Catherine,

whose talent was on view every single day. But in a job like Helen's, the talent was in not showing you were playing a game. And Helen excelled at this.

'Like I said' – Farrah stood up – 'it's a genius idea. So which actresses are in the running for our new bitch then?'

'Oh, I've got one or two ideas,' she purred. She had that look in her eyes that Farrah always liked; it signalled that fun times were coming. 'Now be off with you so I can start working more magic for Jake to take credit for.'

Farrah laughed and exited.

Helen left it a moment, then slid the lock back on the office door and re-entered the bathroom.

'Hey, babe, you got a sec?' Jude said, giving her the same look he used on camera that brought him in thousands of letters from horny housewives every week. But it didn't work on Helen. And she hated being called 'babe', though she decided to let that go, on compassionate grounds. He was, after all, about to be unemployed.

'Not really. You need to go before someone else turns up.'

He blundered on regardless. 'It's just… I wasn't listening on purpose, but I heard what you and Farrah were saying about show changes. I don't want to sound paranoid, but is any of it going to affect me?'

'Oh no. It's just about the new female casting,' she lied, checking her hair in the full-length mirror on the back of the door so as to avoid his eyes.

'Oh, cool,' he said, buttoning up his shirt, blissfully oblivious to his impending life change.

'You'd tell me though, if I had anything to worry about,

wouldn't you?' he asked, his puppy-dog eyes catching hers in the mirror.

'Of course I'd tell you,' she said, turning round to stroke his rugged face with one hand, while crossing the fingers on her other, hoping that would keep her out of hell.

3

When Channel Island TV was first launched in the late sixties by husband-and-wife team Tina and Harry Pearson, it produced local news bulletins and heritage documentaries. In the seventies, with some profit in the bank, the Pearsons took a punt on comedy and ended up selling several sitcoms to the BBC that also aired in Canada. At this point they rebranded, using the initials C.I.TV to make them sound less parochial. In the eighties, they ventured into co-productions across Europe, eventually moving into glossy spy thrillers and period dramas. Each series would go down well for a few years before eventually falling out of fashion.

What C.I.TV really needed was to create something that could be syndicated around the world and generate an audience of millions. Tina and Harry lived for television and wanted viewers to love watching their shows as much as they loved making them; it was never just about the money for them. After much brainstorming, they came up with *Falcon Bay* and it was this initially gentle soap opera that would make their fortune. The Pearsons conceived the show as an everyday drama of beautiful Channel Island folk, set in an idyllic seaside village that would showcase the island of St Augustine's that they adored. There would be residents falling in and out of love with each other, domestic crises and professional triumphs, rivalries and tragedies, but the Pearsons never felt the need to make plotlines or characters overly realistic. Entertainment was key. An instant hit when it launched on Christmas Day 1980, it went on to be watched, at its peak, by nearly a billion people worldwide.

With a global hit on their hands, C.I.TV received offers to sell out and suggestions that they expand and open offices all over the world, but they were devoted to St Augustine's and vowed never to sell their shows or leave their beloved island. And they never did. They died within a few months of each other at the dawn of the new millennium. Both were in their eighties when they passed, working right up to the end, thriving off the bay's daily hustle and bustle, drawing energy from the drama factory they'd created to churn out their global phenomenon.

Tina died of a heart attack on the show's famous board-walk, dropping to the floor, gone in minutes. Harry never recovered from the loss of his darling wife and died in his sleep, in their house overlooking Falcon Bay's beach, just months later. The coroner's report cited natural causes, but everyone on the island knew he'd died of a broken heart. Their ashes were scattered into the sea by Catherine Belle and the cast and crew in a remembrance service that the world's media reported on. 'TV's Golden Couple Together Again' said one headline. Catherine had smiled when she read that and hoped it was true.

After their deaths, the Pearson sons, Guy and Luke, continued to run the shows, but unlike their parents, were very hands off. They were rarely seen on the purpose-built studio set that dominated the south side of St Augustine's, positioned next to the idyllic cove where all the exterior location filming took place, and made even fewer appearances at the production office where their parents had once thrived, an office so big it held more than forty desks, each with a phone, a computer and the inevitable stack of scripts, contracts, plans and memos. But Guy and Luke weren't really interested in oiling the machine that made their much-loved productions, so it was no surprise to anyone when they offloaded their shares to an asset group in 2010. C.I.TV had changed hands several times since and, sadly, never saw the likes of Tina and Harry again.

Inside the vast production office, locked onto their computers with eye-wateringly long daily to-do lists, it was easy for *Falcon Bay* employees to lose all sense of the building's unique location, but every now and then, mid-phone call or mid-argument about what kind of product placement would fit a particular scene, one of them would glance up and catch sight of the arc of golden sand and its gently swaying palm trees and remember that they were working in paradise.

Amanda King, however, never forgot how beautiful Falcon Bay was. Before she had her baby, she used to go for regular morning swims in the sparkling aquamarine sea, and if she could, she'd finish the day with an invigorating walk along the breezy clifftop path. Even though she was second-in-command on the show, she would always find time to enjoy where she worked, to be at one with the lush surroundings. Sometimes she'd just sit for a while, inhaling the scent of the wild thyme bushes as she took in the sights, which never failed to impress her.

Right now, she was taking in another impressive sight: Dan Cochran's bulging crotch. And it was making her blush. She was seated and he was standing, which meant her eyeline was level with his zip. She knew she should avert her gaze, but she couldn't help but linger just a little longer.

Words like 'expenditure', 'taxable recompense' and 'economic fluidity' floated around her, but all she could hear were fantasy moans of tender lovemaking rising into passionate sex and ending with a screaming climax. The executive producer of *Falcon Bay* was imagining having sex with Dan, the new head of finance. This would never happen, Amanda knew. *Never. No way.* But despite her blushes, she found that she was enjoying the fantasy.

Dan wasn't Amanda's type at all. No, scratch that. Physically, he was exactly her type. Muscular, tree-trunk legs, a super pert bum and a toned but not overly developed body, all of which gave her a feeling of butterfly wings fluttering gently between her legs. He looked after himself but clearly didn't feel the need to bulk up; he was confident in what was already there. *And that face…* She sighed. *That boyish smile, the neatly trimmed beard, the cobalt blue eyes. The salt-and-pepper hair, mussed up into an orchestrated casual look.* If she didn't get a grip, she was going to have to sneak off and give herself an orgasm.

Sadly, the reason this would only ever be a fantasy was

that Amanda was married – to Jake Monroe – and she wasn't the cheating type. Marriage to Jake was complicated, and absolutely no bed of roses, but, well, Jake was Jake and she'd known him a long time, been married to him for twelve years and was determined to keep trying to make things work, despite his often horrendously hurtful behaviour. And without Jake, she wouldn't have Olivia. The most perfect thing in her life. Sweet, eight-month-old Olivia, the miracle that doctors said would never happen.

Amanda had been pregnant before, more than once, and by more than one guy. But none of those pregnancies had been viable because her body couldn't carry past the first seven weeks. It was a blessing of sorts that they'd failed in such a short time; a friend of hers had got to eight months and had to go through the pain of delivering, even though she knew she'd never hear her baby cry. Seven weeks was nothing, Amanda used to tell herself. 'Your baby was no bigger than a blueberry,' one doctor told her, and she'd consoled herself with this. She hadn't lost a child, she'd lost a blueberry, and she'd never really liked blueberries.

After her fourth blueberry (her second with Jake), somebody suggested they try IVF. She knew all about it because the character of Lucy Dean had gone through the tribulations of IVF on *Falcon Bay*. When her daughter drowned, Lucy Dean wanted to have another child – even though she had a long-lost son somewhere and a daughter she'd given up as a baby and still hadn't tracked down… That was soap operas. Lucy Dean wanted to be a mother again and thought a baby would make up for her loss. So, despite being forty-nine, the same age as Amanda was now, the character had gone through IVF. Nations wept when it failed and Catherine Belle excelled herself again, picking up yet more awards.

Amanda's own IVF story had a much happier ending. She'd got past the blueberry stage with no complications and was thrilled to finally reach the point where she could look back on her first trimester and go home with a scan of her baby girl (she'd wanted to know the sex, couldn't bear the thought of not knowing). During the second trimester she forgot, at times, that she was pregnant at all. Things at *Falcon Bay* were very tense then. Viewing figures had been in steady decline, and, under pressure from the latest owners to 'move with the times', they'd taken the show into grittier territory, including a controversial paedophile plotline. Critics, as well as the audience, hated the dark, bleak story and that's when ratings really began to fall off their world-famous cliffs.

Falcon Bay had always been known for telling light, joyful, life-affirming stories, and from the start Amanda had been very vocal about wanting to squash the new storyline before it even saw the light of day. But by the time the network execs could see how badly it was playing with viewers, they were in too deep. The show was getting universally panned by a new online audience who did not hold back when it came to calling out *Falcon Bay* on its change of direction.

Amanda was on maternity leave when the global trolling really kicked in. Even the seagulls seemed to be less interested; flocks of them usually circled the bay, but the majority had now flown elsewhere – maybe they'd been able to tell that the show was in real trouble. It had dropped out of the world's top one hundred shows and was on the brink of losing its vital syndication, which left the last remaining custodians of C.I.TV no choice but to sell to a US investor. And while the change of guard was being put into place, Amanda was in Jersey General Hospital on all fours, sucking gas and air and screaming like a trapped bear in the woods.

Jake had not attended the birth. He claimed sudden squeamishness and made no secret of the fact that he'd rather be on set, 'doing some real work and protecting *Falcon Bay* from future shitstorms'. Part of Amanda had admired him for that – for his professionalism, and his honesty. The other part had felt deeply wounded. Though her gorgeous friend Farrah had been a lovely substitute in the birthing room – comforting and funny and foul-mouthed at all the right times – Amanda doubted she'd ever truly forgive Jake for not having been there to welcome Olivia into the world. It had opened a rift of a different order to all the other fractures in their relationship.

Eight months later and she could still smell the hospital room, feel the plastic sheet under her knees and hear the midwife telling her she was 'a good girl'. She remembered every single second of that agony, right up until the moment Olivia emerged. After which she remembered barely anything.

A few days after she'd returned home with Olivia to her beautiful shorefront house that was a cut above most of the condos that housed the cast and crew of *Falcon Bay*, Amanda was scrolling through her social media feeds while breastfeeding her tiny daughter when she noticed a Twitter poll asking which soap should be axed. Although *Falcon Bay* won, with seventy-four per cent (the first award they'd won in years, sadly), she hadn't taken it too seriously. Online was a hateful place. She'd given fifteen years of her life to *Falcon Bay* and she deserved these precious few months bonding with her daughter. So she forced herself to switch off and spent the following weeks lying on the chaise-longue in the glass-walled sunroom, staring out to sea, her baby girl lying on her chest. She had never felt so complete, so lacking in ambition beyond loving her child. Yes, she was sleep deprived and starved of adult company, but – and this was the biggest but in her life – she had never been happier.

Six months later, when her maternity leave came to an end, she put Olivia in *Falcon Bay*'s crèche. Her friends had expected her to employ a live-in nanny and make a swift return to her former lifestyle – Farrah and Helen had already started scheduling girls' nights out, keen to get the partying back on track – but Amanda was adamant that she wanted to be there for Olivia as much as possible. Plus there was the worry that Jake would try to screw any half-decent-looking nanny she hired. So the crèche was the perfect solution.

Many years ago, when she was still a production assistant, Amanda had begun what had seemed like a single-handed battle to get a crèche built on the premises of C.I.TV St Augustine's. She had worked with accountants, the head of HR and anybody else she could enlist, believing it would allow mothers to come back to work earlier. At the back of her mind was the hope that she too would be dropping off her own child there one day. So when that day did finally come and she left Olivia in a room exploding with primary colours and scrawled crayon messes, she had to hold in her tears.

As it turned out, it was her professional life that would cause her to cry real tears that day. Tears of frustration and betrayal.

Before her maternity leave, she and Jake had been co-executive producers on *Falcon Bay*. They shared the top job, took joint responsibility at the helm. Being partners at work as well as at home had its challenges, and they used to argue like Bruce Willis and Cybill Shepherd in *Moonlighting*, but they were equals and the fact that neither of them was in sole charge meant that they always had to somehow find a compromise, an approach that usually benefited the show. They'd done that successfully for ten years, but then came the ratings drop, the network sale and Amanda's maternity leave. A perfect storm. The new owners decided they wanted one boss, accountable for everything. So while Amanda was pushing a pram through the lazy days of her baby bubble, Jake was promoted to controller of *Falcon Bay*.

Amanda returned to work to find that, although she was still exec producer, she had lost her position at the top. It was Jake who now had overall power on the show. And with that effective demotion, she'd also been kicked out of the swanky private office they used to share and into the open-plan bullpen of the main production office. Jake had kept that particularly wounding change very quiet; not even the C.I.TV team knew, or one of her friends would have warned her. She'd burst into tears of humiliation when all was publicly revealed on her first day back. Helen, Farrah and Catherine urged her to fight him on it, but all Jake could muster as a reason for the secrecy, let alone the betrayal, was something about not wanting to blur the boundaries between home and work, and how it was imperative that he had total privacy, now he was controller.

So here she was, sitting at her desk among the many other desks, with Dan Cochran's tantalizing crotch at eye level while he went through last month's expenses. She'd only known Dan for a couple of months – he'd been brought in by the new owners while she was on leave – but she already liked him a lot, and not just because he was so scorchingly sexy. He was also a really nice person, a listener, almost boy-next-door nice. Before Olivia, that lack of edge, his mildness, would have been a turn-off. Jake didn't do nice. He was exciting, unpredictable, mercurial and she'd always been drawn to that in a man. It made her feel alive – or at least it used to.

Out of the corner of her eye, she could see Jake now, lying on a portable massage table in the office she'd lovingly decorated. Everybody knew it was the best office in the building: big enough for ten desks, and still with room to spare. The view over the bay was exquisite: you could see for miles along the shoreline and all the way to the woods that topped the nearby cliffs. There was a balcony you could step out onto whenever you wanted the sea air on your face. Inside, the silk carpet was so invitingly soft, she had sometimes pulled the blinds down and laid down on it to take a nap.

She loved that office. And now she had to make do with a six-by-three desk with drawers that jammed, and no privacy at all.

Through the glass window Amanda was trying not to look at, Jake was sprawled across the table, having a hot-stone massage. A different person might have imagined picking up one of those hot stones and hurling it at his smug head, but that wasn't Amanda. She knew him better than anyone, knew where his vulnerabilities lay, knew that him having a massage in the middle of the day was a sure sign that he was under stress. Anything that helped calm him down was good – for the show, for the staff and for her. She wasn't going to waste her energy begrudging him that.

'It's against company policy,' Dan was saying, pointing again at the figures on his spreadsheet.

His words pulled her back to the moment, back to what they were doing, which was going over her expenses. Her eyes were still level with his crotch, which seemed to be pressing against his tight trousers more than it had been before. The apple red of her cheeks spread down to her neck as it occurred to her that he might be getting an erection. Was he looking down her open-buttoned blouse, which was showing more than a single serving of her ample breasts?

Ordinarily, she'd have been flustered by such a thought, but a strange thing happened: she was suddenly overtaken by the idea that he was looking at her and liking what he saw very, very much. She put it down to postnatal hormones and tried to concentrate.

'You can't put these overnights in your expenses,' he continued.

She got up from her seat, feeling the need to put a stop to her fantasizing. She stretched her arms high in the air, pulling her blouse out of her waistband, not realizing she was showing him her skin in the process. There were a few stretch marks there, but she liked to think of them as battle scars, testaments to the miracle that had happened within.

Dan shifted his weight from one foot to the other, as if trying to covertly move his bulge into a more comfortable position.

'But they were work related,' she said, determined to get this back on a business footing.

'Work-related overnights need to be agreed in advance.'

'With you?'

He stumbled. 'Sorry?'

'I need to work out an overnight with you, in advance?'

He glanced up, swallowed and looked over her shoulder rather than meet her eye. 'Er…'

Seeing his hesitation, Amanda realized what she'd said and how it must have come across. 'I didn't mean…' she stuttered.

'I know.'

'That's just the way it sounded.'

'I know,' he repeated and held up a hand to say it was okay.

She held up hers in the exact same gesture at the exact same moment, which meant their hands awkwardly touched.

They both recoiled as if they'd prodded a burning log. The #MeToo movement rolling through the entertainment industry had everybody on edge.

Amanda could feel her blouse sticking to her skin. Looking down, she noticed her breasts were leaking across her peach Armani blouse. Two circles were spreading from her hard nipples. She quickly turned away so he wouldn't see them. A glance at the computer screen told her it was Olivia's feeding time, which her body clock had just announced in its own way.

Luckily, the phone on her desk rang at that very moment. As she lifted it to her ear, she tried to read Dan's expression. His eyes flicked to her bare neck. She batted away the image of his lips on her exposed skin and focused on the phone. 'Amanda King…' she said hoarsely down the receiver.

'I'm going to let these through this time, but in future… come to me first,' Dan whispered as he readied to go.

'I will,' she whispered back, and watched him walk away.

'Amanda, it's Ross Owen from the *Herald*.'

Amanda scooped up a make-up pad from her desk's bottom drawer and tucked it into the cup of her bra. She'd have to send the blouse to dry-cleaning and get a temporary replacement from wardrobe. Brad would help her out; he was a star when it came to that sort of thing.

As she put a second pad on the other breast, she said to Ross Owen, 'Why do you always say "from the *Herald*"? I've known you for fifteen years.'

'Habit. Listen, you wanna tell me what's going on there?'

Helen had already pinged an email over, explaining that Ross was likely to call. Amanda knew the way to play this: give him nothing but make him think she was hiding something. She let the pause suggest she was actually considering telling him.

'Sorry, I can't tell you anything and I'm due in an emergency meeting, so I've gotta go, Ross Owen from the *Herald*.'

'Let me take you to dinner. You can not tell me anything there instead, while I try to get you drunk enough to let something slip.'

'Last time what slipped was your hand.' Her tone made it sound like she was his mum telling him off. She noted the silence at the other end.

'Yes, sorry about that. Let me take you out as an apology.'

She'd let him, at some point. Keeping the press sweet was all part of the job. And she heard in his silence that there was no way he'd try it on with her again. But right now it was all about keeping him out of the loop so he would do everything he could to get in.

'Another time, definitely. But I really do have to go – things are wild here. Sorry.' She hung up before Ross could ask her anything else, well aware that he'd be speed-dialling another contact at *Falcon Bay*. Right now, though, it was time to feed Olivia. She grabbed her pass, looped it around her neck, and headed for the door.

At the same time, whether by coincidence or design she couldn't be sure, Jake came out of his office, in his tight jeans, stripped to the waist, glistening with massage oil, and planted himself in her path.

'You heard about my idea?' He beamed.

'Your idea?' She returned his smile. 'No. What is it?'

'We're going to audition a load of old cougars.'

A few women looked up from their desks before quickly dropping their gaze when they realized it was Jake speaking.

Not noticing, he continued. 'Helen says she can guarantee them still being hot. The best one will be *Falcon Bay*'s new bitch.'

'Oh!' She nodded, keen to make a speedy exit and prevent

more leakage. 'You mean Helen's idea? Yes, it's great. Sounds really interesting, but I've gotta dash. See you at home and we'll talk about it later.'

She glanced at him. His brow was furrowed.

'What do you mean?' he asked.

'The bitch was Helen's idea, no?'

'I don't care what she told you—'

'*She* didn't tell me – it was in the minutes of the meeting.'

His eyes went wide and then his face flushed when he realized he'd been busted. 'Since when do we minute story conference?'

'Since *you* asked for it. You wanted a record of who spoke in meetings and which writers were coming up with the ideas.'

She could practically hear the synapses firing in his brain. It was like his spirit had literally left his body and the shell was waiting for it to return, which it then did, and his eyes moved again. A smile came. She knew that look; it was classic Jake. He'd clearly figured out that the best Donald Trump way to deal with this trap was to 'fake news' his way out.

'Then somebody doctored the minutes, to make Helen look good. I'll get to the bottom of it, don't you worry.'

'I'm sure you will.'

She tried to slide past him without touching his slippery body. He was in power-games mode and she didn't have the time or the inclination to play. Olivia would be crying with hunger by now.

He put out a glistening arm. A few people popped their heads up from their desks again, sensing something was about to go off.

'Where you going?'

'It's not important,' she said lightly, attempting to get past, while still covering the milk stains on her blouse, not wanting anyone to think being a new mum affected her job in any way.

But Jake was unrelenting. 'I think you'll find that it's important to me. As your boss. The new owner's not going to look kindly on me allowing my wife to sneak off early, is she?'

'Give it a rest, Jake,' she said. And then, lowering her voice so that the room didn't hear, 'Just let me past, okay? I'll fill you in later.'

She continued to try and edge by him, but he stepped closer, blocking her exit.

One of the women nearby couldn't help herself – she sat watching them, transfixed, as if they were characters on set. Jake stared daggers at her, then turned his smarting anger back on Amanda. 'You sit down at your desk and do some work. After all, that's what we're paying you for.'

Not wanting to get into a public argument, she made another attempt to get past him. This time his oily hand grabbed her forearm, catching her blouse. Not even Brad's magic dry-cleaners would be able to get that mark out. She sighed, annoyed now. The room had fallen silent. Nobody knew which way this would go. She leaned in, so close they could kiss, but that was definitely not on offer from either of them.

'Take your hands off me.'

'Don't be so ridiculous.'

She pulled herself up tall, to her full five foot five, let her arms drop, revealing the milk stains on her blouse, and stared at him. As did the female staff around them. The men all looked away.

Finally realizing, and aware he was being watched, he let go and stepped back.

As she passed, embarrassed, Amanda looked deep into his eyes, searching for the Jake Monroe she'd fallen in love with, the one she'd married twelve years ago on the very beach they now found themselves in a turf war over. This new promotion had brought out the absolute worst in him, and becoming a father hadn't mellowed him in the way she'd hoped, but surely he had to still be in there – didn't he?

Desperate not to show the emotion she was feeling, she forced herself to take three deep yoga breaths and tried not to let the lump in her throat develop. She couldn't be seen to be crying in front of the staff, new mother or not, so she plastered on a smile and focused on putting one foot in front of the other. *Once the new owner's settled in*, she reasoned, *Jake will be a lot less stressed. It's just a phase. We can get through this.*

As she reached for the button for the lift, she heard footsteps behind her.

'Wait for me!' shouted Dan from finance.

The last thing she wanted was company right now, but even so, she held the lift door open and he sprinted in.

'I just wanted to check you were okay,' he said, his handsome face tilting ever so slightly to one side.

She gave him a tight smile, mumbled, 'I'm fine, thank you,' and pressed the button for the ground floor, where the crèche was. The lustful thoughts of earlier had entirely vanished. She just hoped the pads she'd popped in her bra would hold back the floodgates till he got out of the lift.

'I know it's not my place,' he continued, 'but I just wanted to say that if you ever want to talk, I'm here.

Amanda was taken aback. Aside from her best friends Farrah, Helen and Catherine, no other member of staff had ever checked in on her like that or asked her if she was alright. She was too high up the ladder, too close to Jake. Being new, Dan probably didn't know that. Or didn't care.

His simple act of kindness brought tears to her eyes. She was on the point of sobbing out loud when the lift doors pinged and she somehow managed to stumble away before she embarrassed herself by falling into his arms, desperately in need of being held.

4

Stacey Stonebrook's apartment was on the fourth floor of a three-hundred-year-old neo-Gothic building overlooking Kensington Gardens in central London. There was a doorman who wore the obligatory uniform and doffed his top hat to any lady who came or went. Through her vast windows Stacey could see the leafy park where she used to jog. Back in the day, she'd spot Princess Diana out there and the two would occasionally chat breathlessly during their daily workouts as they were pursued by paparazzi.

Diana hated having the press intrude on her, but Stacey used to love it. Although no one could ever hold a candle to the princess, on the days she was not around Stacey got the same sort of attention from the paps. Back then, just like the area she lived in, she was A-list. She'd chosen her apartment not simply because anyone who was anyone lived there (Elizabeth Taylor, Cher and Elton John had all had residences on her floor when she moved there), but also because its location was perfect. Central enough to get where she needed to go within minutes, but with a feel of the country thanks to the lush gardens opposite.

In the park, the sun was shining brightly as joggers jogged, children played and lovers kissed. London life was in full swing out there, but inside Stacey's apartment it was a very different vibe.

Stacey was in a fog, but one of her choosing. It was a *Valley of the Dolls* kind of haze that cocooned her as she lay in her freestanding bath. The water, when she moved, splashed over the side onto the marble floor. She'd filled the bath too high and was lying with her head resting on the rim, her chin sunk. As she sipped vintage Krug from a Baccarat champagne flute, she gazed down at the pink glow of the water, produced by the special bath salts she'd had shipped in from the Himalayas. Then she frowned, remembering it was the last of her supply. She could no longer afford the cost of having them specially imported. As she'd not worked in nearly five years, her once formidable bank balance wasn't the paradise mountain it used to be. Although she hated to let the idea even percolate in her addled brain, she knew there would come a time when this apartment would have to go, and that time was probably soon.

She'd miss bathing daily in these salts. She'd read in *Vogue* that their rich minerals fed the natural cells of the skin, leaving it plump and even-textured. She didn't know if they worked, but the pale pink colour they gave off as they dissolved certainly looked lovely; it was like gazing into your lover's eyes and seeing no judgement there, just an open-armed welcome. It occurred to Stacey that this feeling of near wild heaven was most likely the Xanax she'd taken half an hour ago mixing with the fizz.

She slipped beneath the water, everything submerged except two perfect tits and the breathing parts of her face. She knew that mixing bubbles and relaxants was a mistake (they were already causing conflicting messages in her brain), but to then add a warm bath to the cocktail – to be immersed in the heat of the water, the chill of the music playing in the background and the slideable shape of the tub – while it felt like heaven, had all the ingredients for a tragic early death.

Of course, an eighteen-year-old, which was how old she was when she first became famous, looking at Stacey's obituary wouldn't see it as early. Forty-nine to a teenager… well, that would be considered ancient. But when you were taking a too fast run at the big five-o, well it seemed too damn early.

Another downside to mixing fizz and Xanax was that you had no control over when you might fall asleep. Stacey began to think she'd better get out of the bath in case that sleep came too soon and she drowned. Her mind darkened at this thought, then went darker still when she asked herself: would anyone even care if she did?

A decade earlier, it would have been a different story. It would have been on the front page of every newspaper and very likely the lead item on news shows around the world – maybe not quite Whitney Houston coverage, but very close. They'd certainly have run the footage of her and Princess Di jogging through the park on a loop. But if it happened tonight, she'd be the thirty-second segment before throwing to the weather – that's if she was mentioned at all.

As for the papers, well, she'd be lucky to get her picture in one of the gossip columns, and it would be an unflattering pic at that. Maybe the one where she was caught coming out of a Botox centre, headscarf wrapped tightly and her forehead swelling like she'd been caught in a bee swarm. She might trend on Twitter for an afternoon at best, then no doubt all the porn she'd managed to bury with injunctions in her early career would start to appear online; after all, you couldn't libel the dead. The thought of men masturbating over her when she was cold in the grave gave her cause to smirk very briefly, before she realized how tragic that reaction was. God, she must be desperate for attention for that to have prompted a smile.

Feeling the second gear of the pills start to override the champagne, and keen not to die now that she'd imagined the underwhelming reaction to her early exit, she pulled the plug and the water began to gurgle away. How you could be so hot and then so cold within the space of what seemed like the blink of an eye still amazed her.

Rather than get out, she lay and watched the water drain, revealing her still perfect body. At forty-nine, that didn't come easy. Two-hour sessions with Han the hot yoga instructor helped – hot in body and temperature. He visited her three times a week. Also, her three boob jobs had ensured her perky pink breasts could still give a twenty-five-year-old a run for her money.

She got out of the bath, pulled a thousand-count Italian cotton towel around her toned stomach and curvy hips, and stumbled over to the gilt-edged dressing table. Before sitting down, she took in the view and admired herself, then wondered why nobody else seemed to do the same.

Once seated, she stared into the mirror and began her examination. Thanks to the surgeon's scalpel, her almond-shaped eyes were still taut. Rolling her fingers under her chin, she searched for any fat. Finding none, she smiled. Undoing the clips in her wet hair, which were meant to have kept it out of the bath water, she pulled her nonetheless soaked tresses into a ponytail, wrapped a towel around her head and slathered on a layer of La Prairie moisturiser.

She used to be sent masses of products for free, but not any more. In the past, the gift packs had come with Polaroids of cocks and the telephone number of the guy who had packed it on the back. She never called them – well, that's what she told her friends anyway.

Nobody had sent her a cock pic in quite a long time, not even on Instagram, which was flasher central. The doorbell of the apartment next to hers rang more than Stacey's phone, and the woman only lived there part time. Even her neighbour had stopped calling round, now that Stacey could no longer afford to throw the 'help yourself' coke parties.

No, no, no! If you keep following these thoughts, you're gonna end up crying, Stacey told herself. She could already feel her eyes welling up. She needed this moment to pass, needed to avoid becoming sad and tearful. Even though it was only mid-afternoon, she'd decided it was time to sleep, which was why she'd taken the damn pills in the first place. Last night had involved too much drink and nowhere near enough fun. She'd need to book a blow-dry later, after having gone to bed with wet hair, she noted, as, with the slightest stumble, she dropped her towel to the floor and got onto her giant oval bed. Taking a final sip from her glass and placing it on the bedside cabinet, she rubbed her HRT gel onto her perfect thighs, then slipped her naked body onto the cool of her white silk sheets. The erotic sensation of them gliding against her skin had given her an idea.

If she was quick, there'd be just enough time to treat herself to an orgasm, a big one. With one hand, she reached inside her dressing-table drawer, past the eighteen-karat, gold-plated vibrator which had cost a fortune and that she used when she had company, to find what she was really looking for. Not even the best lover in the world could get her off in the way her true secret pleasure-giver could. She'd worn her largest Prada sunglasses when she'd popped into her local Ann Summers store a few years back to purchase her Moregasm Rabbit – a friend had told her it was better than any man and she hadn't been wrong. Knowing what was about to happen, her nipples hardened and she was already wet as she slipped it gently inside herself and pressed on. With her other hand, she flicked on the TV in the wall opposite the bed, pressed a few buttons and suddenly her naked body, surrounded by men all taking turns to fuck her, filled the screen.

She had never wanted the public to see the porn she made before she was famous, but there was something so raw about it, that, just like the Rabbit, it was guaranteed to get her where she needed in under two minutes.

She fast-forwarded to the scene where she was being double-penetrated from behind while two other men were using her mouth for their pleasure and pushed the vibrator hard against her clit. As the vibrations began to shake deep inside her, she focused her face on the events on the screen from years ago. She imagined them all being here in her bed once more, and she flicked the control panel to its highest setting and ground her body down hard against the rabbit ears. Suddenly she was coming. Her back arched as a wet flood released from her body. She'd just begun to catch her breath when she felt the final notch of the drug cocktail kick in.

Here goes, she thought. *Coma bliss*. Any second now, her frettings about the fame that had been ripped from her would be gone. Negative thoughts disappeared from her opioid-filled mind. She turned off the TV, slid the Moregasm to one side and pulled the covers over her still quaking body. She focused her eyes on the gold coving that snaked around the room and melted into the honey wallpaper; the daylight that had snuck in through the heavy velvet curtains painted patterns on the wall opposite. Stacey let this trippy feeling wash over her, let the morphing images push away any dark thoughts of failure or unhappiness. She let the waves of Xanax and the afterglow of her orgasm envelop her as she drifted off to sleep.

She was deep in a dream world of female adoration and male desire when the phone on her bedside table silently lit up, and the name 'Agent' blinked on and off. On and off.

On...

and...

off.

5

At the back of the production building was a set of glorious red double-doors. They were too heavy for a mere mortal to pull open, which was why there was a silver button with a hand logo next to them. It was impossible to push this button without getting a thrill as the doors mechanically parted to reveal the tropical Narnia of the exterior *Falcon Bay* set.

Stepping through them that afternoon, Catherine Belle had, as usual, hesitated briefly to absorb the change in sensations: the gentle caress of the sea breeze on her skin, the sun on her face and the rhythmic whoosh of the waves lapping at the shore. The bay's golden sand became pebbles near the cliffs and on a day as calm as today the little round stones were perfect for skimming across the blue waters. Catherine was tempted, but she was due on set so decided to forego that pleasure.

There were several sea houses built into the cliffs and a couple at each end of the beach. The rugged stone buildings were hundreds of years old and had once been owned by local fishermen, but C.I.TV had snapped them all up when it picked this side of St Augustine's as the setting for its new soap. It had been quite a scandal at the time, buying out islanders whose families had been there for generations, but showbusiness paid well above market rates and Tina and Harry Pearson used to personally invite each of the former owners to the annual cast party so as to stay on friendly terms. The cottages would have been worth a mint now, but filming the show's heavy daily schedules while people were actually living in them would have been a nightmare, so they remained empty.

While the houses were real, the waterfront beach bar, The Cove, was entirely fabricated. Every show needs a place where the community can gather, so the network spent millions building the elaborate facade, which was attached to a wooden dock that stretched fifty feet out into the sea. Small boats were moored around it. They never filmed inside this constructed bar; it was purely for location. The interiors of the bar and the houses in the cliffs were all studio sets.

Every bar needs its landlady and every soap needs its matriarch and in *Falcon Bay* Lucy Dean was both. She had grown up the hard way, learned to fight for everything she had. She was the heart of the show and the heart of the *Falcon Bay* community. Lucy Dean owning The Cove made her the centre of everything.

Catherine Belle, the woman who inhabited the character of Lucy Dean, was without doubt a brilliant actress. She'd been on *Falcon Bay* since its inception, and though the writer of the first season had given Lucy her name, it was Catherine who truly breathed life into her. Catherine made her the most loved soap character of all time. Without Lucy Dean, many believed, there would be no *Falcon Bay*.

Today was a location day. Filming was taking place on the dock of The Cove. Cameras were in place. Sound technicians were at the ready. Farrah was the writer and director of this episode and she was in conversation with her director of photography and her producer, worrying that the clouds in the distance were fast approaching. Filming was on pause while they talked. Which meant the actors were meant to stay in place until Farrah was ready to call 'Action' again.

In the pause, Catherine stepped away from the shade and allowed the sun to wrap her in its glow. After three chemical peels, she was well aware she wasn't supposed to stand in its direct rays, but she couldn't resist the lure of its heat. Her eyes were closed as she listened to the soothing slap of the water against the wooden piles of the jetty and the flapping of the seabirds as they took off en masse from the crest of a wave. She enjoyed the tranquillity of the between-scenes lull that came when working on location. Though there were gaffers and boom boys, techies, DOPs and PAs bustling around her, she was still able to get lost in the soundscape of the natural world around her.

Even though Catherine had been on St Augustine's for the show's full thirty-nine-year duration, she never tired of the island's agreeable climate and unhurried pace. Her onscreen character had every reason to be sick of the place though. Lucy Dean had been married several times, had suffered rape and bereavement, had lost a child, found another, lost another daughter to drowning and then had a son go missing; she'd broken her back in a boating accident for the show's twentieth anniversary, had survived cancer and been menopausal; she'd been shot, was imprisoned for a murder she didn't commit, and had accidentally killed her last husband; and, inevitably, she'd had innumerable affairs of the heart with men she should never have got involved with.

She really should have been exhausted. But luckily it was all an act, it was just a role, and when the cameras stopped, she went back to being Catherine Belle, who was a much, much simpler person.

Feeling a tap on her shoulder, she turned to see Brad from wardrobe. 'Best get you back under the parasol or your dermatologist will kill me.'

'One more minute?' replied Catherine, though Brad was well aware this wasn't a question. Like all stars of her pedigree, Catherine was skilled at deploying a tone of voice and turn of phrase that did not invite denial or contradiction.

As she gazed out at the bobbing boats, Catherine's thoughts turned to the dip in the ratings. She hoped this problem would finally be fixed by the new owners. Ever the optimist, she reasoned that while she and everyone else on the show knew they were failing at the moment, when you looked back on their near forty-year reign, no other soap could beat them. *We'll survive this*, she thought. *We have to.*

She never wearied of being Lucy Dean and nor did she take her good fortune for granted. She was painfully aware that she'd have had a very different life if she hadn't landed this job forty years ago, thanks to a stroke of luck – for which she would be eternally grateful.

Catherine grew up in the rural plains of Oxfordshire, born Susan Lewis. She had once dreamed of becoming a doctor, but that went out the window when, as a teenager at college, she fell in love with a pot-smoking activist who lived in a commune. She abandoned her studies to spend three years attending peace rallies with him and was heartbroken when he left her for a goth who was much thinner. This sparked an eating disorder that would take her into her twenties, where she went from one gaslighting man to another, each seemingly worse than the last. Her last relationship had such a devastating effect on her, she fled to Dublin, a place she'd only ever seen in magazines, and it was there, by chance, that she fell in love again, but this time with a life partner much more suited to her – acting.

She was fast approaching thirty, doing bar work to get by, when she found her true calling. The landlady she worked for, Rosie, had once been in the Royal Shakespeare Company, but, like many actors, had failed to make it and so had returned home to Dublin to run her family's pub. To keep her hand in, Rosie decided to put on an Oscar Wilde play in the empty room above the bar. Thanks to a flu bug, she was one actor short, so she convinced Catherine to stand in, offering to pay her the same rate she got pulling pints of beer. It was a surprise to everyone, especially Catherine, that she was a natural on the stage. And on the third night of the play's short run, fate threw the deserving twenty-nine-year old a break.

Shuffling uncomfortably in her seat made from a beer crate, Caroline St James, head of casting for C.I.TV, was counting down the minutes until she could escape back to her five-star hotel nowhere near that side of town. Truth be told, she'd have paid good money not to have had to come and see her nephew in this tatty pub doing a terrible rendition of *The Importance of Being Earnest* (a play she had seen more times than the recommended dose and which she knew he was going to be terrible in), but family was family, so Caroline had made the visit to be supportive. By the end of the first act, however, the trip had suddenly proved to be worth it. She'd spotted a star in the making playing the role of Gwendolen. The young woman had such energy, Caroline couldn't take her eyes off her. At the interval, she snuck out to use the payphone in the noisy bar.

C.I.TV had high hopes for *Falcon Bay*. They'd spent the past year developing their new soap, which was now in pre-production, almost fully cast and ready to go. There was just one role they'd struggled to cast, the most important role of all: Lucy Dean. They'd seen just about every actress in the country and no one had been right, until tonight.

Although her résumé in the tatty show programme that had been printed on beer mats was blank, this young woman was the real deal, and Caroline knew it. She waited for her at the end of the play and convinced her to travel back to St Augustine's with her to audition. Catherine was hesitant. She'd only been acting for three days – could she really pull off such a ginormous leap to land a role in a television series she'd been reading about in all the papers that got left behind by drinkers in the bar?

Her dilemma became irrelevant when Rosie, furious that she'd not been spotted herself, sacked Catherine, making her homeless as the job came with lodgings. With nothing to lose, she flew back to the Channel Islands with Caroline St James to do her screen test and was hired on the spot.

A quick name change to really give her a fresh start and Catherine Belle was ready to embark on her new life. She'd paid her dues and karma had decided she was deserving of a jackpot.

After everything she'd been through, that hard-to-fabricate combination of homespun but sexy, dependable but exciting, loving but capable of being vitriolic when attacked just shone out of her. As soon as the first episode aired, both Catherine and *Falcon Bay* were a hit. Within weeks she was known to millions as the woman you wanted as your wife, your mother, your daughter or your friend. Without her, it was often argued, *Falcon Bay* wouldn't have been such a success, and she was one of the main reasons millions tuned in. An incandescent Rosie had banned *Falcon Bay* from ever being shown on the TV in her pub. She never got over Catherine's lucky break and for years after continued to regale anyone who'd listen with the story of the girl who'd robbed her of her last chance of fame.

Five hundred miles south of Dublin and nearly forty years on, Catherine once again marvelled, as she had so many times, at just how lucky she'd been. She'd only had two acting roles in her whole life – Gwendolen Fairfax and Lucy Dean – yet she'd been about as successful as it was possible to be in soap terms. She sent up a silent prayer to the soap gods above, requesting that they allow her good fortune to continue, then dutifully stepped back under the giant parasol just as Farrah called out, 'Places, everybody, please.'

Today was one of those deceptively simple scenes: half a

page, that was all. It looked for all the world as if it should be a 'one and done', a scene that was short and straightforward enough to require just a single take. And then it would be 'Moving on, people, please.'

Farrah had written the scene, which was perhaps where the trouble lay. She knew how crucial it was to the storyline as a whole. She knew the nuances needed in those four lines of dialogue. It set up the hour-long double-episode to follow; it was a head-turn moment for the audience. If they got it right, a high audience share the following day would be guaranteed – which was just what *Falcon Bay* really needed right now.

As writer and director of this episode, Farrah's goal was to make it so juicy that the audience would not only stay with the show but would also tell their friends that something big was coming in tomorrow's episode; enough to make them need to see it. While she had absolute faith that Catherine would help her achieve this, she had none in her co-star, even though the script was as simple as could be.

Lucy Dean has been through a lot. As she stares at the sea, she believes her fight has been won. She believes life can go back to normal. Eyes closed, guard down, a slight smile of relief on her face. Until her peace is broken by a voice.

JEREMY: Hope you've got your Factor 50 on.

Lucy opens her eyes but doesn't turn.

JEREMY: I'd hate to see you get burned twice in one day.

He steps between her and the sun, a piece of paper in his hand.

JEREMY: The Cove is mine. Signed, sealed and delivered.

She doesn't have to look at the paper: she knows she's been betrayed. She looks him in the eyes, full-on Lucy Dean mode.

LUCY: Over my dead body.

Now Jeremy's smile grows and in that smile we see his unsaid words, 'God, I hope so.' Despite Lucy's bluffing, she sees it too. The battle is a long way from over. We come out on her fear that she's lost her precious bar.

END OF EPISODE 9048

Lucien Horsefall's CV claimed he'd been in shows all over London's West End, but if he had, it was as an understudy who'd had less audience time than a box-office assistant. He'd come to *Falcon Bay* in its fifth year and had somehow clung on to his role as Jeremy Lloyd, despite several attempts to kill him off. Not because he was a bad actor, which he was, or because he was annoying, which was also not uncommon. It was his inability to learn his lines that had him on everyone's dread-to-work-with list.

Learning lines was the one job every actor was meant to be able to guarantee. Actors like Catherine were exceptional because of their talent and because of their ability to get underneath the lines, to make choices that changed the text. That was the alchemy of acting. Learning lines was the bare minimum. But even that shortcoming might have been forgiven in Lucien if he'd have just admitted it and called for a prompt.

What Lucien did instead of calling for a prompt was to make up lines off the top of his head. This had a terrible knock-on effect for continuity and naturally got the writers' backs up, not to mention infuriating the cast and director. The audience, however, had no idea of the nightmares he caused, and his character was continually popular in the show polls, so everyone ended up having to work around him. And while Catherine was a pro at dealing with Lucien, it took a tremendous amount of effort not to kick him in the balls, which meant Farrah had to also consider Catherine's mood too. The heat today was also a factor; it made the crew lethargic and a bit tetchy. So this half-a-page 'one and done' had suddenly become a powder keg waiting to explode. Which was why Farrah had trepidation in her voice as she called 'Action!'

Catherine stared at the sea, then closed her eyes. She tried to convey the sense that Lucy Dean was tired but relieved. She herself was burying the anxiety that always came when working with Lucien. When his voice piped up from behind her, she knew that anxiety was justified.

JEREMY: 'Have you got some sun cream…?'

The script said she should keep standing there, registering his words but not turning. Couldn't he see the monumental fuck-up he'd just made? She knew Lucien would be pleased that he had remembered the line was about sun cream, but his paraphrasing of the line had changed two important things: firstly, the now benign question would require a different response from Catherine, and secondly he couldn't follow through with his next two lines.

Farrah, however, allowed him to try. Catherine could practically hear his teeth grinding as he ruminated. There was a sudden joy in his voice at remembering his line. Or at least the first part of it.

JEREMY: 'I'd hate to see you get sunburned.'

And that was it: 'Have you got some sun cream, because I'd hate to see you get sunburned.' In this new version, he was a benevolent friend looking out for her. The absolute opposite of what the scene was about.

Finally, Farrah stepped in, calling 'Cut!'

Immediately, a parasol was opened over Catherine to shield her from the sun. She didn't turn to look at Lucien. It was better to stay out of it. Farrah was good; she knew what she was doing.

'Well done, Lucien. Nearly there. Tiny thing… it's "Hope you've got your Factor 50 on",' Farrah said in a voice she might use to a struggling child on a bad school sports day.

Lucien ran a hand through his thick hair. It was no secret that he was proud to have such lovely locks at his age.

He clearly knew he'd messed up his script, but rather than admit it, he tried to rationalize his line changes by using every actor's get-out-of-jail-free card.

'I don't think Jeremy would say that, actually.'

'Okay, okay. I'm fine with that,' said Farrah, displaying her trademark on-set patience. 'So long as the next line is "I'd hate to see you get burned twice in one day." That's the important bit.'

'That's what I said,' he bluffed.

'Hmm,' was Farrah's response. As this was the first take of what could be many, she let it go and took it on the chin. 'My bad,' she said. 'Let's go again. And if you could hammer that line home, to make sure I don't miss it again. Sorry. My fault, people. Let's go again.'

There was a puzzled creasing of Lucien's brow and a few seconds of silence as he visibly prepared himself to double-down on his lie. Then he turned to the male boom operator. 'I mean, she's lovely and everything,' he mumbled, 'but female directors…?'

What she wanted to do was call him out on his comment, or better still smash his teeth in, but like the professional that she was, Farrah bit down on her lip, took up her position and got ready to call 'Action!'

Catherine watched the boom operator shuffle away awkwardly. He obviously didn't want to contradict Lucien, but nor did he want to endorse his sexist comment either – a typical male fence-sitter. Although she could see he was in a difficult position, Catherine still thought it was cowardly. As the matriarch of the show, she had no hesitation about sticking her oar in. 'Us women do so well letting men think they're right,' she said loudly, 'even when they're wrong. It's a skill and a handicap.'

Lucien tried to unpick this complicated sentence and then latched onto the only thing he could. 'I don't think we're allowed to say "handicap" any more.'

'*You* can,' Catherine said. 'For you, it's reclaiming the word.'

Lucien made an O-shape with his mouth as he tried to muddle through another of Catherine's tricky sentences. He was like a Buddhist monk being given a koan by his master and struggling to figure out the truth of it.

Farrah yelled, 'Action!'

And they were off. Catherine stared at the sea, closed her eyes and waited. And waited. And waited. And then…

'Are you saying I'm handicapped? Which should be "disabled" anyway. Which I'm not.'

Oh, for fuck's sake! Catherine was one more wrong take away from throttling him.

Farrah stepped in again. 'Actually, the term is "a person with a disability",' she said. 'And if you don't mind, I'd really like to get this scene done. We've five more to do with you, Lucien, and these clouds won't hold off forever.' She took a breath, hesitated. 'Catherine… for me… could you say sorry?'

Catherine looked Farrah in the eyes, a cold, hard, Lucy Dean stare that said, *Are you fucking serious?*

Farrah mouthed the word 'please'. Hands in prayer, begging.

Lucien had that sanctimonious look men have when they know they're in the wrong but think they've got away with it. This time with the added bonus that the mouthy little lady had been put in her place. His O-shaped mouth was in a full-on smirk that made Catherine want to punch him.

She took a moment. She could, and should, kick off. She had the power here, she was number one on any call list. She could have Lucien fired and, probably, at a push, Farrah too. She'd done it before, got people sacked: crew, cast, even catering. But that wouldn't get the scene done. And what Catherine wanted more than anything was to be inside.

She'd loved her time out there in the September sun and sea breeze, but the heat was getting to her now. Brad had been right; she should have stayed under the parasol. Lesley Reynolds, 'the Queen of Harley Street', the woman who kept her looking so youthful, would have a fit if she knew Catherine had broken the celebrity code by letting the rays touch her well-preserved skin.

So, to further her own ends, an apology was the right response. One thing she knew for sure was that Lucien would give her plenty of opportunities to show him up in the future.

'Lucien, I'm sorry. That was out of order. We're pros – it's the heat. Now, shall we...?'

His smile made her want to explode and he even topped it off by giving a little bow. Then he did the unthinkable and called, 'Action!'

Catherine noted Farrah's reaction, but Farrah swallowed it down, then gave a tiny nod of thanks to her. But Catherine ignored it, because asking *her* to apologize to *him* was a shitty thing to do.

Farrah caught the look Catherine was giving her and knew she'd have to make up for it later, but everybody was tetchy now; the sun might have been bright, but there was a growing sense of bad feeling shading the set and she just wanted this done.

They returned to their marks, Farrah repeated her call for action, Catherine waited and finally Lucien delivered his line.

JEREMY: 'Hope you've got your Factor 50 on.'

Jesus H Christ, thought Catherine, *he's only gone and got it right*. She was about to turn and finish the scene when a booming voice cut through the air.

'Farrah, darling, you've got my star!'

A collective sigh rang out from the crew as Farrah yelled 'Cut!' and turned to see Aiden Anderson striding over the sand dunes. Despite the heat, he was wearing drainpipe-tight ripped blue jeans, a white T-shirt, and a red scarf with the words 'Rock and Roll' around his neck. His shock of blonde hair bounced like a seventies advert for shampoo as he bounded towards them. He really was a walking cliché. Even before his midlife crisis he'd looked like a man smack bang in the middle of one.

You'd think at fifty-two, having survived two motorbike accidents, he might dial it down a bit, Farrah thought as he got closer, chewing gum loudly as he approached. She tried to stop her face from showing how much he irritated her, because, like Hugh Grant, even when Aiden Anderson was being annoying, he was really charming with it. He bumbled his way through faux pas after faux pas with a hamster-cheek smile, dopey eyes and an upper-class, 'So sorry. Sorry all.'

His charm didn't work on her though. Every time Farrah saw Aiden, she wanted to throw a lit match onto his grease-slicked hair. The fact that Aiden was seen as *Falcon Bay*'s number one director really fucked her off, as did his habit of mentioning it in every conversation. She was certain he'd simply said it enough until it became true. A number one tactic of male success. He got all the episodes Farrah wanted. But if she were to complain about it, she'd be considered a jealous bitch. So all she could do was be nice to him and hope the quality of her own work would speak for itself.

'Aiden, how can I help you?' Farrah said, attempting to keep her tone jovial.

'Hate to be a pain and all, but we have the pleasure of Ms Belle's company. Schedules don't lie.'

Farrah was now looking at her schedule. 'I've got her until three.' She tried to show him, but he batted it away.

'For a one and done? I think everybody expected Catherine to be on her way by now. We're all set up and waiting.'

Farrah looked at her watch. It was fifteen minutes to. The sun was scorching, and there was a trickle of sweat descending her brow. She wiped it away, not wanting it to look like this situation was making her perspire. Farrah was well aware that Aiden was calling her on her ability. But everyone knew that Lucien's line issues delayed any director who had scenes with him; it was an unspoken understanding that his scenes always ran over. Plus this scene wasn't done. And without it, she had no end of episode.

She continued to try and keep her cool, even though the sun was now burning her neck. She wished someone would hold a parasol over her like they were over Catherine.

'I've got her till three, and if we go over because of…' – she threw her eyes towards Lucien – 'then that's just how it is. I'll apologize then. But right now I'm within my schedule, which this chitchat is eating into.'

Aiden smiled, trying to disarm her with his dimples. 'I'm not one to pull rank, darling, but I've got to get through my scenes quick as, so I can attend tonight's meeting about the live ep I'm doing.'

It took Farrah a few seconds to deal with both the shock and the disappointment. He'd got the Christmas live episode. The cream of the cream. He'd just been handed it by his best mate Jake. No discussion, no chat with all the directors. It had gone to the old guard, same as always. Farrah had been working on a whole pitch about why she was the right choice for the Christmas live. How they were in exceptional times and the audience wanted something new, *a woman's touch*.

But Jake hadn't even given her the chance. And Farrah realized that he never would. The boys' club was very much alive and kicking in *Falcon Bay*, no matter how many amazing women were working there.

'Farrah, darling…' Catherine said. 'Maybe we should…' And she pointed to the waiting crew.

Farrah looked at the crew and then at Catherine. It was subtle, but it was definitely there. A change in Catherine's manner towards Aiden. And the rest of the crew too. Farrah could see it. The way Catherine had taken a few steps closer to the director who would lead her through an hour of live TV. She was aligning herself with the power on the set. And that was exactly how the boys' club survived, because amazing women didn't stick together, which allowed men to keep the power.

Farrah bit down on her lip, hard. She was furious and disappointed. But she was also hurt. Catherine Belle, of all people! The woman who, at seventy, epitomized the talent that made *Falcon Bay* the powerhouse it was – the talent that also happened to be female. Catherine Belle, who had faced down male execs her whole career. Farrah choked back her fury. She knew there was no point arguing. About the schedule or even about Aiden being the director of the live episode. It was all decided and she'd been kept out of the room where the decisions got made. Worse than that, she didn't even enter their heads when they made their decisions.

'I'm sure we can get this scene done in one take,' Catherine added, aware enough not to look at Farrah because she knew she was letting her down. She hoped Farrah would understand, perhaps trade it against that ludicrous apology she'd asked her to give Lucien.

Actually, Farrah did understand. She understood just fine. And liked Catherine less for it. In that moment, her old and dear friend, the woman who had played her mother on screen and nurtured her through her career, had betrayed her.

Aiden looked at Farrah, aware he'd won, but his eyes were those of a sad puppy asking to be forgiven.

With no choice, Farrah turned to the crew. 'Okay, people – positions.'

Farrah and Catherine walked silently to their places. Catherine, sensing the vibe was bad, was about to apologize, but Farrah cut her off.

'You'd better just hope Lucien delivers,' spat a pissed-off Farrah.

With nothing to lose in the scenario now, Catherine decided to give it back to her. 'Actually, darling, you're in charge. So if Lucien doesn't deliver, I think you'll find the shit's on you, not me.' And to really rub it in, she added, 'Shall we get on with it? Aiden is waiting.'

Farrah glanced over at Aiden, who gave her his trademark killer smile. *No way am I going to give him the pleasure of watching me fail*, she thought as she turned to Catherine.

As angry as she was, Farrah was determined not to show herself up. She needed to find a workaround that even Lucien couldn't mess up. 'Okay, this is what I want you to do,' she said, smiling through gritted teeth as she quietly gave Catherine instructions, then turned to the crew and bellowed, 'People! We're doing this in one take, so let's go. Action!'

Lucy Dean stared at the sea. She tried to communicate the sense that she was tired but relieved. She heard footsteps behind her. Before Jeremy even opened his mouth, Lucy turned and saw he was holding a piece of paper. She crossed to him and snatched it out of his hand.

Lucien was shocked. Jeremy hadn't even said his line yet. But Catherine barrelled on, exactly as Farrah had told her to.

Lucy looked at the contract, looked at Jeremy, then screwed it up and threw it at his feet.

LUCY: 'Over my dead body.'

Still in character, Catherine walked away from her nemesis, determined to fight to the bitter end.

'Cut!' yelled Farrah. 'That's a wrap.' And then, to both Catherine and Aiden, 'Now get the fuck off my set.'

Catherine visibly flinched at this, but Farrah didn't care. She stood and watched the two of them striding towards the beach buggy that would transport them to the next location. She was more angry at Catherine than she was at the men who'd caused this. Falcon Bay*'s star actress will find out what it's like not to be supported next time she's on set*, she thought, shielding her eyes to avoid the spray of sand kicked up by the buggy's tyres as it hurtled across the beach.

6

Hundreds of miles away from the *Falcon Bay* beach, another actress was having a difficult time on a waterside location. This set certainly wasn't as picturesque: it was a warehouse in East London, next to a filthy canal. When her driver finally found the address, she was sure it couldn't be the right place, but, once inside, she sadly found it was. Lydia Chambers couldn't imagine Gwyneth Paltrow being dropped off here. There was no air-con or even windows in the studio. The cameras were so tiny they looked like toys and the lighting was worse than you'd get on a prison mugshot.

As she was led onto the set, Lydia had a bad feeling. When her agent had set the audition up, she'd said, 'It's not for one of the main channels, but it's well paid, and cable channels are very popular these days.' So Lydia had been determined to give it her best.

However, pretty quickly, she realized she'd made a huge mistake. The lights were way too hot and all the powder in the world couldn't prevent her expertly applied make-up beading with sweat and dripping down her face. The crew stared expectantly at her, wondering if this would be a car crash or a comeback.

Lydia's self-help guru had promised the latter. The two of them had screamed at a rock all morning, and she had really gone for it. There was a lot to let go of: her anger at having been forgotten by her fans; her deep sense of betrayal at having been sacked off the second biggest soap in Britain; her pain at being passed over by men who were the same age as her but derided her for being 'past it', ignoring the fact that she was still very attractive, whatever the age on her birth certificate said. And, lastly, she'd screamed at her insecurity, the inner voice that constantly told her all those traitors were right, that she wasn't good enough, was nothing but a has-been, had truly had her day.

Lydia channelled the positive affirmations they'd been working on as the tiny camera zoomed towards her.

'What an amazing locomotion,' she said, squinting at the autocue, then corrected herself – 'I mean "location"!' – before proceeding to get every other word wrong in her dreadful five-minute screen test. 'And finally, Mr Crawford reported that he was petrified of the black face,' she continued. There was a collective gasp and she squinted again. 'Sorry! "Rat race"!'

The room fell silent, bar a few stifled giggles. When her audition was over, Lydia just stood there, in absolute horror at what a monumental screw-up it had been. She'd fumbled from the off; it hadn't just been a car crash, it had been an absolute pile-up. The crew, mainly gay men in their forties who'd fawned over her when she arrived, saying how fabulous she was and how excited they'd been to see her name on the list, looked embarrassed. They were clearly disappointed that the Lydia Chambers they'd adored was from the past, an altogether different being. She had walked on set as a gay icon but had stumbled off as just another actress who'd lost her sparkle. They all smiled awkwardly at her, trying to offer her reassurance, but she knew she'd fucked it up.

And all because she was too vain to wear her bloody glasses. She couldn't wear contact lenses after botched laser surgery in the nineties had wrecked her eyes. This was fine when she was learning lines, as she did that in the privacy of her own home, but she'd be damned if she was going to be seen in public with her glasses on. She'd come to the audition hoping she could wing it, but underestimated just how small the autocue would be. She wasn't just losing her sight, she was losing her shine, buried beneath a slurry of failed auditions and knocked confidence.

As she walked unsteadily towards the exit, she noticed that standing outside were a couple of fans waiting for autographs and pictures. Wiping the last remnants of the sweat off her brow, she fluffed up her hair and readied herself, but as she came out of the door all smiles and teeth, the selfie hunters let her pass with barely a glance. No one was waiting to see her. In fact no one looked at her at all.

Lydia wanted to scream at them, *Don't you know who I am?* But she caught herself as she realized how desperate that sounded. She used to be the face on every magazine, but that was nearly fifteen years ago, a lifetime in television. In her prime, she'd won Soap Bitch of the Year three consecutive times, but then she overestimated her worth by refusing to sign a new contract unless she got a forty per cent increase in her episode fees. Her agent, Sheena McQueen, had strongly advised her not to be so demanding, but Lydia, knowing she was way up on the world's most popular actress list, was belligerently insistent. Just three months later, Lydia's character was crushed to death by a herd of stampeding cows.

The Soap Bitch of the previous year won best comedy scene at the next, but Lydia wasn't there to collect the award. The cow scene brought about not only the death of her character but also the death of her acting career. Nobody would see her for serious or sexy roles again. She tried to embrace her new brand by doing comedy sketch shows and late-night chat interviews, but there was always some cow reference. And it all just got so old.

A bit like she felt now.

She still looked amazing, especially considering she'd just turned sixty, but these days she had to work twice as hard as she used to in order to look not even half as good as she had the year before. It was exhausting.

Sometimes she fantasized about letting nature take its course. Giving in to the ageing process, doing the whole Helen Mirren thing. But then she'd catch sight of women in the street who were letting the years ravage them and she'd remember that without the Helen Mirren award-winning acting jobs, the Helen Mirren thing looked a lot like giving up. So now she went running in the gaps where she wasn't working, which was every day, and when she wasn't jogging, she was toning, preening, pruning and doing whatever nips and tucks were needed to keep her looking this good. At five foot eight, nine stone, flat-bellied, and with shiny, unwrinkled skin, full-bodied flame-red hair and bee-stung lips, she still turned heads. It was just that no one actually recognized her.

She fumbled in her bright red vintage Chanel Boy bag for her mobile. Her fifty-carat citrine-and-diamond cocktail ring caught on the lining as she fished around trying to locate it. When she found it, she dialled Sheena McQueen's number. The call went to voicemail. Lydia swore and the curse was swallowed up by the London traffic. She flicked it back off, leaving no message, as her car pulled up at the roadside for her to get in.

Her long-time driver, Jeff, got out to open the door for her. Jeff had driven Lydia for more than twenty years, so he was pretty good at reading her slumped posture, and it concerned him. He hated seeing her like that. He was very fond of her and she had always looked after his family. He'd decided that the day she got back on her feet and settled into a new job, he'd let a studio driver take over and he would retire, happy in the knowledge that even in the bad times he'd been there for her. His wife Joyce had her heart set on a cottage like she'd seen in *Poldark*. She was obsessed by the show and felt certain she and Jeff should live out their remaining years in Cornwall, but with them both now in their seventies, she kept reminding him that time was running out. Looking at Lydia, despondent and weary, Jeff knew for sure that his wife's dream was still some way off.

'How was it?' he asked. 'I bet you knocked it out of the park, right?' He mimed swinging the bat, watching his imaginary baseball fly across the street.

Lydia didn't answer, afraid she might get choked up. She

loved Jeff; he'd been so loyal to her. One time he even got into a fight to protect her from some French paps. English paps were bad, but the French ones were unstoppable; if you were on a hideaway beach, they'd hire jet skis just to get to you. Like Catherine the Duchess of Cambridge, she'd once sued and won against a French magazine that had printed topless pictures of her, but unlike the duchess, no one would try and take those sorts of pictures of her any more. Looking at his kind face, Lydia struggled to lie to Jeff. He reminded her of her late brother, who'd been dead for more than ten years now. Jeff had that solidity about him, that true essence of gentlemanliness, so she just shrugged and got in the car.

'Well, there's always next time, Ms Chambers,' he said gently as he closed the door.

Lydia wondered if he was right. How many failed 'next times' was she prepared to put herself through? When she was at drama school, they'd told her there was no point going into the business if you didn't have a thick skin. And she had responded with lots of resilience when the work first dried up. She took every knock with grace, shrugging it off and readying herself for the next, just like Liza Minnelli bellowing 'Maybe This Time' and refusing to let anything stop her. *Though looking at Liza now*, Lydia thought, *maybe I should update my role model to somebody more robust.*

She reminded herself that, unlike most out-of-work stars and thanks to wise investments in her heyday, at least her bank balance was still productive, even if she wasn't, so she was better off than most in her position. Suddenly she felt better.

Screw this, was her next thought. Her therapist was always advising her to stay in control. *I'll be my own role model. I'll get myself through this and anybody not on board with Project Lydia can get the hell off the train.*

She straightened the shoulder pads on her lilac Dior jacket, then took her phone out again. As the car weaved in and out of the busy afternoon traffic trying to make its way back to the civilized centre of London, she hit redial.

Once more, it predictably went to voicemail, but this time she decided to leave a message.

'Sheena, it's Lydia. I would appreciate it if you would answer your phone when I ring. You know I've just had that audition, so obviously I'm calling to tell you how it went...' She said this in what most people would consider a polite telephone voice, then she breathed in and really let rip. 'Well, it went fucking abysmally. Which you obviously know, otherwise you'd be picking up. I blame you for this. The job was totally wrong for me. I am an actress, and a bloody good one. I do not want to be reading shitty autocues on some cable channel next to a canal that stinks of piss. I want an acting job. Do you hear me? And no fucking comedy. If you have forgotten who I am, then I suggest you google me to refresh your fucking memory. I am a multi-award-winning actress, so fucking well start treating me like one.'

Jeff closed his ears to the swearing, if there was one thing he couldn't bear, it was swearing. Particularly in a lady. He just hoped she wouldn't use the C-word.

'You make a big thing about the fact that you've never been sacked. Well, I've been a top earner for the McQueen Agency over the years and the fact that I'm not earning now I place entirely at your door. You need to take your share of the responsibility for my stalled career. I'm putting you on notice. So listen up... I want you to find me the best role going. One that when you hear of it, you think, "Lydia Chambers will nail that part."'

She took a breath, allowing the pause to work its magic, and then added the kicker. 'And if I don't land it, then we're done. You and me, we're over, for good. After which I'll be known for two things, the woman who was crushed by a cow, and the actress who sacked Sheena McQueen.'

7

In Christie St John's Hair Salon in a trendy back street off London's Oxford Circus, Sheena McQueen was having a blow-dry on her glossy mahogany-brown hair while reading the latest *Vogue*. She wanted to look her absolute sexiest for her date that evening and she knew Christie, whose client list was a who's who of anyone who was anyone, would not let her down.

She'd just finished her affogato when Lydia Chambers' number flashed up on her mobile. With the noise from the hairdryer, there was little point in answering as she wouldn't be able to hear, plus she already knew that Lydia's screen test had been a washout. A friend on the set had WhatsApped her some footage, next to an emoji of a grimacing face. Lydia was lucky it had been gay guys on the crew, who felt sorry for her, not anyone she'd previously had a run-in with, otherwise this would have gone viral by now and Lydia would have found herself innocently caught up in a race row.

That could still happen. Everything found its way online these days, Sheena mused, watching the clip again. She couldn't hear the sound, but she could tell it was a total wipe-out. If it did leak, then that would be yet another situation she would have to un-fuck. She sighed. What clients like Lydia didn't get was that Sheena had to call in favours and pull strings just to get her on the list for an audition like that. So when they went wrong, it was her rep on the line not theirs.

The McQueen Agency represented TV's hottest stars, on screen and off, and Sheena was its CEO and eponymous founder. She had most of the top female actresses from all the soaps and continuing dramas, with Catherine Belle her top earner. She also represented her oldest and best friend Farrah Adams, who was a writer-director on *Falcon Bay*. Farrah had told Sheena many times that she considered actresses like Lydia to be dry rot in a stack of wood. 'You need to get rid of them before their bad name affects the rest of the pile.' But that just wasn't Sheena. Because while she was a ballbreaker in contract negotiations, she actually had a soft heart. She knew what it was like to have been loved on a soap and then cast aside by the execs. She knew it first hand and not only had she survived, she'd prevailed.

'Happy, darling?' Christie asked in her heavy Brazilian accent, the second she turned off the hairdryer.

Sheena looked at her in the mirror and, admiring Christie's work, said, 'Fabulous, as always.' Glancing down, she saw that her phone was beeping away again. This time it was Farrah, which brought a smile to her face.

She and Farrah had been friends since they were teenagers, since Farrah had effectively saved her life. Later, Sheena had returned the favour.

As girls, they'd both been very successful young actresses, but where Farrah had been a strikingly mature and sensible youngster, Sheena's story had run the depressingly familiar route from precocious child star to teen fuck-up heading for rehab. It had not helped that Sheena's parents could see no further than the sordid mess their daughter's life became and wanted nothing to do with her, despite her tender age. Farrah, on the other hand, had a supportive family and a psychotherapist for a father.

It had all started so well for Sheena. At just eight years old, she landed the role of Linda on a globally syndicated drama set in the British countryside called *Second Chances*. She won best newcomer, reducing everybody to an emotional heap with her humble and cute acceptance speech, but by the time she was fifteen she was damaged goods. Going through puberty in front of millions messed with her mind and made her an easy target for sexual predators, who were rife in an industry filled with minors being treated like adults.

Papers ran photos of her everywhere she went, and in every shot she had a man by her side: socialite Ed Nichols, her sordid abuser, the Jeffrey Epstein of his day. A self-made millionaire studio investor, friend to royals, politicians and the filthy rich, whose true interest lay in grooming impressionable young stars, plying them with drugs and taking them to debauched parties where they were raped and passed between powerful men. Sheena tried to blank out what was done to her, but in the dead of night she'd wake screaming and reach for more booze and drugs to numb the pain. It was no wonder she couldn't perform on set.

To those who didn't know about the grooming and took

Sheena at face value, she just seemed to be yet another famous soap teen who was entitled, rude, at times violent, and addicted to drugs. There were plenty of other 'star children' just like her who were struggling with similar demons. Farrah, luckily, wasn't one of them, but there was a young boy called Calvin Butler who was passed around in the same circles. He played Catherine Belle's son on rival soap *Falcon Bay*. Long before Sheena became Catherine's agent, in what seemed like another life altogether, the teenage Sheena would find herself with Calvin, high on drugs at the same parties, being abused by the same men. Later, when they saw each other at soap awards parties, they'd nod a hello and exchange a few words but would never ever talk about what they were going through.

Eventually Nichols was caught trying to sell a thirteen-year-old he'd groomed to a sheik who was willing to pay millions. The *Herald* got hold of the story and went hard at Nichols, who, after being the subject of a month's worth of daily front-page headlines, killed himself in his prison cell while on remand. But by then the damage to Sheena and many others had been done.

Her name became synonymous with Nichols. Whenever the victims were mentioned, it was her photo that was splashed across the screen because she was instantly recognizable. Had she known? Was she involved? The press hounded her with questions, but, still in denial, she refused to comment. Her days on set became more chaotic, her nights of drugs and drink became never-ending and yet she still couldn't bring herself to tell anyone she'd been a victim too. Inevitably she was suspended from *Second Chances* because of her behaviour; in response, she blurred her pain with more drugs.

After one all-night party she awoke from her stupor to find an overdosed rock star dead in her bath. Realizing she'd had a total blackout, she turned to her bosses at *Second Chances* for help. But when the repeatedly violated, troubled, teenage addict eventually reached out to the very people who had put her in the line of danger, she was betrayed. The minute the news of his death, alongside her picture, was all over the world's tabloids, the producers sacked her, citing the moral clause of her contract and making the fifteen-year-old sign an agreement claiming she was leaving of her own accord.

Her next couple of years were a mess, but then one night Farrah found her at an industry party and rescued her. The two girls barely knew each other then, even though the younger Farrah was being loudly touted in the press as the new Sheena, but Farrah wasn't the daughter of a psychotherapist for nothing. When she saw Sheena on a sofa, dead-eyed, gaunt-faced and high on heroin, with two disgusting men taking advantage of her, Farrah immediately understood that serious help was required. Within minutes, she'd dragged the zonked-out Sheena out of the club, into a cab and into the hands of the one man she knew Sheena could trust – Farrah's father.

Farrah's dad had links to a clinic in the States that specialized in treating teenage addicts and it wasn't long before Sheena found herself in San Francisco, within sight of the skyline silhouette of Alcatraz, which made a perfect metaphor for her own prison of addiction. She stayed there for three years, spending a full year at the clinic and a further two in therapy.

She celebrated her twenty-first birthday alone in a tiny roof apartment in Haight-Ashbury with just the landlady's cat for company. Money was tight, but she had her sobriety, her mind and Farrah, who wrote her weekly letters. For the first time in her life, she felt whole. And she had Farrah to thank for it. Looking back, their early friendship reminded her of CC Bloom and Hillary in the film *Beaches*.

As Christie applied some finishing touches to Sheena's perfect mane, another text popped up on Sheena's phone. It was from her dinner date for later that evening. She'd arranged it online earlier. It was just a no-strings hook-up really, but she liked to do the dinner part first to check there was chemistry. She'd made the mistake of going straight to the bedroom even when things hadn't clicked in the past, so now if she wasn't feeling it by the main course, she'd skip dessert and go home alone. Bad sex was definitely not on any menu she would order from. She never had a problem getting a date, and some developed into affairs, but the last thing Sheena wanted was a live-in lover. She liked the freedom to pick and choose and she knew how to protect herself from heartbreak.

People assumed she'd never settled down because of what happened with Ed Nichols and his paedophile cronies. But it was only when she got to the States that she finally had the space, perspective and privacy to discover what she truly wanted – sexually and professionally. After rehab, she spent the rest of her twenties relishing the freedom to experiment, the freedom that came from being out of the limelight and unrecognized. She lived for a long time in New Zealand, worked on a street art festival there, found her way to New

York and produced some off-Broadway shows, hung out in Laos for months, returned to the States, got a gig as a camera operator on a TV music show and befriended a struggling girl band who'd been dumped by their label. It was here that she finally found her niche. She became their manager, got them a new deal and then went off with them on a sold-out world tour. So, by the time she rocked back into the UK at the age of twenty-eight, she'd packed a hell of a lot into her short life and was a lot wiser than when she'd left.

By this point, Farrah was also looking for a change. She'd done the best part of a decade as Lucy Dean's daughter on *Falcon Bay*, but acting no longer fulfilled her and she wanted to write. Sheena didn't see why that meant Farrah would have to leave the show. Why couldn't she just cross the corridor and join the writing team?

'But that's unheard of in this business,' Farrah said.

Sheena laughed. 'Unheard of just means it's not happened yet. Leave it to me.'

The next morning she popped into the *Falcon Bay* wardrobe to see the new stylist, Brad, a fashion-forward gay guy who had started his career designing costumes for musical theatre but, fed up of being the only black man backstage, had decided to network his way into a more diverse industry. He'd lucked out when he'd done Farrah's hair and make-up for an awards ceremony, and she was so impressed she persuaded C.I.TV to hire him on the spot. As per Farrah's request, Brad kitted Sheena out in a power dress with shoulder pads and a sharp V-cut to her cleavage. Thinking about it today, Sheena marvelled at the stuff she used to wear back then. With a cloud of hairspray hanging around her 'do' and just the right amount of Chanel, she made her way to the exec's office without an appointment.

Falcon Bay's exec back then was Colin O'Connor, who had also been a producer at *Second Chances*, so when he saw Sheena, he was blown away by how well, sorted and together she was. Sheena proudly said she was eight years sober and nothing like the girl she used to be. Colin was genuinely pleased to see that she was okay and told her he thought the bosses above him at *Second Chances* had been wrong to fire her. Technically she'd been a minor, so even with her serious problems, they should have honoured their duty of care to look after her...

But Sheena shut him down. 'Old news,' she said. Which was her default position whenever anybody brought up her difficult past or the spectre of Ed Nichols. 'I want to talk about right now,' she told him firmly.

He assumed she was there for an acting gig. And, funnily enough, they were about to cast a new role. She wouldn't even have to audition...

For one brief moment Sheena had imagined what it would be like to be back on a soap, in the full beam of the spotlight, on one of the world's most adored programmes. Then she thought about the parties, the need to boost her self-esteem every time she got a bad review, the drinking, the drugs... and saw exactly where that story would end.

'No thanks, Colin. You'll never see me in front of a camera again,' she said calmly.

'Then what do you want?'

'Farrah Adams. I'd like to discuss her long-term future.'

'What? Are you her agent now?'

'Yes,' she lied. But her brain fizzed at the thought. The idea of being Farrah's agent gave her such a buzz, she wondered why it hadn't occurred to her before. After all, she'd done it before when managing music groups, so there was no reason why she couldn't be an acting agent. And she'd do it right, unlike the greedy pigs who'd only cared about their cut of her earnings and nothing at all about her wellbeing.

But first there was Farrah to take care of.

'Farrah's an incredible talent and it would be a shame to lose her,' Sheena continued.

'She's thinking of leaving?' Colin gulped.

A major rewrite would be needed if Farrah left without renewing her contract, as her mother-and-daughter storylines with Catherine Belle were a major part of the show. Sheena was well aware of this. She could see the panic in his eyes and knew she had leverage.

'Yes and no,' she said with a smile. 'So let's talk.'

Over the next half an hour she outlined her plan. Farrah would do one more year, allowing the *Bay* to write out her character in a way that would win them awards. In return for staying, Farrah would then move to the writing team with a minimum episode guarantee.

A handshake later, the deal was done.

When Sheena met up with Farrah to give her the good news, Farrah called her old agent, firing her on the spot. Sheena couldn't imagine how awful it must have been for Farrah's agent to receive that phone call out of the blue. One minute she was representing a hot talent, the next minute she wasn't. It sent a chill through Sheena and she decided there and then that she would do whatever it took to never get sacked by a client, to never have to feel that chill. And, so far, she'd managed it.

Though Sheena and Farrah had been close before that point, they became best friends after the deal. It was a perfect outcome for them both. Farrah became the writer she'd always dreamed of being and Sheena began a career in which she would excel beyond all measures.

Once Farrah had signed on as her client, Sheena made advances towards her co-star, with Farrah's blessing. Catherine Belle was the biggest soap star in the world and if Sheena could get her on her books, she knew many other actresses would follow. It wasn't easy. Knowing Sheena's past, Catherine was more than sceptical, but when she saw what a great deal she'd secured for Farrah, she was intrigued but hesitant, so Sheena wooed her slowly. Whenever Catherine needed help (a secret treatment here or a quick nip-and-tuck there), Sheena sorted it, always with unspoken loyalty. Eventually, Sheena became such a trusted friend to Catherine that when her contract negotiations came around again, Catherine (who'd never had an agent, having been hired directly) agreed to see if Sheena could get her a better offer than the network were offering her direct. The deal she came back with was enough to convince Catherine to sign on the dotted line and the McQueen Agency was really off.

It wasn't only her clients who made headlines. 'The troubled teenage starlet who became the most powerful agent in the country' was typical of the praise heaped on Sheena. She was back on the A-List.

And it was a success story that was still writing itself. Sheena was now approaching her sixtieth birthday, still mostly sober (she'd overcome her addictions sufficiently to be able to drink and not lose control, but she went nowhere near drugs), still gorgeous, still ultra successful, still absolutely fabulous. In any given week, up to twenty-five million viewers would be collectively watching her stars. That sort of reach meant she held power with the networks like none of her rivals. And she knew exactly how and when to use it.

Take Lydia, for example. Any other agent would have ditched her the moment the phone stopped ringing. Sheena knew there was a lot of mileage in the menopausal pound and while it had taken a bit of coercion by Sheena to get Lydia to follow the grey train, it had proved lucrative and effective for nearly a decade. Sadly, however, it looked like Lydia had finally reached the end of the line, at just sixty years old.

Sheena was the only client left in the salon now, so, having finished her hair, Christie began rolling the blinds down on the giant windows. Sheena looked in the mirror whilst running her fingertips, coated in tiger-red polish, through her impressive mane. She admired her reflection, happy with what she saw. Her pale, porcelain skin was still fresh and line free, thanks to her weekly facials and the fact that she stayed out of the sun. Her large violet eyes framed by winged liner and half lash extensions gave her the look of a cat-eyed vintage Hollywood star. If she'd stood on camera opposite any of her leading ladies, they'd certainly have felt the competition.

On set visits, she was often shocked at the state of some of her clients, unimpressed at how quickly they'd let themselves go once they landed a regular role. Once under contract, it was almost guaranteed they'd gain a dress size in the first month; after that, the boozing followed and then holidays in the sun. Then invariably there'd be a bad beach shot on a front page, after which they'd come crying to Sheena. After a rap across their knuckles, she would send them off to Harley Street for repair work followed by a game of hide and seek so the paparazzi didn't manage to catch them being restored. No other agent covered their talents' backs like Sheena. And that included Lydia.

She thought about how to answer Lydia's phone message, which she'd now listened to, where she'd threatened to sack her. There was no way on earth Sheena was going to allow that to happen. Which meant only one thing: she'd better get Lydia the gig of her life. And she knew of exactly the right role. She had been planning on pushing just one client for this part, and Stacey really needed this, but now she'd have to work double her usual magic.

Though it was quite usual for agents to set their own talent against the other – a win-win for the agent, doubling the chances of a big fat percentage – Sheena had always been too honourable to do that routinely. But this was an exceptional circumstance: no way was she going to experience being sacked for the first time in thirty years. She had already pushed Stacey Stonebrook forward for the role, but what the hell. Lydia Chambers would certainly hold her own in this bitch battle.

Picking up her phone, she dialled Helen Gold. It was out of hours, and, as expected, the call went to voicemail. She had assumed Helen would be busy, in the best possible way. She had just finished leaving her message as Christie began switching off the lights.

'Do you think you can trust yourself to be alone with

me in the dark?' Sheena said, spinning her chair round to face Christie, who was now standing in the half light, just a faint glow accenting her figure, which looked glorious in her leopard-print wrap dress.

'Darling,' Christie said softly, in that accent that drove Sheena wild, 'you know I'm married.'

'That didn't stop you last time,' Sheena said with a wink as she got up from the chair and sauntered towards her.

Christie stayed perfectly still, and when Sheena reached her, the women looked deeply into each other's eyes.

'Besides,' Sheena purred, 'it's not like real cheating, like with a man.'

As she got closer, Christie's eyes flashed a look of excitement. 'I thought you had dinner plans?' she said.

Sheena leaned over to the door and flicked the catch onto locked before turning her attention back to Christie. She pressed her perfectly glossed lips onto the exposed skin at the nape of Christie's neck, feeling her body tremble as she did so. After working her lips up to her ear, she slid one hand inside Christie's dress and gently squeezed her breasts, circling her hard nipples with her nail tips. The women kissed, their hands roaming the soft curves of the other's body, until Sheena took a small step back.

'I'd rather eat you,' she said, and with that she pulled Christie's dress open and sank to her knees.

8

Meeting Room 6 was once again packed to the rafters. The automatic lights were on maximum because, outside, a storm was exploding. The skies were black and heavy rain was beating against the windows, making the atmosphere even more tense. Waves smashed into the cliffs as if trying to escape the raging sea. Exterior filming had ceased for the day, cast and crew had been brought inside and studio scenes had been doubled-up. Forecasts claimed the weather would settle by the evening, but those in the meeting room saw no sign that their own troubled waters would be calmed anytime soon.

The writers and producers had been brought in to flesh out the live Christmas fortieth anniversary episode. Amanda was sitting at the head of the table, in charge, without Jake in attendance. Meetings led by her were always much more productive, not least because, unlike Jake, she believed that you got the best out of people with kindness. TV was for the most part run by power-crazy people out to avenge past wrongs, but Amanda had trained under Tina and Harry

Pearson and, like them, she loved *Falcon Bay* and cared deeply about both its audience and the team that made it. She wanted to run a show that existed on love, nurture and consideration.

Two producers sat either side of her, both trying to look like sturdy deputies, with notebooks and pens but nothing written on their pages. Further to her right were the storyline team, who had barely slept for several days, and to Amanda's left were the script editors, who had been trying to make sense of the storylines just delivered. Both teams looked frazzled, but if anybody dared to ask if they were okay, each would blame the other for their worries.

As this was an emergency conference, the writers, who were not always included, had been brought in – which meant their already short writing schedule was being eaten into. They were a team of nearly twenty, and in amongst them was Farrah. To say the room was in an edgy mood would be an understatement.

Helen Gold, however, was her usual chipper self, never allowing negativity to bring her down. She loved being in a story conference and she loved problem-solving.

The room was bursting with nearly forty people, but every time Amanda glanced up from her files she caught the same pair of eyes looking at her. Dan, from finance, was sitting next to Helen, making calculations on his jotter and repeatedly giving Amanda the loveliest of supportive smiles. She hadn't seen him since they were in the lift together, and now she wasn't quite sure how to behave.

'Amanda?'

A voice pulled her back into the now. It was Candy, one

of the two producers under her. Candy had worked her way up from script assistant and in truth had hit her ceiling around senior script editor, but her tenacity and Amanda's maternity had collided. So when Amanda had gone on leave to have Olivia, she'd wanted somebody she could trust sharing the helm with Dustin, the producer to Amanda's right. He was definitely too dark and moody for her liking. Everything with him was negative, nothing was possible and when it came to blue-sky thinking you could count on him to introduce metaphorical hailstones as large and noisy as the real ones that were now attacking the meeting room windows like little bullets. Candy's fluffiness was a useful antidote.

'Karyn was just saying,' Candy fed back, 'that it's very hard to storyline the episode when we don't know who the actress is who's coming in.'

'I agree.' Amanda nodded sympathetically. 'It's not ideal.'

'It's a fucking shitstorm,' added Helen. It amused her that Candy struggled with swearing in any form. Candy herself refused to swear, changing 'shit' to 'sugar' and 'fuck' to 'fudge'. And when she heard somebody else swear in conversation, it made her alabaster cheeks flush apple red. So Helen swore around Candy as much as she could. She winked at Amanda. Candy looked everywhere except at Helen; her face was burning and everybody in the room could see it. Amanda gave Helen a hard stare, which made Helen want to laugh all the more.

'Okay, so it's a challenge,' said Farrah, 'but isn't that what we do? Rise to it, show our new bosses that we can handle anything?'

The other writers were slumped in their chairs. Once upon a time, Farrah was one of them, and the best of them too. But since she'd moved over to directing as well as writing, nobody was quite sure whose camp she was in. Farrah knew this and didn't care. She wouldn't let their paranoia hold her back, so she continued. 'But we need to storyline something or this conference will be a blowout.'

'Tell us who our bitch is – and I don't mean the actress, I mean who she really is, what she wants, why she's here – and we can go from there.' This came from Amir, a talented but fairly new writer.

'Jake wants us to cast her first,' said Amanda. 'He feels we'll be informed by who she is. Mould the character to the actress.' In truth, she knew this was a terrible way of doing things, but she didn't want to show her hand just yet.

One of the old-school writers conveyed what he thought of this idea by getting up and shuffling over to the cake table. Amanda wished she could join him; the petit fours looked beyond divine, but Jake's chastising words were on loop in the back of her head.

'You don't lose your baby weight by pretending you're still eating for two' was his favourite saying whenever he saw her eating anything other than salad.

A different tack was needed to get things going. 'Why don't we work on the stunt. We do know that Jude is sadly leaving in the Christmas Day live, so let's storyline the death of Jimmy, our handyman rogue.'

The energy in the room lifted instantly. The one thing writers loved more than anything was a good exit. Jude Roscoe, the actor who played Jimmy, though hugely popular with the show's audience, was not adored around the table. On rare occasions when writers and actors mixed, at the annual summer party or the Christmas one, he would work his way through the writing team, berating them about where they were going wrong with his character and then overloading them with stories of his own.

He'd had some huge storylines too – a bank robbery, a kidney transplant, an affair with two women at the same time – and yet he'd never once done anything but criticize, so there was a crackle of excitement in the air from those who'd been on the receiving end of his ingratitude. They were delighted to come up with ways for the actor to get the chop.

Suddenly ideas were coming thick and fast and Amanda enjoyed listening to all of them. The background noise also allowed her to steal a few glances at Dan. She couldn't understand why this man was occupying so much of her thoughts. She'd been trying, during her yoga practice, to meditate on it. So far she'd come up with two reasons: his decency and his body.

This was new territory for her, and even just thinking that way made her feel disloyal to Jake. Her hormones were definitely playing games with her. She could already hear Helen's voice in her head – 'Forget your bastard husband and go enjoy yourself, darling!' – but Amanda wasn't like her permanently sexed-up friend. She believed in fidelity, and in trying to make things work. Life with Jake was always stormy; she was used to that.

As she mulled on this, the writers were coming up with creative ways of killing Jimmy.

'How about he's walking home in the dark, looking at his messages on his phone, and he just steps off a cliff edge into the sea and drowns. Happened to me.'

'Except you're not dead...?'

'Well, there was a barrier. But still...'

Amanda wasn't sure how long to let the writers brainstorm, but she let them go on for a bit. Sometimes you had to wade through the bad stories to reach the gold.

'A pack of wild horses, come down from the hills, stampeding across the beach... The sea in the background... A kid making sandcastles, the horses coming towards it... Jimmy flings the kid out of the way and is trampled to death. He goes out a hero,' ventured Amir again.

The room buzzed with positive noises. People were impressed.

'Very filmic. I like that,' said Farrah, and then remembered Aiden Anderson would be directing it and tried not to frown.

'Okay,' said another writer, 'let's riff on the stampede but make Jimmy less of a hero. Have him put the kid on the beach. Make it Cheryl's kid, and he's paying her back for the divorce.'

'He's killing the kid?' asked Amanda, not sure they were near the aluminium, let alone the gold.

'Not baby Bjorn? I love baby Bjorn,' Candy felt the need to chip in.

'Exactly. We'll hate Jimmy. And the kid lives – obviously. The horses all run past him and then crush Jimmy, who's watching from the sidelines.'

'Fuck, that's harsh,' said Helen, not entirely dismissing it, and swearing on this occasion because she genuinely felt the need, not just to discomfit Candy.

Dan raised his hand and the chatter stopped.

Amanda found herself thinking that his hand was the perfect size to cup her perfect breasts and then she blushed the same colour as her edit pen. 'Yes, Dan?' she said, trying to keep her breathing even.

All eyes turned to him.

What words of wisdom? Amanda wondered. What could he have to add to what was already pretty crazy?

'Hate to be a downer,' he began, 'but the budget for the live won't allow for a horse stampede.'

And the spell was broken. This was Amanda's problem in a nutshell. He was a lovely guy, no question, but whenever he contributed, it wasn't artistic. It was just about the budget. He wasn't a creative – and might in fact be downright dull if she got to know him better.

'How about just one horse?' she asked.

'That's not much of a stampede,' Helen mumbled.

Dan thought about it and then offered a compromise. 'One horse we can do.'

The room lost interest.

'Can we have an explosion?' asked one of the writers, annoyed at a stunt that wasn't… well, a stunt.

'Depends what you're blowing up,' Dan replied.

'A car?'

He shook his head as the room looked to Amanda once more.

'Hmm,' she said.

'Maybe it's best we leave the stunt specifics for now. We

obviously need more money to plan this out properly, so I'll go back to the station and see if we can up the budget. If we're pulling out all the stops, we need something big.'

As if she had uttered the magic words, the door to the meeting room opened and in walked Jake accompanied by the new owner of the network. People had heard all sorts about Madeline Kane, but no one had met her yet. It was noticeable how all the men in the room turned to check her out. Dan included, which gave Amanda a tiny rush of jealousy that she instantly realized she had no right to feel. A few of the women seemed to be gushing at her too. And, objectively, Amanda could see why.

Madeline Kane was hard to put an age on, but if Amanda had to guess – and she was pretty good at that; she could spot even excellent surgery a mile off – she'd say she was in her early fifties, though she looked at least a decade younger. In her snakeskin Jimmy Choos, she was taller than Jake, standing next to her, but elegant with it. Her long, tanned legs were shapely and she was wearing a pencil skirt that showed off her curvaceous but slim hips. Her ruched, fitted shirt accentuated her tiny waist and tremendous breasts, which were instantly the focus of most of the men in the room.

Despite herself, Amanda did a little seat shuffle, making her own prize assets perk up. Full of baby milk, they were bigger than they used to be. Across the room, Farrah was also sitting forward without realizing it, so that her own breasts were brought into the mix. Helen was too cool for school and she remained laid back, allowing her boobs to do their own talking without any manoeuvring to make them shout.

Above Madeline's cleavage hung a stunning piece of jewellery comprised of a large pearl on a thin gold chain. Its simplicity made her neck appear all the more kissable. Her face was unlined, chalk white with full cherry lips and a nose that was far too perfect not to have been doctored. Fantastic thick eyebrows and a perfect mane of jet-black hair completed the picture. All in all, she was a walking sculpture. And to top it all, she oozed power and wealth, as befitted the owner of the entire network.

Madeline took a tour of the room, talking as she went. '*Falcon Bay* has always been in my heart,' she said with a soft American accent that sounded to Amanda as if she was from the Deep South. 'As a long-term fan of this wonderful show, I've often imagined what it must be like, being in this special place where fates get decided. Oh how I've dreamed of being in this room. Who knew that all I had to do to make it happen was buy the company!'

Jake laughed as if Madeline had told the funniest joke in the world, then turned to the room.

'Everybody, this is Madeline Kane. She's my boss, which makes her your boss too. How about a round of applause to say hi.'

There was an awkward pause for a second. Nobody had ever been applauded in this room just for being who they were. However, she was the boss's boss, so… One by one, each of the writers, editors, storyliners and producers clapped – politely but without particular enthusiasm. Amanda was the only one not to clap. Which, of course, Jake and Madeline both noticed.

Eventually, Madeline feigned embarrassment and told the

room they didn't need to. 'Jake, stop!' She laughed, tossing her head, letting her shiny hair ripple. 'Just being here feels like a privilege. Why, I declare, I already feel at home.'

'It is your home now and we're privileged to have you here.' Jake was truly grovelling now.

Helen stuck a finger down her throat and mimed gagging, which made Amanda want to laugh. Instead, she took a sip of her sparkling water so nobody would see her smile. Madeline didn't pick up on any of this, but Jake did. He scowled at Helen and she returned his gaze with a cool stare.

Madeline walked over to the cast cards and was now face to face with Lucy Dean. 'Ah, there the old dear is,' she said. 'Everybody's favourite mother. The star of this show.'

There was the faintest hint of an edge to Madeline's tone, but her smile was so sincere, most people in the room didn't hear it. Amanda did, though. She'd become attuned to edge. It's what made her so good at running conference; she could read the room perfectly.

'I think Jake's idea of introducing a new femme fatale to *Falcon Bay* is much needed. Somebody who can really challenge Lucy Dean. The viewers will love it,' Madeline drawled. Her accent was part Blanche DuBois from *A Streetcar Named Desire* and part Blanche Devereaux from *The Golden Girls*.

'Thank God for Jake's ideas,' Helen said.

Jake narrowed his eyes.

'Just wish we knew who she was,' Farrah interjected.

Madeline looked at Farrah, expressionless, for longer than was comfortable. And then said, 'Tiffany Dean?'

'Used to be, in a different life. I'm a director now. Writer too.'

All the writers in the room noticed the order she'd said it in. As did Madeline.

'Shouldn't that be writer first, seeing as you're writing the Christmas special? Aiden Anderson is directing, right?' Madeline looked to Jake for confirmation, even though it was clear she knew everything that was going on there, so her question was superfluous.

Jake nodded like an energetic puppy.

'He is, but he shouldn't be,' said Farrah. 'But that's what happens when you give out jobs without interviewing all the potential candidates.'

'Tell me about it,' Amanda added, unable to stop herself. She hadn't planned to express her anger about her effective demotion in public like this, but she was still smouldering from the way Jake had treated her in the office the other day, so it slipped out.

Madeline's head swiftly turned to look at her.

Rachel, from HR, who wasn't usually in these meetings but had been called in to do the minutes, suddenly popped a hand up as if she was trying to get a teacher's attention in class. 'Can I just say—' she started, but Madeline cut her off and waded in.

'Jake told me, Amanda, that with your new baby, now wasn't the right time for you to assume that level of commitment.'

Rachel's face turned pale as she waved her hand, desperately trying to cut into what was threatening to become a legal minefield.

'You mean *our* baby,' Amanda countered, gesturing to Jake but talking to Madeline. 'But it seems you thought now was good timing for him.'

'I guess that's a momma–dadda thing,' Madeline said in her lazy, Louisiana twang, not in the least put out.

The whole room watched as the women traded barbs. Rachel continued waving and was now looking very panicked.

Amanda was incensed. 'As a woman in charge, I was hoping you might redress the old-fashioned gender balance around here.'

'Too right,' Farrah threw in casually.

'There's been no consultation,' Amanda said. 'No attempt to find a workaround.'

Jake shifted uncomfortably at the direction this conversation was taking. 'How about I show you our edit suites, Madeline,' he said hurriedly, trying to stop things from getting any worse. Annoyed at himself for having forgotten to cancel the minuting of all meetings after the fuck-up with Helen's idea being noted down and thrown back at him by Amanda.

Madeline ignored him and turned back to Farrah and Amanda.

'You think just because I'm a woman, I should do y'all some favours?'

'No.' Farrah was holding her ground. 'Amanda should never have been demoted. Jake used her maternity leave – the maternity leave of his *own wife* – to climb the corporate ladder. He's morally corrupt.'

Rachel, now in a full-on panic, cut in. 'Everybody, from an HR point of view, this conversation really must—'

Wanting his response to go on record, Jake cut her off. 'I am not—' he started, but Amanda picked up the baton and talked over him.

'And Farrah's the best director we have, but Aiden is Jake's buddy and as Jake's in charge – thanks to you, Ms Kane – he picked him. Things need to change around here.'

She was trembling now, shocked at herself for bringing Jake into this in front of the whole room. That was a first, and she wished she hadn't. It was unprofessional. She had nothing against Aiden, but she just couldn't stand injustice, couldn't stand the boys' club way of doing things. And Farrah deserved a fair chance.

'Amen,' Farrah said, clenching her fist in appreciative solidarity.

Helen shot Amanda a surprised look too. Amanda was usually the conciliator, the one who'd do anything not to hurt a person's feelings. Never meek, but always kind, always wanting to think the best of everybody. It was a standing joke with Helen, Farrah and Sheena that even when Amanda tried to bring out her bitchy side, it came out all wrong. Not today, though.

Jake looked daggers at Amanda, barely containing his fury. But Madeline was much calmer. Rachel looked like she might faint.

'Oh, I'm all about change, honey. But you can't wait for others to change things for you. That's not change, that's called a handout.'

Amanda and Farrah exchanged glances, now certain Madeline Kane was not a woman's woman. Having already overstepped the invisible line, they sat back in their seats, deflated.

The room went silent. Madeline spoke again, but this time in a softer tone.

'Ladies, let's not get off on the wrong foot. Farrah, I want to congratulate you for having survived life as a soap opera teen. You're truly a rarity. Too much fame too young can send people off the rails, with devastating consequences, so all credit to you for keeping your head. If you're as good as Amanda says you are, then you'll find a way. I mean, look at you: from actor to lead writer and now to director – stands to reason you'll be a lead director soon.'

For all Farrah's anger, she couldn't help but be touched by those nice words. Her ego enjoyed the stroke too.

Madeline then turned to Amanda and her voice sharpened a little. 'Regarding Jake's promotion: we needed somebody who was available 24/7 and new mothers are, quite rightly, clearly not up to that. Exactly the opposite, in fact.'

Rachel's hand shot up and she started to speak. 'Ms Kane, I really don't think you should say things like—'

Once again, she was interrupted.

'What about new dads?' asked Helen, sticking up for her friend.

'Turns out that Jake here is the kind of dad who puts his job first – which is great for us at C.I.TV but not so great for you, darlin',' Madeline said, flashing Amanda a patronizing smile.

Jake was uncharacteristically at a loss for what to say.

A deeper hush fell on the room, until from a quiet corner Dan unexpectedly chipped in. 'Thing is, you could change the system so you don't have to rely on anybody 24/7. That way, it wouldn't be a role determined by gender or parenthood.'

The whole room turned to look at him. He wasn't blushing. Didn't even look nervous. He was just quietly standing his ground and supporting Amanda.

She felt a flush of pride in him. With Jake positioned so close to Dan and also so silent in this discussion, she could compare them side by side: it was no contest at all.

Finally seizing her moment to speak, Rachel interjected. 'I really think things are being said that shouldn't be, and especially not in public. I am not being personal, Ms Kane, I'm just here to protect you from any legal issues.' Having at last managed to finish her sentence, she sat back and waited for the fallout.

'And I appreciate your effort, my dear,' Madeline replied, 'but I don't believe in pussyfooting around the issues at hand. You'll get to know that about me – well, those of you who survive the reboot will. Myself and my legal team can handle any lawsuit that comes my way, and if I have to pay some bills for not being PC to save this network, then so be it. Luckily, my pockets are very deep.' She gave an imperceptible nod and the faintest of smiles, entirely at ease.

Desperate to change the subject, Jake gestured towards Dan. 'He only works in finance, he shouldn't really be in here.'

'And yet here he is,' Madeline said. 'Looks like your wife is effecting change while you're not looking, Jakey.' She raised a perfect eyebrow in Amanda's direction.

This time both Amanda and Dan turned red. Jake stared at the pair of them, chin jutting forward in confusion.

Madeline laughed and shook out her hair once more, in total charge of the room. 'In our first bid to halt these haemorrhaging ratings we've decided to do something unprecedented – a live behind-the-scenes special. It will take place as soon as possible. It will be a full *Falcon Bay* spectacular, a chance for the audience to see how this majestic show works and to meet the talented people who make her.'

There was a scraping of chairs and a clatter of pens on the tabletop as the room took in this bombshell. Jake cleared his throat, wanting to get in on the act, but Madeline was on a roll.

'It will be glamorous, it will be sexy and it will be exciting, and we're calling it the Bitch Party.'

As Candy let out an audible gasp at the B-word, Amanda froze, her head whirring with all that this might entail.

Madeline was very obviously enjoying the different reactions. 'And, yes, the title has been cleared with compliance – which is also me, as I am the network.'

'A Bitch Party?' asked Amir, not quick enough to see the angle.

'As well as the stars of our show, we'll have all the actresses there that we're considering for the role of our new bitch, and to really engage our fans, to show them we care what they think, we'll be asking the online audience to vote on who they want to join our family.' Madeline said this with a slight giggle, clearly excited.

Helen was stunned into silence.

Which was handy as it allowed Jake to finally get a word in. 'Everybody will be talking about it, really creating a buzz in the build-up to the Christmas live. We'll be having cocktails themed to match our characters and a firework display over the sea for the backdrop.'

Madeline turned to a still silent Helen. 'Ms Gold, our casting director, I believe?' She twitched her perfect lips, but it wasn't a smile, and she didn't wait for an answer. 'I want you to get the seven best suitable actresses to our party. Tell them this show is part of their overall audition – they need to make an impression.'

Helen's eyes widened.

'Look, I don't know how things work in the States, Madeline—' she started.

'Ms Kane.'

Helen bit her tongue at the correction. Everyone around the table sensed the atmosphere. Madeline Kane might be beautiful to look at, but she was certainly not to be messed with.

'But around here, *Ms Kane*, actresses act and leave that sort of thing to reality stars,' she said as flatly as she could.

Madeline was unfazed. 'Well, if any of your shortlist wants to be considered for the best part on television, then they'd better deal with the *reality* of it. Times are a-changing, Ms Gold, and we and they must change with them. If they are not in that show, then they will not be in the running.'

Helen couldn't think of anything to say to that, which was a novelty for her, so she kept quiet. Jake, meanwhile, grinned at her like a demented joker.

Madeline began walking towards the exit. 'It's a showcase for us too. I want our audiences to see not just the cast but the whole *Falcon Bay* family.' As she reached the door, she turned back and addressed them once more.

'Speaking of which, The Bitch Party will also be a good test to see which of *Falcon Bay*'s employees can meet the high expectations required to stay on board this ship. As you know, I am *determined* to sail back into the number 1 slot, and I will not hesitate to replace *anyone* who I consider to be a dead weight.' She smiled broadly, and stalked out of the room.

Jake followed her, looking smug.

The entire room looked to Amanda, whose reaction was as professional as she could manage. 'Well, that was... unpleasant,' she said.

'What a prick,' Farrah chipped in.

'Which one?' Helen asked, and the whole room exploded into nervous laughter, like kids after the headmaster has left the room.

Rachel switched off her minutes machine.

'A Bitch Party? I mean... *really*,' Farrah said.

Amanda echoed the sarcasm. 'A bunch of actresses all vying for the same job, plied with alcohol and told to *make an impression* live in front of millions... What could possibly go wrong?'

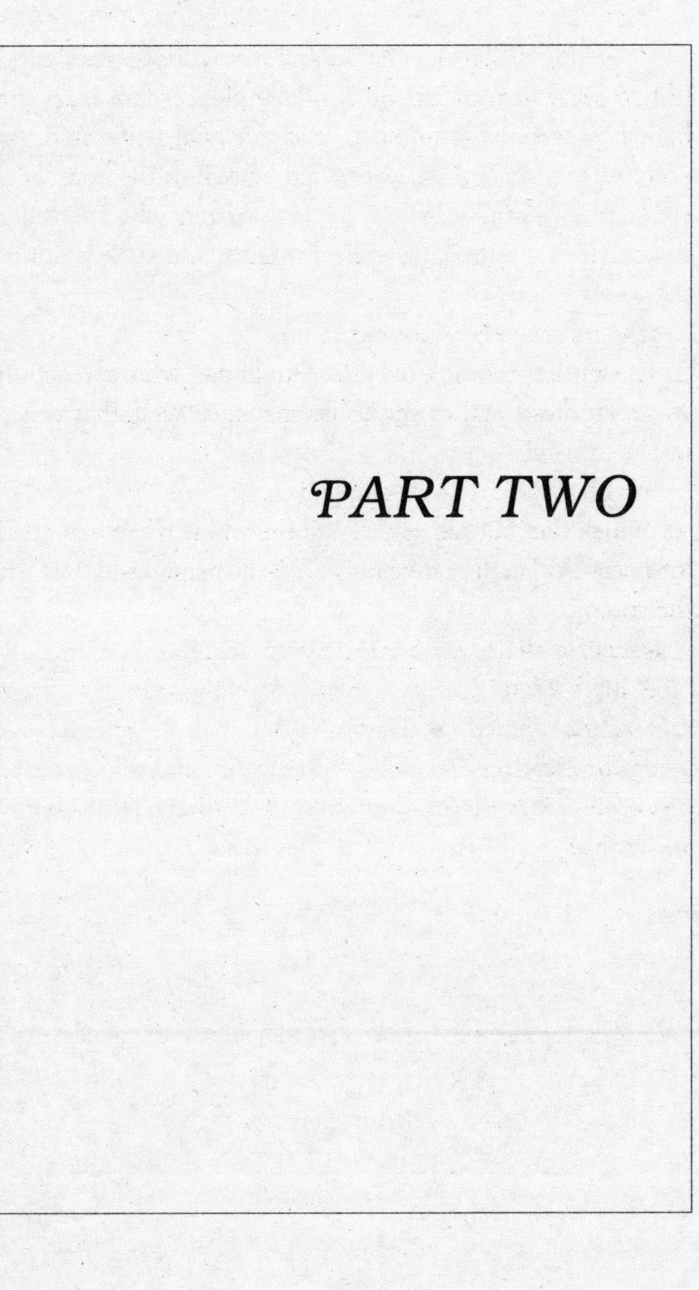

PART TWO

9

Carnaby Street, famous for being the heart of London in the swinging sixties, was now home to Fonda Books, which knew a thing or two about swingers as in the late seventies and early eighties it was the biggest producer of bonkbuster novels in the world. Decades later, when they went out of fashion after the death of Jackie Collins, the Fonda family decided to sell up.

Mickey Taylor, the new owner, bought the business primarily because it came with a freehold building in the heart of the city, but he also kicked Fonda Books into new territory: the celebrity biography. Dripping in money but lacking in taste, Mickey made sure that his revamp of Fonda Books screamed grandeur – the price of a single chair in his silk-walled conference room could help feed a developing country, and there were ten of them. The plush carpets had Swarovski crystals woven into them, and even the gold leaf painted on the coving was twenty-four carat.

Subtle was not Mickey's thing. But, like his dad Frank, who had made the family fortune running second-hand car dealerships, he knew a bargain when he saw it. Only it wasn't broken-down cars that interested Mickey, it was 'off-the-road' celebrities.

He could spot a battered star with a juicy tale to tell a mile off. And he threw money at them to spill all for his publishing company. Other publishing houses looked down on Fonda Books and his gauche ways, but, to his credit, he'd had several number one bestsellers. Though they might never get a review in the *Telegraph* or *Variety*, they shifted millions of copies to stay-at-home housewives desperate to hear celebrities air their dirty linen and tell tales on each other.

Mickey revelled in scandal. If a star couldn't get a publishing contract anywhere else, they'd end up at Mickey's. If you needed a big advance and lots of publicity more than you needed your integrity and dignity, then this was the place to be.

In the reception, Honey Hunter was perched on the edge of a white, fifties-style, leather sofa. Her long legs were encased in skin-tight pink jeans, she was wearing a fitted Hermès blazer in exactly the same shade, and she had towering white ankle boots on. Under the jacket was a low camisole which showed off her generous cleavage. Nestling just above her world-renowned boobs was a large aquamarine encircled by diamonds. She'd been gifted it by the Hollywood studios she'd been contracted to in her teens, where she'd starred in a string of adventure movies, playing a young orphan who'd found millions after discovering a map to buried treasure. In the seventies, this role made her famous around the globe and, like so many teen stars before her, it wasn't long before young Honey was rebelling against her girl-next-door image.

At eighteen, she left the cosy family franchise to make an edgy French movie in which she appeared naked. She also fell in love with its director, Patrice Bernard, who was twice her age. This was three decades before Britney Spears and Miley Cyrus shocked the world by revealing they were not so innocent and, back then, Honey's decision to bare all caused the sort of scandal that made even Fonda Books' back catalogue look tame. By twenty she'd been thrown another chance at Hollywood by her first director, who was now making romcoms with A-listers. She was cast as the innocent Imogen Tate in *Good Guys Go to Heaven*, a box-office smash, which saw her star rise so high that during this period on the showbiz merry-go-round she won an Oscar, an Emmy and a Golden Globe.

But within a year she'd fucked it all up. And love was to blame, again. She'd been cheating on Patrice with rock's baddest boy, Damon Gilligan from the LA band Fader, and was caught out by the tabloids. Damon was a hardcore party boy, and late nights and early call times did not mix. Honey's life descended into one shambles after another: Damon would cheat on her, she would drink, then she would cheat, he would beat her, then she would beat him back – all usually captured by the paparazzi. It was a vicious circle and the tabloids loved it, along with the shoplifting arrest, the three spells in rehab and the several affairs with high-profile married men.

The tabloid hell continued once she returned to England until, at thirty-five, after exhausting the chat-show circuit and lads' magazines shoots, her career finally flatlined. With her Oscar in her Prada handbag, she retreated to Switzerland

and her house on the shores of Lake Geneva (chosen for its tax-haven status in her heyday), and there she'd stayed, out of the media glare, for twenty years. Right up until she'd got a call from Fonda Books offering her an insane amount of money to do her autobiography. Her original movies had been digitally remastered and re-released, creating a new wave of fans, which meant she was having a bit of a resurrection – she'd recently been trending as a gif on Twitter.

The receptionist at Fonda Books was appraising Honey from her desk. She'd already checked out her story online, but in real life Honey looked better than she was expecting. She'd clearly had some work done – those boobs would never be up so high without a bra at her age – and her face had the pillowy look that fillers usually created, but considering the life she'd led, and the fact that, according to Wikipedia, she was in her fifties, Honey Hunter looked good.

The red light flashed on the phone, which meant Mickey was ready for Honey to be shown in. The receptionist usually just called out to the visitor from her station and gestured to the door, but she wanted to get a closer look at Honey, so she walked over to her.

'Mr Taylor is ready for you now,' she said while scanning Honey's puffy but well-made-up face.

Honey, who knew she was being studied, picked up her Valentino tote, brushed some imaginary dust off it and looked around at the reception as she headed towards the opening door. 'That table needs cleaning. If you stared at that the way you've been staring at me, you might have noticed,' she said dismissively and walked into Mickey's office.

Mickey was sitting at his desk, and the ghostwriter, who'd spent more than a hundred hours on the phone to Honey over the last six months, was also there. She offered to get Honey a drink, but as Honey had been sober for more than ten years – a triumph that the ghostwriter had already written about in detail – she declined. She really hoped this meeting wasn't going to take long. She was so uninterested in her own 'autobiography', she hadn't even bothered to read it.

'So what did you think of your book?' Mickey asked, a cigar in his beaming smile, ice clinking in his crystal glass as he swirled his cognac.

'I thought it was excellent,' she lied.

'That's super rad to hear,' the ghost said. 'I was a bit nervous – some of it was so raw. I thought you were very brave.'

Mickey grinned. '*Raw* is what makes people pay big bucks for the hardback.'

A wave of panic washed through Honey. *Raw? Brave?* She dug deep into her failing memory to try and remember what she'd said to the ghost. She knew they'd had conversations late into the night, all of which had been recorded, but specifics…? She didn't think she'd said anything that interesting at all. In fact, she couldn't understand why they'd offered her such a huge advance in the first place. In the era of YouTube uploading and illegal downloading, her rerun royalties were dwindling, so it had seemed like a good idea at the time. But now she was wondering what she'd let herself in for.

'You really think people will like it?' she asked.

'No – people will love it!' Mickey roared from his chair.

She wasn't sure why, but suddenly she felt quite emotional.

'I just thought nobody would be interested in me any more,' she said, reaching for a tissue on his desk.

The ghost moved the box closer to her and touched her hand. 'Mickey's right,' the ghost said. 'And after this, people will remember you for the right reasons.'

Honey visibly relaxed in her seat. 'Maybe this will get me back into acting,' she said quietly.

Mickey leaned over the table, poured himself another drink, took a slug, then grabbed her hand and spoke sincerely for the first time since she'd met him. 'Honey, you are a fantastic actress. More than that – you are a star. Sure, you fucked up – nobody wrote an autobiography that didn't have a dramatic life! But you burned brightly when it mattered and you deserve to be in front of the cameras again, in a role that does you justice.'

She wiped away a tear. She'd barely even dreamed of hearing someone say such things about her again. Gently, she blew her nose. 'I don't even have an agent any more.'

'Yes, you do,' he said. 'Me! And I know the perfect part for you. *Falcon Bay* are looking for a new bitch.'

As the words tumbled out of his mouth, Honey all but stopped breathing.

The ghostwriter chipped in. 'It's all over the papers – there's going to be a live behind-the-scenes episode where all the shortlisted actresses will be introduced to the public.'

Honey's stomach was churning now; this was making her nervous but in a strangely exciting way.

Mickey picked up the thread. 'And whoever they choose,' he added, 'will be brought in on Christmas Day to take over the show. It's the role of a lifetime and they're not looking for a new face, they're looking for someone well known who's been off screen for a while. Someone with gravitas and history.'

'And that's you!' encouraged the ghost. 'You'd be a beacon of hope to women in their fifties. A role model proving that your second act can still be your best!'

Was it possible, wondered Honey. Could she really get back onto a global show like *Falcon Bay*? As she visualized stepping back into the limelight, her heart started beating faster.

'Okay,' she said, retrieving her compact from her tote and repairing her eye make-up. There was no way she'd let that cow of a receptionist see that she'd been crying. 'Get me on that beach.'

10

Over in the interior sets building, Farrah was using her lunch hour to walk through the blocking for the two-hander she would be filming in the afternoon. It was to be an intense, emotional scene between Lucy Dean and her teenage granddaughter, Emily, filmed around the kitchen table of Lucy Dean's beautiful home.

Farrah was pacing out the distance between the door and the sideboard, identifying the exact spot in the kitchen where Lucy Dean would need to be when Emily dropped her bombshell about having fallen pregnant. She was counting the paces out loud to herself when she glanced up and saw that she was being observed.

It was Lara Collins, the sixteen-year-old daughter of one of the writers, Nate. She was on a brief stint of work experience at *Falcon Bay* and, as was often the way in television, nepotism had played a part in getting her through the studio's doors. Farrah had seen her yesterday, on the beach set, where the poor girl had been standing silently in the shadows. Surrounded by some of the most famous faces in the world, she'd really retreated into her shell, barely uttering a single word.

But Farrah had recognized something gutsy in the girl – maybe it was the DMs or maybe it was the book in her pocket – *Everyday Sexism*, which Farrah was a big fan of. Either way, Farrah had gone over and introduced herself. 'Come and find me tomorrow,' she'd said. 'I'll show you something of what I do.'

Lara was like a different girl today, as chatty and confident as anything. Her blonde hair was a new colour too – flamingo pink. 'Thanks so much for inviting me over, Farrah,' she gushed. 'I'm so excited to see you at work. My dad is always talking about you, about how you're the only female writer and director on the show—'

Farrah gave a wry smile. 'Nate usually moans about that to me – thinks I'm disloyal doing both jobs. But let's not worry about pissing off the men, eh, Lara? Me and Amanda King – you've met her, I think? – are always keen to bring more young women into the production side of the business. So, this afternoon I'm directing a two-hander featuring our big star Catherine Belle.'

'She's quite, um, intimidating, Catherine Belle, isn't she?' Lara said. 'I was introduced to her yesterday, but I couldn't think of anything to say. She has this aura—'

Farrah inhaled sharply. 'You know, Lara, at the risk of being indiscreet, Catherine is one of those stars you have to handle very carefully. She's a friend of mine, but sometimes she can be… well… let's just call it high-handed. The thing about this business is, you have to hustle continually to get what you want. Whether you're seventy-years-old and the biggest star on *Falcon Bay*, or whether you're me, forever having to push myself out there to try and get the best episodes, forever getting knocked back by male directors with large egos and insufficient talent.'

Farrah pulled out a couple of chairs from around Lucy Dean's kitchen table and gestured for Lara to take a seat.

'I did notice,' Lara said, 'that there seemed to be a lot more men than women on the production side here. But that hasn't put me off!'

'Good!' Farrah said, pleased she was finding her voice. 'Sadly that is something we have to deal with a lot in this business.'

'I would love to do what you do. Get a real job in TV, a job where I can enjoy going to work and not end up like everyone else, wasting their lives doing something they're not even interested in. You started out as an actress, didn't you? As Catherine Belle's daughter?'

Farrah raised an eyebrow. 'I'm impressed. Nice research, Lara – I like that. Yes, that's where I started, but I really wouldn't recommend it. Teenage actors have to put up with a load of really vile shit—' She hesitated, pictured Sheena all those years ago, decided not to go into details. 'It destroyed a lot of my peers. So I got out – made them kill my character so there was no chance of me changing my mind and returning! Boy, was it a struggle to get them to say yes to me being a writer. And now it's *Groundhog Day* all over again with directing.' She sighed and stood up.

Lara was beaming at her now. She stood up too. 'You're such an inspiration, Farrah,' she said. 'I'm going to take you as my role model. A strong woman in a man's world, clearing the path for future generations.'

Farrah was quite stunned to hear this. Two little tears pricked in her eyes. She never thought of herself like that; she was always too busy fighting to get where she wanted to be rather than acknowledge just how far she'd come already. She cleared her throat, put a friendly hand on Lara's arm.

'I'm honoured, Lara. Thank you. I hope I can live up to your high regard. We probably won't cross paths again before you leave next week, but feel free to get in touch with me directly when you start thinking about your next move into TV.'

As Lara left the studio, all smiles, Farrah had a wicked thought. She would tweak the script of the two-hander and get the props department to give Lucy Dean's granddaughter a copy of *Everyday Sexism*. It would be lying on the kitchen table that afternoon, unmissable. Would Catherine get the message? Farrah was pretty confident she would.

11

The late-afternoon light was painting everything in the production office with a rich, gilt-coloured glow. This was known as the golden hour, a time of day when you could take a photo that didn't need to be Photoshopped, thanks to nature's magnificent filter. Amanda, the only person still at her desk, closed the lid of her MacBook and slid it into her lockable drawer. She wasn't going to need it where she was going.

She was just gathering up a bag of baby paraphernalia from beneath her desk when Dan came through the door.

'So sorry to disturb you, Amanda,' he said hesitantly. 'I need to check a couple of things on last month's accounts, but I can see you're heading off somewhere…' He stayed where he was, as if waiting for permission to come further in.

'Hi, Dan.' Amanda smiled. 'Er, yeah, I am in a bit of a rush, to be honest.' She gestured at the bag of nappies. 'Got to get Olivia's things sorted before I go out for the evening. My first time since she was born, actually.'

'Wow, really? That must be, what, nine months you've not

been out? I bet you're looking forward to it.' He cocked his head in that way he had, reading her conflicted expression. 'Or maybe a bit nervous? Leaving her for the first time, feeling guilty about doing something for yourself?'

Amanda nodded. 'Bit unsure, actually. Yep.' She perched on her desk. 'You got kids, Dan? Sounds like you have some inside knowledge there.'

He shook his head, cracked his knuckles. 'No, sadly not. My ex and I… well, she said she wanted them, then changed her mind after we got married…' He stared out at the streaky pink and orange sky. 'But I do have a niece though.' He smiled. 'She just turned three last week. Mitzi. What a poppet. She's the one person I truly miss since I moved here to St Augustine's.'

Amanda checked her phone – she was going to be late. 'Aw, I'd love to see some photos, Dan. But I'm so sorry, I really have to get a move on now. Could we meet tomorrow about those accounts?'

Rising from her seat, she gathered up a bag of baby paraphernalia and walked towards Jake's office. She entered the open doorway and paused. Jake was licking his fingers as he finished wolfing down the first of two Danish pastries. Then he went back to correcting scripts with the red Montblanc pen he always used, the one she'd bought him for his fiftieth.

Jake had always had a sweet tooth, but Danish pastries had a particular significance for him, and Amanda was probably the only person in the world who knew that. Each bite of the flaky pastry always took him right back to his childhood, when, on returning from the last day of boarding school for the summer break, his mum would be waiting for him at home, with a pile of homemade Danishes with his name written on them in icing. They'd sit together, eating and talking as he filled her in on the previous term's activities. She wasn't a big one for letter writing or phone calls, so all year he'd look forward to the moment the warm pastry hit his lips. He'd told Amanda that this was the only time he'd feel cared for, even if just for a few hours. Once his dad arrived home from work, all cosiness would cease. Amanda knew that even now, as an adult, whenever he saw a Danish, he needed to put it on his plate. Even if it messed up his no-carb, no-sugar diet.

For a moment, with the sun shining on his handsome face, Amanda saw the man she used to love. She was transported to a time when he'd made her feel that they could have it all: careers and children. Except, when their miracle baby finally arrived, it was quickly clear that she was the one who 'had' Olivia. Jake hadn't even fought for her when she was demoted for having become a mother. Even though he looked the same, she barely recognized anything of the man to whom she'd said 'I do'.

Sensing a shadow in the doorway, Jake looked up, staring at her through his half-moon glasses.

'A problem I need to know about?' he said.

It was as if they barely knew each other. Typical Jake. Even when they were alone, he couldn't let the power drop. That was enough to dissipate any romantic nostalgia.

'Yes. The budget for the Christmas live stunt isn't cutting it – we need at least a million to pull this off,' she said flatly as her eyes passed over the two retro leather chairs positioned opposite the windows, where they used to sit together, holding hands, watching the sea.

'The budget has been set in stone. No wiggle room, I'm afraid. Just tell the team to be creative,' he said, barely meeting her eye, returning to his script notes.

Amanda held herself very still, steadied her breathing. She was determined not to let him get to her, not tonight. 'They tried that. We went from an amazing horse stampede across the beach—'

'Nice. I like that.' He raised an eyebrow.

'—to one horse.'

Amanda could almost hear his brain percolating. He knew she was right, so now he'd be calculating how to twist this to his advantage, how to make the whole thing sound like his idea. She knew exactly what to say to get him over the line.

'Look, I'll go back and push the team harder,' she offered. 'I'll say you're going to get them more money, but as you've gone in to bat for them, they'll need to come good on their end and deliver a stunt that will be talked about for years. Plus spending a million on a stunt budget will generate great PR headlines. It's win-win.'

'I was only joking when I said the budget had been set in stone.' He raised both eyebrows, fronting it out. 'I've already told upstairs we need at least a mil, and it's being processed, so rest assured I've already fixed this.'

They looked at each other. She knew he was lying and he knew she knew, but he continued nevertheless.

'I just wanted to see what the team came up with before they knew they had my help,' he said with a patronizing smile.

'Wonderful,' she replied, doing the best Stepford Wife impression she could muster. She placed the baby bag on his desk, then stood back with a smile.

'What's that for?' he asked.

'As agreed last week, you've got Olivia tonight. She's due to be picked up from the crèche in ten.'

'Olivia…?'

'Your daughter,' she said slowly, remaining Stepford-like. 'I know you've not seen much of her lately, but I didn't think you'd forget her name.'

Inside, she was seething. She wanted to scream. But she was determined he wouldn't get to see that and instead focused her eyes on the vein in his neck, which was pulsing like a little bomb about to go off. This was always the sign of an imminent blow-up, but she remained serene as he swivelled in his chair to now fully face her.

He began calmly, mirroring her. 'Oh, right. So it's just' – but then he jumped up from his seat and let rip – 'me saving this fucking show from being cancelled, is it?'

His voice was so loud, anyone still in the building, regardless of what floor they were on, would have been hard pressed not to have heard it.

'I was planning on *working* late, but obviously a night out is more important to you!' He strode towards her, his face beetroot, nostrils flaring.

A spray of spittle grazed her cheeks as he spat his words out like ammo, but she still didn't react.

'It's a working dinner with the girls, so I doubt I'll be too late, but definitely after midnight,' she said, aware the full-on Monroe volcano was about to blow. 'I've expressed milk, so she's got more than enough,' she finished evenly, turning towards the door as Jake continued to fizz.

'And you wonder why you got demoted!'

His voice had risen several octaves, which was usually a sign that he was going to throw something. Amanda knew she shouldn't look back, but when she reached the doorway, she couldn't help herself and turned just as his hand was reaching for a trophy from the cabinet.

'You won't want to throw that one,' she said, nodding at the Golden Globe held high above his head, 'it's got your name on it.'

He glared at her, put it back down, and reached for another.

'Look, I'll have to go, the plane'll be waiting to get us to Paris,' she said, then waved gently, desperate to get out.

Before she'd exited the door, Jake's voice rang out once more. 'I wouldn't have too late a night, if I was you,' he said, his tone mischievousness now, rather than angry.

She should have just ignored him and gone, but curiosity got the better of her. *Damn him.*

'Why, what's tomorrow?'

Jake's face broke into the wolfish grin that said he was back in the game. Amanda's chest tightened. What was he up to?

He began stringing it out. He slowly placed the trophy back in the cabinet and gave it an imaginary polish, then turned towards her and met her gaze.

'Jude Roscoe's become aware his scripts aren't coming through,' he said. 'You need to let him go in the morning.'

'Me?' Amanda gasped in horror. She absolutely hated

sacking people; it was one of her worst nightmares, and everyone knew that. Jake, on the other hand, loved a good sacking and always did it with relish. 'But that's a job for senior management – which has been made very clear is no longer what I am.'

So this was his payback for being made to babysit. All Amanda's Stepford Wifeishness had now gone out the window.

'And senior management can delegate to exec level.' Jake swung an imaginary tennis racket at her. 'So this is in your court now. Unless you want to swap your night out and have Olivia.'

Did he actually just say that? she wondered as the words sank in. *Yes! Yes, he did.*

She took a step back towards him so they were eyeball to eyeball again. 'You're actually offering to sack a man in order to get out of your night with our daughter?'

Sensing he had perhaps gone too far, Jake backtracked. 'That wasn't what I meant,' he muttered.

Amanda stared at him as she regained her composure.

'I'm just grateful that however terribly you handle your first ever solo night with our daughter, the positive is she's still too young to understand what a poor excuse of a man she has for a father.'

Then she turned on her heel and strode out of the office, slamming the door behind her.

12

Several hours later, in the ladies' room of Claude Belrose's Michelin three-star restaurant in Paris, Amanda was propping herself up against the twenty-four-carat-gold sinks with their crystal taps, trying not to make eye contact with her reflection. She hadn't been this drunk in years and could only imagine how terrible the hangover was going to be if this was meant to be the good bit. She considered emptying the milk from her aching breasts into the sink as she tried to recall how she'd got herself into such a state so quickly.

After the run-in with Jake, her evening with the girls had started by downing Krug on the deep-pile sofas of C.I.TV's private exec plane. She must have drunk the best part of a bottle even before the sun had set, trying to forget her troubles as they sped towards Paris.

'I'm just glad someone is finally telling Jude. He's been driving me mad with his paranoia,' Helen had said, gesturing one of the on-board waiters to top her glass up as Amanda revealed it was now her job to dispatch him in the morning.

'It's not paranoia if it's true,' pointed out Catherine, who wasn't a huge fan of Jude's but felt that Helen could have been a bit kinder about it, considering everyone on set knew she was shagging him.

'But why are you the one who's got to tell him?' Farrah said, also shaking her glass towards the waiter for a refill.

'It's Jake's payback for me leaving him on his own with Olivia – for the first time since she was born, I might add,' Amanda said, before knocking back her drink in one.

'What an arsehole,' spat Farrah. 'Sorry, darling, but, really, what the hell are you doing sticking with that idiot? I know we've all said it before, haven't we ladies?'

The others murmured awkwardly. They'd tried to influence Amanda to leave Jake before, but it had only made things more difficult around the office, and they didn't want to get involved. So as Farrah tried to include them in the conversation, Catherine, Helen and Sheena all looked out of the plane windows, suddenly intrigued by the view of the clouds. Amanda focused on her next glass of Krug and also started cloud-gazing, but Farrah was not deterred.

'Jake was good for the IVF, I can see that. He'd for sure have made you destroy those precious embryos if you left him before you'd conceived. But, shit, he didn't even come to Olivia's birth. I mean, what sort of husband does that?'

Amanda continued cloud-gazing, willing Farrah to shut up.

She didn't. 'And then he bloody shafted you over the top job. Typical fucking sexist pig behaviour. I am so sick of this happening on the *Bay*. Every damn time.' She glowered pointedly at Catherine, who did not rise to the bait, it having been several weeks now since their showdown over Aiden.

'You are worth so much more than him, Amanda. And you're the only one who can't see it.'

There were no hard edges to Amanda: her auburn hair was bouncy and despite three workout sessions a week, she was still carrying a bit of baby weight, which actually suited her. Her cheeks were full and had enough red in them to complement her pearly white skin. She was beautiful, in an ordinary but very sexy way. When Amanda came into the room, you wanted to sit next to her, you wanted her to like you and you raised your game accordingly. That was how Farrah felt, and she couldn't bear to see her friend being taken for granted by her pig of a husband.

Amanda finally spoke. 'Look, things are hard for him at the moment, Farrah. He'll come round. He really was nice once, and with Olivia and everything, I still have to believe that the guy he used to be is still in there.'

Farrah rolled her eyes.

'But right now, I just want to get drunk and forget about it all for a bit!' She took a massive gulp of her fizz and spluttered as the bubbles went up her nose.

'Well then,' Sheena said, 'we'd better make it a night to remember!'

'Or at least one that we're incapable of remembering,' laughed Helen, gesturing for a toast. 'Sod Jake. Sod the lot of 'em.'

Farrah reluctantly shrugged and topped up their drinks. In unison, the five friends, including Amanda, raised their middle fingers on one hand and their glasses in the other, gesturing rudely in the general direction of St Augustine's and Jake, then burst into laughter.

By the time they landed in Paris, they were as sparkling as the city lights that greeted them, definitely more tipsy than they'd intended to be at this point in the evening. Somehow, they all squeezed into one yellow cab. The driver had tried to say no, but after thrusting an abundance of euros in his face, they set off for Belrose with Helen lying across the laps of Sheena, Farrah and Amanda in the back. Catherine sat up front trying to placate the huffy cabbie.

As *Falcon Bay* was aired in France (with appalling dubbing, in Catherine's opinion), he soon realized who Catherine was and took great delight in telling her he'd had way more famous people in his cab than her. She didn't react; she was used to the snobbery that was routinely meted out on soap stars. She found it amusing that some people would respect an indie actress who'd appeared in a movie made on an iPhone that maybe a few diehards online were discussing but would look down on someone like her, who, at the height of the show's success, appeared in 100 million homes around the world fifty-two weeks of the year. He wouldn't be getting a tip, that was for sure.

While Sheena, Helen and Amanda screeched lusty catcalls at every half-fit French man they caught sight of through the cab windows, Catherine stared out at a pair of lovers, walking hand-in-hand along the Champs-Élysées towards the Eiffel Tower.

This beautiful, romantic landmark always tugged on her heartstrings. When she and Claude first started their short but passionate affair, he would take her up to the top of the Tower on the last lift of the day, and, with the sun setting over Paris, she would stand in front of him, pushed against the railings, where no one could see his hand sliding round her waist and down between her legs. She tingled at the memory. Claude's womanizing had tainted many memories, but not of those tender moments, or of their vigorous lovemaking. All these years later, she'd never known anything like it.

Catherine wondered if she'd ever have another lover to visit Paris with, instead of her friends. *Falcon Bay* was really the only long-term relationship she'd been in, she thought sadly. But now was not a time for self-pity. Shaking herself out of her reverie, she turned around to join in the drunken gossip being traded in the back seat, and realized that Farrah was looking out of the window in silence. Catherine had heard her phone beep a couple of times, but after Farrah had read the messages, she'd been very quiet, and was now staring at her phone in silence. When Catherine asked her what was wrong, she got a curt 'Nothing' as a reply.

When they reached the 10th arrondissement, Claude himself came to the door of his restaurant to greet them. With his curly mane of black hair, perfect stubble, green eyes and that famously distinctive aroma of his, which came wafting towards them like a warm cloud of a thousand spices, Catherine was transported back in time. There had been nothing more than friendship between them for more than ten years now, but the mere sight of him was still enough to turn her on. There were no air kisses from Claude: he kissed each cheek and added a third kiss on the lips for sincerity.

Even when they were together, it had been hard not to admire his unabashed appreciation of every woman who crossed his path. She'd been kidding herself from the start that they'd had any sort of future. Claude could never belong to one woman – she could see that by the way all the women on reception in the coat-check area were salivating from afar. Perhaps his destiny on earth was to make as many women as possible feel like a goddess – both in bed, and out of it – as only he could. If that was the case, she was in no doubt that he'd be giving Julio Iglesias some competition for bedpost numbers.

Catherine smiled as she watched her friends enjoying being manhandled by him, lapping up his admiring comments about their womanly shapes as he took each coat. 'Proper women,' he drawled in his thick accent, drawing an hourglass with his hands. 'Not like our skinny French girls you don't want to touch in case you snap them.' They took this as a compliment, even though he was also calling them out for not being young or thin. But somehow he could get away with it.

The restaurant was a grand, open space with tall, ornate windows which overlooked the Canal Saint-Martin. Tables full of chattering, well-dressed diners packed the room under a gorgeous low-hanging chandelier which glittered in the centre, giving off a soft glow that could knock ten years off a woman's age. The kitchen could be seen from the tables: a hive of chefs and their assistants bustling around, ducking under plates, reaching around each other, like a beautifully choreographed tango. It was a vibrant place, beloved by the rich, the famous and the powerful. Civilians, as Claude liked to call anyone else, had to wait up to two years for a booking before they could even sip the water in his famous hangout.

Catherine particularly loved Claude's. It wasn't just that she enjoyed the memories of what she and Claude once had; she also felt safe here. This restaurant was as French as they came, and so, unlike in England or America, people didn't come over and bother her.

As Claude led them to their table, he admired Farrah's Dries Van Noten power suit.

'You look *magnifique ce soir*,' he said as he kissed her fingers.

But Farrah's mood had turned snippy. 'You've got caviar on your shirt,' was her reply as she pulled her hand away.

Claude was mortified to be so remiss in his presentation. He called over a waiter, insisted the first bottle was on the house, and went to burn his shirt.

As they allowed the waiter to pull out their seats, Catherine asked Farrah what they'd all been thinking. 'Time of the month...?'

Farrah looked her dead in the eyes. 'I bet you'd love to have that monthly problem again, wouldn't you? Must be decades since the flow last visited your dried-up well,' she said.

Catherine looked shocked. 'I was only joking.'

'But, no, I'm not on my period, as it happens.'

'Did you get some bad news or something earlier?' Amanda asked quietly, putting a supportive hand on Farrah's arm.

'Bad news is one way of describing it,' Farrah said, pulling her phone out of her crocodile-skin Valentino handbag, clicking open her messages and passing it to Amanda. 'Be my guest, read it out.'

Amanda read out the latest one. It was from Aiden Andersen.

> Jake said U took the plane, naughty
> gal! U in London? I am… Let the Bay's
> Number 1 stud give you what you need…
> I know ur pissed I got the big ep, but let
> MY big dick make it up to you!!!

Helen and Sheena squawked with laughter.

'OMG, is he for real? As if!' Helen said when her shoulders had stopped shaking.

'Cheeky bastard,' Sheena chipped in. 'Not surprised you're pissed off, Farrah. You could have him for harassment – hang onto those messages in case we ever need them. Christ! Men… Thank God I'm gay!'

Amanda stole a glance at Catherine, who was determinedly admiring the ikebana arrangement on their table.

Farrah stood up without responding. 'Right, I'm going for a bump.'

Helen was up like a jack-in-the-box. 'One should never bump alone, darling.'

Amanda got up too. Helen and Farrah looked surprised, as Amanda had never taken a non-prescription drug in her life.

'God, no!' She laughed at them for thinking that Jake had finally pushed her off the rails. 'I'm dying for a wee.'

'TMI,' said Helen as they walked off arm in arm, leaving just Catherine and Sheena seated.

'She's being very weird with you tonight, isn't she?' Sheena said, nodding towards Farrah's impressive figure disappearing into the bathrooms.

Catherine, still feeling stung, wanted to move the conversation on. 'You don't miss it?' she said, tapping her nose.

Sheena didn't need time to think about that. 'Absolutely not.'

Catherine smiled, proud of her agent and friend.

Sheena went quiet momentarily, then continued. 'I actually consider myself lucky to have been a drug addict and not an alcoholic. I mean, look at me in here: I still get to be social and not lose my shit. Some people can't even have that,' she said, topping their glasses up.

'Like Honey Hunter,' Catherine said.

'Wow, that's a blast from the past. Poor thing. I can't imagine not being able to at least have a drink, but booze for her was like the drugs for me – lethal. Let's hope the heady air of those Swiss Alps has given her the fresh start she needed.' A memory of herself with Honey from the past filled Sheena's mind for a moment. They'd had a lot in common once. Both of them out on the scene, messed up and messy. They'd lost touch a long time ago, but Sheena still remembered her with affection.

'Well, she's certainly going to struggle handling the Bitch Party sober,' Catherine said, ripping off a piece of bread and dipping it in olive oil. She rarely allowed herself carbs, but it smelled too good to resist.

Sheena looked at Catherine in shock, which Catherine noted.

Catherine bought herself some time by chewing and making a face that signalled that the bread tasted as delicious as it looked. After swallowing, she continued. 'You *did* know she's on the shortlist to be my new nemesis?' she said, trying to give Sheena, who clearly did not know, the chance to pretend she did.

As Sheena took in this news, the others arrived back at the table. Helen and Farrah weren't even trying to disguise what they'd been up to, making exaggerated sniffs and running fingers under their nostrils to check that they weren't leaking. Amanda trailed behind, looking at her phone, which was filled with a ton of childish messages from Jake.

As they took their seats, Sheena confronted Helen. 'You never told me Honey Hunter was up for their new bitch?'

'Amongst many,' Helen said awkwardly.

'You promised you'd do all you could for Stacey and Lydia. My girls.'

'And I will,' Helen said in a voice that was a clear warning for Sheena to stop discussing this in public.

Oblivious to the tension, Farrah chipped in. 'Either of your two would be good, actually.'

'I'd prefer Stacey,' Catherine said, giving the safest choice her blessing. 'She'd be well suited to *Falcon Bay*. On and off screen.'

Amanda shook her head. 'Lydia for me. She's got an unpredictability and edge that would work well for storylining.'

'Just keep her away from the cows.' Farrah laughed and the others joined in, apart from Catherine, who grimaced at the thought of such humiliation. It could happen to any actor.

'See, Helen?' Sheena said. 'Everyone agrees. As lovely as she is, Honey would not be a good choice.'

'Nothing has been decided at this stage,' Helen said, feeling ambushed.

Catherine was keen to back Sheena. 'Honey hasn't worked in decades. She'd be a nightmare on set – even that LA soap she did was only on once a week and she only lasted a year in that. She couldn't handle the pressure of what we have to shoot.' She popped another piece of the delicious bread into her mouth. It quickly disappeared behind her perfectly white veneers.

'What, you mean like screwing over a mate just to pally up with the live ep director?' said Farrah. Thanks to the cocaine that was now trickling down her throat, she had finally revealed why she was in such a foul mood with Catherine.

But before Catherine could respond, Claude arrived at their table bearing a tray of amuse-bouches. 'Ladies, these are on the house for tonight. But I am afraid I must also borrow the most beautiful of your party, to discuss some of the specials we have on this evening's menu.' His eyes roved appreciatively over Catherine's body.

Ignoring the stony expression on Farrah's face, Catherine stood up and allowed Claude to escort her down a small corridor and through a door marked 'Private'.

The door had barely closed when he was on her, licking her neck in that special way that drove her crazy. Then he stood back and stared at her.

'Take your clothes off,' he commanded, whilst undoing his shirt buttons. He knew her well enough to know that Catherine would not want her clothes creased in public.

At the same time as she slid down her dress, he released his belt and let his trousers drop to the floor. Going commando as always, his gorgeous toned body glistened. Her eyes were drawn to the swirling tufts of hair that ran down his manly chest in a line that extended all the way down to his perfect, uncut cock, which was now bobbing around his navel.

Catherine, who never wore a bra, stood in her nude Stella McCartney lace thong, her vagina feeling like a butterfly enclosure with a thousand wings all batting at once.

'Come,' Claude said as he beckoned her towards him.

As their bodies met, he kissed her with the force of a tidal wave flooding an island and moved his fingers down, teasing her soaking clit, then expertly sliding deep inside her. As the intensity grew, she could feel herself coming. Never in her life had anyone but Claude been able to bring her to orgasm in under two minutes.

She moaned aloud as her body arched, and she hovered dangerously close to the butterflies being released.

'Let go, my darling,' he urged. 'Give it to me.' And he changed his rhythm until she was shaking. With his other hand he squeezed her rock-hard nipple, gently at first, then leaning forward to flick his tongue back and forth between each breast, expertly sucking them deep inside his mouth.

'Oh God,' Catherine gasped. This was it; the gate was open, there was no way of stopping now.

'Come for me, my darling,' Claude urged as he took his rhythm up to a speed that no vibrator in the world could match.

Catherine let out a shuddering sigh as she climaxed so deeply, it felt like she might faint.

Sensing her legs were shaking, Claude placed a hand on her back to hold her up and with the other gracefully slid his perfect prick deep inside.

'You're so wet, my Catherine, so beautifully wet,' he breathed as he held her close. 'Now, my darling, it's my turn.'

13

Unbeknownst to the five friends, there was another table of diners from *Falcon Bay* in Claude's restaurant that night, tucked discreetly away in a corner booth.

Seated together, Madeline Kane and her husband Chad were holding court to several key players from C.I.TV's shareholder board. The beautiful couple were facing six men who all appeared to be hanging on Madeline's every word. She was dressed like a flame in a red Chanel dress with matching talon-like nails, and Chad, six foot five and with shoulders like a tank, was rocking a sharp Tom Ford suit, his open shirt revealing a scattering of light brown hair that matched his rugged stubble and well-styled hair. A bright red pocket square in his jacket finished off his look. Next to Chad, the statuesque Madeline looked positively petite.

'Gentlemen,' Chad began in a deep drawl, his accent as Deep South as Madeline's, 'and shareholders,' he added with a wink, then bellowed with laughter. 'Since I arrived, I've been going through *Falcon Bay*'s books with a fine-tooth comb and, while I would never doubt the ability of my wonderful wife to save a sinking ship, it was no secret that C.I.TV and in particular *Falcon Bay* was her passion project. I'm just the money man. I'd have bankrolled whatever she wanted to do to it – anything to keep my darling happy.'

He laughed again as Madeline looked coy and rested her hand on his bulging bicep.

'But I'm happy to say, it turns out there is profit in my adorable wife's love for this show. Her ideas have gone down a storm with syndication. The promise of two live episodes taking us to a year-end boom has already attracted several new advertisers, which covers the deficits from countries we'd lost, and Canada, Italy and Australia have renewed us solely on the basis of Madeline's plans. So, while I'm not saying we're out of the woods yet, we are definitely past the trees.'

He turned to Madeline, who was blushing slightly. 'Honey, take a bow,' he said, leaning in to kiss her cheek.

Madeline knew exactly what sort of bow she'd be wanting to take with her husband once dinner was over. From the moment she'd met Chad, all she ever wanted to do was rip his clothes off, and she positively glowed whenever he was near her. It was obvious to anyone who saw them together that they were both besotted. They fizzed in each other's company, and Madeline felt sexier than ever as she stood there, staring up at Chad's handsome face, losing herself in his chocolate-brown eyes.

To her annoyance, her lustful thoughts were interrupted by loud laughter coming from the other side of the restaurant. As Madeline looked round to see who was causing the disturbance, her gaze fell on Catherine and the other *Falcon*

Bay women. Her jaw tightened. She'd come all this way for some privacy, only to find herself just a few feet from a gaggle of irritating employees. Her rage rose when she realized they must have taken the other C.I.TV plane without bothering to ask her permission.

One of the board members lifted his glass in a toast. 'Gentlemen, if you will. To our noble and beautiful leader. Madeline Kane, the saviour of *Falcon Bay*.'

'Hear, hear,' Chad said, putting his massive hand on her leg.

'Thank you, gentlemen,' she said, almost coquettishly, as she inclined her head in acknowledgement and tried to ignore the noise from across the room. 'You have my word that I will not stop until the deadwood has been shaved off the wonderful oak tree that is *Falcon Bay*. With care and attention, it can go on to live another forty years and make y'all a hell of a lot more money!'

As the men smiled, Catherine Belle's shrill laugh rang out once again. Madeline gritted her perfect teeth.

14

After several delicious if rather tiny courses, Amanda, Catherine and Sheena were full but not stuffed, which was just how they liked it. Farrah and Helen, however, had barely pecked at their food, having made several more toilet visits between plates.

The tension between Catherine and Farrah had continued to simmer through the evening, with Farrah being uncharacteristically taciturn and Catherine making occasional abortive attempts at small talk. As Sheena picked up the tab, adding an overly generous tip, she was also still stewing about the Honey Hunter bombshell. She wasn't going to let Helen off the hook that easily.

'I thought we were friends,' she said to Helen as the waiter scurried off with her AmEx card.

'We are.'

'The talent I've brought to your door over the years, the favours I've done you… I've got two girls who really need this bitch part – either one of them, I don't care.'

'Which is why they're both invited to the party. I did that for you.'

'And your head's been turned by Honey Hunter. Who is a walking lawsuit, for fuck's sake.'

'I can't just give one of your girls the job – the decision goes higher than me. It's going to the audience vote.'

Catherine's eyes widened. 'The public are choosing?' she said, horrified.

Helen nodded.

'You never told me that,' Sheena said, her tone dropping a notch.

Helen shrugged. 'No one is supposed to know yet,' she said. Her tone made it clear she wasn't happy about her own power being given to the people they usually referred to as punters.

Sheena could see there was no point in continuing the conversation for now. After a brief pause of acceptance, the group rose from the table, and as they began to move through the room, Catherine did a double-take. 'It's Madeline!' she said, too loudly, pointing at the corner booth. 'Let's go and say hello.'

Amanda stepped in her way. 'No,' she said, placing her hand on Catherine's arm. 'I'd rather not.'

'Why not?' said Catherine.

Sheena followed Catherine's gaze. The timing was perfect – maybe fate was throwing her a bone and she could slip a few words in for Lydia and Stacey. 'I agree. We really should say hi.' She smiled, linking arms with Catherine, who was fluffing her hair, ready to make an entrance.

'Yes, come on, just a quick hello.' Catherine gestured for the others to follow.

'Amanda said leave it, Cat!' Farrah snapped.

Catherine, who absolutely detested anyone shortening her name, ignored her and walked Sheena towards Madeline's table.

Feeling duty-bound, Amanda, Helen and eventually Farrah all followed.

'Ms Kane, I hope you don't mind the intrusion…' Catherine began as she reached the booth.

'Oh, Catherine, I didn't realize you were here,' Madeline lied, quickly getting to her feet and trying to block the rest of the women before they caught up. But it was too late, and the whole table of men stood up to greet the women.

Chad looked pleased to see Catherine and followed Madeline out of the booth.

My God, he's gorgeous, thought Catherine, who had to look up to take in Chad's full height.

'Ms Belle, I've yet to have the privilege,' Chad said, offering his hand to shake. 'I'm Madeline's husband.'

Madeline squeezed between the two of them, cutting him off, then turned back towards the table.

'My pleasure,' was all Catherine managed to get out before Madeline lightly touched her shoulder and guided her away from the men.

Sheena, who was a few steps further back, looked on curiously. Could Madeline really be that insecure – with those looks? She raised a questioning eyebrow at Amanda, and Amanda gave a little shrug in return, clearly relieved that this path-crossing was going to be brief.

'Gentlemen, please excuse me for a moment,' Madeline said, flashing a large smile. 'Girl talk.' She finished with a wink and began gently herding the women towards the exit.

'Sorry not to be able to chat tonight, ladies,' she said sweetly, almost waving them off. 'Important network business – all very exciting, but I'd hate to ruin any surprises for you by having you overhear something you shouldn't. See you all back at the ranch.'

She'd got just a few steps away when Sheena called after her.

'I'm Sheena McQueen, by the way. We should schedule a meeting sometime,' she said.

Madeline stopped in her tracks and after a mini pause turned round.

She really was quite breathtaking close up. A lot of grace and poise. She'd have made a great soap star herself, Sheena thought.

'But of course I know who you are, Ms McQueen.' Madeline smiled.

Happy to have been recognized as Catherine's agent, Sheena confidently reached out her hand to shake Madeline's and the two women drew closer.

'I used to love you in *Second Chances*,' Madeline said. 'You were a bit of a tearaway on and off screen, I seem to remember.'

Sheena had to consciously stop herself from blanching at the reference. 'That's a long time ago.'

'It's good you never let that Ed Nichols scandal ruin your life,' Madeline said casually, as if they were talking about an annoying next-door neighbour rather than a child abuser.

It had been years since Sheena had heard somebody speak his name. Generally, people in entertainment didn't want to bring him up. She looked into Madeline's eyes, trying to find an agenda, but discovered none. In fact, she looked like butter wouldn't melt.

'He ruined my past; I wasn't about to let him ruin my future,' she said, glancing over her shoulder to see whether other people were listening in. She had nothing to hide from her friends – they knew pretty much everything – but she didn't want the sordid details shared with the whole of Claude's.

'Good for you,' Madeline said, sounding like she meant it. 'From what I remember in the papers of the day, not everyone involved was so lucky.'

'True,' replied Sheena.

The rest of the group were picking up on the awkwardness of the exchange, even if they couldn't hear the substance of it. Helen, leaning on the cloakroom counter to stop herself from swaying, was about to fall over. Catherine rushed over to prop her up as Farrah and Amanda fastened their coats. Amanda was desperate to leave before she said something she shouldn't.

'As the new owner of C.I.TV, I am proud to say we'll never allow predators like Ed Nichols to get their hands on our precious young stars.'

'Well, that's a positive thing to hear,' Sheena said.

'You've done very well for yourself, all things considered,' Madeline said, smiling but with a touch of ice in her tone. Her face might have given the illusion that the two of them were merely discussing something relevant to their industry, but, subtle or not, Sheena could sense when she was under attack.

Some people reacted like that – as if Sheena having gone

on to make a success of her life somehow tarnished her innocence, made her less of a victim. It was tiresome and narrow-minded, but she was used to it.

'Well, I'm not sure that sort of behaviour will ever entirely be consigned to history, sadly, but it's good to know someone is on guard to protect the vulnerable. That's important in TV.'

'On guard I am, Ms McQueen,' Madeline said with another smile.

Maybe it was an American thing, Sheena thought. This hyper vigilance and keenness to lay it all on the table from the get-go. In which case, insensitive or not, she was all for it. Madeline Kane could be just what *Falcon Bay* needed to keep it going. And every agent wanted their clients to be as well protected as possible. Sheena knew more than many exactly what that meant.

Catherine, glad whatever was going on between Sheena and Madeline was now over, steered Sheena towards the exit.

But before they were out the door, Madeline called out to Amanda. 'Oh, Ms King, I do hope you're not going to be too hungover in the morning.'

Amanda gave a drunken, childlike shrug.

'You've an important meeting first thing with Jude Roscoe, remember,' Madeline said, with what definitely looked like a glint in her eye.

So Jake had told her. The bastard. And now here Madeline was, looking at Amanda in a way that suggested she'd made the right call overlooking her for the job. Amanda wanted to find the perfect put-down, the ultimate riposte that showed she was eloquent and had been wronged. But before she could find the right words, the wrong ones came out.

'Oh, fuck off,' she said, and staggered out to the street.

Helen gave a surprised cackle that echoed back into the restaurant. A lot of well-coiffed heads turned in their direction.

As soon as her heels hit the pavement, Amanda knew she'd made a horrible, awful, mistake.

Catherine was furious. 'I cannot believe you just said that,' she said, while frantically trying to hail a cab.

Farrah was laughing, which incensed Catherine even more. 'And you could have stepped in. You could see the way it was going.'

Farrah stormed towards her, face flushed with outrage. 'Me! You're the one that was so desperate to be liked by the new boss that you dragged your friend over to kiss the arse of the woman who stabbed her in the back.'

'Jake stabbed Amanda in the back, not Madeline,' Catherine snapped back.

'Yeah, keep telling yourself that, Cat.'

'Stopping calling me Cat.'

'Why? You go rubbing yourself along the leg of anybody who'll feed and stroke your ego – it's the perfect name for you.'

Catherine snarled, her composure crumbling.

Farrah was right beside her now. 'As soon as Aiden Anderson came on my set and told you he'd got the live episode, you were all over him like a Siamese on heat. "Oh, Aiden. Purr, purr. I'm sure little old Farrah can do this in one and you and me can go running off together."'

'I didn't want it coming back on you,' Catherine said smoothly, 'so I tried to help out.'

'My arse, you did. You threw me under a bus and Aiden was driving.'

'Girls! Girls!' Helen managed to wave down a cab, which pulled up next to them. 'Let's stop this and get back to partying. What club are we going to?' she said, gesturing to the driver to hang on.

'I don't think you're the best person to be peacemaking here.' Sheena lit a cigarette, which made the driver tap his 'No Smoking' sign on the window as a warning.

Amanda watched the two sets of bickering women and wasn't sure who would be left standing if things got physical. She wasn't certain if she still had a job, after what she'd just said. Her head was spinning. What a nightmare evening. First the altercation with Jake, and all so she could have a night of drinking and dancing, and now even that had turned into a full-on disaster.

Catherine pressed her point. 'What was I supposed to do? You're both directors – I treat you both the same.'

'But we're not the same. Aiden's been handed everything on a silver platter, thanks to the boys' club, whereas I have to work twice as hard to even get half a look-in.'

'You're being ridiculous,' Catherine snapped.

'Oh, am I?' Farrah was swaying now. 'You should know better. When you see the chance to lift up a fellow woman, you should leap at it.'

'I want you to demand a woman directs the live episode.'

'By "woman", you mean you.'

'Yeah, but not 'cos it's me, because I'm a woman.'

'There's never been a woman director do a live ep on TV,' Catherine said, as if this was proof of her argument.

'Exactly!' Farrah bellowed.

'You know what, Farrah, you didn't come up the hard way. Thanks to Helen and me fighting for you, first you were a well-paid actress, then Sheena talked the execs into putting you on the writing team. I'm not the only one who sidles up to people for food. So don't come to me for handouts – you've already had more than enough from all of us! You want the live gig? Then fight for it, 'cos you've used up your favours in this group.'

The two women squared up. Amanda thought she'd better get in the middle of them, but Sheena seemed to be on top of it and pulled Farrah away from Catherine mid-rant.

'Oh, I will fight for it. And you'll be sorry when I get it, Cat,' Farrah screamed. She pushed Sheena away and got in the cab on her own. A door slam later and she was gone.

15

Above the sounds of horse-drawn carriages taking tourists on early-morning sightseeing tours, in a room in one of London's finest hotels, a TV flickered silently while Amy Winehouse's voice floated out of a pair of Bose surround speakers. The hotel room bore the signs of an all-night party: trays of uneaten room-service food were strewn across the dining table and the floor, several lines of partially hoovered-up cocaine were visible next to a black Amex card and a couple of rolled banknotes, some white pills lay nearby, and there were empty bottles of wine, champagne and whisky upturned in ice buckets.

Although it looked like there'd been lots of guests, only two people had been at this party: a man and a woman. Both lay motionless on the crumpled bed. Both were naked. He was asleep, she was awake.

The woman was Farrah, and she felt like death warmed up.

Farrah tried to ignore the pain as she first lifted her head and then raised her body into a seated position. Her power suit was crumpled in the corner and she was scanning the room for her underwear. She spotted it at the base of a chair. As she quietly got out of bed and bent down to pick up her bra, her head thumped from the booze and dehydration. Her nose was sore from the coke, her lips felt chapped and her teeth were still numb.

While she was putting her lingerie on, Aiden Anderson began to stir.

She took a good look at him in the few seconds before his eyes opened, this man who represented everything she despised about the cliquishness and endemic sexism of television drama.

Perhaps aware he was being stared at, the way humans tend to notice, Aiden's eyes popped open. 'Morning,' he said, as if this was the most normal situation in the world. 'That…' He sat himself up, groaned a couple of times, creaked a joint or three. 'Was…' He glanced around the room, taking in the jettisoned clothes, the drink and drug carnage, and then Farrah in her knickers and bra. 'Epic!'

Farrah managed a smile, which made her cheek crack.

'When you ignored those texts I thought there was no chance you'd come and play. But then I see your name calling. And I'm like. Boom. It's on!'

Jesus Christ, thought Farrah. She couldn't bear his short sentences and rat-a-tat cadence. She knew other women loved it and hung on his painfully slow delivery of every word. But it made her want to dunk his head in one of the ice buckets.

On unsteady feet, she crossed over to her scrunched-up clothes while he continued to relate his story to what he clearly thought was a captivated audience.

'And when I answered. And you told me to meet you here. I was like, yes! Finally!'

'I was drunk,' she said.

He smiled a cheeky-chappie Hugh Grant dimple grin, a heartbeat away from a wink. 'You knew what you were doing, and to even bring the gear…' He gestured towards the drugs strewn around the room. 'You're the dream lady!' he said, then patted the bed for her to join him again.

Farrah had to turn her back; she didn't want him to see the truth in her eyes. Yes, she'd known exactly what she was doing when she'd booked herself a helicopter that had cost nearly ten grand to get her from Paris to this hotel to carry out the angry, drunken plan she'd hatched during her night out with the girls. She'd been planning on ignoring his grubby text messages, or possibly even following Sheena's advice and using them for a tribunal, but her fight with Catherine had lit a touchpaper that changed everything. This was only half of the plan though; she'd come this far, now she needed to see it through.

She picked up her wallet, stuffed her coke-smeared Amex in it and started putting her jewellery back on.

Aiden shook his hair like a proud lion and punched the air. 'You called. I came running.' He smiled and threw a wink in her direction, which made her feel even more nauseous. 'Thank you. From here.' He patted his chest, meaning to touch his heart, but he got the wrong side.

Looking at her watch, she knew she was almost out of time. She leaned forward and stroked his face, which made him smile all over again, then gestured towards the bathroom. 'I'm just going to brush my teeth.'

'I'm ready for some breakfast.' Aiden grinned at the lined-up cocaine. 'Join me. Then let's get ready for another rumble.'

'Can't wait,' she said, disappearing into the bathroom.

Behind her, Aiden was now bent over the table with a rolled-up fifty in his hand.

She only had moments to escape. When she'd rented the two rooms late last night (paying with cash and booked under a false name, of course), she'd made sure to check that the adjoining balcony went under both bathrooms. Standing on the loo, she pulled open the window and, as quietly as she could, climbed through it. As she slipped onto the terrace that overlooked Hyde Park, the fresh air made her nauseous, but there was no time to worry about that.

Just as she pulled the window closed behind her, she heard a full-bodied knock on Aiden's room door. Her plan was now in full swing.

She let herself into the adjoining suite via the balcony door she'd left open when she'd checked in, then went to the exit and peeped into the hall. Through the crack of her door she saw the hotel's head of security outside Aiden's room. Following closely behind were the *Herald*'s editor, Ross Owen, and two photographers.

Inside his suite, Aiden's smug grin of moments before had been replaced by a panicked grimace as the knocking on the door and the voices from the hall grew louder.

'I hope you're decent, sir. I'm coming in,' said the voice as a card swiped through his lock and the door swung open.

Farrah immediately walked as fast as she could down the corridor. As she was pressing the button for the lift, she could hear a flustered Aiden.

'It's not what you think! Don't come in here – there's a lady present,' he protested, but it was too late. Camera flashes were going off at a rapid rate, snapping shots of a naked and wild-eyed Aiden standing next to the lines of cocaine, pile of pills and empty booze bottles that would make the front page of tomorrow's *Herald*.

The moment the lift pinged open, Farrah slid between the doors and out of sight. She couldn't quite believe she'd pulled it off. As she slipped out of the hotel unnoticed and walked towards the high street where she'd lose herself in the crowds, she felt confident that once Aiden's name was dragged through the mud, linked with drugs and drink, there was absolutely no way *Falcon Bay* would allow him to stay on the show, let alone direct the Christmas live episode. Which meant there would be a Farrah-shaped hole just waiting for her.

16

Every phone ring, chair scrape and low-voiced conversation in the open-plan production office resounded in Amanda's ear canals as if amplified to thunderous levels via the surround sound of an IMAX cinema. Her brain throbbed. She felt as if she was in the middle of a climactic scene in one of the old *Star Wars* movies, like the ones she'd sat through with Jake when they were first dating.

She didn't know if she wanted to be sick or to actually die. She had never, ever had a hangover this bad in her life.

The night was a messy haze. After Farrah had stormed off, Helen had persuaded them not to end the evening on a low and took them off to Chez Raspoutine, a club that had been running in Paris since the seventies. Brigitte Bardot and Serge Gainsbourg had once had a legendary dance-off on its brightly lit disco floor, and more than fifty years later it was still the place to go if you wanted to 'parr-tee' as the cute French boys kept telling them. She'd managed an hour's sleep on the journey back; then, knowing that Jake would relish seeing her in such a state, instead of heading home she'd gone straight to C.I.TV at around 5 a.m., where she showered, changed into something from wardrobe, then slept for another couple of hours in Lucy Dean's internal set.

Just after nine she snuck out of the set department and took the lift back up to the main floor. Its jerky motion made her delicate stomach turn. She'd have preferred the air of the stairs but knew she wouldn't make the five flights. After what felt like hours, as beads of alcohol-infused sweat dripped from her brow, the lift finally juddered to her floor.

The corridor was spinning, but she somehow made her way to her desk and into her seat. It was early, but the room was full of movement, walkie-talkie static and chattering conversation. Everything was far too loud for her fragile head. She was just thinking about creeping back down to the internal sets for another nap – it was an outdoor day, so there wouldn't be anyone down there – when Jake appeared at her station.

'You didn't come home.' There was accusation in his tone as he leaned on her partition wall.

'Erm, I did... but you were asleep, so I slept downstairs, then came in early,' she said hurriedly. 'How was Olivia?'

'Madeline said she saw you last night,' he said with a raised eyebrow.

Oh God, she thought, as the 'fuck you' she'd said to her boss came flooding back.

Jake smiled broadly. Amanda never misbehaved like that, and she guessed he was enjoying the tables having been turned for once.

'Don't worry,' he said, adopting a semi-hushed tone that was so melodramatic it made the people around them zone in even more, 'I covered your back. Said you'd been under pressure lately and were still hormonal from the baby thing.'

The baby thing? She ran the words over in her brain. My God he could be vile.

'She said she forgives you—'

'How decent of her,' she murmured, taking a sip from the bottle of Evian on her desk.

'—and that she was right to bypass you and promote me if this is how you handle pressure.'

Amanda was just about to snap when she saw that he was pointing towards his office. She slowly followed his arm with her eyes until she spotted Jude Roscoe sitting in one of the leather chairs.

'Figured it was better for you to do it in private than out here,' he said with a grin.

Amanda's heart sank. After the catfight, in the haze of the party night, the fun of the dancing, the lights of the club and the seemingly endless journey home, she had completely forgotten that she had to sack Jude Roscoe.

This really was becoming one of the worst mornings of her life.

Silently, she got up from her chair and started walking towards Jake's office.

'Good luck,' he called after her.

Fine, she thought, steeling herself. *You and Madeline think I can't do this? Watch me.*

If you wanted to get to the top, you needed to be tough. Wasn't that the message peddled by all those management books on Jake's bedside table? So she would be tough; tough but kind.

As she entered Jake's office, Jude looked up from the copy of *Variety* that he was pretending to read.

'Morning, Amanda. And to what do I owe this pleasure?' he asked in an overly chirpy manner that made Amanda feel even worse, if that were possible.

'Hi, Jude,' she said, unsteady on her legs, unsteady in her voice. 'Thanks for coming in.' She made her way towards the desk and leaned on it for a second, to keep her balance.

'You okay? You don't look too good,' Jude asked, genuine in his concern.

He started to get up and come over to her, but she gestured for him to stay where he was.

'No, you sit. I'm okay. Sorry, bit of a head cold.' She sniffed unconvincingly.

'Ah, poor you. We can do this meeting – whatever it's about – another time, if that would help?' His upbeat manner was clearly a front; he knew something was wrong.

'No. No. Now is fine. Better to get it done,' she said, more sombrely than she'd intended. 'Jude. I'm sorry but—'

Suddenly he was out of his chair, had dropped to his knees and was at her feet. 'Please, don't say it! I've been loyal to the show. Never been late, never forgot my lines. Not like Lucien – sack him instead!' He was pleading now.

She looked down at him, shocked that he would show such desperation, such need. Most actors would rather die than let a whole open-plan office see them begging on the floor, but Jude clearly had no qualms about appearing undignified.

'Please, get up,' she said gently, her head swimming again. 'It's nothing you've done, it's not personal – you've been brilliant, but the Christmas special needs a death.'

As the words came out of her mouth, his eyes widened and he let out what she could only describe as a shriek. Whatever it was, it was hell on her ears.

'I'm going to die?' he screamed.

The sound of his voice was like a pinball blasting around her head. Even so, she genuinely felt bad for him. Killing a soap character was like killing the actor who played them too. They lost their professional family, their status with the public, their income, their marketability. It meant zero prospect of them ever returning to the show. It was massive. God, Jake really had been cavalier about this. And Jude definitely wasn't going to go quietly.

She tried to calm him while still clutching the side of Jake's desk to steady herself.

'Please stop this, Jude. You've been a professional throughout your time here, don't let yourself down now – people are watching.' She gestured towards the windows, where most of the production office, including Jake, were standing staring at them.

'I don't care!' Jude said and started to sob.

Oh God. Now he's crying! Give me strength.

She attempted one last time to wrap things up professionally so she could get the hell out of that office and try and pull herself together. 'Everyone here is grateful for everything you've given the show, but as you know, it's never a guarantee that an actor gets their contract renewed each year. That's the nature of the beast, and having met your guarantee, your last episode will be the Christmas live.'

Still on his knees, he was full-on weeping now. She handed him a tissue from Jake's desk, and then continued.

'You'll be given some very juicy scenes between now and then. We'll do our best to give you the kind of send-off that will get you good reviews. A press statement will make it clear that it's nothing you've done, it's purely a story decision.' She placed a hand on his shoulder.

Yes, and the fact your photo fell on the floor when Jake slammed the door, she thought bitterly to herself as she glanced across to where Jake was watching with interest.

Jude blew his nose and the foghorn noise nearly took Amanda's head off. But she was proud of herself. She'd actually done it. She'd said everything she needed to, maintained a calm, respectful tone, and ended it on a note of affection and understanding. Bearing in mind just how battered she was feeling, had there been score cards on her performance, she reckoned she'd be getting nines and tens all round.

'Come on now. Get up,' she said kindly, stretching out her hand to help him to his feet.

He was heavier than she'd expected and the weight of him pulling against her caused a blood rush to her head. She wobbled a little, which made her brain spin. Suddenly, every cocktail, every drink she'd had – the glasses of fizz, the expensive wine, the even more expensive whisky – came surging up her throat. Before she could attempt to even turn her head towards Jake's wastepaper basket, let alone get anywhere near it, she lost control of the contents of her stomach and threw up all over him.

Now covered in her vomit, Jude stared at her with a mix of horror and shock, then hurtled out of the room and past all his colleagues.

Dan, who, like the rest of the production office, had seen the whole unfortunate episode unfold in front of his eyes, immediately raced to the water cooler, grabbed a glass and several paper towels, and hurried into Jake's room.

Amanda watched in surprise as he threw the paper on the floor to cover the mess and placed the glass in her shaking hand. If she'd not been feeling so crap, she'd have been mortified at having hunky Dan see her like this. As it was, she was pathetically grateful.

She turned her fragile head towards the production room to see who had witnessed this horrendous act, and saw Jake standing by her desk giving her a slow handclap. Jake's eyes bored through the glass wall of the office and glared witheringly at Dan, before he turned on his heel and stalked out of the room.

Dan quickly clicked the door shut, curled a muscular arm around Amanda's shivering shoulders and led her towards one of the big armchairs in the window. Before she could stop herself, she had buried her face in his neck and collapsed into him.

They stood like that for a good minute, Dan shielding her from the goggle-eyed stares of the production office as he stroked her hair away from her sweaty forehead. Amanda knew she shouldn't let him comfort her like this, with all the office watching, but for once she really didn't care. Somewhere in the back of her mind she was aware she should feel shame and revulsion at what she'd just done. But in Dan's arms, stinking of last night's booze, she didn't feel any guilt. She felt only an overwhelming sense of deep relief.

17

At the exact same moment the production office witnessed Amanda splattering Jude Roscoe in vomit, an even bigger mess was heading *Falcon Bay*'s way. News of Aiden Anderson's drug arrest had hit the wires. Newspapers and online tabloids worldwide were listing all of the drugs found in his room: ten grams of cocaine, fifteen ecstasy pills and thirty Xanax pills. To say it was all for personal consumption made Aiden either a liar or somebody with very serious drug issues. Either way, the photo of a naked Aiden doing a line as the security guard opened the door, alongside the news that he'd been arrested on suspicion of selling drugs, meant all hell had broken loose in the syndication office. Every international network that syndicated the show wanted to know what C.I.TV was doing to 'fix the situation'.

To make matters worse, someone's iPhone footage of Amanda being sick had been leaked online. She'd already been turned into a meme, and people were faking videos of her in crazy situations, all of them resulting in her throwing up on someone. Amanda kneeling before the Queen and being sick into her crown. Amanda meeting the Pope, going to kiss his ring and then barfing over his hand. Amanda having dinner with Meghan and Prince Harry and then vomiting all over their baby.

Amanda was mortified, but Farrah, Catherine, Sheena and Helen kept sending her funny, supportive WhatsApps, trying to make light of it and telling her it was pretty mild stuff compared to *Falcon Bay*'s own Pablo Escobar. Then Helen finally asked the question she knew her friends were all dying to ask.

> Everyone is talking about how Dan from Finance put his arms around you. He was on my to-do list, but it looks like you've got there first. That butt makes me want to tear his clothes off and get down to some calculations featuring the numbers 6 and 9!

Amanda blushed, glad she was on her own, and pointedly didn't reply. She was just about to go into the Aiden crisis meeting, and now wasn't the time to discuss what had just happened with Dan. It was blindingly obvious they fancied each other, but that hug in Jake's office had been something different. She couldn't stop picturing him as a knight in shining armour – always coming to her rescue when she needed him most.

The others, meanwhile, were still having fun at her expense. Cue a stream of erotic mathematical memes from Sheena, and from Farrah the pithy if predictable:

So much better for you than that bastard
husband of yours!

Amanda's head was all over the place when she walked into Meeting Room 6, but at the sight of a sombre-looking Madeline and a blank-faced Jake she immediately clicked into professional, problem-solving mode. Avoiding eye-contact helped.

On Madeline's instruction, the network had already sent a solicitor to the police station where Aiden was being held, to find out exactly how serious the charges would be. The three of them had only just begun discussing how to handle Aiden's official exit when Helen burst through the door.

Madeline looked unimpressed. 'Ms Gold, have you heard of knocking?' she said, eyeing a breathless Helen with disdain.

Helen waved her hands towards the whiteboard on the wall. 'Tonight's episode!' she said with urgency.

'What about it?' Jake asked.

Amanda looked at the production number on the board. 'Oh no,' she said, instantly understanding the problem. 'It's the ep where Sam gets Jeanie to try cocaine at the house party.'

Helen nodded, her chest still heaving from the three-corridor run she'd just done in six-inch heels. 'Directed by Aiden!' she added.

Madeline's feline eyes swung from the whiteboard back towards Jake. 'Pull it,' she said decisively.

'But what will we put out tonight?' he said nervously.

'You tell me,' Madeline shot back in a tone that prompted him to look to Amanda for an answer.

But before Amanda could speak, Helen took her chance.

'We have a two-hander due to be aired next week. We could use that.' She said this as if it had come to her like a bolt from the blue, whereas in truth she was hitting every mark that Farrah had coached her on. As soon as Aiden's demise had become public knowledge, Farrah had flagged that rather than stand back and see their beloved network damaged further, they could not only help but actually benefit from Aiden's fuck-up. All that was needed was a bit of strategic planning around the reveal of the problem with tonight's show.

'Oh my God, that's brilliant,' said Amanda. 'It's a stand-alone story, so we can simply slot it in.'

'Do it,' said Madeline.

Helen picked up the phone and called scheduling, while Amanda went through the episodes for the week ahead, looking for other potential issues. Jake, meanwhile, stood there like a nodding dog in the back of a car.

Madeline watched, taking careful note.

Amanda glanced up from the planning sheets. 'There's an aftermath episode that was due to go out a week later, but if we reshoot the first scene, we can make it a pick-up and show both episodes in a row. That will give us time to reshoot the party scenes and change the drugs to alcohol. Once we take Aiden's name off it, we can carry on the story arc as is.'

Madeline exhaled loudly. 'Your heads-up has saved the day, Helen,' she said. 'Seriously, you're a star.' She then turned to Amanda. 'Go and tell the team, and make sure not a word leaks out about what we've done. And do try not to be sick on anybody else, please.'

Reddening a little, Amanda left Meeting Room 6 alongside Helen and, still fighting her hangover, rose to the challenge. After a quick dash to scheduling and syndication, the party episode was pulled and replaced with the heartbreaking but ultimately life-affirming two-hander between Lucy Dean and her pregnant granddaughter Emily that just so happened to have been written and directed by Farrah Adams.

18

Falcon Bay's online fans absolutely loved the Lucy and Emily Dean episode. Social media was buzzing with comments about 'emotional authenticity' and how the relationship had been portrayed 'just right'.

Farrah had a big grin on her face as she sat at her desk, wolfing down her lunch and scrolling through the feeds. She was pleased that fans in Lucy Dean's age-group were happy – 'If I was Lucy, that's exactly how I'd have reacted: disappointed in my granddaughter but forgiving' was a typical post – but she was even more thrilled at the response from younger fans, ones for whom Emily's storyline really resonated. Farrah hoped Lara Collins had been watching.

The tabloids followed up with articles on the importance of grandmothers in a child's life and the 'special bond' that skipped a generation. It had not gone unnoticed by the press or the board that during the middle of a male-made shitstorm, *Falcon Bay* had wowed its audiences with a female-driven, female-written and female-directed episode which had also seen their audience share go up by ten per cent. On Twitter,

#FarrahForTheLiveEp was trending. This had actually been initiated by Sheena, who was very hot on social media. Within hours, Farrah got the call to say she was being considered as director for the Christmas special.

If she said so herself, Farrah had played this to absolute perfection. The scandal of Aiden Anderson was everywhere. Though she was fully expecting to see him back on the premises shortly, released on bail but in the doghouse, she had maximized the brief window of his absence and shown the world – and the execs – exactly what she could do.

It had been a gamble, but Farrah had learned to her cost that being nice all the time didn't get you the top job. Being ruthless paid off. She'd seen that time and again. Helen and Sheena were living proof. As was Catherine bloody Belle. She didn't hate Aiden personally – he may have been an annoying fop, and not nearly as talented as he or his boys' club mates would have people believe, but he wasn't interesting enough to actually hate. What she did hate with a passion was the aura of entitlement, the privileged position, the fact that everything landed in his lap without him even trying.

She had wanted to give him a bit of a scare, and force the execs to notice her, so she'd been careful to limit the drugs and make sure he wouldn't get done for intent to supply. Celebs always just got cautioned, did a mea culpa press interview and then everyone moved on.

But then some unexpected news emerged. The police had found a gun in his flat on St Augustine's and were keeping him in custody pending further enquiries. This caused a whole new wave of press speculation, with Aiden now being nicknamed 'the Beast of the *Bay*'. It quickly became apparent that the gun was a replica which Aiden had stolen from the props department 'to role-play with the ladies in one of his kinky sex videos – which his female co-star was now selling online via her only-fans sex site', according to the *Herald*. All this new evidence meant there was now a delay in him being charged.

For Farrah, the vision of a dick-swinging, gun-toting Aiden triggered unpleasant flashbacks to their night in the hotel. She immediately lost her appetite, jettisoned the rest of her salad and headed out the door in search of some fresh air.

At exactly the same time as Farrah came out of her office, Catherine stepped out of her dressing room. Somehow they'd managed to avoid each other since Paris, but now there was nowhere to hide. The corridor was so vast, it took a good thirty seconds before they crossed paths, enough time for them to work out what, if anything, they were going to say to each other.

By the time they finally came face to face, the best that Farrah had come up with was a simple 'Hey.' Their argument still sat heavy in her heart.

'Hey, you,' replied Catherine in a similar tone. One that said I know we need to talk, but I'm just not sure what to say.

So Farrah went for an industry icebreaker. 'You were magnificent in last night's ep. Hope you've been on Twitter and read what people are saying.'

Catherine was pleased with the compliment. She'd been getting lots of messages and she was genuinely proud of what she'd done. As Farrah was clearly holding out a proverbial olive branch, she decided to return it. 'Well, you were the power behind that ep. Your words, your direction.'

As Farrah looked into her friend's face, she knew the first apology should come from her. She'd been the most out of order – which didn't let Catherine off the hook, but it would get the ball rolling. And now that Aiden had fallen from grace, she was more inclined to forgive her for her betrayal. 'Look, I'm sorry about the other night,' she said. 'I was a bitch.'

Catherine was relieved. She hated them not talking, but without an apology she hadn't been able to see a way forward. Now she'd had it though, she could reciprocate. 'You were,' she said softly, 'but I had it coming. I didn't back you on set in the way I should have. I can honestly say my intentions were right, but I got it totally wrong and I am sorry.'

'I guess it all worked out in the end,' Farrah said, with a little smile.

Catherine smiled too. 'Seems like it.' She tilted her head, appraising Farrah, her one-time onscreen daughter and long-time real-life friend. 'You've become quite steely recently, haven't you?'

For a second, Farrah wondered if that was an insult, but before she could pick up on it, Catherine was on the move.

'Got to run. I'm shooting dubbing all afternoon as the waves were so loud yesterday we might as well have been miming,' she said, walking away. Without turning round, she called, 'And for what it's worth, I told Jake and Madeline that you should get the Christmas special.' She disappeared through the studio doors.

Farrah stayed rooted to the spot as a big smile spread across her face.

19

It had been a rollercoaster few days at C.I.TV. What had begun as an all-out shitshow for the *Bay* – Aiden being arrested and Amanda covering an actor in vomit – had somehow ended with massive ratings and credit for how swiftly and respectfully the cast and crew had come together to unite and overcome. The two standalone episodes were being talked about in awards terms, and the press had now returned to their favourite topic: the imminent Bitch Party.

Amanda had been keeping her head down, waiting for her vomiting gif to stop trending, but as her own week from hell drew to a close, she was thrown yet another curveball.

When the police strode purposefully into the production office mid-morning, she'd assumed they were there to interview more people about Aiden, so she simply glanced up and then returned to the script she was reading. Next thing she knew, the two officers were at her desk, delivering the news that Jude Roscoe had lodged an official complaint against her. He was claiming that her being sick on him constituted 'actual bodily harm'.

The old Amanda would have laughed that off and might even have created a meme of her own featuring a bare-chested Jude in all sorts of situations where 'actual bodily harm' might befall him. But the post-Olivia, post-Paris Amanda was stressed, emotional and sleep-deprived. The situation with Jake was dire. They'd ignored each other since his nasty slow handclap. Although he'd left the room before Dan embraced her, the whole office had been gossiping about it. Jake was surely aware of it too, and every night since then, Amanda had taken to lying awake in one of the spare bedrooms, taking solace in Olivia's snuffling company, wondering if Farrah and the others were right and it was finally time to call it quits with her cruelly cool husband.

So when the female sergeant had said, 'We have to warn you, Ms King, that should Mr Roscoe press charges, you will need to come to the station for questioning,' she couldn't stop herself from bursting into loud sobs. Too upset to fight her corner, she sat there speechless, carefully dabbing at her mascara and imagining that instead of going home to inhale the comforting sweetness of Olivia's fresh baby scent, she might find herself banged up in the same holding wing as Aiden.

Luckily, someone in the production office had the wit to alert Helen, and within minutes she had strutted in and taken control.

'Officers,' Helen said sternly, 'this is quite clearly a ridiculous publicity stunt by Mr Roscoe. As casting director, I know the gentleman well and it is obvious that he is aiming to cause the show and Ms King embarrassment. It's outright blackmail, hoping we might change our mind about dropping him from the show in exchange for him failing to press charges against Ms King.' Helen smiled graciously at the two officers and ushered them towards the exit. 'If you would be so kind as to leave this with me, I will talk to Mr Roscoe and sort this out.'

If anyone could save Amanda from doing the cell-block tango, it was Helen. As soon as the officers were out the building, she went straight to Jude's dressing-room door, popped her head round the corner, and said, 'I just wanted to check which you'd prefer – to leave on Christmas Day after heroically saving someone from a burning building or after being found in bed with baby Bjorn and your six-year-old niece?'

On hearing this, and knowing how the public often confused drama with real life, Jude himself threw up in his dressing-room toilet and immediately withdrew his complaint. He spent the next few hours as white as a sheet, telling everybody how much he loved the show and assuring anybody who would listen that he intended on being professional to the end. He also phoned the real-life mother of his onscreen niece and paid her a lot of money to pretend her daughter was ill and unable to work for the next month.

Just in case.

A couple of hours after the police visit, Catherine caught sight of Amanda heading towards the studio. It had turned into a crisp, blue-sky autumn day and Catherine was looking forward to a rare afternoon off. She hadn't yet decided how to spend the next few hours, but seeing Amanda, she recalled Helen's concerned text from earlier.

'Sweetie!' she called. 'Do you happen to be free for lunch? I was planning to walk over to Seafood Joe's for a lobster bisque. I have a sudden craving, and it's a gorgeous day for a stroll.'

Amanda hesitated. There was so much going on just now, and her tears in front of the police officers earlier had left her shaken.

'There's a couple of things I wanted to talk through with you,' Catherine prodded. 'My treat.'

Twenty minutes later, the two of them were deep in conversation as they threaded their way past the fishermen's cottages of Falcon Bay and up the road to the cluster of shops and restaurants on the clifftop. Catherine was wearing her Dolce & Gabbana shades in a vain attempt not to be recognized, but her classic coat and elegant dancer's poise naturally caused every passer-by to do a double-take. Regardless, St Augustine's was such a small island that every resident would have recognized her even if she was wearing a baseball cap – which, naturally, Catherine wouldn't have been seen dead in.

'How are you doing, Amanda?' she said, deliberately slowing her pace and then stopping for a rest on a bench at the top of the cliff road. 'I've hardly seen you since Paris and, um…'

'The vomiting?' Amanda said, unable to suppress a little sigh.

Catherine nodded. 'Yes. That.' She paused, focused on the beautiful array of bright pink Guernsey lilies in the flowerbed in front of them. 'You know, I so admire you, Amanda. You run our show with such compassion and integrity. But lately…'

Startled, Amanda turned to look at her friend and colleague, over twenty years her senior and someone she always felt safe with. Catherine wore her seventy years well, but there was a lot of hard-won life experience there, and Amanda respected that. Was she about to be reprimanded?

'I'm going to come out with it straight, my love. When I was young, before *Falcon Bay*, I was a lot like you when it came to men. I used to forgive all sorts of behaviour, find any number of excuses, blame myself.'

Amanda knew where this was going. She stared at her hands. Her shellac needed redoing.

'No one could understand how I managed to be perfectly intelligent about everything else but terribly weak when it came to partners. That was always my flaw: my terrible taste in men.' She picked a stray thread off her coat. 'I've never told anyone this, but the reason I moved to Dublin – which was where I was spotted for the *Bay*, as you know – was because I was in fear for my life.'

Amanda gasped. 'My God, Catherine, I had no idea…'

'I was in a relationship with a bloke whose friends called him Psycho Joe. The clue should have been in the name, but it was only me who didn't twig it. It was lovely at first, but once I was in love with him, he changed.' Catherine spoke quietly now. 'I never like to admit this, as I pride myself on being a strong woman, but behind closed doors he used to beat me.'

Amanda tried to hide her shock. She couldn't imagine

Catherine letting anyone treat her like that. Before she could express her sympathy, Catherine continued.

'It was obvious to everyone, including the police, but I denied it every time. It was only when he got arrested for pushing a stranger through a restaurant window – on Christmas Eve, of all times – that I got the help I needed to break my cycle of denial. He got eighteen months and I fled to Ireland for fear of recriminations from his associates for not standing by him.'

'I'm so sorry to hear that, Catherine. I really am.'

Catherine gave a tight smile. 'I learned a lot from that experience, learned that you have to put yourself first every time. Personally and professionally. I'm not saying Jake is as bad as Joe, but psychological abuse – gaslighting, I think is what the young people call it now? – is just as damaging. So while you might not have the bruises on show like I did, they are definitely there. You need to look after yourself, Amanda. Yourself and Olivia.'

She uncrossed her ankles and rose to her feet in a single balletic move.

'And now, let's change the subject and go devour that lobster bisque. I've been meaning to ask you, do you think Lucy Dean might get away with wearing a flame-red dress like Madeline was sporting the other night? You know, the one that was slit all the way up to her thigh bone. I know it can't be an actual Chanel, on Lucy's budget, and we rarely have red in the bar as it clashes with the beer pumps, but I think in the right scene it would really make me pop…'

20

Seated at her favourite table in the Palm Court restaurant of the plush Langham Hotel in the centre of London, Sheena was waiting to meet her two clients. Outside, the city screeched and jostled; inside, however, she could lose herself in the quintessential English experience.

The wonderful pianist John was playing movie scores in the corner. He always launched into the Bond theme 'Diamonds Are Forever' whenever Sheena walked in, and she never failed to get a kick out of that. Calm, low-voiced conversations, the clink of cutlery on plates, the stirring of a spoon on bone china – these were the only other sounds audible in the Palm Court, because decorum in the Langham was paramount and all savages were kept at bay.

If there was even the subtlest sign that a conversation was becoming heated, the ever-watchful maître d' would politely escort out the uncouth diners, with minimum fuss and maximum efficiency. This was why Sheena loved to dine here. You were guaranteed a calm experience. It was as if, alongside the climate-control thermostat that kept the temperature cool and perfect – an absolute must for any woman over forty – there was also some sort of emotion-control regulator that did the same with people's moods. Everyone was always serene in the Langham, which was just the way Sheena liked it.

A flurry of activity at the entrance told her that her first client had arrived.

Sheena watched as Lydia Chambers entered. Lydia was not particularly tall, but in her hot-pink Gucci stilettos and white figure-hugging Stella McCartney suit, and with her hair piled into what was meant to look like a casual updo but in reality would have taken at least an hour, she looked larger than life.

People turned to look as Tom, the coat-check clerk, attended to her. They whispered to each other and tried not to make it obvious they were having a jolly good gawp. But Lydia didn't mind being looked at; in fact, she practically lived for it. She hadn't been to the Langham in a while, and she loved that the staff were now making a big fuss of her. It wasn't the cost that had stopped her frequenting its fabulous location, it was those inevitable questions. *What are you doing now, and when will we see you back on screen?* God, how she hated those questions when she didn't have an answer worth giving.

But as the world's media had been printing pictures of all the actresses rumoured to be in the running for *Falcon Bay*'s new bitch, her face had been everywhere recently, including on the front cover of several global tabloids. She'd even gained an extra fifty thousand followers on Insta – not that she really knew what Insta was. Wayne, one of her gay fans from back in the day, ran all her online stuff for her. She didn't have to pay him – he said it was a privilege to be her digital voice, as it were – and he'd excitedly told her that she'd been 'trending' on Twitter (which apparently was a good thing). Daytime TV had also been discussing the show's upcoming new star-signing a great deal recently, so lots of her best clips had also been played. Thankfully, no one had shown the cow clip, but probably only because it was pre-watershed, so they weren't allowed to. And judging by the reactions she was getting today, all this exposure seemed to have brought her back into the public's consciousness.

Now, as she glided past staring eyes, she pretended she was completely unaware and avoided meeting anyone's gaze. She didn't need to see their faces to know when she'd been noticed, and when it was 'good noticing' she practically glowed.

Tammo, the gorgeous Dutch maître d', walked Lydia over towards Sheena's table, and he couldn't help but ask her the question on everybody's lips. 'I hear we will be seeing your beautiful face once again upon our screens, Ms Chambers,' he said in an accent that gave Lydia a tingle, where tingles rarely tingled these days.

As she looked into his bright green eyes and then at his bee-stung lips, she was tempted, for a nanosecond, to lean in and kiss him full on the mouth, but she settled for some flirtatious words instead.

'Well, you didn't hear it from me, but watch the Bitch Party live next Wednesday evening – I don't think you'll be disappointed with what I'll be wearing...' She winked and walked on, giving her best wiggle as she went.

In stark contrast, when Stacey Stonebrook entered the Langham's lobby, she was barely recognizable as the woman who'd once graced every magazine cover and TV screen. From beneath the large floppy hat she always wore in public spaces, she was delighted to spot Lydia's attention-seeking sashay through the giant restaurant because it meant she herself could now slip past the packed tables unnoticed.

Taking the opposite side of the room, she headed for Sheena's table without a single person even registering that she was there – which was just how she liked it. Conversations with fans these days always went one of two routes. Either they mocked her for the way her career had taken a nosedive following her exit from the soap world or they were overly sympathetic about how things had turned out. Both attitudes were hard to bear. She thought longingly of the days when people had been pleased just to meet her and tell her how much they loved her work; they'd maybe have a picture together, then she'd give them an autograph and they'd be away. That had always been enough for her.

Although Stacey and Lydia were both from the same bygone era, they had very different ways of dealing with this. Lydia loved to bloom and would, in Stacey's opinion, go to the opening of an envelope, where Stacey herself would stay inside her apartment, often just reaching around the door to grab a Deliveroo or an Uber Eats without even making eye contact. She knew that being invisible didn't help her public profile, but it suited her battered self-confidence just fine.

From the best vantage point in the restaurant, Sheena studied her two actresses as they made their way towards her. She wasn't happy with either of their performances. Lydia was far too flash, bordering on tacky, and Stacey, well, she was a disaster – Sheena had seen more presence in a ghost. Where was her star power, she wondered as she studied Stacey's dowdy body language. It was ridiculous because she still had the figure and looks to kill for.

No, this would never do. Sheena had put too much on the line for either of them to mess up this last chance. She twiddled her diamond-encrusted cocktail ring in circles around her finger and pondered how best to handle what was quite clearly going to be a difficult situation. With a final twist of the ring, she decided that she'd been nice when she got them on the list, so today they would get the other side of Sheena McQueen. Which meant that when Lydia and Stacey reached her table, she let her dissatisfaction be known by ordering for the both of them without so much as a greeting.

'I'll have my usual please, Alicia,' she said to the waitress who'd been hovering nearby. Her eyes lingered on Alicia's lithe, athletic figure. She and Alicia had history – a single, spontaneous night spent together a few months back – and she wondered if today they might get to pick up where they'd left off. But not right now. She refocused, and before Alicia could ask Stacey or Lydia what they would like, Sheena spoke for them. 'They'll be fine with water,' she said and then dismissed Alicia before either of them could get a word in.

Lydia immediately looked at Sheena with concern. 'Only water? Why – do I look big? I shouldn't, I've been working out every single day and I've not had a carb in weeks!' She suddenly felt humongous in the white suit that just minutes earlier had made her feel like Sharon Stone.

Sheena remained poker-straight in her seat. 'No, you look fantastic, as it happens.'

A beaming smile spread across Lydia's face.

'But you've got a big mouth, haven't you?'

The corner of Lydia's mouth turned down, and Stacey looked on, worried and a little frightened.

'You signed an NDA, Lydia, which strictly forbids you from mentioning *Falcon Bay* to anyone or even alluding to it. "You didn't hear it from me, but watch the Bitch Party live next Wednesday evening,"' she said in an unnervingly accurate impersonation of Lydia's voice, which made Lydia gasp.

'I take it you did not see that two people had their phones out filming you at the exact same moment you were using the Bitch Party to try and get your leg over with the Dutch boy?'

As the realization of what Sheena was saying sank in, the colour drained from Lydia's face.

Pleased that her message was getting across loud and clear, Sheena persisted. 'If those are posted online, you'll be out of the running to become C.I.TV's new star before you've even auditioned.'

Lydia steadied herself in her seat as Stacey fidgeted in hers, pulling a strand of hair with her finger.

'They wouldn't, would they – not in here, surely?' Lydia croaked, grasping at her neck as if clutching some imaginary pearls.

Sheena didn't answer. She wanted the seriousness of this to sink in. Instead, she stared off, searching for Alicia, wondering where her mimosa was.

Sheena's silence was causing Lydia to really panic. Her brain was going into overdrive; she needed this job, needed this last chance. So when she next spoke, she was almost pleading. 'Sheena, I'm sorry, I didn't think. You've got to do something – please!'

Just as she finished her plea, Alicia arrived at the table to make Sheena's mimosa. Sheena gave her her full attention as she poured Cristal champagne three quarters of the way up the flute, then finished it off with a dash of fresh orange juice. Ever since Sheena had escaped the hellish clutches of Ed Nichols all those years ago, she'd always insisted on seeing exactly what went into her glass. She took an appreciative sip, thanked Alicia and gestured for her to leave the bottle.

'Shall I bring more glasses, Ms McQueen?' Alicia said, her voice deliciously sexy.

'Not today, Alicia,' Sheena said, keeping her tone neutral and professional.

Once she'd gone, Sheena finally turned back to Lydia.

'Luckily for you, thanks to me spotting it and texting hotel security, they'll be deleting their videos.'

Lydia almost collapsed on the table at this news and downed her glass of water as if it was the finest wine available to humankind. 'Oh God,' she said breathlessly, then added, 'Thank you, thank you.'

Sheena now turned her attention to Stacey, who, content in the knowledge that she hadn't said a word to anyone about *Falcon Bay* (because she had nobody to tell), had relaxed a little and started nibbling on a breadstick.

'And as for you...' Sheena began.

Lydia looked on, hoping that whatever Stacey had done would make her faux pas seem insignificant. Stacey, however, was focused on the breadstick, unaware that Sheena was now talking to her. Lydia gave her a nudge and Stacey glanced up to find herself directly in the glare of Sheena's violet-eyed headlights.

'Did you take a Xanax before you came here? And don't lie.'

'Only a half, for my nerves,' Stacey said quietly.

Lydia raised an eyebrow, trying to get in Sheena's good books, but her effort was ignored as Sheena leaned closer to Stacey.

'Well that's got to stop right now. Next week you will be live in front of millions, and if *I* can see you are off it – even on a half and with that stupid hat covering most of your face – then the audience and more importantly the network will too!'

Stacey pulled herself up in her seat and lowered her voice to match Sheena's.

'I only use them to take the edge off being in public – which, as you know, I get anxious about. I don't feel the same way in a studio or on a set. I'm not stupid, Sheena. I wouldn't take one on screen.' She was quite proud that she'd stuck up for herself, but she was sure there'd be a backlash.

Sheena looked at them both, then took another sip of her mimosa.

'Now listen to me very carefully. Next Wednesday, you'll be officially announced, along with four others, as the contenders to be *Falcon Bay*'s new bitch. So far it's all been speculation, but once it's official, everything you do will be fully scrutinized by the world's press. And these days it's not just the professionals who can do you harm – every single punter with an internet connection is potentially your worst nightmare. The public will give their opinion on everything from your dress size to your surgery scars.'

Even hazy Stacey was now hanging on her every word as Sheena took another sip of her mimosa, paused, and then asked the most important question of the day. 'So, if you don't think you can handle it, I need to know right now. Then I can replace you on that list.'

Lydia was aghast at the very thought of being removed from the running and chipped in straightaway. 'I can absolutely handle it. I made a silly mistake today, but I was made for this role – and I'm determined to get it.' She sat bolt upright and completely ignored Stacey. This stirred something in her rival.

'Me too,' Stacey countered, enthusiastically but with less conviction. Realizing she'd not quite matched Lydia's passion, she added, 'I know I've work to do on my confidence, but as an actress, I will not let you down. I am right for this role and I'm not going to blow it.'

For the first time since they'd arrived, Sheena smiled, finally hearing the determination she was looking for. 'I'm glad to hear that, because there's something I haven't told you. The real reason I asked you here today is so I can share with you a little secret I've been keeping.'

Both their eyes lit up. Sheena was loving having them on the hook, now that she'd put them in their places. She signalled for Alicia to bring extra glasses.

'I brought you here to celebrate the fact that although

there will be a group of you publicly announced at the Bitch Party live show next week, it's really down to just the two of you as to who will win.'

Alicia arrived and filled their glasses with champagne, while they both excitedly looked at Sheena to continue with her bombshell news.

'One of you,' she said, 'and I genuinely don't know which one, is going to be picked as *Falcon Bay*'s new bitch. So instead of a one-in-seven chance, it's a straight fifty-fifty between you both.'

'How can that be? Isn't it a public vote?' asked Lydia, doing her best to keep her voice low to avoid another telling off, though her excitement was mounting.

Sheena nodded, then tapped her surgically sculpted nose. 'There may be a public vote, but trust me. I've got my sources, and I've got the experience. There are strings I'll be pulling behind the scenes to tip the balance.' She wasn't about to ruin it all and tell them that Helen Gold had betrayed their friendship of many years and allowed Honey Hunter – Honey Hunter, of all people! – to sneak in and disrupt her well-laid plans. 'I'm telling you it doesn't matter about the other girls, and it doesn't matter about the public vote. I know it will be between one of you two.'

'Which one of us?' Stacey asked nervously.

'That's up to you.'

Lydia and Stacey exchanged glances, realizing this was now a very different ball game.

'But this news is absolutely not an excuse for you to relax. Quite the opposite. The fight is now stronger than ever because you know how close you both are to clinching it.

I've done everything to get you this far; the rest is down to you. On that live show you have got to give them the very best bitch you've got in you – it's vital you steal the limelight from the others and get the audience on your side.'

She put a real emphasis on this last part because it was crucial. They still had to stand out ahead of everybody else or they'd never get selected by the audience vote.

'Whoever gets the highest approval rating out of the two of you on the night will win.'

She finished by handing them both the filled champagne flutes.

Stacey's hand shook slightly as she lifted hers and took a sip. To know she was so close to being back in the land of being beloved, wanted again, admired once more. Even if she couldn't ever love herself, the audience would fill that void for her. No more sleeping away her days – she'd have a purpose, a career again. The Xanax and champagne were mixing in her brain, but a half and alcohol couldn't make her sleepy today, not with the most exciting news she'd had in years buzzing inside her head. She found herself smiling for real, for the first time she could remember in a long time.

Lydia's hands also had a slight tremor. But she wasn't nervous: electricity was coursing through her as she too sipped the Cristal and allowed herself to dream. No more shitty auditions, no more tacky jobs, no more pitying looks. She was going to be back in the big time; this role was the part of a lifetime, even better than the wonderful role that had made her a star. This was the plum pie and knowing now that the only woman she had to beat was the drug-addled mouse sitting next to her, well then, that pie was hers and she was going to devour every bite. There was no doubt in her mind: Stacey was toast and she'd got this in the bag.

'Now, ladies, I want to add one more thing before we all celebrate this wonderful news,' Sheena said with a glint in her eye. 'As I represent you both, I don't want any dirty tricks. Just remember, you're representing the McQueen Agency as well as yourselves.'

They both nodded.

'Obviously you can do whatever you like to outshine the other contestants – I'm not their agent, so quite frankly I don't care. But right here and now I want to see you two shake hands and agree to fight fair. And whoever wins, let's promise that the other will wish them all the best and be publicly supportive.'

Stacey and Lydia slowly turned to face each other. Lydia offered a hand for Stacey to shake and Stacey took it.

'We will,' they lied in unison.

Sheena smiled as she gestured for them to raise their glasses.

'Cheers!' she said, and watched as Lydia and Stacey clinked their glasses so hard she thought the flutes would break.

21

This morning's meeting was about the Christmas live and more importantly about who would direct it, following Aiden Anderson's arrest. With the Bitch Party looming, Madeline wanted to announce the new director and move the press coverage on. There'd been a lot of speculation within the building as to who would take over the role. Everyone was waiting to find out who would get the prize.

Jake had his back to the door of Meeting Room 6. He was polishing off the second Danish pastry he'd taken from the snack trolley, so he didn't notice Dan and Amanda entering together, looking very chummy. They were late. This was not lost on Helen, who winked at Dan playfully. He duly blushed.

'Right, now everybody is here, let's get this show back on track,' said Madeline, who was seated at the head of the meeting room table. She raised an eyebrow at Dan and Amanda, who, along with Jake, had filled the last three seats.

It was clear to Amanda that her lateness had been noted, but for once in her professional life she actually didn't care. She was only a couple of minutes late anyway, but it was still out of character. She'd got distracted talking to Dan on their way there and they'd both lost track of time. She didn't even bother to try and catch Jake's eye, though she had noticed him brushing the pastry crumbs off his shirt and knew that he'd be feeling even more prickly than usual. She immediately busied herself flicking through the storyline documents that were laid out in front of each seat.

'I've been told,' Madeline continued, 'that details of the charges Aiden will face will be finalized shortly. The board want to make a swift decision on the termination of his contract, but I feel that we'll be in a better legal position if we wait until we have more information. As he's not yet been *officially* charged or bailed, it's a hard one to call.'

She sounded businesslike and more sanguine than the Madeline they were usually faced with, Amanda thought. It was an effective approach and put everyone at ease.

'Aiden's lawyers,' Madeline continued, 'have asked if anyone at C.I.TV might be willing to provide a character witness statement, and I want you all to know that if you wish to do so, we won't stop you.'

'I'll happily tell the police what I think of him, if that helps,' Helen chipped in, a wicked grin on her face.

'I agree with Madeline,' said Amanda, ignoring Helen's contribution. 'Aiden can be a loose cannon for sure, but he's been a really solid director on this show for years, and as we all know, the tabloids love to embellish. So let's see what the actual charges are in the morning and take it from there.'

'That seems very fair and sensible to me,' Dan said. 'And if we need to post bail for him, I can organize that within the space of an hour.' He nodded supportively at Amanda.

Helen smirked, forever on the lookout for signs that Amanda and Dan might finally be about to actually get it together. Jake, however, scowled at Dan, the interfering money man who always seemed to be popping up where he was least wanted and siding with Amanda.

Jake was determined to take back control and show Madeline who was in charge. 'I think that's fucking ridiculous,' he roared in Amanda's direction. 'I gave Aiden the biggest chance of his career,' he said, melodramatically gesturing to himself, 'directing the live ep, and this is how he repays me? By putting our show in jeopardy. And what was he doing with a replica gun from our props department anyway? So that's theft we can add to the list, along with the drug dealing!'

With the rest of the room now giving him their full attention, Jake stood up and stepped back from the others. 'What's the point in waiting till tomorrow?' he said. 'The damage has been done. As far as I'm concerned, I hope they send Aiden down and he gets passed around like a teddy bear in an orphanage.'

The whole table looked surprised – even Helen, whose face rarely showed much expression due to her love of Botox. Everyone knew Jake and Aiden were old friends.

'Have some heart, Jake,' Amanda said. 'It's not as if he's been in trouble with the law before. And you guys go back decades – he was your best man.'

'Well he won't be my next,' Jake snapped.

'Planning on remarrying, are you?' Amanda batted back, quick as a flash. Then, remembering who else was in the room, and realizing what Jake's words actually meant, she quickly focused on her sheaf of papers, ignoring the tears that were pricking at her eyes.

Jake, unable to think of anything to top Amanda's reply, decided he needed to leave the room on a win. 'Farrah Adams is directing the Christmas live and Aiden Anderson will not spend another second in the studio or on set. He's finished at *Falcon Bay*.'

Everyone watched in silence as he stormed out, slamming the door behind him.

Madeline sat completely still, observing everything.

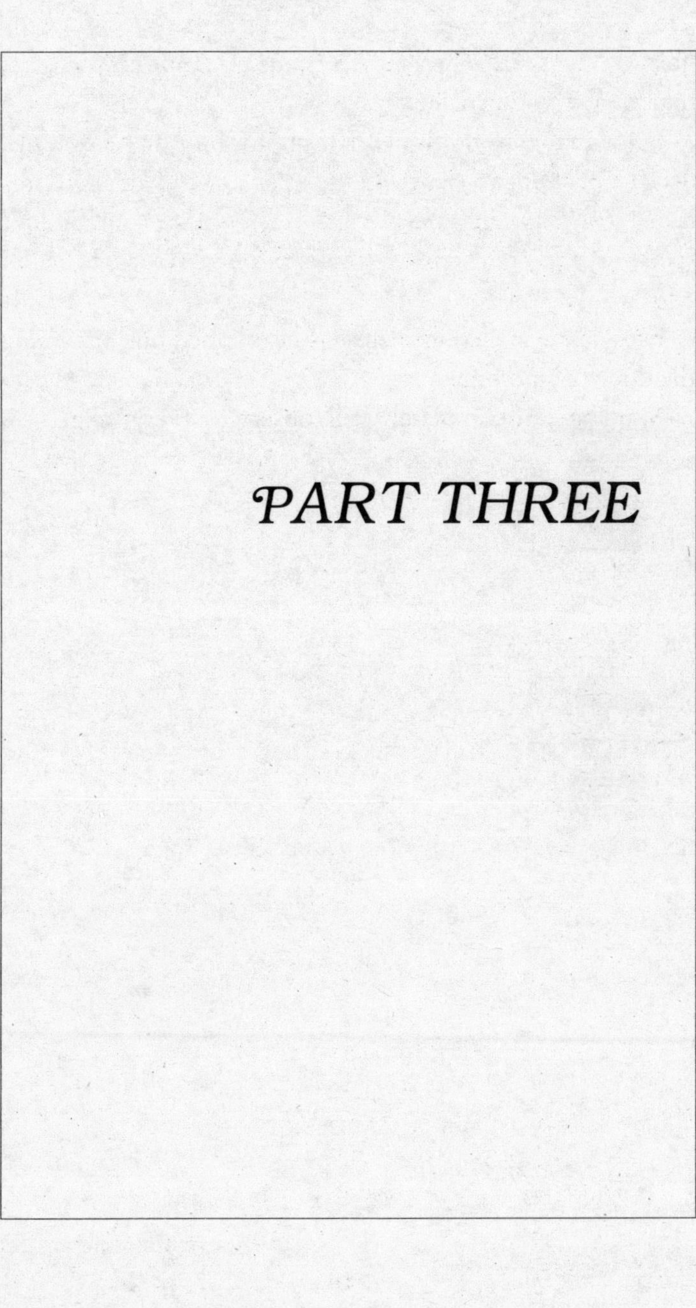

PART THREE

22

The *Falcon Bay* edit suites were a rare place of calm and concentration. Their low lighting, soundproofing and absence of windows allowed an editor total tranquillity as they spent hour upon hour editing the episodes until they were just right. An editor's chair was comfortable but firm, supporting the back but not so rigid that it caused aches after a short time.

Directors would come into the edit suite when the rough version was ready and together they'd finesse the episode into a final cut fit to be beamed around the world to millions of fans eager to get their latest fix of their favourite show. Farrah was in Edit Suite 9. She liked 9 best as it was bigger than the others and had a sofa she could lie on as she watched the screens while her editor sat in the chair. They were trying to work out how to cut around Lucien's latest scenes, where he'd ad-libbed his way through what had been written as a pin-sharp piece of dialogue but now sounded like a verbal car crash. The only upside to Farrah being down here meant she'd missed the meeting taking place upstairs to decide Aiden's fate.

Ever since Aiden had been arrested, Farrah had played it super cool. When he'd called her from the police station, she'd prepared herself for an onslaught of accusations and had been ready to deny all knowledge and say she'd hidden in the bathroom because she was scared of all the voices she'd heard. But instead Aiden had asked her how *she* was. That had made her feel bad. He'd then carefully spoken in code, in case the call was being recorded, and via their jumbled conversation had made it clear he'd be keeping her name out of it.

She still couldn't quite believe he'd been so nice about it. It was possible she'd misjudged him, but as long as she reminded herself about the sexts and the perverted videos – a new one that emerged where he was using the fake gun as a sex toy had shocked even her – she could push any guilt she was feeling to one side. The prospect of him going to prison, though, had been weighing heavily on her mind. That had absolutely not been her intention. So she defended him around the studios, condemning him for his life choices but making it obvious that in her view prison would be way too severe a punishment for him having 'gone a bit wild'.

Whenever she was asked if she'd like to direct the Christmas special, her standard line was 'If it's available and they ask me, I'd love to, but right now I'm just focusing on my current block.' But behind closed doors, Farrah was watching the clock. She'd been waiting for that all-important nod from the moment Aiden was arrested. It was killing her having to act so nonchalant. She desperately wanted to storm right into

Madeleine's office, brag that she'd been right about Aiden being the wrong choice for the live and demand to be given it to prove what she could do. But, no, she'd had to play the waiting game. She didn't imagine it would be much longer, though, especially with all the fan comments and rumours of an Emmy single-episode nomination for her two-hander.

She was just choosing between cutaway shots of crashing waves to cover Lucien's muffled lines when the door burst open and light suddenly filling the darkened room.

Ordinarily, she'd tear a strip off whoever was interrupting her when the sign outside said 'Do Not Disturb', but then she saw that it was Jake, who must have come straight from *the big meeting*.

'My office – now!' he said, then smiled. 'You won't be disappointed.'

The little girl in Farrah wanted to squeal.

23

Back in Meeting Room 6, just Helen, Amanda and Madeline remained. They were seated in a row at the top of the table, but no one was talking.

Amanda looked at Madeline, considering what to say after Jake's dramatic exit. Madeline waited her out, which Helen was aware of, so she too stayed quiet. The seagulls were circling overhead, like a playground of curious kids wondering if there was about to be a fight. Finally, Madeline broke the silence.

'Is he like that at home?' she asked.

Amanda was surprised that during such a crucial meeting about the show, Madeline would choose to go down a personal route. It was embarrassing. She sighed. 'Er, he can be. Yes. He's been a lot more like that recently. Which is why I let rip at you at Claude's…'

Helen gently nudged her seat away from the table by a few inches so she was no longer right in the middle of them.

'Let's forget that nonsense,' Madeline countered, in a tone

that seemed much more reasonable than when they had all first met her.

Helen shifted her chair ever so slightly further back.

'I did have my reasons for that "nonsense", as you call it,' Amanda said with a definite edge to her voice. 'As I assume you now appreciate.' She raised her eyebrows and looked Madeline full in the face. 'You promoted Jake without even considering me, which I hope you now realize was the wrong decision. As you've seen, we bring very different qualities to the role. He is not known for being calm in a crisis. And he is famously tactless and self-serving when it comes to dealing with cast and creatives.' She wasn't going to make any more excuses for him now, not after his horrible 'remarrying' comment.

Madeline visibly straightened in her seat at this questioning of her judgement. 'You were on maternity,' she said icily. 'It was just bad timing. Anyone who says you can have it all is a liar – as any woman knows.' She froze Amanda with the sort of stare a rattlesnake assumes just before it strikes.

Helen could hold herself back no longer. 'Jake has always been a nightmare. Everybody round here knows Amanda is the talent.'

Silence fell once more.

Madeline turned away to pour herself a glass of still water from the bottle of Fiji in front of her. She took her time, sipped it slowly, then looked back at them.

'I went with the person that I could sell to the investors, who, as I'm sure you know, are nearly all men. Wrongly or not, they were never going to back a woman who wasn't even in the building.'

Amanda and Helen's eyes followed Madeline as she refilled her glass.

'I'm going to have a lot of battles over the next year or two,' she said, drawing the words out in her Deep South accent, which made her sound like a Tennessee Williams character. 'I needed somebody in charge that the board wouldn't fight me over.'

'It seems to me that you wanted somebody whose strings you could pull,' Amanda said with unusual bluntness.

Madeline's perfect lips curled into a wry smile, which immediately and depressingly confirmed to Amanda that she was right. In her head, Amanda heard Farrah's voice, raging at the sexist system, the unfairness of it all. She sighed. It was patently obvious to Amanda that she had hit her ceiling at *Falcon Bay* for as long as Madeline owned the network.

'Supposing you were in charge instead of Jake,' Madeline said provocatively. 'What would you do about Aiden Anderson?'

Amanda chose her words carefully. The question might only be hypothetical, but she wanted to really show Madeline it wasn't personal to her about being passed over – it was professional. She loved *Falcon Bay* and didn't let her ego or her friendships affect her judgement on what was right for the show. What she elected to say next would at least prove that if she had been given the job she deserved, she'd have known exactly what she was doing.

'Personally, I do not agree with Jake's plans to sack Aiden today. As you pointed out at the start of the meeting, none of us know what, if any, real charges will be brought tomorrow.

This could just be media hype. Drugs are rarely the end of anyone's career in entertainment, as long as he was only taking them and not selling them.'

She turned to Helen for confirmation that she was right about this.

'Is Aiden a coke head? Yes, he is,' Helen said. 'But a coke dealer? Nope.'

Madeline stayed silent and listened.

'Then we can't kick him off the show without trying to help him with his addictions, which, to be fair, have never affected his work here – up to this point.' Amanda held Madeline's gaze. 'At the end of the day, we have a duty of care, and Jake is about to break that. If you were worried about the board thinking a pregnant woman was a hassle, then just wait till this blows up. If Aiden is sacked in the way Jake intends, and then he doesn't get charged by the police – well, then you really will have an issue on your hands.'

Amanda let these words hang for a few moments. Doing the right thing by Aiden, by all that she stood for as exec producer on *Falcon Bay*, meant doing wrong by her friend Farrah. Wrong for the right reasons.

'In many ways,' she continued sincerely, 'his failings are our failings. Showbusiness is the strangest world I know. Living in a bubble of make-believe can take its toll on people's minds – not everyone is strong enough to handle it.'

Madeline took another sip of her water as Helen picked up the baton from Amanda.

'She's right. Nobody comes out of TV unscathed, and unfortunately for some, "unscathed" doesn't begin to describe it. You remember Sheena McQueen, who was with us in Paris, and the scandal she was once involved in?'

'I do,' Madeline said.

'Her show – *Second Chances* – sacked her even though she was never charged with anything.'

'She was hardly a good example for the network!' Madeline cut in. 'I don't think many shows would tolerate dead rock stars being found in their talent's bathtub. She also seems to have come out of the whole Ed Nichols scandal pretty well in the end, so I'm not sure what her relevance is to our issue.'

'The point is,' Amanda said, 'later on, she sued the network for breaching their duty of care to her.' She looked to Helen.

Helen nodded. 'It was a hell of a risk, dredging up all that bad publicity, but – as she frequently reminds us, usually after her third or fourth V&T – that gorgeous building that the McQueen Agency occupies had to be paid for somehow. She took the *Second Chances* production company to court over their safeguarding failings, and let's just say there were a hell of a lot of zeros on her compensation cheque. So much so that *Second Chances* got cancelled not long after.'

'Yes,' Amanda said. 'She'd brought negative attention on the network, but if they'd done things properly, they could actually have turned it to their advantage and made it work for them.'

Madeline hadn't moved a muscle since the conversation had turned to money.

'Tomorrow,' Amanda continued, 'if we find Aiden's not charged with anything other than drug use and possession – which, if we're honest, is sadly pretty standard in our business anyway – we can treat him like a victim and publicly get him the help he needs to get back on track. We'll use his recovery as a way of warning others not to follow that path. The press will eat that up, we'll be seen as a network that cares and we'll be praised for our socially responsible attitude. And we'll let him keep the live ep, which will ensure it's all very high-profile. It's a win-win.'

Except for poor Farrah, Amanda thought. *For her it's lose-lose. Again.* Her stomach churned at the prospect of having to break this to her friend – even though it was the right decision. She would pick her moment, maybe delay it a bit. She poured a glass of water for herself and another for Helen, who had pulled her seat back in and was nodding approvingly, clearly impressed.

The two women looked to Madeline, whose perfect face was giving nothing away as to what she thought of Amanda's speech.

24

When Jake pulled open his office door for Farrah to enter, he got a delicious waft of her alluring scent. They were usually separated by a ten-foot table in meeting rooms and Amanda did all her appraisals, so he was rarely close enough to notice how divine she smelled.

As Farrah leaned over the desk, the sunlight streaming through the window made her shapely figure visible beneath her white dress. Suddenly, Jake's body responded and he found himself desperately trying to focus. He prayed that Farrah hadn't noticed the growing bulge which was now straining against his tight jeans. He'd never even looked at her in that way before, and yet now his dick felt like it was going to explode. In the hope that talking business would make it deflate, he made a swift move to one of the leather chairs, which meant he could avoid getting any closer to her.

'Firstly, and most importantly,' he said, sitting down and crossing his leg uncomfortably, 'I consider you our best writer and director. Hands down. No bullshit.'

Farrah was very aware of the effect she was having on him. She'd positioned herself between him and the window on purpose and had worn this dress today deliberately. It was crunch day for the live ep choice and this was going to be her victory day – she wanted not only for him to give her the job she longed for but also to mess with his mind. Her outfit and the decision to wear nothing underneath it certainly seemed to be doing the trick.

'Thank you,' she said. She was sure 'bullshit' was exactly what this was, but she'd wanted to hear those words for so long, she no longer cared what was motivating them.

'I also want you to know that before all the shit hit the fan about Aiden, I had already argued with Madeline about you directing our prestigious live episode,' he said, regaining his composure from the safety of his leather seat.

Farrah was genuinely taken aback by that. It couldn't be true, could it? She walked over to the chair next to his and sat on its arm as he continued.

'Madeline wanted Aiden simply because on paper he's directed more episodes than anyone else. Which to her makes him the most experienced. But I fought for you from the start. I told her that you're special. People say Catherine is the beating heart of this show – well, I say you are its blood. You inject *Falcon Bay* with oxygen and energy. You drive us all to be better people. I'm just glad that the Christmas live is yours now – you truly deserve it.'

Farrah had come to Jake's office with a very firm plan: get confirmation she was directing the live episode, tease him with her outfit, leave him hot under the collar and disappointed in the knowledge that he'd never get anywhere near her, then get the hell out of there. But now she found herself flushing over his every word of praise.

'That means so much to me, Jake,' she said, surprising herself by placing a hand on his shoulder.

Thanks to her careful plan, she'd been confident they would make her the director of the live, but having that decision finally out in the world, dancing about in front of her, floating in the air… it made her head spin. Everything she'd put herself through to get here had been worth it.

Electricity fizzed inside her and suddenly she lost all sense of reality. She wasn't even aware of her impulse to kiss him, but she was glad it was happening. His tongue gently touched hers, tentatively, suggesting it would like more but waiting to be invited in. She pulled it into her mouth with her lips and suddenly this wasn't a kiss, it was foreplay. Particularly with the way their hands were caressing each other's bodies.

What am I doing? she thought as her brain finally kicked itself back into gear, just as she was tearing Jake's trousers off. But it was too late: her body had taken over and she couldn't stop herself from mounting his hard cock right there on the leather chair he was sitting in. As she pulled her dress over her head, releasing her perfect breasts, which went straight into Jake's hungry mouth, he clapped his hands for the electronic blinds to close, shrouding their secret shag in darkness.

25

Hundreds of miles away from Falcon Bay, another woman was hurriedly getting undressed with a lecherous man nearby. Honey Hunter was in one of London's finest appointment-only boutiques and had been climbing in and out of outfits all morning, desperate to find the perfect look for the Bitch Party. The place didn't look like much from the outside – its grey-tinted windows let light in but kept prying eyes out, and there wasn't even a sign to identify what the shop was; just its number, 77, marked it out as findable on Chelsea's famous King's Road. The thing about the Jani Collective was if you didn't already know about it then you weren't the kind of person that was meant to shop there.

It was as stark inside as out. There were no chairs for friends or partners to sit on and wait, just a vast empty space with all the dresses kept out of sight. You didn't pick them, you didn't even see what was available. Instead, Ms Jani asked you to describe what you wanted your dress to achieve and then disappeared behind one of the many white doors. Minutes later, she would reappear flanked by two silent assistants carrying a selection of the finest haute couture that was somehow magically close to whatever the shopper had described.

The problem for Honey was that her imagination was pretty vivid, hence she'd been trying on outfits for nearly two hours and was now running out of time. The Jani Collective only allocated ninety minutes per slot because only one client was allowed in the building at a time. This ensured ultimate privacy.

As one of the assistants silently pulled the zip up on the final outfit on the rail, Honey turned to look at her reflection and smiled. 'This is it!' she exclaimed and gave the assistant a hug, which was not returned. It was lucky Honey had finally found what she was looking for as at that very moment Ms Jani appeared at the door of the dressing room and clicked her fingers for both assistants to leave. This signalled that Honey's time in the shop was well and truly up.

Even if she thought so herself, Honey looked amazing in the Valentino embroidered tulle gown. The sheer emerald fabric clung to her body like a second skin and the bodice held her curves lovingly. She opened the dressing room door so Mickey could see.

'Isn't it gorgeous?' she said and did a little twirl.

Mickey Taylor, publishing entrepreneur, purveyor of celebrity biographies and currently Honey's attentive new agent, grinned. 'Wow, sweetheart! You wear that at the party and the cameras won't leave your side all night. It's almost as beautiful as you are,' he said and gave her his signature double-thumbs-up.

She liked the glow on Mickey's face. She'd gone through

so many dresses, she was worried she might have lost perspective.

As if sensing her hesitation, he reinforced his approval. 'That's absolutely the one,' he exclaimed, 'but as you're going to be so busy from now on and we probably won't get a chance to come shopping for a while, why don't we take all the other ones you liked as well.'

Honey beamed as if she were a little girl on Christmas Day seeing a pile of presents under the tree with her name on. 'Are you serious?' she said, looking down at him. Not in a judgemental way – she was four inches taller than Mickey, who had not been blessed in the height department.

'Totally. We'll need the rest for photoshoots to celebrate you becoming *Falcon Bay*'s new leading lady,' he said with a wink.

He was being so kind to Honey, she wanted to hug him, but she'd never be able to bend that low in this skin-tight dress, so instead she patted his chubby cheek, the only man in years who seemed to be really looking out for her, the only one who believed she was still talented and deserved another break.

'Only if you're sure.' She beamed.

'Course I am, darling. Now listen, I got a friend to tell a few paps you'd be here. So they're going to want to take some snaps. You go outside wearing the first dress you tried on, the short red one. Papers always love a pop of colour, and that won't blow the reveal of the one you'll be wearing for the show. Go and show 'em what you're made of, then hail a cab to the hotel. They'll get plenty of pics of you getting in the back of it that should make for great coverage with legs like yours! I'll sort out the bill and meet you there.'

She looked back at the red dress on the rack. It wasn't right for the Bitch Party, but he was spot on – she'd look good on the celeb pages wearing that. 'Mickey, did anyone ever tell you you're a diamond?'

'Babe, you're the diamond. Every penny I spend to help you get back into the spotlight is a thousand pennies returned. When your book hits the shops, you're going to be number one in the bestseller list and number one in the soap bitches list too. And that means double-bubble for both of us.'

He laughed as he rubbed his fingers together, then gave her a kiss on her cheek, which was definitely platonic and made her feel content at his almost parental attention, and then left her to change.

Once in the red dress, she gathered up the other outfits she was keeping, and her Chanel, then looked in the mirror to fix her hair and make-up ready to be papped. She made her way out of the shop, musing on how lucky she was to have Mickey taking care of her the way he did.

As she stepped beyond the tinted doorway, she was blinded by what felt like a hundred camera flashes. There were paps out there, but not just 'a few' like Mickey had said. She was about to say hello to one she recognized from back in the day when a wailing noise sounded and a light above the top of the door started flashing. *Damn*, she thought, *I've come out with a tag still on.* She was just about to turn back when two big security guards rushed out and grabbed both her arms while she was standing on the pavement.

'Madam, I have to ask you to come back into the store,' said the biggest one, forcibly guiding her back towards the shop.

She could hear cameras snapping even more frantically and some passers-by had crowded onto the street too, holding up iPhones to film her.

'It's not what it looks like,' she protested, turning her head back towards the photographers and speaking loudly so the fans filming her would hear too. 'My manager's inside. He's paying for them – it's just a mix-up,' she managed before she was swept back through the door of Number 77.

But no one was listening, and the damage was already done, just like before…

26

When Amanda and Jake's marriage would finally end was the group's unofficial sweepstake. Sheena had chosen after the live ep, Catherine said it wouldn't last that long, and Helen had gone with Sheena. Back in Jake Monroe's office, the realization hit Farrah that perhaps she'd just handed Catherine the win.

How the sweepstake should have even crossed her mind was a mystery to her as the main words on repeat in her brain right now were, *Fuck, fuck, fuckety fuck.*

As she watched Jake getting dressed, Farrah couldn't believe what she'd done. Yes, Amanda was obviously deeply unhappy in her marriage and needed to get the hell out of it as soon as possible, but Farrah had still just shagged the husband of one of her best friends, and, worse than that, a man she truly despised.

She was lying in the centre of his office, balanced on the cushions that he'd dragged off his work sofa, and she seriously didn't know if she could feel any more wretched. It wasn't just breaking the girl code – which, surprisingly, she'd never done before. The main reason Farrah felt awful was that now everybody at C.I.TV would think she'd shagged Jake for the gig. Once she walked out of Jake's office and announced she was doing the Christmas ep, they'd assume she'd got down on her knees for it. Especially given that they'd been seen.

All of her clever planning to take Aiden down had gone out of the window now for a below-average bonk. And that's all it had been. He'd had a couple of interesting moves, including a circular motion with his hips that had given her an orgasm, but once she'd spotted that was his only trick, it had felt a bit rehearsed and repetitive. Sensing she was perhaps not that impressed with his skills, Jake had attempted to switch it up and started to spank her. Farrah wasn't someone who liked it rough, but hoping it might hurry this dreadful situation up, she had looked enthusiastic, which was definitely a mistake because the next whack he delivered to her bottom not only really hurt but also made a slapping sound so loud that she was sure the whole office must have heard it.

And she was right.

Outside Jake's office, Lara Collins was on the last day of her work experience at *Falcon Bay*. For most of her time there she'd been tentative about intruding on people's work schedules too much and had mainly been happy to loiter on the fringes and soak up the atmosphere. Seeing people rush about with purpose, some of them only a few years older than herself, had been a revelation. She marvelled at how confident and content everyone was in their work. Most of the production staff had been really kind and she'd learned a lot, but the highlight of her time there was unquestionably the chat she'd had with Farrah in Lucy Dean's kitchen.

Lara was in the production office photocopying the call sheets as instructed when she heard the loud, hard slap. She looked up to see where it had come from at exactly the same time as the sound-activated blinds in Jake Monroe's office responded to the noise and mechanically opened.

Intrigued, Lara glanced up from the photocopier and into the office. A few seconds later, she realized she was looking at Farrah Adams, naked, on all fours, with Jake Monroe behind her.

As Lara and Farrah's eyes met, a look of horror appeared on both their faces. Then for no reason that Lara could understand, Farrah started applauding.

Behind the glass windows of Jake's office, Farrah frantically clapped her hands, trying to get the automatic blinds to close.

'Well, I knew I was good…' Jake laughed, mid-thrust, but Farrah pushed herself off him, rolled onto the floor and tried to hide behind the desk.

'The blinds!' she said from under the desk, her voice raised in panic.

Jake then looked up to see the pink-haired kid by the photocopier looking in on them. Utter panic came over him at the realization he was exposing himself to a teenager in the workplace. He too rolled to the floor, keeping low, crawled over to the desk and grabbed the override control, bringing the blinds down to an instant close.

Farrah wanted to cry. Not only had she'd let herself down, she'd been a major disappointment to a teenage girl who'd called her a role model. So much for being 'a strong woman in a man's world, clearing the path for future generations.'

Shagging the boss couldn't have been a more damaging message to give to a girl like Lara.

What on earth had she been thinking? And how could she have done this to her best friend, Amanda?

She pulled on her dress, which suddenly seemed really inappropriate for the workplace, and walked to the door just as Jake was yanking up his trousers.

'This was a mistake,' she said as she reached for the door, praying that Lara wouldn't still be at the photocopier when she opened it.

27

Aiden Anderson was languishing in a cell that was just minutes away from where he'd been arrested five days earlier. The Old Police House was a station that not even most Londoners were aware of, even though it was slap bang in the middle of Hyde Park. Tourists, however, knew all about it and a continuous stream of them posed outside with their selfie sticks, smiling as they snapped the picturesque Queen Anne-style building that first began holding criminals in 1902. It still had its original street lanterns and was especially atmospheric of an evening, when it gave off a real Jack the Ripper vibe.

On the first day of his incarceration, during gruelling interviews and still full of coke, Aiden had raged. On the second day he'd opted for denial, and on day three he'd tried arguing. None of that had worked, so he'd resorted to banging his tin cup on the steel door of his cell day and night, demanding that someone higher up than a PC come to see him. Nobody came except his solicitor, who emphasized that, serious though the circumstances of Aiden's arrest were, the fact that he'd not yet been charged was a good sign. Aiden took this to heart and duly turned his rage into gritted-teeth politeness. He stuck to his story that all of the drugs were recreational, and acted outraged at any suggestion the replica gun was to be used for criminal purposes, muttering that the last time he checked, using a prop gun as a dildo for a private porno may be unseemly, but wasn't a crime.

On the fifth day a voice woke him from his surprisingly deep sleep. He was amazed at how quickly he'd got used to the rock-hard mattress and had already decided that if he was released, he would change his home mattress for one of a similar style.

'Anderson,' the custody sergeant boomed solemnly through the bars, 'come with me.' He began unlocking the gate.

Aiden slowly pulled himself up from the bed. His solicitor had warned him this was coming. The police had limits on how long they could hold someone, and five days was the maximum. After that, it was charge you or let you go, and with what they'd found him with in that hotel room, it would take a small miracle for it to be the latter.

With his solicitor's words ringing in his ears and images from *The Green Mile* in his head, he followed the duty sergeant through the corridors of the police station, trying not to make eye contact with anybody as they headed towards a door at the end of the long walkway. When the officer pushed it open, it revealed not only that he'd been led back out into the reception area but that Helen Gold was standing there.

'What are you doing here?' he said, unable to hide his shock and disappointment. He assumed she was there in an official capacity to sever his contract face to face, a sure sign that he was about to be charged.

Helen looked him up and down with disdain. She took a moment to enjoy his obvious panic before answering.

'I'm here to take you home.' She nodded towards the envelope on the desk. 'Grab your stuff and let's go.'

Aiden's mouth dropped wide open, almost cartoonlike, as her words sank in. 'What?' he said, looking at the officer for confirmation she wasn't joking.

The officer calmly nodded.

'You mean I'm… I'm free…?'

Helen's eyes narrowed. 'Yes and no.'

Aiden looked stricken again.

Helen paused once more, savouring his discomfort.

'What do you mean?'

'Our lawyers have struck you a plea deal,' she said, her tone serious now, 'so instead of incarceration, which, to be quite frank, I think you deserved, there'll be a schedule of compulsory public atonements you'll have to do.'

She left the words hanging as she glanced around the police station. She was aware that several admiring pairs of eyes were trained on her shapely figure, shown off to perfection in her white jeans, low cami and the hot pink Chloé blazer that really emphasized her waist. She could sense that the rugged, middle-aged detective inspector behind the desk wanted her, and was surprised to feel a tug of desire in return. She rarely looked twice at men her own age, but there was definitely a quiet chemistry between them. She made a mental note of his name badge and planned to look him up on social media later.

'So yes, you are free to leave, *but* you will be doing active rehabilitation, going to NA and seeing a C.I.TV-approved therapist weekly,' she continued. 'And you'll be volunteering on the young offenders' film-making scheme for two years. I do hope none of your bad habits rub off on them.' She turned away from him and made eye contact with the detective inspector, who she was now absolutely sure wanted her as much as she wanted him.

Still stunned, Aiden wasn't really listening. All he'd really paid attention to was the word 'free', and by the sound of it, he hadn't been sacked, so whatever the conditions, this was bloody good news.

Helen gestured towards the exit door and as Aiden passed her, she decided not to bother waiting to contact the hottie detective online but to just go ahead and make sure he knew how to find her.

'Detective inspector…' she said, pivoting towards the desk.

The inspector stood up, his chiselled face catching the light.

'Here is my card.' She placed it on the counter. 'If there is anything else we need to do regarding Mr Anderson's exit – perhaps a donation to the station for looking after him so well, or anything else I can help with – do get in contact with me *personally* and let me know.' She finished off her little speech with the slightest smile that made it crystal clear why she had handed over her details.

With that, she strutted past a dawdling Aiden, flung the doors open and shoved him through them. Aiden immediately clamped a hand to his brow with a melodramatic flourish, shading his sensitive eyes from the blinding daylight.

Once outside, Helen let rip. 'Now listen to me, you shitbag. Lots of favours were called in to get you out of this mess. I would have left you to rot, but the top brass decided to give you another chance, so I really suggest you don't blow it,' she said with a hiss.

'I knew Jake wouldn't let me down,' Aiden said, too relieved to take issue with Helen's tone.

'You really are an idiot, aren't you.' Helen laughed. 'This wasn't Jake's doing,' she said, leaning towards him with a smile. '*He* wanted you *sacked*!'

She could see by the look on his face that Aiden was really hurt by this revelation, but she didn't care. He was going to hang on to what should have been Farrah's gig, which would break her friend's heart, so the very least she could do was fuck up their bromance.

Aiden, still shielding his eyes from the sun, squinted at her in confusion. Jake was his best friend and his only ally at the network that he knew of. Then clarity settled. Helen must be trying to create trouble between the men at the network by making him believe Jake had turned against him. Well, he wouldn't fall for her bitchy tricks.

'I know you're lying', he said, serenely. 'Me and Jake are blood brothers.' He held up a scarred thumb, no doubt marked by some drugged-up blokey bonding ritual.

Helen looked at him and raised a scathing eyebrow. 'You really are as stupid as you look,' she said, walking towards a cab she'd hailed and leaving Aiden standing amongst the chattering tourists taking selfies outside the Old Police House.

28

The meeting in Dan's office the next afternoon had been perfectly innocent. Although the chemistry was undeniable between the two of them, Amanda was determined to keep things professional. This was not an easy task, as ever since Dan had held her in Jake's office, she'd fantasized about him non-stop. This made her feel guilty – for all his faults, Jake was still her husband – but not so guilty that she didn't seek out excuses to be around Dan when she could. She'd recently got into the habit of dropping by his office for tea, making sure to leave the door open so as not to give in to temptation.

That afternoon, they'd been discussing last-minute insurance details for the Bitch Party, which were a real minefield, given the live audience and the outdoor set, when Jake appeared at the open door.

'Together again. What a surprise. Not,' he said drily. He looked at them with an expression that would be more befitting of having caught them making love on the desk rather than poring over a pie chart.

Dan was quick to defend Amanda's honour and tried to explain that they were working, but Jake wasn't interested.

'Save it, I only popped in to give you my official blessing. Enjoy your ride on my wife, pal.'

Amanda stared at Jake in shock, but he wasn't finished. He took a step back into the hall to make sure he had an audience for his parting shot.

'Fill your boots with my cast-offs, mate. Oh yes, it's all sexual swings and roundabouts here at C.I.TV.' He smirked. 'I'm fucking Farrah now – and let me tell you, I know who's got the better deal.'

Jake barked a laugh, turned on his heel and stalked out.

Amanda stood in horror and disbelief. Had she heard him right? This was a new low, even for him. But yes, that triumphant sneer he'd had on his face was the one he used when he was telling the truth. How could Farrah do this to her?

Dan tried to comfort her, but, heart thumping, she fled the building in tears, stumbled home, locked herself in her bedroom and sat staring out at the slate-grey sea as she processed this latest revelation. About Jake's infidelity she felt very little. He'd been unfaithful many times before. Was this the final straw? Perhaps. It was Farrah's betrayal that really hurt. All that shit from her about female solidarity and how Amanda shouldn't be putting up with Jake's crap. Some fucking friend she'd turned out to be.

She sat there stewing until long past sunset, ignoring all text messages and calls. She toyed with the idea of going round to Farrah's apartment and slapping the truth out of her, *Dynasty*-style, but that just wasn't her. But she did decide on a plan: one which would bring her some much-needed joy rather than plunge her deeper into misery. Instead of storming her so-called friend's condo, she organized a babysitter for Olivia and set off for the other end of the beach. Before she left the house, she pulled out her phone and texted Dan.

The hideaway cabin beneath the little grove of palms at the furthest end of the bay was Amanda's favourite place. It was an old-fashioned beach hut, just big enough for a bed, an armchair and a cocktail cabinet, with a cute little deck out front and a shower room to the side. She'd decorated it in shabby-chic style, which Helen dismissed as 'way too hippy, darling', but it was cosy, bohemian – and hers.

Amanda adjusted the flame of the paraffin lantern, refilled her glass of wine and sat motionless on the deck in front of the cabin, staring out into the dark evening sky. It was a good four hours since the showdown with Jake, and she was feeling unexpectedly calm. The weather had turned chilly and rain was forecast, but she was snug with the blanket round her shoulders.

A lone figure was making its way slowly through the ink-black darkness towards her. She kept her eyes trained, enjoying the sight of Dan's handsome form becoming more and more solid as he strode across the sand, dodging boulders, light on his feet, closing the distance between them.

She stood up and let the blanket drop to the deck, enjoying the feel of the chill sea breeze on her bare skin, her nipples hardening beneath the delicious slipperiness of her black satin camisole, her groin tingling in anticipation.

Her breasts jiggled invitingly as she hopped down the wooden steps and jumped into his arms. Dan scooped her up, kissed her deeply, then carried her over the cabin threshold and onto the bed.

Not a word was spoken as they began urgently, feverishly exploring each other, skin to skin at last, tongues circling, fingertips caressing, gasps and moans filling the space around them. The lamp flickered and went out. Amanda closed her eyes, yielded to the darkness and pulled him deeper inside her. 'Don't stop,' she whispered in his ear, then kissed him deeply. She ran her hands down his back, feeling a faint glaze of sweat upon it, then placed both hands on his gorgeous firm bum and pushed him harder, eager to keep the rhythm that was just about to make her insides light up like a box of sparklers. They came in unison, gasping and panting in uninhibited exhilaration.

She'd left the cabin shutters open and the moonlight flooded in, spotlighting his strong cheekbones and salt-and-pepper stubble. His eyes glittered and crinkled as she ran her fingertips along his biceps. They were both grinning at each other, no other language necessary. Amanda couldn't recall the last time her body had felt so alive, or so desired.

She kissed him passionately once more and instantly she felt his cock, which was still inside her, harden. They went at it again. She couldn't remember ever physically wanting a man so badly as she wanted Dan. She'd had great sex in the past – even Jake had been pretty good in bed in the old days – but this was on a different level. It was as if her actual vagina wanted Dan as much as she did, as if their body parts were designed to fit together.

She dug her perfectly manicured pale pink nails into his firm arse once more and Dan responded by pushing her up against the mound of pillows and spreading her legs wider with every thrust. He intensified his rhythm, at the same time lifting one of her ample breasts to his mouth and licking her nipple in a way that made her feel a million miles from the baby-milk machine she'd started to see herself as. She was close to climax again.

As he bit down on her neck then ran his tongue up towards her ear, it happened again – more fireworks, more stars, more everything! She screamed out in ecstasy as her wetness flooded him. As soon as Dan felt her come, he released again. Now they were shuddering together, legs like jelly, then clutching at each other, laughing and sighing and smiling in a tender embrace.

The threatened storm finally materialized and the rain began drumming against the cabin windows. Amanda lay with her head on Dan's toned chest, listening to the loud, comforting thump of his heartbeat. With the rain pattering in harmony and the thick down duvet now cocooning their conjoined form, she was the happiest she'd felt in years.

29

It was the day of the live Bitch Party. At Falcon Bay, the sea was tranquil, like it was having a disco nap, knowing it had a huge night ahead.

Large walkways had been built either side of the golden beach and huge studio lights were hanging from temporary scaffolding. Sound technicians were rigging speakers strategically and the show's famous theme tune was playing softly. Site supervisors raced around signing off different areas of the set in a desperate rush to be ready for tonight's live behind-the-scenes special. Heaters disguised as fake palm trees had been dotted all over, but the weather was unusually warm for mid-November and so far there'd been no sign that they'd be needed.

There was a palpable air of excitement about the whole event. International news stations were setting up in the C.I.TV media area, ready to host live links during the broadcast, and reporters from other networks had spent all day gathering footage for their own showings later on. Seldom-seen network executives were giving rare interviews and minor members of the cast had been sent to mingle with the news crews. Even the parking valets and security guards, usually the moodiest people on the set, seemed in high spirits, watching everyone arrive.

Social media was abuzz with fans swapping rumours and describing their plans for the evening. Many of the *Bay*'s loyal cohort of gay fans had arranged screening nights in their favourite bars, and Twitter feeds were busy with updates from drag queens, many of whom had dressed as Lucy Dean for the occasion and were downing cocktails as they waited to discover which seven actresses would be competing for the new leading lady crown.

The whole world seemed to be not only talking about *Falcon Bay* but watching it again. Viewing figures had stayed high since the Lucy and Emily two-hander and the *Bay*'s audience share and approval ratings were the best they'd been in a decade. There were reports of people in other countries staying up through the night or bunking off work just to see the contenders. The Bitch Party was featured on every news update, on every chat show and in every newspaper, and the hashtags relating to the soap, its characters and the Bitch Party itself were at an all-time high. For the first time ever, this classic show, whose core audience had never really been the online generation, was making digital waves as big as the real waves lapping at its shore. #FalconBayBitchParty was the number one trend.

In her beachside apartment not far from the set, Catherine Belle stepped out of the shower, dripping wet and feeling refreshed inside and out. Production had called 'Wrap' early that morning so everybody could get ready for the party, and Catherine had used the time very productively indeed.

First she'd called by Jacinta's, her favourite aesthetician, where she'd had the most expensive treatment, the stem-cell facial. At two grand, it wasn't cheap, but on special occasions like this, Catherine didn't hesitate. As Jacinta worked the magic ingredients into her skin, running a wand that punctured tiny holes all over her famous face, allowing the potion to sink deep into the contours, Catherine pictured her cells receiving this 'fertiliser' nourishment and generating natural collagen. This elixir of youth was, for any woman over forty, as rare as a unicorn, and for Catherine no price was too high to make sure she looked her best for the live show. Whereas in the studio she had a say over the lighting and was also able to go into the edit suite and pull any shots she didn't like, tonight would be out of her control, so she wasn't taking any chances.

When the treatment was finished and she was handed a mirror, both Catherine and Jacinta had smiled at how smooth, young and dewy she looked. But Catherine wasn't stopping there. Her next visit had been to the hotel suite of Dr Pascal Beaulieu, France's top haematologist, who she'd had flown in, at further extravagant cost, for a very special blood transfusion.

Dr Beaulieu was a well-kept secret among the rich and famous. Rumour had it that she looked after the ageless icon Tina Turner, who had spoken publicly about having her blood removed annually to encourage it to regenerate. What she hadn't shared was whether she too was part of the 'infusion club', whose members – famous women, and some men – received pints of the finest teenage blood. Full of oxygen, youth and (Catherine liked to think) hope. The blood came from models who were well paid for their donations; it gave new meaning to the term 'beauty industry'.

As she air-dried her naked body on the balcony overlooking the perfectly still sea, Catherine not only looked twenty years younger but also felt it. *A new leading lady may well be on her way to my set, desperate to make an impression on the public*, she mused as she poured herself a glass of Cristal champagne, *but there's no way she'll be taking my crown.*

She raised her glass and gave a silent toast to the sea.

Elsewhere on the bay, Amanda was getting ready to leave for the party. She was in the hallway of her family home, doing final checks in the mirror and surprising herself by actually liking what she saw. She hadn't felt great about herself since she'd been pregnant and Jake's jibes about her 'baby body' had really affected her self-confidence, but since Dan had come along she was starting to feel like her old self again.

Her reflection showed almost the exact same figure she'd had before giving birth, but thanks to the fact that she was still breastfeeding, her tits were considerably more voluptuous. She didn't mind the cleavage spilling out of her off-the-shoulder sapphire-coloured Chloé Bardot dress; she felt womanly and amazing and somehow sexy.

Her rare moment of self-appreciation was broken when

the front door swung open and Jake appeared, looking annoyingly handsome in his black suit and tie. He was carrying what looked like a gift bag and seemed to be concerned about something.

Ah, thought Amanda, *here we go*. Jake was no doubt about to deliver some reason as to why she couldn't attend. They were still at each other's throats on a daily basis, still sleeping in different bedrooms, but they'd agreed to put on a united front at the Bitch Party.

'Had to cancel the babysitter,' he said, then waited for a reply.

Amanda gave none, so he was forced to continue.

'She's been sick all day, apparently, was still planning on coming, but we don't want her giving whatever she's got to Olivia, so I told her to stay home and get better.' He smiled.

Damn him, she thought. Using their daughter's health like that was a clever strategy and she didn't really have a comeback, so she steeled herself for the inevitable. There was no time to get someone else in to look after Olivia, so she would have to stay at home. She didn't even have the energy to fight him over it, so she slipped off one of her nude Stella McCartney stilettos and accepted that she'd miss the party she'd worked so hard to get ready for. She was just about to slip the other one off when Jake got down on bended knee, picked up the discarded shoe with one hand and placed his other hand on her naked foot.

'What are you doing?' she asked, totally confused.

'Fear not,' he said, sliding her shoe back on, then standing up and grabbing the bag he'd come in with, 'Cinderella shall still go to the ball.' He winked and pulled out a papoose.

Amanda was almost lost for words but eventually managed to utter, 'Are you serious?'

'Absolutely.' He smiled. 'We'll go as a family.'

Amanda's heart fluttered. There, standing in front of her, appeared to be the old Jake, the man she'd married, the one to whom she'd said 'I do' to at the altar, the one she'd fully intended to spend the rest of her life with. Had she overreacted – about his nasty jibes, his thing with Farrah? Should she gently break it off with Dan, stay with Jake and give their marriage everything she had left in her to make it succeed?

Just as she was framing her response, Jake's next words brought her crashing back to reality.

'I mean, imagine the press headlines and pap shots I'll get when I arrive – not to mention if I take her on set with me. Daddy with his baby strapped to his chest? The audience will go crazy for it – it's so modern man. Have we got any Calpol? I want to dose her up so she's groggy and sleeps. We don't want her crying on camera.'

And with that he waltzed up the stairs to retrieve and drug their sleeping child.

30

Helen was seconds away from an orgasm when a bundle of padded envelopes landed on her head. Breathlessly close, she swiped them away and pulled the handsome detective inspector she'd picked up at Aiden's police station deeper inside her.

'Don't stop,' she moaned, then kissed him passionately. She dug her nails into his thick, firm thighs, widening her legs as he thrust into her faster and faster.

'I want you to come. Are you close? he whispered, running his tongue up her neck and pinching her nipple between his fingers.

'Yes,' Helen groaned in ecstasy, then kissed him again. As her tongue darted into his mouth, he let out an animalistic grunt and with one final thrust flooded his seed into her. Helen let go, soaking him with her own orgasm, which was so shockingly intense she had to bite her lip to stay quiet and avoid alerting anyone passing the six-foot-square store cupboard they were in. She was so used to being in control, she'd forgotten what it was like to be matched sexually. And she liked it.

Helen would never normally have been caught dead shagging in a cupboard, not when she had her lovely and, more importantly, soundproofed office in which to have her wicked way. But when Detective Matthew – 'call me Matt' – Rutland had turned up unannounced just hours before the Bitch Party live, she'd been careful not to move in straight for the kill, in case she'd read the signals wrong. She was sure she hadn't, but with things so strained at the *Bay* after the Jude scenario, the last thing she needed was to be accused of improper conduct by an inspector.

Under the guise of a quick tour before she got changed for the show, she'd been showing him round when, as they reached the third floor and with no one in sight, Matt had gone in for the kill. He'd practically knocked her off her feet with a deep kiss and roaming hands that had left her pushing open the first door she could find.

Pushed up against the wall piled with stationery and stacks of cast photos lined up in rows ready to be posted to fans (she noted that Catherine Belle had the biggest stack of requests, which pleased her), it was hardly the most comfortable place in the world – but so far she'd had three knee-trembling orgasms. She was used to being the older woman, which left her in charge. But this man couldn't have been much younger than her, and she was surprised to find how turned on she was by his air of experience and authority.

'I knew you wanted me that day we met,' he said, before kissing her passionately.

His still hard cock was pumping her so forcefully, it made

her vagina's lips want to burst into song. For once she was speechless; she couldn't remember having ever physically enjoyed a man as much as DI Rutland, which was saying something, given her hundreds of conquests.

As he continued the rhythm that was bringing her dangerously close to orgasm number four, she decided it had to be the role reversal. If this was what it was like to lose control, then she'd be doing this more often, she thought, as she gripped his firm thighs once more. He responded by pushing her up against the shelves and spreading her legs even wider.

Thank God there was no CCTV in there, Helen thought, as Matt intensified his pace at the same time as licking her neck and ears – her secret pleasure spot. Usually she'd be barking out the orders, telling him just how she liked it, but this guy was doing things his way and she was loving it.

As they lay, drenched in sweat, with her head on his chest, she really didn't want to get up. Had she had the time, she'd have straddled him right there and then and helped herself to number five, but she knew she had to move quick if she was going to be ready to welcome the guests to the Bitch Party.

As she began to stand up, his arm took her leg and pulled her back into him. 'This isn't going to be a one-off, is it?' he said, his green eyes looking at her with lust, the lines on his forehead furrowing gently.

For once in her life, Helen hoped very much that it wouldn't be a one-off. There was something about this man which made her thoughts turn to dinners and flowers, and naked swims in the bay. But before she could answer, her phone sounded a text alert, and all post-sex glow was replaced by panic.

'Oh, shit, they're looking for me on set,' she said, jumping to her feet and pulling on her clothes. 'You wait here and let yourself out ten minutes after I've gone,' she said, handing him a guest pass.

As she strode towards the exit, he called out to her again. 'You never answered my question,' he said with an eyebrow raised.

God, he is sure of himself, she thought as she suddenly found her face flushing.

'I'll be in touch,' was all she could manage as she rushed out of the cupboard, her thoughts racing. Were these feelings just because she'd had four orgasms, or was she seriously considering asking him to go out to dinner with her? She only had about thirty minutes to shower, do her make-up and get her dress on, so she pushed the thought aside and concentrated on the task ahead.

31

In The Grove, the closest hotel to the *Falcon Bay* set, Stacey Stonebrook was pulling up the zip on the dress she'd chosen for the evening, a rose-gold Donatella Versace number which was both floaty and fabulous, exactly mirroring how she felt right now. Despite Sheena's orders not to take any more Xanax, she'd dropped one just to take the edge off her anxiety, which had been off the scale when she'd checked in.

The receptionist, well aware of why she was there, had whispered to her when she handed over the room key, 'Good luck tonight. I hope you get it, Ms Stonebrook.' Stacey was touched and thanked her with a generous tip, which was very odd for someone checking in not out. But once she was in her room, the fear hit her, alongside a tidal wave of emotion.

Was she really still good enough to do this? The voices in her head that made her doubt herself were louder than usual. *You're past it, Stacey*, they said. *No one will be impressed by you*, they taunted.

She opened the mini bar and made herself a large vodka and tonic, then reached for her magic pills and dropped another one.

The Xanax kicked in within ten minutes and the voices were replaced by the soundtrack of Jane Wiedlin's 'Rush Hour', playing loudly on her iPhone.

She danced around the room singing along, using Jane's words as her mantra for the evening.

Finally, after two more large V&Ts, she was ready to face the night, ready to answer questions, ready to be cherished by strangers, ready for her close-up once more.

By the time she was in the car that had been sent by the studio to collect her, she'd started to see herself like the receptionist saw her. She was a star. This was *her* time. Even though the sky-high gold Alexander McQueen heels made her stumble on the way to the lift, nothing could take away the sense that she was walking on air.

Farrah was most definitely not walking on air. She was on her knees in her bathroom, heaving.

She'd been checking out her outrageous outfit in the mirror – the full-on, all-white James Bond tuxedo showed off her gleaming skin and toned silhouette to perfection – with Missy Elliot's 'Work It' blaring from her iPod, when a message alert pinged on her phone. Picking up her mobile, she saw Amanda's text.

> Need to talk to you before the show starts.

The sudden sensation that she needed to vomit overcame her with bullet speed. She'd eaten nothing all day, to make sure she looked amazing for the evening, so it couldn't be food poisoning. As she hung her perfectly made-up face over the toilet bowl, she ran over the text in her head. There'd been no kiss on it, which was unlike Amanda, who usually added at least three kisses and very often an emoji.

She *must* know.

She retched again, bringing up bile from her empty stomach, then wiped her mouth, got up from the floor and walked back into the lounge.

'Fuck,' she said out loud, then downed the glass of champagne that she'd set down on the side and looked at herself once again in the full-length mirror. This time it was a Bond villain she saw staring back.

When Lydia Chambers' studio driver had been told who he was collecting from the St Agnes Hotel, he'd had to google the name; being twenty-five-years-old, he'd never heard of her. After he'd scanned the images online and had a quick flick through her Wikipedia entry, he vaguely recognized her from one of the soaps his mum used to watch when he was a kid, but when he pulled the tinted-windowed car up to the hotel's entrance and took in Lydia, who was standing under a huge palm tree talking on her phone, she looked nothing like he remembered. As he flashed his lights at her to indicate he was there, the beams pierced her outfit, a barely-there, sheer white dress with a dangerous split up one side that showed off every inch of what looked like gorgeously toned legs. *Fuck!* he thought. He had no idea how old she was, but she looked sexy as hell. He got out of the habit of opening car doors for clients after the coronavirus a while back, but tonight he was going to make an exception.

As Lydia's heels crunched along the gravel towards the car door being held open, she felt a flutter between her legs that she hadn't experienced in some time. Being post-menopausal, and despite the HRT, her sex drive was precarious at the best of times. Tonight, though, the young driver's muscular frame, shaved head and tattoo creeping up his neck was sending thunderbolts and lighting right between her thighs.

As she got closer, she couldn't understand why her body was reacting like this to someone so brutish. In her dating days she'd always preferred the young-Jude-Law look and this driver wouldn't have been out of place on an episode of *Breaking Bad* or even a police line-up. But there was something hypnotic about him that turned her nipples as hard and erect as bullets – and in this dress that was not going to go unnoticed. As she reached him, she told herself she was being ridiculous; he was clearly less than half her age and wouldn't be interested in her, so, avoiding his gaze, she slipped into the back seat without a word.

As she passed him, the driver noticed that even up close Lydia looked flawless; she also smelled delicious. An intoxicating mist had wafted over him as she'd climbed into the car. He could have sworn the dress had parted to reveal she had no knickers on, which made his cock spring to life and begin pushing at his light grey suit trousers.

For a moment neither spoke or moved as their eyes locked and chemistry crackled between them.

Surprising herself, Lydia extended one long, lean leg, slid herself further into the car and pushed her gold heel against the door, keeping it open. The way the material had fallen aside as she did so left the driver in absolutely no doubt that under that dress she was completely naked.

Maybe it was the excitement of knowing she was just hours away from millions around the world seeing her big comeback, or that – against her doctor's orders – she'd doubled her hormone dose a few days back, but suddenly her body was alive, and it was hungry. It wanted this driver and it wanted him now.

In an almost out-of-body trance, Lydia heard herself purring at the young man. It was the same voice she'd once used in a series of famous coffee ads whose final frames had seen her flirting with her neighbour then coyly closing the door before he could have his way with her.

'Is that for me?' she said, moving her shoe over his groin and prodding his bulge with the tip of her toe.

The driver looked her deep in the eyes. 'It is, if you—' he began.

Before he could finish, she leaned forward and slid down his trouser zip. As her perfectly manicured hand reached in to grip his velvety smooth yet hard-as-steel throbbing flesh, she used her other hand to undo the last button and nudged his trousers down. There, waving in front of her, was quite possibly the biggest dick she'd ever seen. She drew him into the car by his perfect balls, shifted her dress to one side and spread her legs. As the tip of his dripping wet shaft began to enter her and his mouth sucked hungrily on her bright pink nipples, she gasped with ecstasy. She just managed to use the heel on her shoe to pull the car door closed as he slid fully inside her.

Up in her penthouse apartment above the *Falcon Bay* set, Madeline Kane stood naked before a wall of floor-to-ceiling mirrors. She loved looking at herself and slowly ran her eyes over every inch of her immaculately fashioned body. After a few more moments spent admiring her reflection, she picked up her phone and called Chad. He was on a business trip to Australia, so because of the time difference, she knew it would go to voicemail.

'Baby,' she said in her softest, sexiest accent, 'I just wanted to tell you how much I love you.' She breathed seductively down the phone. 'I'm about to make you a little present, darlin'. Hope you enjoy it…'

She positioned the phone on the dressing table, slipped on a red silk robe, angled the three-way mirrors just so, and pressed record on the camera app.

It was a tradition of hers that whenever they were apart she would surprise him with a sexy little something to remind him of what he was missing. This evening she decided she would replay a scene she'd performed for him when they had first got together.

From the moment Madeline and Chad had locked eyes at a street market in Louisiana, she'd known he was *the one*. As a child, she'd been obsessed with Greek mythology, and if ever a man resembled a god, then it was Chad: tall and rugged, with light brown curls that haloed his handsome face and hazel eyes. She'd never seen anyone like him.

The attraction was mutual. As the son of a devout Southern Baptist who'd made his millions via ethical trading, Chad was one of the most sought-after bachelors in the US, but the moment he took in Madeline, her supermodel body, height and feline beauty, it was love at first sight. He invited her to lunch there and then, but they never even made it to the aperitifs. They booked into the nearest five-star hotel, only just kept their clothes on in the lift and didn't leave their suite again for seventy-two hours.

One of the many exhilarating discoveries they made in those ecstatic first days and nights was how exciting it was to watch each other masturbate. And in their fifteen years of marriage since, they had never tired of it. Seeing Madeline bring herself to orgasm sent Chad wild every time and the thought of his inevitable, urgent, frantic response was making Madeline wet right now.

She sat down at her dressing table, let the robe fall open to reveal her right breast, cupped her artfully manicured left hand around it and began fondling her nipple. As her neck arched in pleasure, she pouted provocatively into the phone camera, placed two fingers in her mouth, moistened them and then ran her hand down between her legs. She was already soaking wet as she slipped her fingers inside herself.

32

The bay's cliff face was dotted with thousands of twinkling lights, making the sea shimmer like it was full of diamonds. It was a magical meeting of TV and nature and the result was magnificent. The Bitch Party area was centred on The Cove, Lucy Dean's infamous beach bar. Decking had been laid on the sand in a U-shaped walkway, creating an island within an island, and cameras were everywhere – on spider wires, on erected towers. Press drones floated high above the set in the clear sky.

Ross Owen had been one of the first members of the press to receive his invite to the party. It was his reward for having given the show so much positive coverage lately. He'd declined the champagne offered to him on arrival, because as much as he liked to party, he knew that getting him drunk was all part of the network's plans to give the evening the rosiest of glows, and Ross was determined not to miss a thing. Also, he was interviewing the cast and crew for the TV show, and he'd be writing it all up for the *Herald* in the morning, and doing all that with a hangover would frankly be more hassle than getting wasted merited.

On the main stage, on a podium draped in sequins, stood Jake Monroe, ready to open the show with microphone in hand and a sleeping Olivia strapped to his chest. He'd been surprised when Madeline had asked him to officiate by himself. He'd expected her to want to co-host at least, as she was certainly no shrinking violet, but he relished taking the lead.

As the floor manager counted down, gesturing to him that they were five seconds to live, camera operators whizzed around the packed audience area with cable bashers following them, making sure no one tripped on the long black wires that led to the gallery feed. A crane-camera assistant rushed around too, moving people out of the way as the crane swirled above their heads, capturing wide shots.

The 'On Air' signs flashed red, the first few bars of *Falcon Bay*'s instantly recognizable theme tune filled the air, and Jake began to speak into Camera 1.

'Hello and welcome to *Falcon Bay Behind the Scenes*! I'm Jake Monroe, director of continuing drama here at C.I.TV, and this is my baby…' He gestured at Olivia, which caused the crowd to sigh 'Ahhh', and then with open arms and a big smile he added, 'And this is my other baby – *Falcon Bay* – but she's much less sleepy!'

A round of applause and laughter broke out at his seemingly cute joke.

'Throughout tonight's exclusive episode, we'll be looking back at the history of our show, showing you people and places you've never seen before *and* introducing the seven actresses we've shortlisted to become our new soap bitch!'

Another round of applause rang out, this time with some wolf whistles on top.

'So to get this party started, let's take a trip down memory lane and remind you just how fabulous the last thirty-nine years of *Falcon Bay* have been.'

As the crane camera panned around the bay, everybody lifted their flutes of champagne high in the air.

'Cheers!' Jake smiled as the live feed cut to the montage and they came off air. He swiftly moved off the podium and signalled for a runner to unstrap Olivia's papoose from him. Leaving her in the runner's arms, he walked over to Ross and high-fived him.

Watching Jake from behind the sound desk, Amanda picked up two flutes of champagne from a passing waiter, and downed them both. 'God, what a performance,' she said quietly under her breath.

Through the crowd she saw Dan making his way towards her, also bearing two glasses of fizz. He was not the dull accountant she'd originally seen him as, Amanda thought, allowing her gaze to linger on his toned chest, its contours clearly visible under his modishly close-fitting shirt. Just the sight of him these days gave her a major flutter; she'd truly never known anything like it.

He came and stood with her behind the sound desk, and as the two of them watched the clips in full view of the crowd, he very subtly snaked his left hand around her and began cupping and caressing her buttocks through the silky fabric of her dress. Her nerve endings sizzled as his fingers crept down the back of her thigh and began rucking up the hem. He drew his fingertips slowly up her stockings to the flesh above her panty line and she inhaled deeply, doing her utmost to keep a professional expression on her face. Inside, she was melting. The gentle, insistent strokes of his fingers probed and circled and teased until finally she could hold it no longer. She gripped the sound desk as she came, every sensation heightened as she bit her lip and panted as quietly as she could manage, the pleasure flooding out of her. He moved behind her and pressed up against her, his cock hard and urgent, champagne glass still in hand as they both pretended they were merely watching the show.

From down among the crowd, Farrah caught a distant glimpse of them. The screen was showing thirty-one-year-old footage of her final scene as Lucy Dean's soon-to-be-drowned daughter. It was a truly heart-rending performance and Dan raised his glass at her and mouthed 'Bravo!' Amanda managed only a half-smile. She still hadn't had her talk with Farrah about the episode, and now it was too late. But before she could beat herself up over that, she felt Dan's hot breath in her ear.

'I'm going to have to sort myself out,' he murmured. Christ, even his voice was enough to make her breasts burn. 'Just being this close to you has got me close to exploding,' he whispered, gently pressing his body against her, making it clear he was telling the truth.

As his lips lightly touched the nape of her neck, she desperately wanted to sneak off with him, to feel him inside her, to smell his body next to her, but there was no way she could disappear in the middle of this, so she forced herself to step to one side so as not to give in to her body's temptation – again.

'See you later,' she managed with a wry smile, as Dan shuffled off into the crowd, trying to hide his bulge. Amanda hoped the flush she could feel creeping up her neck wasn't going to show on her face.

As the montage came to an end, Jake minus Olivia returned to the podium, this time with Ross in tow. The 'On Air' light went red again.

'Wasn't that amazing?' Jake began. 'What a journey our show has been on over the last four decades – and that's just the warm-up! Over the course of tonight's show, we'll be chatting to our current cast, as well as meeting the women vying to make sure our fortieth anniversary really goes with a bang! *And* to celebrate us turning the big four-oh in December, tonight I can exclusively reveal that *Falcon Bay* will be going fully live for our Christmas Day episode!'

There were more whoops and cheers, including a very loud one from Farrah. Just hearing the words and knowing that this was her big moment made her heart race with excitement. She would talk to Amanda later, deal with the terrible mistake she'd made and pray she'd forgive her, but before that, which she knew would be bad, she was going to enjoy her moment of glory – she'd certainly worked hard enough to get it.

'A special episode needs a special director—' continued Jake.

This is it, Farrah thought and started striding towards the stage, ready to be in position for a camera to throw to her when he called out her name.

'—and the director we've chosen to steer us on Christmas Day is well known to you. In fact, this past week, thanks to Ross here, a bit too well known.'

Ross looked smug. Confusion washed through Farrah.

'But if there's one thing our characters' lives on *Falcon Bay* prove, it's that second chances are vital.'

A cold chill ran up Farrah's spine.

'All the stories we tell on this show have a single principle at their heart,' Jake burbled on. 'They are stories about good people who sometimes do bad things. Well, we want the world to know that if you're sorry and you're willing to change, then you too will get a second chance. So I'd like to announce that the director of our very special Christmas live episode is none other than *Falcon Bay*'s number one director, Aiden Anderson!'

The crowd cheered his name as they parted and Aiden, with a follow spotlight, joined Jake on the podium. The cameras zoomed in on the duo as the men hugged one another to a round of applause – started by the warm-up man, as per Jake's instructions.

Farrah, rooted to the spot, was seething as Aiden took the microphone from Jake and geared up to speak. She snatched a whole bottle of champagne from a passing waiter's tray and swigged at it.

'Thank you,' began Aiden in his best Hugh Grant 'I've just been caught with a hooker but I'm still a nice guy' tone. 'It's been a rough week.'

Ross raised his hands. 'Sorry, man!' he said, clearly in on the game.

The audience laughed as all three men made light of what would usually mean the end of someone's career, not glorification in front of millions. After a short pause to mark a change in tone, Aiden went for the Oscar.

'But, seriously,' he continued, 'it's been the wake-up call I needed. I made some bad, bad choices, but I'm a good person and thanks to the support of C.I.TV and our wonderful fans, I've been given another chance – and not just at my job, which I care about so much, but at life. I went to my first NA meeting earlier today and I am proud to say I am now getting the help I need.'

Another big round of applause rang out as Jake took Aiden's hand and shook it in a manly and respectful way. It was as if they were in a boxing ring and Jake was declaring a win.

Farrah looked away. She couldn't bear one more second of this. She was about to leave when she spotted Madeline Kane on the VIP platform at the back of the audience. She stormed over, bottle in hand.

'This is bullshit!' she shouted as she climbed the two steps to where Madeline, in a crystal-embellished catsuit, met her with perfect calm.

'Makes good TV though, and that's the point of tonight,' Madeline replied icily, not even taking her eyes off the stage where Aiden was still talking.

'I am proud to announce that I will be teaching the art of film-making to young offenders and disenfranchised youth, with one of them getting a placement here at *Falcon Bay* as part of the New Directors Scheme. Thank you from the bottom of my heart for giving me this shot at redemption.'

As he finished his speech, Jake patted him on the back. The crowd roared its approval and Jake took back the microphone.

'We're going to an ad break now, but when we come back, we'll be meeting some bitches!'

As the red lights on the camera went off, Farrah stepped towards Madeline, who, aware of how close she was now, turned to face her. She cast an eye over the bottle in Farrah's hand.

'Do you actually believe that bullshit from Aiden?' Farrah spat before taking another swig.

'It's not whether I believe it, it's whether the show wins because we gave him the chance. I have to say, I'm surprised to see you so shocked at the news,' Madeline said, a half-smile on her lips. 'Considering how close you and Amanda are, I assumed she would have told you since Aiden's redemption and this public penance were her idea.'

Farrah suddenly felt breathless, as if she'd been kicked in the stomach. Then she remembered the text message – had that been what Amanda was going to tell her?

Madeline touched Farrah's arm. 'I want you to know that when Jake gave you the Christmas live gig, he meant it. Aiden was dead to him. But Amanda reminded me about the Sheena McQueen court case and that whether we like it or not, we had a duty of care to support Aiden.'

Farrah stepped back, reeling from everything she was hearing.

Madeline seemed intent on rubbing it in. 'I wasn't sure

myself, but when Helen backed her up, they convinced me that this was the way to go.'

Farrah couldn't believe what she was hearing. First Amanda and now Helen, and neither of them had had the guts to tell her. She took another gulp from the now nearly empty bottle.

'So whether he fucks up again remains to be seen, but right now this is TV gold.' Madeline picked up an empty champagne flute from a drinks table and passed it to Farrah. 'Use this, please. We don't want everyone to think this place is full of feral employees, do we?'

And with that, Madeline walked away, just as Jake once again took his place on the podium.

33

'Welcome back!' boomed Jake from the stage. 'Now it's time for me to introduce you to our first contender for *Falcon Bay*'s Lady Be-atch. It's Miss Honey Hunter.'

At the far end of the boardwalk, sparkly curtains opened and Honey, looking like absolute perfection, sauntered out as the crowd went wild and the show's theme music kicked back in. She looked magnificent, she felt larger than life, and as the drone circled her she waved to all the viewers at home and gave them her biggest, warmest smile.

The crowd cheered again, and Ross Owen, who was now seated in his own interview area (part of the deal he'd struck with Jake when he agreed to do a U-turn on Aiden), was waiting for her.

'Honey, darling, this is well timed after Aiden – and you've had quite the week yourself,' he said, mugging for the camera and using the fact that they were live to show off. 'I'm beginning to wonder if *Falcon Bay* is a drama or a crime series!' He laughed, then pointed the microphone at Honey, who was now seated in the chair opposite him.

'As everyone already knows, Ross,' she began in her silky-smooth voice, 'I was innocent of that little *misunderstanding*' – Ross raised an eyebrow – 'but I *am* guilty,' she continued, 'guilty of being the right woman to take over this show.'

She turned, searching for the one camera out of the three filming them that had the red light above it. Talking into that one, she knew she was looking directly at the viewers at home.

'*Falcon Bay* audience, I'm your bitch. It's down to you now, so vote for this *sinner* and make me your *winner*!' She then gave her best bitch smile and finished it with a wink.

The audience in the studio and the millions of fans at home erupted with catcalls and thunderous applause.

Catherine had joined Amanda on the balcony and they were observing the goings-on below. Honey was now taking selfies with fans as the screens played clips from her career, including the night she won her Oscar.

'Showing the Oscar win is a clever move,' Catherine said.

Amanda nodded.

'And she looks good. I'd say she's in with a strong chance.' Catherine sipped her drink.

'If she gets it, are you going to be okay working with her?'

Catherine shrugged. 'I'm a pro, darling. I'll work with anybody. Even you.'

Amanda was taken aback by the dig, but before she could ask Catherine what her problem was, they both noticed Madeline approaching.

Catherine ramped up the volume of her voice so that Madeline could hear. 'You're wrong to have backed Aiden Anderson in this debacle.'

'Why?' Amanda was genuinely surprised. She wasn't aware Catherine had such a strong opinion on Aiden.

'I'm all for forgiveness, but it doesn't work when it comes to drugs. People want it to, but it doesn't. When drugs are involved, what's needed is a short, sharp and painful shock.'

Madeline reached them, picked up a fresh glass of champagne and raised it at them while narrowing her eyes.

Amanda was mesmerized by her make-up: her inky black eyelash extensions were set off by eyeliner flicked up in a deliciously feline curl, and the shimmering emerald eyeshadow complemented her irises perfectly. She looked extraordinary.

'Sounds like you have personal experience, Catherine,' Madeline said. 'Are you talking about Sheena?'

'No. Though she'd be the first to tell you that being removed from the spotlight saved her life. It's the only thing that works with the wild and wayward.'

Amanda fixed Catherine with a pointed stare, hoping she'd stop, but Madeline gestured with her glass that she should continue.

'We had a similar situation here many years ago. A young boy who played my son.'

'Calvin Butler?' Madeline said.

Both Amanda and Catherine were surprised that she knew the name of a long-forgotten cast member.

'Yes.' Catherine nodded. 'Young Cal was all over the place, addicted to drugs, life in a total mess and heading for disaster. Just like Sheena was back in those days.'

Madeline was all ears now. She'd stopped sipping from her glass and was giving Catherine her full attention. It was making Amanda nervous. Clearly, Catherine was gearing up to send another hit in her direction, and right in front of her boss. Just what she didn't need.

On the stage beneath them, the next actress trying out for the bitch role was strutting down the boardwalk and trading witticisms with Ross as the cameras rolled.

'He was a good kid at heart,' Catherine continued, 'but he couldn't handle the fame. Both his parents died when he was tiny, and with no one looking out for him at home he went off the rails quickly. I tried to mother him in my own way, but it was tough love he needed. Not everyone is suited to this business – TV can kill people.'

'You've done alright by it,' Madeline replied drily.

Catherine nodded. 'I have, because I was made for this – and I came to it relatively late. But others are not so robust. You need a constitution of steel to survive all the negative press, the relentless scrutiny. The pressure of being continually in the world's eye lays bare all your insecurities and magnifies them for all to see. Those that can't cope try and fill the holes with something. For some actors, it's endless shagging – cast and crew, anyone and anything. Some go the other way – getting fit, running marathons, tiring themselves out, finding religion. And some turn to drugs.' She pointed her glass towards Aiden, who was flirting with Honey in the crowd below. 'But I didn't want Calvin to end up like him,' she said, pulling a face. 'I just knew he had to get out of TV. He was so young and vulnerable, I was certain that he would end up dead, like Sheena very nearly did. And now, thanks to this "second chance" that Jake's just announced to the nation, Aiden Anderson will go the same way, I guarantee you both that.'

Amanda took a moment to consider this. Had they signed Aiden's death warrant by keeping him on?

'At least I *know* I saved young Calvin's life,' Catherine said, with such confidence in her tone, it caused Madeline to look up abruptly.

'How?' she asked, arching her carefully shaped eyebrows.

'I got his contract on the show terminated.'

Madeline inhaled sharply and Amanda looked surprised. 'I didn't know that,' she said.

'Well, it was for his own good,' Catherine continued. 'I could see what was happening, where he would end up, and I knew I had to do something. He wasn't all over the tabloids yet, like Sheena was, so there was still time to save him before the world knew what a mess he was. I went to the producers and told them that either he had to leave or I would. And I *know* it saved him because I never heard anything of him ever again. He didn't go to another show, wasn't ripped apart by the press and never worked in TV again. Which means he *got out*. He probably met somebody, somebody who loved him for him and not because he was famous. I'll bet he had a family, lived a normal life. And that's how you help people like Aiden Anderson, by removing them from what's going to kill them. Sheena is living proof of that – as is the fact that no one ever heard of Calvin again. All you've done here is put Aiden right back in with his demons.'

Madeline stared at Catherine long and hard.

'That was a long time ago, Catherine, before support was understood,' Amanda said, finally breaking what felt like a deathly silence. 'Aiden is going to NA and helping young offenders. He's determined to turn things around, and I believe he will.'

Catherine sipped from her glass then widened her eyes. 'Then I guess it can't have been him I saw doing a line of coke in the make-up trailer about an hour ago,' she said, before walking off, knowing she'd won the argument.

Amanda was stunned into silence. She looked at Madeline, who had a scarily grim expression on her face. 'What shall we do?' Amanda said, but Madeline was already stalking away.

In the wings, surrounded by make-up assistants and runners, Stacey was in position, waiting for her entrance and watching the monitors. She'd already seen Honey and two of the other auditionees receiving air hugs and good wishes in the press pen. Two more potential bitches had been announced and while they had some pedigree, none were the same class as Honey; she was definitely Stacey's only competition so far.

As her lipstick was touched up and her hair adjusted, Stacey looked around once more for Lydia. Sheena had pulled strings to ensure that they would be the last ones on, to give them extra airtime, but Stacey had seen no sign of her yet, which was odd, especially for something as important as this. She scanned the backstage area yet again and suddenly felt buoyed up. If Lydia, who was at the very least on a par with Honey, was missing, then that meant it was really down to her. That made her feel a whole lot better. She fished in her clutch for another Xanax, then reached for the champagne next to her to wash it down.

⋆

Behind the *Falcon Bay* set, by the waterside, with a clipboard in her hand, stood Helen. With minutes to spare, she'd made it. She was resplendent in a canary-yellow off-the-shoulder Stella McCartney dress that was so bright it was as if someone had plucked the sun from the sky and turned it into the very material that clung to her perfect figure. Her bronzed skin set it off beautifully and in the reflection from the soft lights above the boardwalk she appeared to be literally glowing – which she was, but not for reasons anyone looking at her might imagine.

The madness of the live broadcast was all around her; it was now or never. Whilst she'd been unable to guarantee one of Sheena's girls the role, she'd worked hard to make sure that both of them had the best chance on the night of getting the most votes, divvying up the camera time and adjusting the order to place her girls either side of advert breaks so as to give them two minutes longer than their rivals. She'd seen Stacey, but there was still no sign of Lydia. And Sheena wasn't answering her phone, no doubt still furious that Madeline had put a ban on agents attending the event. After getting Lydia's mobile number from the car company, she'd just been patched through to the driver, who'd told her they'd been delayed but that he was just dropping Lydia at the studios now.

Usually she'd have ripped the driver a new earhole for bringing talent to a live broadcast so close to the wire, but in truth she was just grateful that the event was now nearly done and they would soon be off air. And whilst she'd just shagged

Detective Inspector Rutland in the office store cupboard, she wouldn't dream of drinking, so she was eager to well and truly hit the hospitality tent the moment the credits rolled.

She was just musing over what it was about Matt that already had her responding to his text messages, when a shadow fell over her. Looking up, she saw a drunken Jude Roscoe stumbling towards her.

'What are you doing here?' she said, searching around for security guards but aware that she was on the far end of the boardwalk where there were none.

'I came here,' he slurred, 'because you are a two-faced blackmailing slut who ruined my life and I've decided that tonight the whole world is going to hear about it.' And with that he stumbled off in the direction of the set.

'Shit!' A genuinely panicked Helen cursed under her breath and started to chase after him.

Gazing down from the podium, Jake couldn't quite believe what a successful night this had been. Aiden's confessional had gone down a storm, the montage clips were already being tweeted all over the world, and all five of the wannabe bitches they'd introduced so far had been hits with the audience.

Honey Hunter was clearly leading the way. Some of the others had been sexy, or had good nostalgia value, but they didn't have her wow factor. Checking the list, he noted that Stacey Stonebrook was up next. He'd glimpsed her backstage and was surprised how hot she looked, but she lacked Honey's pizazz, so unless Lydia Chambers, who he'd just heard on his earpiece had finally arrived on the set, had something no one was expecting, then Oscar-winning Honey was set to be *Falcon Bay*'s new bitch.

He grinned at the prospect of Catherine Belle knowing she was no longer the belle of the *Bay*. There was fourteen years between her and Honey, and as good as Catherine looked – and she had looked surprisingly fresh when he'd seen her earlier – he knew that Honey calling her 'Mother' would stick in her throat like a barbed-wire smoothie.

It was strange that Helen was nowhere to be seen. She'd made it perfectly clear she was gunning for either Lydia or Stacey to be cast, and her scheduling of them at the end of the show hadn't gone unnoticed. But Helen had argued that by saving them till last, it guaranteed a good ending to the show; she'd promised they'd both deliver the goods and prove her right, so she'd got her way.

The studio floor manager began the silent countdown to back on air, and Jake reached for the microphone and announced Stacey's name.

As Stacey stepped onto the boardwalk runway and made her way towards Ross's interview area, she stumbled. It looked like she'd tripped on the hem of her dress and as she wobbled, trying to keep upright, the crowd laughed and clapped. She reached out to grab the railing to her left but missed it, and before she could stop herself, she tumbled over the edge and down into the audience.

Loud gasps rippled through the crowd. Ross rushed over to the edge of the stage and the cameras zoomed in on a dishevelled Stacey, sprawled on the sand and with her dress split up the side. A panicky Jake raced over to Ross, praying for the sake of their insurance alone that Stacey's body wouldn't be as badly injured as her pride was sure to be. But before he'd even reached the spot, a shaky Stacey had got to her feet and was waving from the crowd.

'I'm okay!' she said, though she looked far from it.

Jake took the reins. 'Well, that was Stacey Stonebrook, folks!' he said.

Everyone looked embarrassed, and radio earpieces from the gallery were aflutter, telling Jake they now had to call Lydia as otherwise they'd have four whole minutes to fill. Cameras followed Stacey as she was helped away.

Desperate to push on, Jake put the microphone to his lips once more. 'Ladies and gentlemen, it's time to welcome our final contender of the night. You all know and love her from her many years on television, but will you choose her as *Falcon Bay*'s new uber-bitch? Let's find out – it's Miss Lydia Chambers.'

Knowing she had extra time thanks to Stacey's early exit, Lydia entered the set beaming, really milking her entrance by sashaying slowly along the boardwalk and leaning down to the fans below, touching hands Mariah-Carey-style. She was the only one who'd done this, so the crowd went crazy.

Jake was impressed. There was something different about Lydia – maybe Helen did know a thing or three.

This was a million-dollar entrance in her sheer dress that showed off her legs and pretty much everything else too. After touching the last hand and gesturing her thanks to the audience the way a Broadway star did for a standing ovation, Lydia took her seat opposite Ross, doing a *Basic Instinct* leg cross that came dangerously close to revealing all on camera.

Grabbing a glass of champagne, she raised it to the watching masses.

'They clearly saved the best bitch till last, so let's get this party started!' she squealed.

The crowd were ecstatic – there were yells and whoops and a full minute of cheering and clapping.

In a restricted area backstage, Helen was desperately trying to reason with Jude, but he was having none of it. Luckily, he was so drunk, he'd gone in the wrong direction for the set, so at least they were away from the cameras, but as Helen watched him step into a hole in the sand then fall flat on his face, she suddenly felt pity.

'Jude,' she said softly, holding out her hand to help him up.

He swatted it away. 'Don't need your help!'

'I can talk to upstairs – we'll find you a role on another show. I know you're angry and I should have told you, but I honestly didn't know,' she lied, desperately thinking of things she could say to calm him down as she tried to pull him up by his arm. They were nose to nose and he stank of whisky.

'You'd do that?' he said, his face a forlorn picture of desperate hope.

'Yes, of course I would,' she lied again, supporting him as she steered him towards the exit and closer to where she knew security would be able to dispatch him.

'Really?' He came to a sudden standstill and gazed drunkenly at her.

'Yes, really. We'll find you something really explosive on another of Madeline's networks,' she said, not meeting his eyes as she glanced down at her watch. There was just five minutes of airtime left and she'd do whatever it took to keep him away from the cameras until the live broadcast was over.

He might have been drunk, but he noticed her checking her watch and immediately knew what she was up to.

'You're lying again!' he raged.

He pulled a packet of cigarettes from his pocket, stuck a cigarette in his mouth and brought out a Zippo lighter. The flame flickered in the sea breeze as he tried to light it.

As he turned away to try and shield the flame, he spotted a crate of fireworks.

'I'll give you explosive, you fucking bitch,' he snarled, staggering towards the crate, lit Zippo in hand, as Helen screamed out for him to stop.

Down in the party pit, people were shaking champagne bottles and spraying them in the air. The music was full-on party. Everyone was dancing and screaming. The atmosphere was electric.

A devastated Stacey, flanked by two medics, was seated on the observation deck watching as Lydia and Honey had a dance-off in the sand. She wasn't injured, but her heart was broken. Not only had she humiliated herself in front of millions – which would no doubt become billions once her fall had gone viral – but if Sheena was right, and it really was between the two of them, she'd just handed Lydia the win.

On the podium, Jake picked up the microphone and prepared to read the farewell speech from the autocue. He was full of himself; the night had been a huge success. While running over the words on the screen, he spotted Farrah making a beeline for Amanda on the beach set. He'd been waiting for that all night. He just hoped they wouldn't be heard on camera as the red lights came on once more and he began the show's farewell.

With teeth clenched and fury in her eyes, Farrah reached Amanda and went straight for her.

Ross, who had finished his interview duties and was now enjoying the party, saw something was happening and gestured for the *Herald*'s live-feed web-camera team to head towards them.

Farrah zoned in on her prey. 'How could you do this to me! And behind my back? That live ep was my gig. Jake gave it to me,' she shouted.

She was now so close, Amanda felt Farrah's spittle on her cheek. 'That wasn't all my husband gave you, was it?' she shot back.

Farrah recoiled in horror. Amanda did indeed know about her and Jake.

'Oh yes, he couldn't wait to tell me.'

Farrah was searching for an appropriate response when from down in the party pit Helen Gold appeared, screaming at everybody in sight.

'You've got to get away from here!' she shrieked. 'He's going to set off the—'

The second half of her sentence was drowned out by the ear-splitting bangs and pops of a crateload of fireworks suddenly exploding into the air. Jake, startled by the noise, tried to continue the exit speech, but inside he raged. These were meant to be for the show's big finale, which was ninety seconds away, and as he looked down, he saw that the guests hadn't been moved past the safety barriers either. There had been a strict and very boring health and safety meeting he'd been forced to endure earlier that day, so he knew the intention had been to move everybody back from the danger zone so that they could safely watch the spectacular firework display to end the party. He couldn't understand why they were going off now.

As Helen pushed as many people back through the barriers as she could, the explosions kept on detonating. It sounded like a warzone. Aware that something was now very wrong, people began running away from the soaring rockets, trying to avoid them as they rained down from the heavens. It was more like a scene from *Saving Private Ryan* than the glossy shores of *Falcon Bay*.

Helen raced towards Catherine, grabbed her arm and just managed to pull her out of the way of a giant rocket before it smashed into a speaker. She glanced up just in time to see Dan shoving his way through the throngs of screaming fans on the boardwalk, but then she lost track of him in the smoke and chaos. Amanda and Farrah were nowhere to be seen.

Explosions popped all over the decked beach area, and the sparkly curtains at the start of the walkway went up in flames. Through his earpiece, Jake was ordered to get off the stage and into the building immediately. Surreally, the show's theme tune began to blare out of the speakers as on the montage screen the titles rolled over the madness. People were running into the sea, afraid for their lives, as more fireworks exploded in every direction and the stage continued to burn.

Madeline, who'd returned to the internal gallery for the last part of the show, was calmly watching the madness unfold through the panoramic windows. When a breathless Jake raced in in a panic, she cut his ramblings off midway.

'After all this *drama* tonight, the audience are going to want something way bigger than Jude Roscoe's death for our fortieth anniversary episode,' she said, her eyes still focused on the chaos below.

Jake did a double-take and wondered if he'd heard her right. Why wasn't she yelling, pacing up and down or at the very least breaking a sweat? The scene through the windows was apocalyptic – he suddenly wondered if this was some sort of bizarre publicity stunt that she'd deliberately kept from him.

'You couldn't plan this, but it's certainly gone with a bang,' she said, as if reading his thoughts and correcting his curiosity.

Knowing he wasn't out of the loop, he took a deep breath, calmed himself, and looked at her standing there as controlled and undemonstrative as ever whilst watching a dozen firefighters trying to stop the blaze that was now licking at the edges of Lucy Dean's infamous beach bar. If Madeline wasn't freaked by this mayhem, and, more importantly, was seemingly not blaming him for whatever had caused it, then he wasn't about to try and change her mind.

'Er, okay,' he mumbled. 'So, the fortieth...' he continued.

It was unreal that they were discussing everyday business while flames were raging below them. 'Shall I get the team to put together some ideas about—'

As she turned towards him, reflections of the fireworks flashed in her beautiful eyes.

'That won't be necessary. I've already decided what needs to be done,' she said, with the hint of a smirk running across her lips. 'Lucy Dean will die instead. So tomorrow, after you've sorted out whatever was behind this mess, I want you to inform the team *and* Catherine Belle that we'll be filming her death scenes – live – on Christmas Day.'

34

By the following morning, all evidence of the Bitch Party fire had vanished.

Set painters had repaired the scorched corner of The Cove and a cleaning team had worked through the night de-rigging the set and collecting the stray fireworks that had littered the bay all the way to the waterline. Even the sand on the beach had been raked. The whole place was back to its idyllic former self, silent once again except for the rhythmic clonking of the tied-up boats as they gently nudged the wooden mooring raft when the waves lapped against their sides.

In Meeting Room 6, the writers, producers, execs and heads of departments looked in a lot worse shape than the bay, but they were very much still buzzing, recounting the choice moments from the night before as they watched the big screens along the wall tuned in to various morning chat shows. Every one of them was talking about *Falcon Bay*. Candy was scrolling through the interactive hub stats, which were open on another screen. Last night's show was still trending globally. All seven actresses had their own hashtags and memes, but clearly the most talked about – for all the wrong reasons, sadly – was Stacey Stonebrook and her epic tumble from the boardwalk.

As they watched Stacey's fall being replayed in slow motion from several angles, the door to the meeting room swung open and in walked Jake and Madeline. Candy stood up and started a round of applause and the whole team, even Helen, got to their feet and joined in.

For once, Helen's applause wasn't sarcastic. Last night had been a massive success and even the fuck-ups had played into *Falcon Bay*'s hands. Having to double-up as the show's press officer had finally come good as it had been her duty to smooth-talk the oleaginous Ross Owen, which she'd done with ease. After trapping him in the hospitality tent while the fireworks were still popping, and plying him with champagne, she'd dictated a nice little spiel about the fire having been intentional as a metaphor for the new firebrand about to take over at *Falcon Bay*. It was all utter bollocks, but Ross had bought it because she'd promised that if he posted it on the *Herald*'s website immediately, he'd get a shag from her in gratitude. That was to be Helen's penance for the whole Jude Roscoe fiasco. Luckily, Ross had been too pissed by that stage to manage anything, which was a blessing after the night she'd had. The *Herald*'s story was copied by all the news agencies within the hour, and Helen's work was done. Or so she thought.

Breaking into a smile, Jake took a theatrical bow, arm across his waist, doubling over. 'Thank you. Thank you very much,' he said, sounding like an Elvis impersonator.

Madeline looked on, impassive as ever, and Jake quickly remembered his place, stood up straight and dropped a step back so he was now facing the room.

'Congratulations, everyone,' Madeline said. 'As you can all see,' she continued, waving an immaculately manicured hand at the TV screens, 'last night achieved everything we wanted.'

Helen breathed a small sigh of relief, which soon stuck in her throat, as Madeline turned in her direction.

'There was of course the unfortunate timing of the fireworks incident,' she said, as Jake followed her gaze, both now pausing in Helen's direction long enough for her to be in no doubt that Jude had filled them in on their altercation. Once she knew Helen had felt the burn, Madeline turned to the wider audience, and, like a shadow, Jake did likewise.

'But the whole world is talking about us!' Madeline said with what was almost a squeal, clearly delighted. 'In fact, the episode that followed the Bitch Party last night was the most viewed episode we've had in eighteen years. Which has meant that, with our combined audience for the two shows, we've become the number one soap in the world – again!'

The room cheered, apart from Helen, who was still squirming in her seat.

Jake cut in. 'Everything we've been aiming for is working. We are relevant once again. And more than anything, viewers are saying that they can't wait for the Christmas episode.'

'But one night does not a revival make,' Madeline said, more serious now. 'We must deliver on our promise to make the Christmas Day live episode unmissable. And Jude Roscoe' – she cast her eyes once again in Helen's direction – 'just isn't an important enough character to sacrifice to meet our audience's expectations. His death, no matter how good the stunt, just won't bring the emotional depth we need.'

Helen's blood froze in her veins. She had a horrible feeling she knew what was coming next.

'Which is why,' Madeline said, 'we've taken the decision to reprieve Jude and give the audience a much more meaningful character to mourn.'

She shot Helen another glance, and quite possibly a smirk too.

The room began to chatter. This was big news. Madeline allowed the mutterings to continue for a moment, letting the tension build. Helen spun her Cartier watch around her wrist, the way she always did when she sensed something terrible was about to happen.

'So, on Christmas Day, when we will introduce our show's new star – I'll tell you who we've chosen in a moment – her first act on screen will be to end the life of one of our most loved characters.'

The murmurs in the room got louder and Jake grinned like an excited teenager on Bonfire Night who'd been chosen to throw the guy into the flames.

'Killing one of our most central characters will not only secure our new bad girl a place in soap history, it will breathe life into the future of *Falcon Bay*, a place where anything can and will happen.' Madeline took a long pause, savouring the drama. 'So for our fortieth anniversary special we will be saying goodbye to Lucy Dean.'

A series of gasps echoed round the room.

Helen snapped her watchstrap as the words sank in. *After*

forty years of loyal service, she thought, *they're going to kill the show's most popular actress. Live and on Christmas Day.* It was unthinkable; cold-hearted but horribly genius.

And it would break Catherine's heart.

After the room settled down, Jake said with a wide smile, 'So your job now is to work out how our new star kills Lucy Dean.'

'I've been through the archives,' Madeline said. 'The new bitch will be playing *another* of Lucy's children that she abandoned as a teenager. Tanya, her missing daughter, is in Lucy's backstory and gives you the perfect dynamic to work from. Most importantly, I want a stunt that has never been seen on TV. I want cinematic quality, so don't talk to me about car crashes – or fires. I want something that's exclusively *Falcon Bay*. Something that could never happen anywhere else, something epic.'

Helen knew it was a risk to raise her head above the parapet when she was very much fair game. But she'd been quiet for too long in her capacity as casting director and thought she should at least pose the question that the room – and since last night, millions around the world – must now be wondering. 'So, which of the actresses is looking like the favourite? Because if they're going to write for her, the writers will need to know.'

Candy took her chance to chip in. 'The Twitter polls have Lydia Chambers way ahead of the others,' she said perkily.

Helen smiled. At least that was one positive in this terrible mess. She would call Sheena right away.

Madeline shook her head. 'Honey Hunter is our new star,' she said, in a tone that made it clear the decision had been made, no matter how the viewers voted. 'Signing an Oscar winner to be *Falcon Bay*'s new leading lady is great for our US distribution. Plus, being English, she's great for Europe too – it's a double whammy.'

Candy flushed and began stammering out her objections. Very unusually for someone who worked in TV, she hated dishonesty just as much as she hated swearing. 'But the audience have voted for Lyd—'

Before she could finish, Madeline flashed her perfect teeth into a smile and cut in. 'That's just the Twitter polls,' she said with a lilt to her voice. The whole room knew she was lying, but no one dared correct her. 'The overall vote is already in Honey's direction and although it was a good idea to have the vote stay open for a month, to milk the publicity, after last night we simply don't need it. So while I agree Lydia Chambers was on top form last night, we've already offered the part to Honey, and she has accepted.'

Everyone in the room looked at Helen, who as head of casting was clearly being humiliated by this public revelation. In return, desperate not to look defeated, Helen threw on a smile and tried to score some respect back.

'I'm so glad I was able to give you such a fabulous shortlist to choose from,' was all she could manage before bending down to pick up her watch from the floor.

Madeline ignored her comment and made to leave, with Jake following her. As she reached the door she turned back.

'I want to see storyline reasons for why and how the bitch kills Lucy Dean sent to Jake by the end of the day.'

35

Neither Farrah nor Amanda had wanted to go to A&E, but C.I.TV's insurance team were insistent. They'd both received minor cuts and grazes when the crowd had surged past them as people tried to escape the fireworks, knocking the two of them onto the rough wooden decking just as they had begun their row.

St George's was a tiny hospital about three miles from the set. Upon their arrival, Matron Jones had insisted that they both stay overnight, for fear of delayed concussion. She also placed them in the same tiny ward, in adjacent beds.

Amanda decided to finally break the silence that had consumed them since they'd got there. One of them was going to have to be the bigger person and she decided it might as well be her.

'Quite a night,' she said.

'I'd say it's up there,' Farrah replied.

'I should have told you about Aiden—' Amanda started.

'Christ, Amanda – too bloody right you should have told me! You should have stuck up for me in the first place –

fought my corner. How long have we been friends?' Amanda tried to interject, but Farrah wasn't having it. 'Of all people, you know how hard I've worked to get this far. How fucking impossible it is to break into that bloody inner circle. You loved that two-hander of mine – everyone did. I would have been a brilliant director on the Christmas live – you know it. Everyone knows it. But oh no, Aiden bloody Anderson not only gets to keep his bloody job – but *also* that episode. Shit!'

She was quivering with rage now, unable to continue as tears of frustration streamed down her face.

Amanda nodded, swallowing repeatedly at the sight of her friend so upset. She took a deep breath and plunged in. 'I know all that, Farrah. And I'm truly sorry that it was you Aiden was up against. But I'm not sorry we gave him a second chance. It wasn't personal. I only ever think about what's best for the show and I believed what I was doing reflected best on the network.'

She sighed and shook her head.

'But after Catherine told me she'd seen him taking drugs on the set last night, I've realized I made a bad judgement call. Even though I did it with the best intentions. I should have come to you and explained my position. For that, I'm truly sorry.'

Farrah couldn't bring herself to look her friend in the eye. But she could hear the sincerity in her voice. And she was in no position to take the moral high ground after what had happened with Jake. So she just nodded and continued picking at a hole in the hospital blanket.

Amanda took that as acceptance, and they both fell silent again, but Farrah knew what was coming.

'I just hope you didn't shag Jake as a thank you.'

Farrah glanced up at that, and Amanda held her stare. Unflinching.

But Farrah couldn't sustain it. She was too ashamed. She felt a deep sense of failure, of having let her friend down. 'It wasn't to say thank you,' she said quietly. If there was one thing she needed to make clear, it was that. 'I don't even know why it happened. I was just so excited to get the live ep—'

'So excited your knickers fell off?' Amanda snipped.

Farrah glanced round at the patients in the other beds. In such a tiny space, they had no option but to listen in. 'I'm sorry,' she said. 'I can't even explain why I did it. You know how much I hate him! I swear it was just one time, the biggest mistake I've ever made, and it was over in minutes.'

'Nothing new there,' Amanda said.

Farrah noted the lighter tone. 'Even at the time, I knew I'd massively fucked up.' She reached for her friend's hand. 'I don't know what else to say other than I am truly, truly sorry.'

Amanda knew Farrah well enough to know this was a genuine, heartfelt apology. She decided to accept it. She took Farrah's hand in return. 'It's lucky for you that a few days ago I decided to leave him.'

'For real?'

'Yes. We're done – so I guess if we look back at the dates, we can sort of pretend it happened after I'd ended it.'

Farrah sighed. 'Thank you.'

'I haven't told *him* yet though – so keep it to yourself,' Amanda continued. 'I need to sort my finances out first. You know what a tricky bastard he is. Even though he clearly couldn't care less about me or Olivia, the moment the great Jake is abandoned, he'll be hiding every penny and making my life hell at work, so I want to be prepared. And Dan's been so good to me – he's reminded me what life could be like.'

'So, things *are* moving in that direction then.' Farrah smiled. The women had suspected something, but with everything that had been going on at the *Bay*, there'd been no time for a girls' night out, which would have been the best time to bring it up.

Amanda suddenly dropped her tone and spoke more quietly, trying to keep it private. 'Oh, Farrah, he's so special. The other day....' she began, but before she could go into details, the ward door opened and Dr Grant came in.

'Good morning, ladies,' he said, facing their beds but keeping his eyes on the medical file he was reading.

'Everything okay?' Amanda asked, causing him to look up.

'Yes, you're good to go. Absolutely nothing to worry about.'

'Brilliant,' said Farrah, and both women began to get off their beds and gather their belongings.

'I saw you ladies on TV,' Dr Grant said with a smile. 'Looked like quite a party.'

Farrah and Amanda were both too embarrassed to reply, so they just grabbed their bags and followed him to the door.

As they passed him, Dr Grant leaned in towards Farrah and dropped his voice.

'Hate to be a killjoy,' he said, deadpan, 'but alcohol isn't great for the baby.'

36

All Stacey wanted as she entered the grand foyer of the Langham was to make her way to Sheena's discreet corner booth without anyone recognizing her. But despite her Valentino hat-and-scarf combo, as soon as she'd got past the maître d', multiple sets of eyes turned in her direction. Luckily, because the Langham crowd were A-list, they were too posh to admit they'd tuned in to last week's Bitch Party and actually make any comments to her. Nevertheless, Stacey could feel their gaze following her through the room.

After what felt like ten miles, Stacey finally reached Sheena's table. Lydia was already there, dressed in a killer pink Escada trouser suit that, unlike Stacey's outfit, was intended to gain attention.

Lydia air-kissed her as she sat down.

'How are you feeling after, well, you know…' Lydia said, grimacing as she mimed Stacey falling off the boardwalk.

Sheena reached out and patted Stacey's hand. 'Thanks for coming,' she said in a comforting tone that Stacey found as insulting as Lydia's mime. 'I know things didn't go exactly as planned,' she continued, pulling the bottle of Cristal from the ice bucket and filling the glasses placed out for them, 'but I want you to know how proud I am – of you both.' She lifted her glass and proposed a toast.

But Lydia, not pleased to have had her successful appearance at the Bitch Party lumped in with Stacey's epic fail, did not raise hers. 'Cut straight to the chase, Sheena, and then let's toast the winner,' she said with a grin. 'We're both big girls.' Lydia touched Stacey's arm with obvious sympathy, absolutely certain the gig was hers. 'So, which one of us got it?' she asked, picking up her glass in anticipation.

Sheena looked at them both, then drank from her glass as they waited.

Stacey might have been beneath a hat that was half covering her eyes, and full of Xanax, but she suddenly knew. 'They don't want either of us, do they?' she said.

Lydia eyeballed Sheena, urging her to speak. This was business and Sheena needed to get on with it, however awkward for Stacey.

For a couple of seconds the only sounds in the room were of fine silver knives clinking against bone-china plates. Finally, the famous Langham bubble of calm was popped by an expletive from Lydia.

'What the actual fuck?' she exclaimed. 'Apart from the fact that I absolutely killed it on the night, and I know I'm ahead in the polls, you said it was practically guaranteed that one of us would be cast.'

'It was,' Sheena said. 'You girls were ahead in the polls all the way. But Madeline used her control of the network to override everything—'

'So who got it then? Lydia shouted, her face reddening with rage.

Diners on nearby tables turned to look.

'Honey Hunter,' Sheena said quietly.

'So much for us having a month to campaign and keep the audience fucking voting!' Lydia spat.

'Yes,' Stacey chipped in. 'This is immoral.'

'It is – but sadly, that's TV,' Sheena said, filling her glass again. She'd known this meeting was going to be bad, but she'd need to drink a whole bottle at this rate, and she usually rationed herself to two glasses in public. 'Look, I know it's a horrible disappointment, and I made you that promise in good faith,' she continued, reaching for her notebook, 'but on the upside, the exposure has been amazing for both of you.'

Both women looked at her as she flicked the pages open.

'Lydia, I've got you an amazing deal with a fashion house.'

Lydia looked hopeful.

'It's a catalogue company for a fifty-plus style guide, but the money is unbelievable. And, Stacey, every sketch show in the world wants you to guest appear.'

Lydia was incandescent. 'Are you for fucking real? Trying to palm us off with this shit after we've been used and thrown away like a couple of castoffs,' she hissed, aware people were watching and possibly even recording her, as they had tried to do last time. The last thing she wanted was Honey Hunter knowing how badly she was taking this.

Sheena tried to push through. 'If you just trust me, I'll milk the Bitch Party for more money for each of you than you would have earned on *Falcon Bay*.' She waved her book in the air, exasperated. 'I've got a schedule in here that will keep you both busy for at least two years, and that's just the start…'

Stacey might have completely screwed up her appearance at the Bitch Party, but Lydia had stolen the show, and Sheena still felt terribly guilty that she'd not been able to honour the promise she'd made that the best one would win. It was horrible seeing their dreams shattering right before their eyes. And all thanks to that Yankee bitch Madeline Kane. What was Madeline playing at, Sheena wondered for the hundredth time. She really didn't understand her behaviour; she'd never known a network controller like this, and she'd known them all.

'So that's it,' said Lydia bitterly.

'Sadly, for *Falcon Bay,* yes,' confirmed Sheena. 'The decision has been made, but I can still use all the publicity to rebuild your careers.'

'A career made of guest appearances as the butt of people's jokes? No thanks,' said Stacey.

'And you can keep your fucking over-fifties catalogue,' said Lydia, slumping back in her cushioned chair. Reality was settling in. 'I told you that day I called you from that shitty presenter audition that I only want to act.'

'Me too.' Stacey shuffled her seat closer to Lydia, so now it was clearly two against one.

This wasn't the way Sheena had intended the meeting to go. She didn't like where it was heading.

'Girls, girls… I get it,' she said in her best negotiator's voice. 'You're understandably upset. Let's take some time out, sit with the news.' She signalled for the waiter to bring the bill. She needed to get out of there before things escalated any further. 'We'll regroup in a few days.'

But they weren't listening. They were talking to each other, and so quietly, Sheena couldn't quite catch what they were saying. She leaned closer and they both turned back to her.

Lydia took charge, her eyes flashing like ice-cold emeralds. 'I think we're done here,' she said.

'What do you mean?' asked Sheena, her voice suddenly tiny.

Stacey's eyes weren't cold or bitter, but they were as determined as Lydia's. 'Sheena, you've been good to us over the years and we thank you for that, but we won't be needing you any more.'

Something truly awful was happening here. Sheena had come in with some bad news, that was for sure. But she'd delivered worse in the past. She'd spent the last twenty-four hours filling their diaries, scheduling every type of compensation she could arrange. *Falcon Bay* might have turned them down, but she, Sheena McQueen, had come good for them. Anger rose in her throat.

'Now hang on a minute. I think you—'

She never got to finish her sentence. Lydia and Stacey stood up in unison, grabbed their things and began heading for the exit. After just a few steps, Lydia turned back and said as loud as she could, to ensure the whole room heard her, 'And just in case there was any doubt – you're fired.'

37

Inside one of the world's most famous department stores, Harrods, in London's uber-exclusive Knightsbridge, Mickey Taylor was watching the queue. It stretched all the way around the building and down three flights of stairs – far longer than any book-signing queue he could remember. Every person was a 'ker-ching' sound that went off at the imaginary cash register in his head and Mickey couldn't get the smile off his face

Honey Hunter's memoir was now a number one bestseller, having sold more than a million books on pre-order. When he'd first pitched it to the bookshops, most of them had been sniffy, agreeing to stock only a small order. But now Honey's face was plastered across every window of every bookstore he passed.

Thanks to her appointment as *Falcon Bay*'s new leading lady following her sensational appearance at the Bitch Party, and the serial deal with the *Herald* courtesy of Ross Owen, Honey's life secrets had been splattered over the tabloids day after day and picked up internationally. It had made her a global A-lister once more. And all because of some canny game-playing by himself. Mickey allowed that thought to wash through him. His old dad would have been proud; once again, he'd turned a battered old banger back into a Porsche.

From behind the signing table she'd been at for hours, Honey looked out at the line in front of her and, just like Mickey, she couldn't stop smiling. Was she dreaming? An acting role from the heavens, number one in the charts, and, with every signature she made, yet more fans telling her they'd voted for her to win the bitch contest. She truly felt loved.

It had actually been quite fun to see the juiciest episodes from her past splashed all over the tabloids. Big chunks of her story felt like someone else's life: so much of the detail had been lost in the alcoholic haze that had engulfed her through her twenties and early thirties. A whole chapter had been dedicated to the time when, at thirty-five, with three failed marriages behind her, she'd been hired as 'the good wife' in one of America's most popular dramas, where she'd surprised everyone, even herself, by being really, really good. The critics had loved her – until, once again, she'd been caught in the wrong sort of headlines after she started an affair with a pregnant co-star's husband.

Looking at the photos of the man now, dredged up again in the national papers to sell her book, she couldn't imagine what she'd seen in him. But that was then – different time, different Honey. She'd even picked up a best newcomer award for her stint in that role, which was rather ironic, considering she'd been acting for twenty years. But that couldn't save her as the bad publicity meant the producers didn't renew her contract.

Desperate to claw back some good press, she'd posed naked for the cover of *Playboy*. Honey still loved that shot. It was one of her finest. It had been for the Christmas issue, which was always the biggest seller of the year, no doubt because husbands were stuck at home with the family, so they probably all had a copy hidden away to de-stress with on the quiet. The photos inside, even if she thought so herself, were stunning. First she was skiing naked across the Swiss Alps; then they'd had her rolling in the snow with an open fur coat and sixty-carat emerald earrings, the cold of the ice making her nipples look like lipsticks. For the cover, she'd been gift-wrapped in a huge red ribbon, the edges of the bow just grazing her breasts. Hugh Hefner had liked it so much, he'd hung a framed version in his office.

In the late nineties, *Playboy* was still a huge gig, and the half-a-million-dollar fee had got her some good investments and her place in Switzerland. It had been one of her best moments. Until now.

She was just signing a copy of her book for a geeky girl with glasses, who had a barely pronounceable let alone writable name, when Mickey came up with a paparazzo. A waiter was following close behind them, carrying a bottle of champagne and two glasses.

'Darling, just a quick pic toasting your success,' Mickey said, gesturing for the waiter to pour her a glass and hand it to her. 'And make sure you take wide shots, getting all the queue in,' he said as the photographer snapped away.

'Mickey, you know I don't drink,' Honey said, glaring at the glass.

'Just hold it to your lips for the picture,' he said. 'It's a celebration – we've got to have a bit of bubbly in the shot. And besides, one won't hurt you.'

As she lifted the champagne flute and posed for the pictures, she could feel the bubbles popping under her nose, smell the aroma. Oh, it smelled so good – she wanted to taste it so badly.

Still posing, this time with the geeky girl in the shot, her mind raced. Her inner self, her good side, the one who'd kept her sober all these years, told her not to let it pass her lips. But, she reasoned, if ever she was due one drink – just one – then this was that time. She raised the glass to her mouth and drank it down in one go, then immediately gestured to the waiter to pour her another.

38

Through his office window, Jake was watching Catherine filming a full-on row as Lucy Dean opposite Jude Roscoe's character on the beach bar set. Seeing her flounce around the set in her floaty dress, he had to admit she wasn't bad-looking for an old broad.

For a fleeting moment he had what he assumed was a pang of guilt. Not because she was being fired – she'd had a good run and at seventy her time was definitely up – but because it had already been a couple of weeks since Madeline had demanded they kill off Lucy Dean and he knew that Catherine still hadn't been officially told. He was meant to do it. Helen refused to even tell Catherine's agent, which he considered totally unprofessional. For days now, he'd intended to go down to Catherine's dressing room and tell her, but he still hadn't got around to it.

From her seat in the production office, Amanda caught sight of Jake in his office window and a wave of agitation flowed through her. She didn't even have to be in the same room to be irritated by him these days. She let the dappling sun blind her momentarily so she didn't have to look at the man she used to live with. He still hadn't noticed, but five days earlier she'd taken some of her things, and Olivia, and moved into one of the beach houses. They'd been in separate rooms for months anyway, and Olivia had been in with her, plus Jake often slept in his office (or so he claimed). Him not even registering her absence had actually worked out quite well, giving her a head start on squirrelling away money from their joint account for her new life.

Suddenly she was aware of Jake's presence at her desk.

'I'm off to see Honey Hunter,' he said.

'And you are telling me why?' she replied without looking up.

'While I'm away, tell Catherine we're terminating her contract.'

He said it so casually, as if he was asking her to feed the cat, that it took Amanda several seconds to fully understand what he meant. He was halfway to the door when she found her voice.

'You're not seriously expecting *me* to do it?'

Crew members on other desks were now watching what was clearly another War of the Roses brewing.

'What's not serious about me asking you to do your job?' he said, raising his voice.

An incensed Amanda stood up to face him. 'She's my friend,' she said. 'Which might not mean anything to you – but it does to me.' This was truly the last straw. 'I'm not like you, Jake.'

She was quivering with fury now as the full horror of what was about to be done to Catherine sank in. She squeezed the headrest of her chair to stop herself from thumping him. 'Talking, respectfully, to Catherine is *your* job, Jake. *If* you're the big boss here, the one Madeline bloody Kane thinks has the quality to lead us mere minions into the future—' She gestured wildly at the room, her voice at full volume, and rows of mesmerized faces hurriedly turned away from her, like skittles falling in a bowling alley, 'then why are you asking me once again to do your dirty work?'

Before Jake could reply, she was in full flow again.

'Are you afraid Catherine will fight back? Is that it, *Mr Boss Man*?'

She was close enough to Jake to slap him now, but somehow she restrained herself.

'After all the years Catherine has served at *Falcon Bay*, you have the gall, the affront, the sheer bloody arrogance to not only accept Madeline's ridiculous decision to axe her, but to then ask someone else to tell her that her forty years of service to the show is now at an end – when I know for a fact Madeline told you to do it.'

Jake, who so far had not reacted to what he considered to be his wife's emotional meltdown, did look surprised to learn that Amanda had perhaps spoken to Madeline behind his back.

Amanda took a breath. Tears were spiralling down her cheeks. She'd reached the point of no return now and was no longer in control of what she was saying. Her truth pot was finally spilling over.

'Thanks to you and *her*, *Falcon Bay* is no longer recognizable as the show I've worked my guts out for. The show I have loved. The show I used to feel privileged to work on.

The two of you are ruining it. And I really don't understand why.'

She gulped down a sob and Jake grabbed his moment.

'Stop being so dramatic. It's *because* you and Catherine are *such* good friends,' he said acidly, 'and that you obviously care *so* much about her' – he flicked his hand dismissively at her tear-stained face and heaving chest – 'that it will clearly be so much *kinder* for her, coming from you.' He looked around the room to make sure everyone had heard him, and then added, 'I thought that would be obvious,' just for good measure.

'That is bullshit! I won't do it,' Amanda shouted.

Jake flinched and jerked his head to look her full in the face. This was unexpected and embarrassing. No way could he let her get away with this in front of the whole team. Candy, who was hovering nearby, looked like she might faint at Amanda's loud use of the B-word.

'You will do as you're told, or you can clear your desk,' he barked.

Everybody in the room held their breath. Including Jake.

There was a long pause as Amanda and Jake stood eye-balling each other.

Amanda's heart was thumping wildly and her mind was racing with what she was about to say, but she suddenly felt totally calm. This decision was absolutely the right one. *Falcon Bay* had been her life, but not any more. She was done.

'Fine,' she said, throwing her laptop into her bag and grabbing some pictures in frames.

'I officially quit,' she said. 'I quit you. And I quit this show.

So do your own dirty work. 'It'll be a lot quicker leaving here than when I packed my bags and left our home.'

'What?' Jake stammered.

'I moved out on Monday with Olivia and – surprise, surprise! – it's been nearly a week and you haven't even noticed!' She managed a wry laugh.

Jake was, for once, stunned into silence.

As she pushed her chair in and threw her drawer keys on the desk, she leaned in to him once more. 'And whilst it's doubtful you'll be worried about losing access to Oliva, maybe you can fill the void with Farrah's blueberry.'

'Farrah…?' Jake asked, now totally confused

'Yes, there's another kid on the way for you to ignore too.'

Jake was paralyzed with too much information. He looked like he might explode. Those nearest to him widened the exclusion zone as Candy steadied herself on a desk.

'You'll be hearing from my solicitor on Monday. I want a divorce.'

With that, Amanda pushed past him, walking out on the man she didn't love and the TV show she did.

39

In the studio gantry, high above the internal set of The Cove, Farrah and Helen were observing Catherine and Jude film the reverse scene from the one Jake had been watching from his room before all hell broke loose with Amanda. Crew busied around as Catherine had her windswept hair restyled.

A text pinged on Helen's mobile. It was from Amanda.

> Can't speak now but needed to warn you – I've quit and left the building. Someone has to tell Catherine what's happening to her character before she hears the gossip from the bust-up – which was about her exit BTW. I will ring soon, but please get to her before someone else does. Amanda xxx

'Fuck,' said Helen, reading it, then showing it to Farrah.

Farrah's phone pinged with a message also from Amanda. She and Helen read it together.

> SO sorry, I blew up at Jake in the production office (I've quit – but I'll tell you about that later) and just wanted to warn you (and apologize) that I told him about the baby (sorry, sorry, sorry). It wasn't on purpose – just happened. Will call you later. Amanda xxx

Neither of them spoke for a moment, taking in these two bombshells.

'Is it true?' Helen said gently.

'I wish she hadn't told him. I've already dealt with it,' Farrah said flatly. 'I know that sounds harsh, but there was no way I was going to be linked to him forever for a minute and a half's mistake.'

Helen nodded. There was no judgement in her expression.

'I can't believe she's gone,' Farrah said.

'I'm proud of her,' Helen replied. 'She deserves so much better than the way Jake and Madeline treated her. And while I've no idea what possessed you to let that monster give you one, and I don't even want the details' – Farrah's eyes flashed in horror at the thought of having to recall the event – 'if it helped Amanda finally cut her ties with that prick, then you've done her a favour.'

They both returned their gaze to Catherine, who was now set up to film a new scene opposite Lucien Horsefall.

'Right, on that bombshell, we'd better get to Catherine, quick,' Farrah said. She shook her head despondently. Things were suddenly looking very different for *Falcon Bay*.

'I had a feeling this would be coming to a head today,'

Helen said. 'Tomorrow they'll be rebuilding the set and she'd have started asking questions. It really was Jake's job, as head executive, to tell her, you know.' She grimaced, feeling like she needed to explain why she hadn't forewarned Catherine herself. 'But when I saw her still blissfully unaware this morning, I messaged Sheena to come down to the set today.'

She got her phone out and started making a call. 'Sheena, how far away are you? Oh, you're already here? Perfect, go straight to set and I'll meet you there. You need to hear this face to face.'

Farrah kept her eyes on Catherine, knowing her whole world was about to collapse.

In her office in the *Falcon Bay* studios, Madeline's door was locked. She and Chad were making love on the large sofa that took up the entirety of one wall. They were in the spoons position and Chad was without doubt the big spoon in every way. With each thrust he kissed her neck as she groaned with pleasure.

'I've missed you so much,' he said, flipping her over so she was now on top of him and pulling her into a deep kiss which sent shivers down her spine. As he re-entered her, he used one hand to push her hips down on him and the other to gently and rhythmically stroke her clit with his thumb.

Madeline let out a moan as she climaxed just moments later. Watching his wife orgasm brought Chad to his own and he pumped what felt like electricity into her. They embraced tightly, both glowing with sweat, skin to skin.

Madeline buried her face in his thick neck and breathed in

his manly scent. 'I love you,' she said as she kissed him once again. 'I'll never be able to show you just how much.'

'And I love you,' he replied, then pulled her in so tightly, their bodies felt moulded into one. 'Oh, I think you showed me in your little present, my darlin',' he whispered. 'That was one hot gift,' he breathed, and hugged her tightly once more. 'Kept me entertained through many a lonesome night.'

He lifted her up like she weighed nothing, and proceeded to take her once more.

Minutes after being filled in by Helen, Sheena McQueen flung open the red double doors of the internal studio set and pushed aside the production assistant who was desperately pointing at the red 'Recording' light. She was too furious to give a damn about studio etiquette.

Dressed in black leather and a pair of YSL boots, she stormed past Aiden, into the Lucy Dean set and right up to Catherine.

'What the fuck?' shouted Aiden, who was directing. 'Cut!'

'Sheena, what are you doing?' Catherine gasped, horrified at her unprofessionalism.

'I want you off this set now!' Sheena said, linking her arm with Catherine's and guiding her towards the exit.

Aiden was off his seat and now making his way towards them. 'Would someone like to tell me what the hell is happening?' he bellowed.

Catherine turned to her agent, stunned. 'What's going on?'

Sheena gave Aiden a look that suggested if he came any

closer, he'd be feeling the spiked heels of her YSLs somewhere very unpleasant and held a hand up.

'My client is downing tools. Not one more line of *Falcon Bay*'s dialogue will be filmed with her until we've sat down with Madeline Kane.' She continued half dragging Catherine through the packed studio.

Jude Roscoe chased after them and stood in their way, blocking their exit. 'You okay, Cat?' he said, trying to look as rugged and heroic as possible. He knew Sheena McQueen was the best agent in the business – he'd tried to get a meeting with her several times but had never even got a reply – so he was seizing his opportunity and attempting to catch her attention.

Sheena was forced to stop.

Catherine took the moment to speak. 'Sheena, what is going on?' she said, now visibly pale, the worry loud in her voice.

'I'll tell you in the corridor,' Sheena replied, trying to push past Jude.

Catherine didn't move. 'No, tell me now,' she said firmly.

Jude smiled at Sheena, but she scowled and then turned to Catherine.

'Did you not wonder how this talentless idiot got un-sacked?' she said, pointing at Jude.

He was about to defend himself against the claim of being talentless, but seeing the fury in Sheena's eyes, thought better of it and stepped out of their way.

Sheena continued marching Catherine towards the door. 'Apparently it's been decided that his character's exit on Christmas Day won't be dramatic enough. So they've chosen somebody bigger, somebody who's been here longer.'

The blood drained from Catherine's face. She clutched at Sheena's arm as they emerged into the corridor and headed for the lifts.

'And not only have they not had the balls to tell me so that I could tell you,' Sheena said, 'but everyone around here already knows. Let's go.' She punched the lift button.

Catherine's chest was rising and falling at a frighteningly rapid rate. She began to gasp. Sheena saw what was coming and put an arm around her as the lift lurched upwards.

Before they reached Madeline's floor, Catherine began to sob. Her body shook and then she let out what Sheena could only describe as the sort of primal scream an injured animal might make when caught in a poacher's trap.

Sheena pulled her close and held her tight. 'It's going to be okay. I've got your back and we're gonna make the bastards pay,' she said as the lift doors pinged open opposite Madeline Kane's office.

As he made his way to Honey Hunter's penthouse suite at the Savoy in central London, Jake tried to let go of the stress of the past few hours. Though he liked to think of himself as being fully Teflon coated, discovering that he'd got Farrah pregnant at the same time as finding out his wife and baby had left him felt like an episode of *Falcon Bay*.

Amanda making her announcement in front of the whole office had hurt his pride, but, if he was being completely truthful, he'd never really bonded with Olivia. Though he hated to admit it, Amanda had been right about his own childhood having an effect. He'd been scared of his dad as a boy and had no idea how a loving, normal father should behave, so when Farrah texted him saying she'd already aborted his baby, he was actually relieved.

Shaking his head as if to try and get all the madness of the day out of his brain, he pressed the bell to Honey's suite.

He wanted to make a good impression on their new star and as she wouldn't be aware of the shitshow of a day he'd had, he intended to get back in the celebratory mood. After all, this was a big moment for both of them.

There was about a minute's wait and then the door opened. A visibly tipsy Honey appeared, barely clad in a sheer black silk gown that was loosely tied around her waist, exposing her generous cleavage. She threw her arms out to embrace him.

'Hello, boss man!' She giggled and pulled him into her.

He could feel her breasts against his chest. He thought she'd let go any moment, but instead she held on and breathed into his neck. He was surprised to smell the alcohol on her – according to the tabloids, which she was in daily, she was 'many years sober'.

'I'm so thankful you chose me out of all those girls,' she slurred, her lips catching his ear. She stepped backwards into the room and faced him. 'In fact, let me show you just how grateful I am.'

She wobbled and dropped the robe to reveal her buxom body, which was now totally naked apart from her high-heeled gold stilettos.

Jake paused for a second. He never fucked the talent. Execs and staff, yes, but never the stars. Until now. As he stood looking at her, Honey ran her hands over her perfect breasts and gave her nipples a tweak. And with that he closed the door and let her rip off his clothes.

Without bothering to knock, Sheena angrily pressed the handle on Madeline Kane's office door. It was locked. She could hear music playing from inside, so she rapped her knuckles hard on the door, the rings on her fingers making the sound echo around the long corridor.

Inside, Madeline and Chad were lying on the sofa naked and sated, holding hands and gazing out at the sea.

'Ignore it. They'll go away,' Madeline whispered, not wanting to disturb this moment of paradise with her husband. 'There's nothing that can be more important than us being together right now.'

Chad smiled, then gently shook his head. 'That's so sweet of you, darlin', but it does sound very urgent…' He sat up and reached for his clothes.

Madeline kissed him affectionately, sighed, and began searching for her bra.

She was in no hurry to answer the door, but as the knocking got louder and louder, she smoothed down her dress, checked her hair and prepared herself.

As soon as Sheena heard the lock turn, she pushed down on the handle and flung the door wide. Madeline would have been hit by it if she hadn't jumped out of the way. Chad rushed over to stand by her side, his shirt still only partially buttoned.

'What the hell do you think you're doing?' Madeline roared.

Sheena pushed past, almost dragging a broken Catherine

Belle behind her. 'What the hell do you think *you're* doing is the question,' she spat as she settled Catherine on the sofa where, minutes earlier, the Kanes had been enjoying a perfect moment of marital bliss. She pivoted round to face Madeline and Chad.

Chad stepped forward. 'Don't speak to my wife like that,' he started, but Madeline placed a hand on his rippling bicep to stop him.

'It's fine, darling. I know what this is about and I can handle it.' She flashed him an appreciative smile. 'Why don't you head out to the dock and I'll join you for dinner once I've got this cleared up.'

'Are you sure?' he said, looking like he didn't want to leave her. Then he turned to eyeball Sheena, who met his stare with an arcing of her left eyebrow. She'd not missed the fact that he'd clearly got dressed in a hurry.

'I'm sure.' Madeline purred like a kitten – saving her inner cat for Sheena.

Grabbing his jacket and phone, he glanced over at Catherine, who was staring out at the sea. 'Ms Belle,' he said respectfully. He shot Sheena another warning look and left the room.

Perspiration misted her Botoxed brow as Sheena began to let rip.

'Four decades, this woman has given to this show,' she said, pointing to Catherine, who was looking away from them, hoping that at any moment she'd wake up and find this was all a terrible nightmare.

'Technically it's thirty-nine years, but do go on,' Madeline said with a smirk, which enraged Sheena further.

'In *nearly* forty years, she's never once been late, ill-prepared or unprofessional. She's given her all to this show and helped make it the success it is.'

'Was,' Madeline corrected, as she made her way over to her desk and took a seat. 'Yes, it's true, your client has been an audience draw in this show's history, but those days are over. Ms Belle can take no credit for our recent upswing. That, you'll find, is down to me alone.'

Sheena stepped closer, undeterred. 'When she miscarried her baby five months into her pregnancy, she turned up for work the next day so as not to disrupt *Falcon Bay*'s shooting schedule. She buried her parents within months of each other and yet never took time off to grieve. She's been putting this show first in her life for decades and never once has she complained.'

Madeline cut in again. 'Well, there was that one time, concerning a co-star she wanted to be rid of,' she said, tripping up Sheena for the second time.

Catherine, who'd started to listen as Sheena had been describing her, turned around. 'That's twisting what I told you. I did that to help Calvin Butler.'

Madeleine rolled her eyes. 'Tomayto, tomahto,' she said with a giggle.

The mention of Calvin's name threw Sheena. Decades-old memories flooded into her mind the way the coke she used to snort had once rushed to her brain. Ed Nichols escorting her and Calvin to his bedroom filled with naked older men and locking the door. So many memories…

'I'd say *demanding* a cast member get sacked is rather at odds with this angelic picture you're trying to paint, Sheena,'

Madeline said coolly, gazing out of the window at a wild horse galloping along the clifftops.

With Sheena temporarily struck wordless by Madeline's crass raking up of the past, Catherine began to find her voice. She stood up and came over to stand with Sheena.

'Stop trying to misinterpret my intentions,' Catherine said quietly. 'I told you about that in good faith.' She shook her head wearily. 'I don't understand this decision to axe me when my character *leads* this show. There are so many others that don't have my history with the audience? Why does it have to be her? Lucy Dean is the heart of *Falcon Bay*.'

'And all hearts cease to beat eventually, Catherine. Fact or fiction, it's the way of the world,' said Madeline icily as she looked over. 'And while the network *is* grateful for your long service, this decision is right for our show. As we all know, no matter how popular a character *used* to be, the show is the star. So if you've said your piece' – she smiled – 'my husband is waiting for me.'

Sheena and Catherine looked at each other, both shocked at Madeline's coldness.

But Sheena, who'd faced down many powerful people over the years, wasn't done yet.

'If *Falcon Bay* were truly grateful,' she said, 'one of you would have told Catherine in person. Not even I, her agent, had an official phone call, which is not only beyond unprofessional, it's actually a breach of her contract.'

Madeline leaned towards Catherine. 'For that, on behalf of C.I.TV, I would like to formally apologize,' she said with what sounded like sincerity. 'Until you *barged* in here, I had no idea you hadn't been informed. I instructed Jake to tell you personally – *weeks ago*,' she said, casting an eye towards Sheena, 'so please be assured that I will be taking that up with him.'

'Putting how I found out aside,' Catherine said, desperately trying to find a way to salvage the situation, 'can you at least tell me why I was chosen to go?'

'Because your death will matter,' Madeline said, holding her stare.

Catherine's legs wobbled and she grabbed at the back of the sofa to steady herself.

'You're *killing* Lucy Dean?' she stuttered, her voice thick with emotion.

Catherine's one safety net had now been dramatically cut. She'd been trying to convince herself that it probably wouldn't be long before the network was sold yet again, and then the new owner would bring her character back, as was so often the way in soap. But if Lucy Dean was now being killed, then this truly was the end of the line.

Madeline reached over to take a sip of water then nudged a box of tissues in Catherine's direction. 'Your reaction just then to the news of Lucy Dean's demise is just a ripple in the sea compared to how deeply our global audience will be affected. A hundred million viewers' hearts will break like yours did just then, which is absolute proof we've made the right decision. As painful as it is for you, no other character's death would give us the ratings we need. It's the right choice for *Falcon Bay*, and even you, Sheena, must understand that the show has to come first.'

Neither Sheena nor Catherine responded.

'Look…' Madeline leaned across the desk and surprised

Catherine by taking her hand. 'As a viewer of this show, I feel like Lucy Dean is my family. And as we all know, *that's* the sign of a great soap. People will grieve for you just as they do when somebody they've known all their life dies. The viewers having these feelings is exactly what a successful show hinges on: our audience's investment and their need to keep tuning in.'

Catherine couldn't help it: a tiny tear had come to her eye. Madeline's impassioned speech had moved her, but above all she was truly devastated that Lucy Dean, a character in whom she was so deeply invested, into whom she'd actually put so much of herself, was about to reach the end of the line.

'I understand,' she said, then turned to Sheena and nodded, giving her old friend and agent her blessing.

'Well then,' Sheena said, 'it's been *terribly* handled, but now we've heard your reasons, there won't be any stand-offs. Catherine will be what she's always been: a consummate pro. She'll give you everything she's got.'

'Thank you,' said Madeline. 'And when on Christmas Day we get the largest viewer numbers ever recorded, I guarantee your death will go down in television history.'

'How will Lucy die?' asked Catherine.

'Now that, I can't share with you yet, as we're still working on the finer details, but it will be an exit worthy of the woman you are. Audiences all over the world will never forget your last episode of *Falcon Bay*. I pinky promise.'

As Madeline raised her little finger to demonstrate the point, dark and jumbled-up memories began to flash in Sheena's brain.

40

Jake and a sleeping, quite possibly passed-out Honey Hunter were being chauffeur-driven from her London hotel the hundreds of miles to a very private beach house C.I.TV had rented for her just a few miles from the *Falcon Bay* set. As the car sped along the open roads of southern England towards the port for St Augustine's, Jake looked at her and hoped that when they arrived, she'd be up for round two.

An Oscar winner as a notch on your bedpost was one thing, but Honey had given him what he decided was probably the best sex of his life. It was amazing, he mused with a smile on his face, how a day could start off so badly but end so well.

Honey was to remain holed up in the beach house – close enough for wardrobe fittings, publicity shoots and, if recent events were anything to go by, many more monumental shags – until Christmas Day, when she would film her first scene.

She stirred as an alarm pinged on his mobile. Popping his headphones in, Jake logged into the conference call app the production team used.

Thanks to Amanda's sudden departure, he'd been forced to jointly promote Candy and Dustin into acting exec producer roles until he could find a suitable replacement. Just the thought of dizzy Candy running this conference call was enough to irritate Jake; neither she nor Dustin had ever had a decent idea between them. As annoying as Amanda was, she was the one person he trusted not to drop the ball.

Farrah was on the call too, which felt a bit odd given they'd not seen each other since the abortion bombshell, but as all of the writers were logged in, there was no way she was going to bring that up. Madeline, who'd joined the line under a separate login that didn't show her name, was listening in secret. She'd made it clear to Jake, with whom she was simultaneously communicating via text message, that she didn't want anyone to know she was there.

'Okay,' said Jake, 'now we're all here, let's get started. What stunt have you got for Lucy Dean's Christmas Day death?'

Beside him, Honey woke up and looked confused as to where she was. Jake side-eyed her and put his finger to his lips so that no one would hear she was with him. She shrugged and dug in her bag for a little black bottle, which she brought out and lifted to her mouth. God, she was so utterly sexy, thought Jake; he was getting a semi just sitting next to her. Viewers were going to love her.

'So here's the list so far—' Farrah began, jolting his attention back to the call.

'Just give me the top five,' he interrupted.

Just hearing his voice made her absolutely certain she'd done the right thing about the baby. Now, if she could just forget about that awful encounter in his office, she might be able to find some self-respect again. Clearing her throat, Farrah got ready to be professional. She already knew what Jake would think of the list; she knew it because she thought the same – it was dire. Candy and Dustin had been dreadful in the story conference meeting, the results of which she was about to deliver.

'So, we have an explosion in The Cove,' she began. 'We have a siege in which Lucy offers herself as the sole hostage in exchange for letting the others go, but she gets caught in police crossfire.' She was picturing the steam coming out of Jake's ears, so she rattled the last three off quickly. 'Or Lucy is accidentally killed in a fight with her new boyfriend after she finds out he's mortgaged the bar behind her back. Or an armed robber on the run stumbles into the beach bar and she gets shot. Or—'

Jake cut in. 'That's enough.' He allowed at least ten seconds to pass before he spoke. 'So, let me get this straight. The siege and armed robbery are pretty much the same thing and have both been done to death. Domestic violence is what they're doing on *Heartlands* right now, so that's not going to work. Which leaves the explosion in the bar, which is basically what we did last year when she survived.'

Candy chipped in. 'The explosion could be a fire, set off by the new barmaid as revenge against Lucy for sacking her on Christmas Eve.'

Farrah looked at the list. Candy hadn't suggested this in the conference, sneaky cow. She was clearly not as ditzy as she'd made out. It actually wasn't a bad idea.

Jake didn't feel the same.

'It's all of you I'll be sacking for having shit ideas like this,' he boomed.

Madeline chimed in with a text.

Jake, focus! Stay calm, tell them this...

She followed up with a series of texts that left him in no doubt as to what the plan was.

'We are less than four weeks away from the live episode...' Jake began as evenly as he could, then pretty much read word for word what Madeline had written. 'I want a stunt that couldn't be done on any other soap. I want something that screams "*Falcon Bay*". People watch us all around the world and some of our highest-rated shows ever have been episodes set on our beach or in our sea. So I want the one woman everyone associates with the name *Falcon Bay* to die by the hand of our famous bay.'

As he finished, he felt a bit like the Queen reading her Christmas Day message to the nation.

'Okay,' said Farrah. 'That's very clear. Thanks.' She meant it too. There was none of Jake's usual frothing at the mouth. Maybe she could work with him if he stayed like this.

'How about a boat accident?' tried Candy.

No! texted Madeline.

So Jake shot her down. 'Bigger,' he said.

'Drowning?' asked Farrah.

Madeline texted, and again he repeated her words.

'I want nature to kill her, but it must be personal.'

Even he balked at that. He wished Honey wasn't in the car; this was not the image of himself he wanted her to have at all. None of it sounded like anything he'd say. Perhaps he should stop reading out the texts and try and paraphrase, but the problem was he couldn't translate them into Jake-speak quickly enough to keep up with Madeline's messages.

Farrah was wondering what the hell had got into him. 'So you want her singled out by nature?' she asked.

Before he could give his own answer, Madeline's next text arrived. He had to read it twice just to be sure he'd understood it right. He really didn't want to say it out loud.

'Well?' Farrah prompted.

Madeline texted again.

> Say it now.

Despite himself, he did as instructed. 'Yes. Singled out by a shark,' he said.

Laughter erupted on the conference call and Honey stared at him with wide eyes.

But Madeline was unperturbed.

> Sell it to them. It's what I want. It's what we're doing.

'I'm being deadly serious,' Jake said.

'Good one!' Farrah laughed.

'I'm not joking,' Jake snapped.

'Don't sharks need to be in warm water?' Candy said hesitantly. 'Ours is too cold, surely.'

'We could build a tank that can regulate the water temperature,' Dustin interjected, wanting to get in with Jake.

'It will be CGI, Dustin,' Jake said, trying to regain control of the conversation. 'And we'll deal with the temperature issue one way or another. All that Greta Thunberg climate stuff will help us out there – we'll blame it on the environment.' This was more like him, he thought, smiling to himself for having pulled it round.

'Come on, Jake,' Farrah argued. 'You can't be serious. If Amanda was here—'

Madeline's final text came in.

> Shut it down now. Tell them to make it happen.

Jake's heart sank. In truth, he thought a shark attack in winter was a ludicrous idea, but he'd already lost his wife and kid, so he wasn't about to lose his job. And if he took a second to think about it, a shark would look pretty cool. Soaps were not always about reality, after all. He continued justifying it in his head, trying to get behind his puppet master's moves.

'Yeah, well, Amanda's not here, Farrah. I am and I'm in charge. Lucy Dean will be eaten by a shark *live* on Christmas Day and our audiences will be talking about it for decades to come.'

'Not in a good way,' Farrah replied flatly.

'The decision has been made, and tomorrow we'll storyline how our fabulous new star will be involved in that scene.' He disconnected the call.

Back in the C.I.TV production office, the team looked at Candy and Dustin in silence.

Farrah got up from her chair. 'Well, I'm delighted for Aiden that he's going to be directing this,' she said. And she meant it.

41

On the coast twenty miles from the *Falcon Bay* studios, in a hammock strung up beneath the roof of a vast glass-walled sunroom, Olivia was sleeping in her mother's arms. As a mild breeze wafted through the patio doors, Amanda took a moment to acknowledge just how relaxed and happy she was.

The sunroom was a new addition to the clifftop café, where tired mums with babies in tow ate something yummy from the simple menu, then snoozed to the sound of the sea. Since quitting her job and leaving Jake, she'd visited the café every day. It had become her sanctuary, but even as Amanda used her leg to gently swing the hammock and her daughter made the sweetest little snuffling noises, she knew this uninterrupted bliss couldn't last.

As she'd expected, Jake was being downright shady over their finances. Her legal team had confirmed he was already squirrelling funds away in offshore accounts so that she would never get her hands on them.

'I don't care about the money. I just want out,' she'd said

to her solicitor, desperate to be free of Jake whatever the cost.

'You say that now, but think about Olivia.'

'I am.' She'd made up her mind. She wanted to be done with him and she'd come up with a way to achieve that. 'Tell him I'll walk away with nothing in exchange for full custody. We can arrange weekends and holiday access, although I doubt he'll even want that,' she'd said.

She'd used the money she'd salvaged from their joint account to take a short-term let on a little holiday cottage near one of her favourite ports. She knew she'd be able to get work. She was good at what she did and had already put out some feelers that she was available.

Being away from *Falcon Bay* was hard though. The show had consumed her life for decades, and at every hour of the working day she could picture exactly who would be where and what they'd be doing. She worried for Catherine and how she was coping in her last weeks on set, and she missed Helen and Farrah. Occasional WhatsApp updates were no substitute. But although part of her wished she was still there, helping dream up ideas for the live ep, another part of her was just glad to be miles away from Madeline the nightmare and Jake the monster.

She was just thinking what a great fit the two of them were when her phone pinged. She'd forgotten to put it on silent, but luckily it didn't wake Olivia. She carefully reached into her back pocket.

> Shall I cook for us tonight? Carrot mush for one, beef bourguignon for two?

She giggled. It was like Dan had a psychic link to her: every time something seemed shaky in her future or she was facing an uphill struggle, there he was, thinking about her and Olivia, making sure she knew she wasn't alone.

Amanda knew she was falling in love with him, but she was trying to squash it down. She wasn't sure she could ever entrust her heart to somebody again, even though she wanted to.

She was about to text him back when the phone rang, making her jump. It was a withheld number, so she was cautious as she answered.

'Amanda?' said a posh but friendly voice that she couldn't quite place. 'This is Lucia Brady from *Heartlands*.'

Amanda nearly sat bolt upright but remembered just in time that she had Olivia on her chest, so she forced herself to remain calm. Lucia Brady was the CEO of Graystone Productions, the makers of *Heartlands*, *Falcon Bay*'s biggest rival. A couple of years ago, Lucia had spent six months trying to poach Amanda. She'd been tempted too. *Falcon Bay* was in the middle of its dip and the old owners were throwing blame around like it was toxic dust, sprinkling it on everybody but themselves. She'd liked the idea of being in sole charge rather than continuing as co-exec producer and having to battle for everything. But then she'd fallen pregnant. And when she had at last managed to get through the twelve-week danger zone, after so many losses, Jake had persuaded her not to make any rash, life-changing decisions. But had she known that when she came off maternity leave, her husband would have become her boss, she would, without a doubt, have gone.

'So, now that you're officially free,' Lucia said, 'shall we pick up where we left off?'

Ten minutes later, Amanda King was appointed director of programming for Graystone Productions, with immediate effect. Running *Heartlands* was to be her main priority. The financial package meant her new life could really begin.

Heartlands was a soap set hundreds of miles away in the English countryside, so it would truly be a new beginning. Amanda looked out to sea and took in the sparkling water and emphatic cliffs that hid the wondrous coves that had captured her heart when she'd arrived there full of hope all those years ago. She would miss this beautiful island, but, like her late mum had always said, 'nothing is better than a fresh start' and that's what this would be.

She glanced down at Dan's message again and wondered how she'd tell him she was leaving.

42

After Jake had run an hour on the treadmill, stretched his muscles and cooled down with a bracing dip in the sea, he made his way back to the production office. The clouds were low, there was a hint of rain in them and soon the night would be upon them. Anyone not hardened to proper TV hours had returned home to their loved ones. Those that remained were either true professionals who put the show ahead of their private lives or they were there because Jake had insisted they stay after hours so he could get his ten-mile run done.

As he made his way to the screening room, Jake tried to put Honey out of his mind. Since she'd relocated to St Augustine's, they'd been having sex every day, but she wouldn't let him stay over and she always seemed drunk. He'd started to have a bad feeling about her drinking, but she denied there was a problem and soothed Jake's concerns with quite frankly the best blowjobs he'd ever had. But as soon as he was away from her intoxicating presence, he began to worry that she might be too fragile to handle the pressure of the schedule that was ahead of her; she was like a china doll, one slip away from shattering.

He was confident she'd handle the live episode well and that her arrival would go down a storm, but after that... He wasn't sure how long she'd last in their studio system or being fully back in the public eye. Her every movement would be tracked by the press, her every utterance scrutinized, her every single human encounter filmed on nearby iPhones.

If he was honest with himself, he knew that Honey was a meltdown in waiting, but he hoped he still had time to fix her.

It was as if Madeline could read his mind. 'How is our new star?' she asked as he walked into the screening room.

The room was like a mini cinema, soundproofed and with seats for about twenty people. The screen was half the size of a cinema's, but the resolution was top-class. Bose speakers provided the surround sound. Jake loved the place – he often used it for late-night parties with Aiden, where they'd get drunk, watch porn and hire some escorts to provide a live show.

'She can't wait to get started,' he lied. Jake just didn't do honesty. Not his style.

Madeline was dressed in an orange side-split halter-neck dress that accentuated every one of her glorious curves; she was obviously going on somewhere afterwards. Jake found himself checking her out. He was fantasizing about how wild an animal she must be in bed when she caught the look in his eyes and raised one eyebrow in a response designed to shoot him down.

'So your wife is now working for our TV rivals, I hear,' she said, clearly not happy.

'She won't be my wife for much longer,' Jake said, pouring himself a Bourbon, catching a whiff of her perfume and liking it.

'Do you think she can do any damage to us at *Heartlands*? All our plans are contingent on us regaining the number one slot at Christmas, and she knows exactly what we have planned.' Her tone indicated that she blamed Jake for Amanda's departure.

'She's got three weeks before our live. There's nothing she can do in that time.'

Madeline raised her eyebrow again. 'I hope you're right.'

As Candy, Dustin, Farrah, Helen and the writers all took their seats in the screening room, the CGI tech team at the back by the mixing desk began to look excited. Aiden turned up and took a seat alongside Jake and Madeline, clearly showing his allegiances.

'Oh Aiden, you deigned to join us,' Madeline said pointedly. 'Do help yourself to a soft drink before we start. Anything but *coke*.'

There was an awkward pause, and Aiden looked at the floor. Jake decided to press on. 'Right, guys, he said, turning to the CGI team, show us *Falcon Bay*'s answer to *Jaws*.'

The lights faded as an inviting world of blues and greens filled the screen, plunging them deep underwater. The camera snaked through shoals of shimmering fish and between groves of strange sea plants in rainbow colours. Everything looked beautiful until a quiet, ominous sound began to play, like a bow being drawn across a cello, as finally the shark came into view. It was magnificent: vast and hefty, with wrinkly grey skin and eye-wateringly sharp yellow teeth.

Everybody in the audience gasped as it sped through the water, circling the bay in ever tighter loops, coming closer and closer, homing in on the dock next to The Cove.

Wow, thought Jake, *this is actually going to work*. As the lights began to rise, applause broke out in the room. The CGI team took a little bow and Aiden wolf-whistled. Looking around at how united his team were, Jake beamed proudly. But one person was not clapping. Madeline.

'Oh my God,' said Candy, beside herself, 'it looks so real, it's scary!'

The others were about to agree when Madeline cut in. 'It didn't scare me,' she said, pulling the plug on the upbeat atmosphere. 'It's fake.'

Helen, who, like Farrah, was surprised at how impressive it was, found herself speaking out. 'Well it is fake, isn't it? But that doesn't mean it's not fabulous. I mean, everyone knows *Jurassic Park* is CGI and no one calls that fake, do they?'

'If you could tell me where you think it looks fake,' interjected one of the tech team, 'I'll fix it, Ms Kane.'

'It's not that it *looks* fake, it's that I know it *is* fake, and because of that I'm not scared.'

Helen, ever the fearless diplomat, wanted to help out the techie, who she'd fucked several times. 'That's as realistic as CGI gets,' she said as he smiled at her.

'But not realistic enough to make us the number one show this Christmas,' Madeline said dismissively. She turned her best smile on the tech team. 'It's not a slight on your excellent work, it's because it's CGI. I know Lucy Dean isn't really in danger – and *danger* is what we need for ratings.'

'So what are you saying?' Jake asked, trying to get his head around this. 'That we use a real shark?'

'That's a great idea, Jake!' she said, patting his hand.

Farrah knew how to rile Jake. She went in for the kill. 'So, David Attenborough, how do we put a warm-water shark in cold water?'

'Well...' Jake began, but Aiden, wanting to get back into Madeline's good books after her earlier comment, spoke over him.

'We build a clear tank, heat its water to a temperature a shark can live in, and set it within the bay. To the viewers the shark will be real because it'll be swimming right up to the boardwalk.'

A smiling Madeline turned to him. 'See, Helen, anything is possible when creatives put their minds to it.'

Helen bit her lip – hard.

Unusually for Jake, he was beginning to panic that a real shark, with all its obvious unpredictability, coupled with the live filming, could be a total disaster. 'So you really want a live shark?' he said to Madeline, hoping she'd laugh and say, *Don't be ridiculous*, and they could return to the realistic-enough and, more importantly, reliable CGI.

'Yes, I want you to realize your vision, Jake,' she said with sincerity. 'And I agree, a real live shark on Christmas Day is definitely going to bring in the viewers.'

Jake's brain was scrambled. The CGI was brilliant; why on earth would she want a real shark? How would that even work with the actors?

Sensing his unease, Madeline continued. 'Now I'm not a stunt specialist,' she said, sounding more Deep South than she had in days, 'but I imagine we could build two tanks – an inner one, made from protective, unbreakable glass, for Catherine to swim in, and an outer one for the shark. Our two animals would look as if they were swimming in the same water, but Catherine would of course be perfectly safe.'

Animals? Farrah shook her head in disgust. What the hell did Madeline mean by calling Catherine an animal? She was about to pull her up on that when Aiden clicked his fingers in excitement.

'Perfect! A mate of mine directed *The Shallows* and they used real sharks. I'll find out who made their tanks. All Catherine will have to do is make sure she jumps into the inner tank and the shark will come at her. It'll look fucking amazing.'

'And how is she supposed to jump into a see-through and therefore invisible space?' asked Farrah. This was the most insane meeting she'd ever been at – which was saying something for the soap world.

'Oh it'll be fine,' Aiden said. 'The stunt people will deal with all that.'

Jake was warming to the idea. 'A live shark, Catherine in the water with it… I mean, we are talking quite a spectacle, something that no other soap could do. We'd be guaranteed the number one rating. How could you not watch?' he said, reclaiming what he had now decided was a wonderful idea after all.

Madeline smiled.

Helen wanted to scream.

'So it's been decided. That's our new plan – a real shark for Christmas Day,' Jake said, rising to his feet.

Madeline also stood up. 'Tell the press. This will make them go absolutely bonkers.'

'They'll think *we're* bonkers, more like,' Farrah hissed to Helen, who was rolling her eyes.

43

In the run-up to the Christmas live episode, Jake made several chat-show appearances to drum up interest in *Falcon Bay*'s exciting new plans. He announced that they would be saying a sad farewell to one of their most beloved characters but kept secret the identity of the show's new villain. Thanks to a series of bitter Tweets by Lydia Chambers, everyone pretty much knew Honey Hunter had got the role, but he refused to either confirm or deny. When he revealed that *Falcon Bay* would have a real-life shark on the set, the internet went wild. The press did too. News crews were dispatched to film the shark being transported from an aquatic park to the purpose-built tank in *Falcon Bay* and for two whole days it was all anybody could talk about; the footage even made it on to CNN.

With killer instincts of her own, Amanda timed her first interview as the new head of *Heartlands* to knock Jake and his shark out of the headlines.

At a press conference, she mocked *Falcon Bay*'s storyline, saying that this sort of preposterousness was what had prompted her to join their biggest competitor and that the *Bay*'s plans to kill one of their audience's favourite characters in such a ludicrous way was a sign that they had well and truly lost the plot. But she did concede that going fully live on Christmas Day was a brave move and something that audiences would relish in this ever-changing world of entertainment. In light of which, she announced that *Heartlands* had decided to match its rival by also going live, head to head in the same time slot. 'There'll be no sharks in our show,' she laughed down the lens, 'just unmissable drama that will touch even the coldest hearts.' She picked her words carefully.

From that moment, the press war was on.

'TV's Super Soaps Go Head to Head' screamed the headlines.

#FalconVHeartlandsWhichWillYouWatch trended globally, with plenty in each camp. Even within the same households, people were arguing about it, and with both shows being broadcast live, you had to pick one for the experience. Everybody was talking about it.

Amanda had performed a masterstroke. With just days to prepare, she couldn't compete with *Falcon Bay*'s stunt or the bitch search, but by piggybacking on their live episode, she'd ensured that *Heartlands* would be mentioned every time *Falcon Bay* was. She knew Jake would be fuming.

44

It was mid-afternoon on Christmas Eve and the cast and crew had a mere twenty-four hours to finalize everything for the live broadcast. Everybody had gathered down at the bay for the tech rehearsal of the shark stunt. To get the lighting and special effects right, it was important they did the run at about the same time as the show would be filmed tomorrow. The afternoon was cold and gloomy: the skies were overcast and a biting wind was blowing off the water. Between takes, the cast were shrouded in blankets and coats; some even had hot-water bottles. A new behind-the-scenes crew who'd been filming the making of the shark tank and the transporting of the shark itself were also on set. The sense of nervous excitement was palpable – everyone was on edge; the entire episode would stand or fall on the quality of this stunt.

Over the years, Catherine Belle had shared the camera with many predators. Actors who felt it was appropriate to have a bit of a grope in a kissing scene; actresses who would slip their shoes off on the reverse shot, causing her to have to look down, creating a double chin; and producers who thought that letting themselves into her dressing room and watching her while she showered was perfectly acceptable. But this was the first time Catherine had acted with an actual shark.

The bay had been sectioned off and flags bobbing on buoys surrounded the heated tank. Underwater cameras were filming the shark as it swam round and round within its enclosure. It was a truly spine-tingling sight: a sixteen-foot monster of menacing bulk with dark, expressionless eyes and a jaw packed with flesh-ripping teeth. Catherine felt nauseous just looking at it. The longer it circled, the angrier it seemed. The fact that it was a female shark strangely gave it an even more sinister presence.

Sheena, who rarely came to the set but wanted to be there for Catherine, was standing beside her on the specially built deck outside Lucy Dean's bar. Catherine was her focus right now. If that nonsense with Stacey and Lydia had told her anything, it was that her A-star needed her full attention and she wouldn't be taking her eye off the ball again. She was back to feeling powerful and dynamic again, full of her legendary kickass energy. When the chips were down, Sheena's shoulder pads were always up.

'How are you feeling?' she asked Catherine, who was understandably cold but also unusually quiet.

'I think I'm still in shock that this is really happening,' Catherine replied. 'Forty years on this show, forty years of my life and it has to end like this? With Lucy dying in the gaping jaws of… that thing!' She flicked a trembling hand in the direction of the monitor.

Sheena wrapped an arm around her, sensing that she was on the verge of crying. 'Don't waste your tears on them. As much as we hate this, it's going to go down in history as the most watched soap episode ever, and no one will ever be able to take that away from you.'

'Or people will be laughing at me for decades to come and Lydia will finally have someone to replace her trampled-to death-by-cows clip on all those "Embarrassing TV" shows. That was bad, but this is even worse!'

Sheena couldn't disagree, but there was no way she was going to share that with Catherine. The poor woman would fall apart. So she stayed silent.

'This will be my legacy,' Catherine continued. 'Whatever I do next, I will be forever asked about the shark.'

Sheena turned to face her and placed her hands on both of her shoulders. 'I won't let that happen and do you know why?'

Catherine glanced up at her, desperate for some hope.

'You are the world's number one soap actress and you will be exiting this show as that – nothing less. When people look back at your *Falcon Bay* career, they'll have forty years of memories, not just the final curtain. And you're not done yet. Your best role is still to come.'

Given her age, Catherine wasn't sure about that last bit, but she was grateful for Sheena's efforts. The two women hugged. Then Catherine walked to her mark and stood in the cold, waiting for Honey's stand-in to slap her so hard she would then topple into the dark, forbidding sea. It didn't say much for Honey Hunter that she couldn't even be bothered to do the tech run, Catherine thought. *Just wait till she's done forty years*, she mused, staring down at the circling shark and shivering as she gazed out to the horizon. *I give her twelve months, max*.

'You okay, Cat?' yelled Aiden from a decked area where they had set up camp to watch. They usually used walkie-talkies from the internal studio, but everything about this episode was different.

'Catherine's fine,' snapped Sheena from the sidelines. 'Just waiting on you. Like we all are.'

Not fazed in the least, Aiden treated Sheena to one his roguishly charming smiles.

'Cool. Won't be long now.'

He looked rough today, Catherine thought. The crew had told her that he'd been partying all night, and were joking about the size of the coke mountain on the mirror in his dressing room. She looked him over again. *At least I won't have to mix with scum like him any more*, she thought, desperately trying to get a hold on herself. All this negativity wasn't doing her any good.

The icy breeze coming off the water was cutting her to the core. She wouldn't miss freezing outside like this either. Once this was all over, she would take some me-time, she decided. She'd always wanted to see the world, visit South Asia and New Zealand, go on safari in South Africa. She certainly had enough money not to be in a rush to work. After the live show, she would tell Sheena that she wanted to step off the acting merry-go-round for a while. The prospect cheered her. And maybe, just maybe, she might even fall in love again.

'Cat?' Aiden shouted, breaking into her thoughts 'Soon as you're ready…'

'I'm ready,' she said, as wardrobe came and took her warm parka coat from her, exposing her to the elements in her flimsy Christmas Day party-dress outfit.

'Good, then let's do this thing. Places, guys. Dress rehearsal for the shark attack.'

Catherine had only discovered what was expected of her earlier that morning when she was introduced to the stuntwoman. It had taken her several minutes to translate what she was being asked to do. 'You want *me* to actually jump in with the shark?' she'd said, genuinely shocked.

Nobody had even mentioned this to her before. She'd only found out that it was to be a real shark, not CGI, when she'd seen it on the news. She knew that no one at *Falcon Bay* cared about her any more now that she was leaving, but she'd assumed at the very least it would be her on a pier then a cutaway to a stuntwoman dressed as Lucy in the sea.

Sheena had immediately gone to battle with Jake over it.

'She'll fall into the inner tank, which will keep her perfectly safe,' he'd said, as if the question of Catherine's health and safety was an annoying trifle.

'Says you,' Sheena had snapped.

'Say the makers,' claimed Jake, 'who would be sued for millions if anything went wrong.'

Catherine stared at the water, shivering from head to toe, trying to locate the tank Aiden was talking about. Sensing her confusion, the stuntwoman pointed her towards it. Catherine could see the edges.

Jake, togged up in a black Puffa jacket, wandered up the bayside to where she was standing. 'I know it's a big ask, but I promise you it will be worth it,' he said, giving her the full charm offensive. 'We have cameras down there, built into the tank. They'll be on you and on the shark at the same time and although the protective glass wall is between you, it will look amazingly real on screen, I promise you.'

Catherine took in his words. A promise from Jake was about as reliable as a chocolate teapot.

'How am I supposed to act underwater?'

'You won't need to act – you'll be genuinely scared. We'll see that fear. And the shark. Coming at you…'

Catherine was suddenly very nervous. 'I'm not sure I can do this,' she said quietly.

Jake beckoned the stuntwoman over.

'Ms Belle,' the woman said, a professional smile plastered across her face, 'you are perfectly safe. Now watch me.' She walked to the end of the pier. 'This is your mark on the deck. It's very clear. You can see it.' She turned to Aiden. 'Get the cameras rolling and I'll show her.'

Aiden made a gesture in the air and people went to work.

The stuntwoman stood looking at Catherine, exuding total confidence. 'So when you reach your mark, you don't jump, you just fall. The tank has a good margin for error. So long as you just drop into it exactly where I showed you, you'll be totally fine, I promise. It'll be like toppling into a warm swimming pool. Now watch me.'

The fearless young woman held out her arms. The last of the sun was trying its best to break through the grey cloud and tiny speckles of sunlight bounced off the choppy sea. Keeping her eyes on Catherine's face, the stuntwoman allowed her body to relax, then fell into the water as the shark's fin hovered nearby.

Catherine rushed over to the monitors where Sheena was watching. Everybody was transfixed by the screens, tracking the stuntwoman as she dropped through the water. At the noise, the massive shark immediately switched direction. They all saw it happen, the shark turning a circle. Catherine's heart was in her mouth. The stuntwoman thrashed about, attempting to tread water, and the shark made a beeline for her.

As the shark sped towards her, Catherine realized she was holding her breath.

'Fuck, it's fast,' whispered Jake, as if only now realizing they were dealing with a killer.

'Yeah,' agreed Aiden, 'and it looks amazing.'

The shark was almost on the stuntwoman, its cold, beady eyes unblinking, its mouth gaping, its nightmarish teeth in full view. A few feet to go… Certain death was seconds away.

'Cut… to Camera 3,' Aiden shouted, and suddenly from inside the protective tank Catherine could see the ferocity of its attack, interspersed with close-ups of the stunt double screaming and fake blood being released from her costume. It truly did look gut-churningly real.

On a second monitor, Catherine watched in frozen horror as the shark repeatedly hurled itself against its invisible glass tank. The tank that enclosed the stuntwoman shuddered as she screamed.

'And cut!' yelled Aiden.

The whole studio floor gave the stuntwoman a round of applause as she was helped back onto the boardwalk.

'You got it, Catherine?' Jake shouted out as Sheena looked on.

Catherine glanced at Aiden, then at the crew, who were all staring at her. Suddenly the finality of it all was too much to bear.

As tears began to stream down her face, 'I'm sorry – I can't,' were the only words she could get out of her mouth before she fled from the water's edge and raced up the boardwalk towards the studio.

'Where the fuck is she going?' Jake shouted to Sheena, who was already rushing after her.

45

In Catherine's dressing room, Sheena held her as she sobbed, with Farrah and Helen standing either side, all three encircling her with love. The tinsel garlands and strings of Christmas cards made a poignant backdrop, but there was nothing jolly about this gathering.

'Try and take deep breaths,' Helen said, but Catherine sobbed on.

The women looked at each other helplessly. It was heartbreaking to see their friend so distraught. Farrah wished Amanda was there – she'd have known what to do.

Without any knocking, the dressing room door opened, and in walked Madeline Kane, wearing a long red faux-fur coat. The women could see a crowd had gathered behind her in the corridor, but Madeline closed the door firmly on their peering eyes.

'When I heard there was an issue, I thought it best to come myself,' she said, ignoring the state Catherine was in and adopting the same tone one might use if noting there were no tea bags.

She scanned Farrah and Helen authoritatively. '*I'll* deal with this,' she said. 'So please return to your posts.' She gestured towards the door dismissively, but neither Farrah nor Helen budged.

Madeline raised an eyebrow at their defiance, then turned to Sheena.

'Ms McQueen, as you are well aware, your client is needed for the tech run. So whatever *this* is' – she waved condescendingly in the direction of a still sobbing Catherine – 'kindly sort it out so we can get things moving.'

Farrah decided it was time to speak up. 'Have some respect! Can't you see that Catherine's on the verge of a breakdown? She's been pushed to her edge – it's all gone too far.'

Madeline eyed her coldly. 'No, it's not gone far enough, actually,' she snapped in her Savannah drawl. 'We'd have wrapped by now if it wasn't for Tiny Tears here.'

'Madeline!' Helen interjected. 'That's no way to talk about Catherine. She's very upset.'

'So am I,' Madeline shot back. 'I have a whole crew, plus a shark and its wildlife expert – all of whom we are paying overtime – waiting outside to rehearse, but thanks to Ms Belle's behaviour, our *live* show – due to be watched by millions tomorrow – is *still* not ready.'

Helen, Farrah and Sheena exchanged looks, trying to decide what to do.

'You've had your diva moment now, Catherine *dear*,' Madeline continued, 'so let's just get this done so we can all go home.' She began casually examining her nails, as if wondering whether they were the right colour or not.

'Look,' Farrah said, stepping closer to Catherine, 'she's in this state because not only is this shark thing an insane idea, it's been terribly handled.'

Madeline glanced at her like she was an annoying fly circling her head, about to be swatted, but Farrah continued.

'She's been given one surprise after another, but she's been soldiering on, and now… well, it's obviously all hit her. Catherine is always professionalism personified, and she would never have left a crew waiting if she wasn't deeply traumatized.'

Catherine's sobs intensified as she took in the truth of Farrah's words.

'If Amanda was still here, this wouldn't have happened – she would have done things properly,' Farrah said. Any opportunity to have a dig at Jake was worth exploiting.

'Let's not forget that Amanda left you all,' Madeline sneered. But she took off her coat, sensing she would be here for a while.

Catherine sat upright. 'Only because she wouldn't sack me,' she said, dabbing at her eyes, determined to stop crying and thinking how awful this was. It certainly wasn't the way she'd wanted to spend her last twenty-four hours on the show she'd given her life to.

'But off she went,' Madeline goaded, 'and straight to our rivals, who are aiming to outshine our show as well as *you*, Catherine, the "dear friend" she "couldn't sack". Yet tomorrow, she's quite happy to go head to head with your farewell episode – which we are all working so hard to make an amazing send off *for you*. That's a funny sort of friendship if you ask me.'

As Madeline walked over to the window, the brightly lit shark tank was making the whole bay glow. The reflected light illuminated her strong, sensual body, accentuating her narrow hips and slim torso, making every curve of her bust visible through her flowing dress. Sheena couldn't believe that right now, of all times, she was thinking about Madeline's body, but there was something about her that she was drawn to. Did she fancy her – was that it, she wondered? No, this wasn't attraction; Madeline wasn't her type. But there was something about her that made Sheena's brain fizz.

Unaware she was being scrutinized, Madeline continued to speak. 'I have to say I'm disappointed to see you two join in this pity party, Farrah and Helen,' she said without turning round. 'It's now perfectly clear you don't like the direction *my* series is going in. So unless you can get on board with my vision, you're welcome to leave the show with Catherine tomorrow.'

She swivelled round to face them.

For a moment nobody spoke. Catherine, sensing that her meltdown was now putting her friends' jobs at risk, started to wipe her tears and get ready to stand up. Farrah threw her a look that told her to stay put.

Madeline remained perfectly still, fixing Helen and Farrah with her unreadable stare.

Was she calling their bluff? Farrah shivered at the thought of leaving *Falcon Bay*. Like Catherine, she'd been here most of her life. But things were very different now. The show was twisting her; she'd never have done the terrible things she'd done – set up Aiden and betrayed Amanda by sleeping with Jake – if Madeline hadn't taken over. The toxicity of the show was changing her – and not for the good. She took a deep breath and made a momentous decision. She was better than this. Clearly her time on *Falcon Bay* had come to an end.

'Actually, I was going to leave after Catherine's last episode anyway, so that suits me just fine,' she said, eyeing Helen, urging her to say something. But Helen stayed quiet.

Madeline laughed. 'Sure. You keep telling yourself that. But when you try and get work somewhere else, you'll find that I'll be informing them that you were asked to leave.'

Farrah stared at her – she really was a stone-cold bitch – but Madeline wasn't finished. She now looked past Farrah and fixed her eyes on Helen.

'If you're staying, Ms Gold, please do your job and escort the talent back to set,' she said, staring her out.

Helen's head was whirling. She loved *Falcon Bay* and, like the others, she'd been here so long. But Farrah was right; it was time to go. 'I won't be doing that, as I'll be leaving with Farrah,' she said, surprising herself.

'What a loss!' Madeline practically cackled. 'Please do come to me for a reference. I'll be happy to share just how many incidents of you taking advantage of actors we've had to deal with. By the time I've spoken to the *Herald* and Jude has shared his front-page story about how you abused him – tearful and topless, no doubt – you'll be the female Weinstein. We might even make a series for Netflix about you. I can see it now – *Surviving Helen*.' She was properly laughing now.

Helen was stunned.

Catherine could take no more and rose from her chair to face Madeline. Her eyes flicked over to Sheena, who appeared to be lost in her own thoughts. 'Sheena, say something,' she begged.

Madeline smirked. 'There's nothing she can say. This is *my* show and *my* network. I own it and everybody on it.'

Catherine snapped. 'Well I won't film it! And while I'm sorry to let the cast and crew down, you are a *hideous* woman. I am leaving right now and I won't be coming back. Good luck with your ridiculous *Jaws* episode – because I won't be there.' She checked the mirror, wiping her streaked make-up away, then glanced again at Sheena, wanting her to echo her statement. But Sheena still seemed to be in a trance.

'Oh really?' Madeline said calmly.

'Yes, really,' Catherine said, mimicking her Southern twang.

'Well, my darling, I'd advise you or your zonked-out agent, who looks like she's back on the drugs, by the way' – she gave Sheena an appraising stare – 'to check your contract. When you do so, you'll find that if you don't appear in tomorrow's episode, you will be liable for not only that episode not being filmed – because I will pull it – but also for costs and damages claimed against you for loss of global revenue. This clause also applies to the pre-production of the live episode, with all of its exorbitant costs' – she gestured out of the window towards the shark tank – 'and all the knock-on consequences, including the entire advertising spend we've put into it.'

Catherine went deathly pale.

'And, Helen, given your previous role as head of casting here, you will be able to confirm to Ms Belle that breaching her contract at this stage will cost her more than she's earned in her entire thirty-nine years on *Falcon Bay*.'

Catherine shot Helen an anxious look, seeking reassurance that Madeline was just needling her.

But Helen's eyes confirmed that Madeline was not making this up. 'I'm so sorry,' she said. She's right; your contract does make you liable.' She could barely meet Catherine's eye, ashamed that being so good at her job had now boxed her friend into a corner.

Catherine wobbled and sat down again. She felt like she'd been punched in the stomach. She stared pointedly at Sheena, wanting her to step in, but again Sheena said nothing.

'Bitch,' Farrah hissed.

Madeline nodded, taking that as a compliment, then put on her big red coat and touched up her make-up in the mirror as she spoke. 'So I'll see you down at the tank, Ms Belle, in ten minutes.' She strode to the dressing room door, then turned. 'Oh, and now we've got that sorted, I might as well tell you that we're about to acquire three other networks, including the one that makes *Heartlands*.'

Farrah, Helen and Catherine all knew what was coming. Sheena was still in a world of her own.

'And after tonight's antics, I guarantee that none of you will ever work in TV again. You're done. And that includes you too, Sheena,' she called out in Sheena's direction.

Hearing Madeline say her name seemed to bring her out of whatever mind-spin she'd been in.

'Me?' she said, confused.

'Yes. You.' Madeline smiled. 'None of my networks will ever employ any of your clients, so you can join this lot on the scrapheap. You're *all* over.' She looked victorious as she fastened her coat and delivered her parting shot. 'And there's absolutely nothing any of you can do about it,' she said, grinning broadly.

Farrah, Helen and Catherine were speechless, but Sheena had sprung up out of her seat and was moving like lighting to catch up with Madeline at the door.

'Not so fast…' she said, pushing the door closed again and stepping into Madeline's space so that they were face to face, the fabric of their clothes almost touching.

For months now, Sheena had been trying to work out what it was about Madeline that seemed familiar, and just moments earlier, when Madeline had stood in profile at the window, illuminated, it had come to her – a nightmare, another memory she'd blocked out for years. She was suddenly back in *that* room, surrounded by men who were abusing her, and by a light in the corner stood a young boy who was also going through his own personal hell at the hands of these monsters. As Ed Nichols held the boy bent over so they could use him, the teenage Sheena could see his nudity; could see the shape of his torso and his slim hips.

'I know who you are,' Sheena said, looking deep into Madeline's eyes.

The others looked on in bemusement. Had Sheena slipped – was she back on drugs?

Sheena sensed their disquiet, turned her face half towards them and then back to Madeline.

'You can drop the accent now, bitch – or should I say bastard?' she said, stepping back from Madeline as if she'd pulled the pin on a grenade and thrown it.

Helen grimaced at Farrah, convinced now that Sheena must have taken something.

'Catherine...' Sheena gesticulated dramatically with her arms, as if she were a glamorous assistant about to reveal the secrets behind a magician's trick. 'Behold your long-lost son.'

'What?' Catherine said, shaking her head, concerned at Sheena's increasingly bizarre behaviour.

'Sorry. I should say, Lucy Dean's son,' Sheena continued, giving a hollow laugh. 'And they say soaps are unrealistic! Ladies, I give you *Calvin Butler* reincarnated,' she said with a triumphant flourish.

Madeline's feline eyes widened in shock.

THE END?

46

At the studio-rented mansion on the marina a few miles from the set, Honey paced the vast stone terrace, looking out to the deep dark sea. In the distance she could just about make out *Falcon Bay*'s studio lights further along the coast; the sight filled her with dread. She'd barely slept the previous night, knowing she had less than forty-eight hours until the live show.

What was meant to have been a single celebratory glass at her book signing had turned into a month-long bender that she knew from experience was only going to end one way – badly. After a decade of being sober, when she'd not even consumed food cooked with alcoholic ingredients, which was not easy in Switzerland, she'd hoped that even after this blip she'd have been able to stop again. She'd tried, but she'd only lasted twelve hours.

With her hands shaking and her heart beating like a conga drum, she'd cracked and downed one of the bottles of Cristal that Jake had left in the bar. After that she'd moved on to the spirits and then spent the night scrolling through the freakshow footage of the shark being transported into the studio bay.

Poring over the endless comments about what she'd be like in the new star role, she felt the pressure choking her. Millions of people – billions, it seemed – were now waiting for the moment when *Falcon Bay*'s new bitch would step out of the shadows. And they weren't just interested in her role on the show – they were already discussing her real life too. Every mistake she'd ever made was already being reposted online for the world to see. She cast her eyes towards *Falcon Bay* and once again suddenly found herself being sick.

She retched and splattered the terrace with sick. Oh, how she wished she could go back in time and say no to Mickey and that damn book, no to leaving her Swiss sanctuary where she'd been clean and sober, no to returning into the limelight of supposed global fame and acclaim. She was already a car crash; a drunken wreck on the verge of a breakdown just like before. And she hadn't even filmed her first scene.

She tried to steady herself as it all swirled around in her booze-soaked brain. Even if, by some miracle, she did manage to get through the live episode, the call sheet showed her filming six days a week; she'd never cope with that drunk, and now there was no time left to get sober.

The wind blew her silk dressing gown off her shoulders as she staggered along the terrace's edge, wobbling as she stared down at the deep drop below her.

'What have I done?' She sobbed as she began hurling bottles from her stacked cocktail trolley into the sea. If her Oscar had been to hand, she'd have thrown that in too.

She should never have come back. This sort of pressure

had ruined her life before. She'd barely survived it the first time around, and she'd been young and stupidly fearless then.

Gazing down at the bleak sea, she knew it was time to end this now.

47

In her heels, Madeline wasn't exactly running – she'd never give them the pleasure of that – but she was certainly moving at speed. She'd stormed out of Catherine Belle's dressing room and the women were now chasing her down the long corridor that led towards the studio and the lifts to the upper floors.

She quickened her pace, hoping to reach the lift that would take her to her office before they caught up with her. At least there she could have a few moments alone and prepare for what was coming. The moment the lift door pinged open she rushed inside, frantically pressing the button. She felt a rush of relief when the door closed and it began ascending to the executive floor.

'Shit!' shouted Sheena.

'Let's take the stairs,' Farrah said, pointing to the lift's illuminated numbers. 'She's going to her office.'

Helen caught them up, along with Catherine, who was still very shaken.

'How certain are you, Sheena?' Helen said as their heels

clacked on the metal stair trims. 'I cast Calvin back then. Surely I'd know...'

'I just can't believe it,' Catherine puffed, more out of breath than the others by the time they all reached the executive floor.

Sheena was already bolting towards Madeline's office door. '*Believe it*,' she yelled, without looking back.

The others looked at each other in shock as it began to sink in.

Sheena placed her fingers on the office door handle. 'Get ready, ladies,' she said, turning it, 'because this is about to get ugly.'

Madeline, still in her long red coat and with a glass of wine in her hand, was standing on the balcony looking down on the set of her beloved *Falcon Bay* when they burst into her office. She hadn't bothered to lock the door; there was no point. And while she knew they were there, she didn't turn round.

'If you're going to jump, I'd do it quickly,' Sheena said snidely. 'Otherwise, we want answers.'

The four women stood staring at Madeline with new eyes, trying to peer beneath her glitz, poise and beauty and into her past.

'Cal?' Catherine said softly, breaking the group's line, stepping towards her.

She took in Madeline's profile. Her hair was lit by the glow of the beach lights, making her look more beautiful than ever.

Madeline kept her eyes on the sea.

'Are you sure about this?' Farrah whispered to Sheena.

In the silence of the room, everyone heard her.

'Oh, there's no doubt as to who we have here,' boomed Sheena, who was in no mood to whisper, wanting Madeline to hear every word. 'I pinky promise it,' she said, repeating the phrase of Madeline's that had first alerted Sheena to something familiar about her.

Madeline took a sip of her wine and slowly turned to face them. As all their eyes met, an expectant silence filled the room.

The journey Madeline had been on to reach this point flashed through her mind as she prepared to speak. After successfully building a new life and identity in the Deep South of America, with the wealthy husband who adored her, she'd known that coming back to St Augustine's was a risk. But, like a moth to a flame, when *Falcon Bay* had come up for sale again, she just hadn't been able to stop herself from purchasing it.

Once back on the lot, the comforting familiarity of it all confirmed to her that she'd made the right decision, but seeing Sheena in Paris had been a mind-fuck. Horrendous flashbacks of what had happened to the person she no longer was had flooded her brain on sight of her.

She'd successfully blocked out the terrible damage that Ed Nichols had inflicted on both of them and so many others by reasoning with herself that the body Ed and his friends had violated was a body she too wanted to destroy – and she had. She'd buried *their victim* thanks to a serious of painful and difficult procedures before rising like the proverbial phoenix from the ashes – reborn fresh, as the woman she should always have been, ready to start again.

Finally, she spoke, aiming her words towards Sheena.

'Ed Nichols was a monster,' she said as the two locked eyes.

Sheena's face crumpled, knowing exactly what she was talking about as the others watched their exchange.

The way Madeline spoke those five words, the other women instantly knew that Sheena was right.

Catherine looked deeply into Madeline's eyes, trying to see the teenage boy that she'd had fired. 'Is it really you…?'

'Yes and no,' Madeline said, her Deep South accent now replaced by English tones.

'I never knew you were one of his victims,' Catherine said, now looking doubly shocked.

Madeline raised an eyebrow, which made it clear she didn't believe her.

'It's true. She didn't. I never told anyone what they did to you.' Sheena's tone had softened.

Farrah and Helen watched as the three women's history unfolded.

Catherine stepped towards Madeline gently. 'I swear, if I had known, I wouldn't have done things the way I did. I *really* thought that I was—'

Madeline cut in. 'Oh, I know what you thought. You gloated about it at the Bitch Party, didn't you?' she snapped. 'You said you'd saved me. But, back then, you didn't even try to find out what was wrong. You didn't even *ask*, did you?' Madeline was accusatory. 'Did it never occur to you that the drinking, the drugs, was a cry for help? I was self-medicating to deal with the pain. Not only was I being abused, but you have no idea what it's like to have been born in the wrong body – and what that does to you. I was vulnerable, I was desperate, I was lost.'

Catherine looked remorseful.

'And how did you choose to help me? You got me sacked from the *one* thing I had, the *only* thing I loved. *This show*,' Madeline spat like a caged cobra, the venom rising in her words. 'Even when I couldn't love myself, I still loved *Falcon Bay*. You knew I had no family. You knew I had no other home. *Falcon Bay* was my *everything*, until you took it from me. Yes, Ed Nichols destroyed my innocence, but he's dead, so I consider that case closed. But you… You had me thrown into the gutter when I most needed help. You'll never know the sort of things I had to do to survive because of you. You destroyed my dreams, Catherine, and now I'm about to destroy yours too.'

She knocked back her wine.

The women looked on now as Madeline and Catherine drew closer.

'So, all this – my character's death tomorrow – is your revenge?' Catherine said, still not quite believing what she was hearing.

'It wasn't my plan – originally.' Madeline smiled. 'I was intending to just fix the show that I *love*, and, yes, at some point I would have probably put you out to pasture – as, let's be honest, you are well past your prime in TV terms.' She cast her eyes over Catherine slyly. 'But then, when you told me at the Bitch Party that it was because of *you* that the network cast me aside, you became the focus of my attention. Before that, you were barely on my radar.'

All the women looked shocked as Madeline continued. 'So, as you can see, you brought this on yourself.'

'But I've told you, I *didn't know*,' Catherine shouted.

'And I'm *showing you* that I *don't believe you.*' Madeline smirked. 'I was weak when you took *Falcon Bay* away from me, but I'm not any more, and now I'm taking it away from you. It's just a game of showbiz snakes and ladders, really, isn't it, Catherine? And you've lost, so down you go, all the way to the bottom of the board – or to the sea, in this case!' She laughed.

'That's not showbiz, that's corruption and misguided revenge, and this isn't a game – it's her life!' Sheena was raging, and sensed that Catherine didn't have much fight left in her. 'She honestly did not know what happened to you and thought what she did was for the best. She's told you the truth and I'm backing her up – which with our history should count for something – and yet still you want to make her pay? You might look like a woman, Madeline,' Sheena said angrily, 'but you are acting like a silly little girl.'

'Well, this *little girl* is in charge of this network,' Madeline said, checking her make-up in the mirror. 'And what I say goes.' She smiled, then pulled the walkie-talkie from her pocket and called down to production.

'Problem resolved,' she drawled, her Deep South accent strongly back in place. 'Please reset and Ms Belle will be there in five minutes. Over.'

She clicked the radio off, put it in her bag, then flicked her eyes over all the women as she spoke. 'So, despite you all having worked out my past – which is exactly what it is: ancient history – whether you like it or not, everything I said in Catherine's dressing room still stands.'

Helen, Farrah and Catherine exchanged defeated looks. She was right; knowing that this was a personal vendetta against Catherine made no difference. As the owner of the network, Madeline was still in the driving seat.

'Catherine, if you still pride yourself on being a professional and don't want to be made bankrupt, I suggest you go back to the set and finish this rehearsal.' Madeline fluffed up her hair and put the strap of her Chanel bag over her shoulder. 'And to prove I'm not *totally* heartless,' she said sarcastically, turning to Helen and Farrah, 'you can both leave now and I'll even pay you for tomorrow – it is Christmas, after all.'

Catherine, eyes down, exhausted from the constant see-sawing battle and the fact that her friends' fate was now as bleak as her own, began to leave. Farrah and Helen, also out of words, followed her out of the room, heads held high but pride dented.

As the others reached the hall, Madeline gestured for Sheena to follow, but Sheena ostentatiously drew out a chair from beside Madeline's desk, sat down and pulled open her bag.

'Not so fast,' she said with a smile.

48

Madeline rolled her eyes as the others hovered in the doorway. 'God, this is getting boring. What have you got on me now, Miss Marple? I hope you don't carry an old photo of me in your bag – I know you're into women now but you're really not my type.'

'Don't flatter yourself,' Sheena said, not rising to Madeline's bait but pulling her mobile out and beginning to dial.

Madeline eyed her with a confident smile. 'Well, if you're calling the press to try and out me, save your breath – printing private medical information is illegal so no one would run the story.'

She was right. Years earlier, a history like hers would have been the front page of the *Herald* by morning, and Ross Owens would have been rubbing his hands with glee, but there were new privacy laws in place now that protected her. All traces of Madeline's old life had been replaced with her new one, and no media organization would be allowed to report on her medical past even if Sheena did tell them.

'*You* might be bored of this conversation, Madeline, but I know someone who won't be.' Sheena smiled. 'Your father-in-law.'

Madeline's cool facade dropped and her beautiful feline eyes began to twitch like they had in Catherine's dressing room earlier. Sheena knew she had her again.

'When I couldn't quite work out what it was about you that wasn't sitting right with me, I did plenty of research into that rich family you married into.'

Madeline remained silent.

'Very religious, the Deep South, isn't it?' Sheena continued. 'And Chad's father is rather *conservative*, shall we say, and a strong believer in old family values, which he's obviously instilled in his gorgeous son. Quite a catch you bagged there, Madeline.'

Madeline carried on staring at her as Sheena went in for the kill.

'So even if you have told your husband about your past – which by the way I very much doubt – I know for a fact that his dearest daddy,' she said, expertly mimicking the Southern belle accent that Madeline was no longer using, 'would not be funding Chad's wife's twisted whims if he knew who she used to be.'

'I've always been *me*!' Madeline shouted.

'Try explaining that to him.' Sheena winked. 'Anyway, like you said earlier, let's just get this wrapped up. You might as well go back on set while I make the call – I think it's going to be a long one.'

Madeline went silent as her eye continued to twitch. Sheena knew she'd regained the upper hand, but she wasn't without sympathy for Madeline. As twisted as she was, her reincarnation was undoubtedly impressive. And Sheena understood, because she'd rebuilt herself too – not in the same way, but it had been tough enough. She understood that ruthless decisions were par for the reinvention course. Once you'd been a victim, like they had, something was instilled in you that made you put your own interests first. But Madeline's unjustified revenge was going way beyond that; it was something Sheena could never condone. Especially when it directly concerned her friend and client, Catherine Belle.

'You'll be interested to know that, as an agent, I've had clients with histories similar to yours. And, whilst you're right, you are protected by the law here in Europe. But you and I both know that the Wild West of the American press is not bound by those rules. So after I've filled in Big Daddy, I'll be straight onto the *National Enquirer*.'

Madeline's face paled as Sheena started dialling, each digit pressed deliberately. It was like a countdown to a bomb going off, a bomb that would destroy Madeline's life.

'It's been a long time since you had a front cover, hasn't it?' Sheena said. 'So, to prove I'm not *totally* heartless,' she said, mimicking what Madeline had said earlier, 'I won't take commission – you can have this on the house.'

She was about to dial the last digit, the one that would connect her to Chad's father's office, when Madeline finally spoke.

'Wait...'

Sheena smiled at Madeline's tone. It was a tone she recognized, a tone which acknowledged that the power had shifted. It featured in all negotiations, big and small, irrespective of the individual's accent or status. She glanced at the others, standing by the door, eyes glued to the unfolding scene. She was glad to have her friends here to share this moment.

She didn't once take her eyes off Madeline. It was time to bring this home. 'Make it worth my while,' she teased.

Madeline cracked her fingers, the noise resounding loudly around her office and making the others, who were watching this verbal ping-pong from the doorway, wince. 'Yes, if you make that call, there's every chance you'll ruin my marriage. But – Chad might understand why I kept what happened to me from him. I don't know...' She said this without emotion as she walked over to her desk and took a seat, gearing up to negotiate.

'Your point is...?' Sheena said.

'My point,' Madeline replied, staring out from behind her desk, trying to regain an air of control, 'is that although it will hurt if he rejects me, I can survive that. I've survived far worse.' She let that hang in the air before continuing. 'So even if Chad and his family do disown me, this network is still in my name, which means that while I *might* lose the love of my life, it still won't change anything at *Falcon Bay*.'

The women all looked at each other, then over to Madeline and Sheena. Once again, Madeline was in the driving seat, albeit in a different lane.

'Unless,' Madeline continued, 'we can come to some sort of *arrangement*.'

Sheena and Madeline locked eyes long enough for both to understand they'd reached a stand-off.

After a pause, Sheena slowly put the phone down. She was

back in her agent's comfort zone. 'Ladies,' she said, gesturing towards Catherine, Farrah and Helen, 'go back to set. I'll follow when we have concluded our business.'

Madeline avoided eye contact with them as they finally left the hallway, then poured herself another glass of wine. The negotiations began.

49

After parking outside Honey's waterside hideout, Jake made his way up the gravel drive. The moon hung low, casting a magical glow over the elegant limestone facade. It really was a magnificent property. Perhaps he should buy it, Jake thought as he neared the impressive entrance with its two stone lions either side of the door. Maybe Olivia would want to come and live there one day – perhaps when she was a teenager and old enough to understand what a bitch her mother was.

He was looking forward to seeing Honey. So much so that he'd skipped out of the tech rehearsal halfway through. His need to have sex with Honey was a hell of a lot more compelling than his need to wait around in the cold to see what time Catherine would bother to show up and finish the practice run. He thought privately that it would serve her right if she fell in the shark tank, after the unprofessional way she was behaving.

Yes, it was a casual arrangement with Honey, and she had some problems, but what woman wasn't crazy in one way or another? He let himself into the grand hall. If they stayed together, the showrunner and the show's star, they'd be a true power couple. No doubt they'd get features together in all the glossy magazines and this house would be perfect for that. He checked his reflection in a gilt-framed mirror on the wall, pushed his hair off his face and loosened his collar. He'd look good in those and that would really piss Amanda off. He smiled.

'Honey!' he called out as he reached the vast lounge that overlooked the terrace.

No reply came. She must be in the shower or, even better, in bed waiting for him. Yes, that was just what he needed to wash away the last twenty-four hours of stress – a killer Christmas Eve session with Honey in the sack. He hardened at the thought.

He slipped off his jacket and made his way to the bedroom. 'I hope you're ready for me,' he called out seductively, 'Because I'm ready for you.' He unzipped his trousers and stroked his throbbing cock as he opened the bedroom door.

But the bed was empty. He took the rest of his clothes off and headed back down towards the living room, thinking she must be on the terrace. The house was so big, it was no wonder she hadn't heard him. He imagined doing her on the sun lounger under the stars – he loved outdoor sex, even in the winter. There was nothing like a cold night to make a woman's nipples extra hard.

He was naked by the time he reached the terrace and noticed that on the window a single Post-it note was flapping in the breeze. A bad feeling washed over him. It took only a single second for him to read her spidery writing, but several more to understand it.

I'm sorry. I can't. Don't hate me. Honey x

'Fuck!' Jake roared into the sky, like a werewolf beneath a full moon.

50

On the TV screen in the corner of Catherine Belle's dressing room, a trailer for the live special was playing. Catherine watched it in her mirror as she expertly lined her eyes. She'd wanted to do her own face today, not feeling up to the hubbub of the packed make-up room where everyone would see that her eyes were red-rimmed from crying. Ever the professional, though, she was now in costume for the first scene, a polka-dot off-the-shoulder party dress. As she watched the advert for what felt like the hundredth time that day, she expertly swept her long hair into an updo.

One of the props team had put a mini Christmas tree with fairy lights and presents all around it in Catherine's dressing room as a surprise. The gesture had made her want to cry all over again.

After completing the tech run yesterday following the showdown with Madeline, Catherine had returned to her dressing room soaked to the skin but in one piece. Despite her head being all over the place, somehow she'd managed to land in the right place in the water. She'd barely even looked at the shark – she'd had a different predator on her mind.

She'd just finished drying off and was about to head home when Sheena called, summoning her to join Farrah and Helen back in Madeline's office. Madeline stayed quiet as Sheena went through what the two of them had agreed.

'In return for our silence over Madeline's past,' Sheena began, nodding coolly in Madeline's direction, 'there will be a number of significant changes regarding not only tomorrow's live ep but also the future management of the show itself.' Her eyes flashed wickedly as she glanced at the expectant faces of her three friends.

Catherine was ready to throw her arms around her agent, but Sheena was in full flow.

'Jake is out, with immediate effect.'

Helen's eyes widened and Farrah grinned at the news. Catherine smiled, waiting to hear her part in the new plans.

'Amanda is returning, and replacing Jake as *Falcon Bay's* showrunner. We'll be talking to her on the phone in a minute. As Madeline is buying *Heartlands*, there's no contract minefield so Amanda is in charge as of now, and will be responsible for tomorrow's show.'

Madeline's face remained emotionless, as Sheena went on to tell them that Aiden would be fired, that Farrah was to be promoted to his position, and confirmed that Helen would stay too. Almost the whole room was smiling now – this was the best Christmas present any of them could have asked for. Only Catherine, who had not been mentioned, looked worried.

'So that's you all sorted,' Catherine said, genuinely pleased that Amanda was coming back but horribly anxious that no one had mentioned her own future. 'What about me? What happens to Lucy?'

There was a pause, and Sheena looked uncomfortable. Catherine saw what she thought was the faintest hint of a smirk cross Madeline's lips.

But before Sheena could speak, the phone in her hand rang out loudly. She put it on speakerphone and Amanda's disembodied voice spoke out into the room.

'Girls, we'll all be together again tomorrow and I can't wait for that, I've missed you all so much. But the clock is ticking and there's a mess to unpick, so we need to cut straight to the chase. Farrah, I'll be emailing you a breakdown so you can start rewriting tomorrow's episode.'

Catherine's eyes filled with hope. Maybe Lucy Dean would be saved after all.

Amanda continued, 'Farrah, you need to give Lucy several key monologues designed to get the nation behind her, before Honey Hunter arrives after the last ad break.'

Catherine's spirits lifted. 'So what happens to me after Honey arrives? Does she still push me into the water, or not?'

'Catherine…' Amanda's voice echoed bodilessly from the phone. 'As much as it pains me to say this,' she said hesitantly, 'at this late hour, having promised the audience that Lucy Dean will die on Christmas Day, we can't just abandon that storyline altogether. If we do, viewers will turn off and we'll all be left with no show to run.'

Catherine's eyes widened with anger. 'Oh that's great – so you all get to live happily ever after while I'm eaten by a fucking shark. Thanks very much!' For the first time, she totally lost her composure. She turned to Sheena and screamed at her. 'I expected better from you!'

Sheena put her hand up, desperately trying to stop Catherine from saying anything that might derail her plans. 'Stay calm, please, Catherine. You haven't heard what else Amanda has to say.'

Catherine gulped and stared up at the ceiling, trying to stop the tears that were welling in her eyes from pouring down her face at this betrayal by her closest friends.

'But…' Amanda's voice rang out again. 'We've come up with the best solution possible to avoid it.'

Madeline didn't take her eyes off Catherine, who was now looking at Sheena suspiciously.

Through the speakerphone, Amanda said, 'We're going to let the audience decide Lucy's fate.'

'What does that mean?' Catherine immediately shot back, utterly confused.

'In addition to your extra monologues, Farrah will be rewriting the last five minutes of the show, to give us two alternative endings. The viewers will decide which one they want to happen with a live text vote that will only close in the final ad break.'

Catherine spun round to Sheena. 'And you agreed to this?' she said, her voice trembling.

Sheena stepped towards her and placed a hand on her shoulder. 'Listen, you're in shock right now, but this is a great idea.'

Farrah and Helen nodded.

'Think about it,' Farrah offered. 'The viewers love you

and Lucy – there's no way they'll vote to kill you, not now it's in their hands.'

Catherine looked to Sheena for reassurance as Madeline continued to play it cool.

'And with this new episode playing to all your strengths,' Amanda continued, 'the audience will be with you – we are sure of it.'

As much as Helen didn't want to appear to be onside with anything Madeline had had a hand in, she agreed. 'If we could go back in time,' she said, glaring at Madeline, then turning back to Catherine, 'we'd never have seen you put in this position. But Amanda's right, the whole world is tuning in to see if Lucy Dean will really be killed by a shark. We can't totally remove the jeopardy, or the whole show will sink, but by putting it in their hands, we can give them the choice. So when *they* choose you to stay – which we know they will – there won't be a backlash and everything can go back to normal.'

Catherine's eyes were still full of tears. 'But what if they don't choose to save me?' she asked quietly.

Before Sheena could answer, Madeline, who could bite her tongue no longer, broke her silence.

'It's very simple. You keep telling us that you're the most popular character on this show. *So*, if you're right and the audience *are* with you, they'll vote to save you. And if you're wrong, they won't.' A smile crossed her luscious red lips.

Catherine felt like she'd been punched in the stomach. This really was personal; Madeline's total lack of empathy and the way she was relishing this was evil.

Sheena eyed Madeline, wondering whether to put her

in her place again, but decided to throw her energy into boosting Catherine instead. 'It will work, Catherine. You've been here for forty years – they'll vote for you.' She looked at Farrah and Helen, who both nodded. But Catherine was not so sure.

And now here she was, just an hour away from her moment of truth, unable to tear her eyes away from the TV advert for the show, even though it made her want to vomit.

On the screen, a sweeping aerial shot showed off the stunning bay, with the shadow of a shark swimming through its wintry sea and a voiceover dripping with melodrama. 'Will it be a merry Christmas for Lucy? In just an hour's time, we'll be airing *Falcon Bay*'s historic fortieth anniversary episode, broadcast live from the set. And *you* get to decide *whether Lucy Dean lives or dies* with our interactive text vote. Her fate is in your hands.'

Grabbing the remote, Catherine switched it to mute, and took a deep breath. She reminded herself she had been a 'dead soap star walking' on her way into Madeline's office; at least now she had a chance. And if the audience decided to save her, then there could be no greater vindication.

She finished her make-up by adding a touch of Dior Sugar and Spice blush to her cheekbones and unmuted the TV.

Another advert was on, with the announcer explaining the rules of the vote as the numbers flashed up on screen. 'Text "Lucy Lives" to keep Lucy Dean in the show. Text "Lucy Dies" to let the shark have its way,' the voiceover said, sending another shiver down her spine.

51

In the bed in which just a few days ago he'd felt like the king of the world lay the forlorn figure of Jake Monroe. The silk sheets still smelled of Honey's perfume and splashes of alcohol. He hadn't been able to face going home – it contained too many reminders of Amanda, the last person he wanted to think about. Conniving, scheming bitch that she was.

He'd seen Ross Owen blabbering away over Twitter this morning about his 'parting of the ways' with *Falcon Bay*, making it very clear with use of punctuation that Jake had not walked but had been sacked. He made a mental note to add Ross to his hit list. When this was all over, he'd come back for him. He'd come back for all of them. Especially Amanda.

He still wasn't sure how she'd done it, but his best guess was that she and her coven of witches had found something to use against Madeline, forcing her hand. He wasn't excusing Madeline by any means, she would also be going on his list, but he knew she despised all of them, so she was clearly being steered. There was no way she'd have wanted to give

Catherine a chance to survive, so whatever it was they had on her must be bad.

A phone call to Aiden, also turfed out on his arse, had made him feel a bit better. He'd decided to tell Aiden that he now thought Farrah had set him up for his arrest and had also been involved in his exit from the show. It had surprised him that Aiden had never seemed to guess about Farrah and the hotel incident; once Aiden had told him she'd 'managed to hide in the bathroom' it was obvious to Jake what she'd done. Whilst he might have been too dopey, or maybe just too high, to notice her vendetta back then, by the time Jake had got off the phone with him, he was sure Aiden had started his own list too – with Farrah's name firmly at the top.

As Jake slumped back on the bed, he desperately tried to work out what the witches had unearthed that was so bad they'd used it to gain control. If he'd been thinking straight when Madeline had summoned him into her office late last night, about to turn his world upside down, he'd have tried to find it out for himself. But, like a lamb to the slaughter, he'd arrived worried he was about to let Madeline down. As a waft of Honey's perfume hit him again, he closed his eyes and went over their meeting in his head.

He'd got there just before midnight. Madeline, who was standing in the breeze on her balcony above the angry sea, looked like she'd had quite a bit to drink from the way her body was gently swaying, which was unlike her. The waves crashing against the cliff face below were so loud, she hadn't heard him coming in.

He approached her with Honey's Post-it in his hand. 'We've got problems,' he announced as he reached the balcony.

'More than you know,' Madeline replied, turning to him, ashen-faced and yet somehow still utterly gorgeous.

Determined to get his bad news out of the way before whatever crisis Madeline was going to land him with, he pushed on. 'Honey's gone,' he said, handing Madeline the note.

Instead of the shocked reaction he'd been expecting, she simply screwed the note up and tossed it into the sea.

'Have you told anyone else?'

'Of course not.'

'Well don't. Not even production.'

She was definitely drunk, he thought. Wondering if she was taking in what he'd said, he decided to press the problem home again.

'But casting will have to replace her or we'll have no one for the finale,' he said. 'God knows who Helen can find at this late hour that the audience won't be disappointed in. The whole world is expecting Honey.'

'Don't worry about it, it's not your problem,' she said with unnerving calmness.

'Of course it's my problem,' he snapped, suddenly very tired. 'Everything that happens here is my problem.'

Madeline reached for the glass next to her and took a sip. 'Sorry, Jake, I meant to say it's not your problem *any more*.'

Jake stared at her, dumbstruck. Did she mean...?

'I can't go into it now, because frankly there just isn't time,' she said, the wind blowing her hair wildly as she gazed out at the sea. 'But things are not working out with you in charge. People are unhappy and an unhappy ship is not what we need on a soap set on the sea.'

As her words sank in, Jake was so stunned, it was all he could manage to utter a few words loud enough that she could hear them over the waves.

'What? Why?'

'Let's just say I picked the wrong half of the husband-and-wife team and leave it at that,' Madeline said casually. 'As you would expect, in accordance with protocol, your office has already been cleared out and your personal belongings have already been sent to your house. Security are waiting downstairs to revoke your pass and escort you off the premises.'

Jake was almost choking now. His heart was racing so fast, he thought he might be about to have a stroke.

Madeline turned towards him and patted his cold cheek rather hard. 'Don't worry, Jake, you'll get a hefty severance package, and publicly we're calling it a "parting of ways".'

Finally some words stumbled out of his mouth. 'But... I don't want... to part.'

But Madeline just shrugged and turned back away.

And there it was. What he'd done to so many on *Falcon Bay* had just been done to him.

Moments later, Jake had been frogmarched out of the building.

Another waft of Honey's scent from the silk sheets brought him back into the present.

'Jake,' he said to himself out loud – he'd always been fond of talking about himself in the third person – 'you will not let these ruthless women get the better of you. They have no idea who they're dealing with, but they soon will.' He jumped out of the bed, pulled on his clothes and made his way outside to his car.

52

Farrah was less than an hour away from calling 'Action' on her first ever live episode. In TV, this was as big as it got. Amanda walked over to where she was standing by the camera. There was no need for words; each understood exactly how the other was feeling. It was time to board this rollercoaster, with neither of them knowing how the ride would end.

In the air above them, Christmas carols were playing through the speakers, but the mood on set was far from celebratory; everyone was on edge.

Up on a specially built VIP platform, the world's press, including Ross Owen, were looking down, waiting to witness television history as Farrah made the short walk from the camera to her director's chair.

As Amanda watched her take her seat, not even the nerves of being live, the uncertainty over Catherine's fate nor the chill wind gusting off the gloomy sea could dull the warm feeling of pride she felt at the sight of her friend taking the helm. It had been a whirlwind twenty-four hours, but Amanda and

Olivia had made it to St Augustine's from the *Heartlands* set without so much as a backwards glance. Looking around at Lucy Dean's beach bar set and all the cast and crew dotted across the deck and the sand, Amanda was unquestionably back where she belonged.

After everything that had happened, she'd thought she might never see Falcon Bay again. During her brief stint at *Heartlands* she'd put everything she had into helping them craft their live episode, which would be broadcast at any moment. She felt incredibly guilty about walking out on them in their own most nerve-wracking hour, but when she'd got the call from Madeline last evening, she'd not hesitated. Her soap family needed her, and her talent had finally been recognized at the highest levels. *Falcon Bay* was where her heart lay. As Dorothy once said to Toto, there was no place like home.

Suddenly strong arms circled her waist and soft lips kissed her cheek.

'How's my girl doing?' Dan said softly as he held her, his body hot against her cold, windblown skin.

She turned to face him, conscious that the whole set was watching, and the press too. Not only was she still officially married to Jake, but she had also been parachuted back into the job he'd just been sacked from.

'She's doing well and you've played a big part in that,' she said. 'God, I've missed you – you've no idea how much.' She flashed him a big smile. 'And so has Olivia.' She nodded in the direction of the warm production office, where Olivia was being cooed over by one of the admin staff. 'This is the best Christmas present either of us could have asked for.'

Looking deep into her eyes, Dan grinned. 'Well that's good, because I've got turkey, wine and a whole gang of cuddly toys waiting for the two of you back at mine.'

Amanda wrapped her arms tightly around him, leaned in closer and kissed him on the lips. She couldn't have cared less who saw it.

Catherine smiled as she watched Amanda and Dan embrace from her place further down the set. She loved happy endings and as she stood on her mark waiting for Farrah to call action, she wondered whether, if she survived tonight's vote, she would get her own. She'd had to work even harder than usual to prepare for this live episode. She always learned her lines word perfect, but because the script had two endings, she'd had to use all of her skillset to bank them in different parts of her brain. She just prayed she'd only be saying the lines of the scene that would let her live.

Seconds away from Farrah calling action, Catherine put her self-doubt to one side. This was live TV beamed around the globe and whatever her fate was to be, the fans who'd been with her for four decades deserved the very best she could give them. She was determined that whatever the ending, she would not let them down.

From her position by the monitors, Sheena was keeping a close eye on Catherine.

Farrah and Amanda also caught her gaze and looked up at her, smiling hopefully.

Unlike her friends, Helen was neither calm nor excited – she was panicking. Madeline Kane had just summoned her to the corridor outside the production office, where she informed her that Honey Hunter would not be appearing in the final scenes. In less than an hour's time, an unnamed actress would be revealed as the show's new super bitch instead. Clearly Farrah and Amanda didn't know; if they did, they'd have been as freaked out as she was.

As if reading her mind, Madeline spoke. 'Honey not being here is too long a story to tell everyone else when we're seconds from going on air,' she said firmly. 'I'll deal with the fallout – if there is any – after the show, but in the meantime please rest assured that we have a fine actress replacing her. The show must go on.'

Helen was desperate to know who this actress was, but prising information out of Madeline was like getting blood out of a stone at the best of times. With just seconds to go till they were live, Helen tried a different route.

'We won't be insured if she doesn't sign a contract, so whoever she is, will you at least please have her do that, and get it back to me. I'll email you a standard one-episode release for her now and we'll sort the rest out tomorrow,' she called down the corridor as Madeline strode off with purpose.

'I'll personally stand over her while she does so,' Madeline replied without looking back.

Knowing that everyone in the business would assume she had cast whoever turned up on screen in those final scenes, Helen suddenly couldn't resist asking for more reassurance. 'Just tell me she's good?' she called out, this time with a touch of alarm in her voice.

Madeline stopped and turned back towards her.

'Helen,' she said, with total confidence in her voice, 'she's the absolute best. I pinky promise.' And with that, she disappeared down another corridor.

53

A taxi pulled into Mulholland Drive in Los Angeles and Honey emerged wearing a simple lounge suit and carrying only the smallest piece of hand luggage. She tilted her beautiful face, entirely free of make-up, and gazed up at the familiar facade of her old rehab facility. It would be her home once more for however long it took to conquer her demons, and she was glad to be here. She was thousands of miles from her retreat on Lake Geneva and her stay here would not be pleasant, she was well aware of that, but she'd get through it. And once she had, she would return to her sanctuary and pick up her life again, a life untarnished by the chaos of fame and alcohol.

A nurse opened the gate and accompanied her to reception, where a door opened and Dr Andrew Durand appeared. 'Welcome once more,' he said.

Honey smiled. It was more than a decade since she'd last been within these walls. Her time here had been hellish and she'd always imagined that if she were ever obliged to come back, it would be under duress and with a great deal of kicking and screaming. But now she saw it for the haven it really was.

'I'm so happy to be back,' she said as the nurse led her to her room. Just a few months, Honey reassured herself as she placed her things in the sparse space and heard the key turn in the lock, then she'd be well again and ready to go home.

Even in tracksuit pants and a shapeless top, Honey was still beautiful; Dr Durand was in no doubt about that. The day she'd been released all those years ago had been one of the worst he could remember and there hadn't been a day since when he hadn't thought of her. At one point, she'd been off the radar for so long, he'd had to make do with watching and rewatching all her old movies daily, as well as his nightly routine of masturbating to her Christmas *Playboy* centrefold. Then, suddenly, boom, his Google alerts had gone crazy – thanks to *Falcon Bay*, she was everywhere.

As her star rose once more, despite his doctor's oath to do no harm, he hoped fervently that Honey wouldn't be able to cope and that she would turn to drink again, knowing that if she did, she'd end up back here, where he'd been waiting for her all this time.

As he walked up to the room she was in, peered through the glass and saw her resting on the bed, he made a promise to the devil himself that this time he'd never let her go.

54

Catherine was by the water's edge, waiting for the word. She'd managed to push her spiralling thoughts to one side. The pro was back. She was going to nail this scene and every scene that followed; she was going to fight to save Lucy Dean's life with everything she had.

Amanda was on the podium that gave her a view of the entire set. As she watched the skilfully choreographed dance of cameras happening beneath her, she made every effort not to show the nerves that were rippling through her. She had to stay calm and be everybody's rock.

Helen had popped into the VIP area to get a drink. This casting issue was really getting to her and she needed something to take the edge off. A waiter from whom she'd previously taken more than a glass of champagne tried to catch her eye, but for once she wasn't in the mood for that. She slipped behind the bar to help herself.

A few feet away, Ross Owen caught sight of her and grinned. 'Doing a bit of moonlighting, are we?' He laughed at his own joke as Helen raised a glass to him and mouthed 'prick' under her breath.

Undeterred, he headed towards her.

'So what do you reckon? Lucy Dean – will they kill her or save her?'

For him it was all part of the day's fun: just another soap character facing the axe. But for Helen and all the girls, if the audience went against Catherine, today would mark the end of an era. Luckily, before she had to answer, Farrah's strong and confident voice rang out.

'And action.'

On screens around the world, in sitting rooms where Christmas tree lights flickered and sweet wrappers crinkled, *Falcon Bay* viewers saw Lucy Dean appear on its famous shoreline. The camera followed her across the beach, her heels crunching on the walkway wreathed in Christmas lights. She had a calmness about her which proved what a good actress Catherine Belle was, because her insides were shaking like jelly.

Lucy Dean walks into her world famous beachside bar, weary but happy. The bar is packed with the residents of Falcon Bay. Lucy Dean takes them in: these neighbours of hers, these people she'd had run-ins with, these people she'd loved and hated. The camera moves from face to face and settles on Lucy, now behind the bar. Lucy Dean looks straight into the lens.

LUCY DEAN: Merry Christmas, to each and every one of you.

To the audiences at home, it felt like she was addressing them personally and many raised a toast to her. As the cameras pulled back to reveal everybody in The Cove cheering, pulling crackers and toasting each other, Lucy waited for the hubbub to die down then finished her opening speech.

LUCY DEAN: We can never know how many Christmases we have left, so let's make it a good one.

The live feed cut from the packed bar to some pre-recorded exterior scenes.

'Lucy Lives' and 'Lucy Dies' flashed up, with numbers for voters to text. The countdown had begun.

On screen, Lucy Dean was reaching out to local mechanic, Tyson.

Tyson was Lucy's husband for a brief stint ten years ago until he cheated on her with her best friend. Nobody has seen him in weeks. Lucy Dean has just found him alone on the beach.

LUCY DEAN: Once, long ago, you broke my heart in two. But no one should be on their own at Christmas.

She gives his shoulder a sympathetic squeeze, and takes him back to the bar

TYSON: Lucy, you're an angel. God will pay you back when he sees you.

Tyson has tears in his eyes. Lucy Dean gives a rueful smile

LUCY DEAN: I hope I won't be seeing God for a long while yet.

Throughout this whole scene, the 'Lucy Lives' and 'Lucy Dies' phone numbers remained on screen.

Farrah cut to a wide camera crane shot which panned over the cove and revealed that a shark was swimming towards Falcon Bay's dockside. The theme tune kicked in, the cameras stopped rolling and she called, 'Cut!' It was the adverts. Farrah let out a deep breath that she hadn't realized she'd been holding.

Catherine emerged from the bar and began to make her way across the sand to the dockside. Knowing they were in an advert break, Sheena rushed over from where she was standing to reach her. Usually this would be the ultimate in unprofessionalism, but these were not usual times.

'You're killing it,' Sheena said in her most positive and supportive voice. Realizing that she could have chosen her words better, she followed up with, 'I'm so proud of you.'

Catherine gripped her hand. 'How's the vote looking?' She'd sworn to herself that she wouldn't ask, but the words came tumbling out anyway.

Sheena looked her deep in the eyes. 'We won't know until it's in,' she said, 'but with the performance you're giving today, I can't believe anyone would vote to kill Lucy. It's Christmas, the season of generosity, and they love you. I'm sure it's going to be fine.'

'Catherine!' yelled Farrah from her position. 'One minute to go. We need you on the launch decking for the stand-off with your daughter. We've got a pre-recorded scene at the marina first, but we're cutting that in from a live shot of you.'

Catherine nodded and looked at her agent once more before walking over to the marina. There should have been at least some indication of which way the vote was going by now, she thought, as a camera assistant helped her onto the decking and to her mark. If she'd had an overwhelming majority, Sheena would have tipped her off. The live or die vote was obviously going to go to the wire. She could feel it in her heart, which was beating as loud as a drum.

Helen, meanwhile, was leading a bunch of extras out of the bar as crew were scurrying around getting ready to film the final scene.

Amanda appeared. 'Where's Honey, our bitch?' she asked Helen.

Helen gestured for a crew member to take over, then took Amanda to one side. 'Look, I didn't want to panic you, so don't go mad...'

Amanda's face went white.

'Honey is a no-show.'

'Oh my God!' Amanda gasped. 'How could you not tell me?'

Helen grabbed her by the shoulders. 'Exactly for this reason.

Hold yourself together,' she said. Amanda was shaking now, looking as if she might faint.

'Madeline has recast the role.'

Amanda's eyes widened even further.

'I know, don't even say it.' Helen shook her head in disbelief.

'Who is it?' Amanda asked breathlessly.

Helen was saved from a full-blown awkward conversation by Farrah calling 'Action'. 'We'll find out in about ten minutes,' she whispered, throwing her hands in the air to show Amanda that even she didn't know. Amanda looked like she'd been tasered.

55

Backstage, in the wardrobe department, standing before the full-length mirror, was Madeline Kane. She was wearing the sexiest dress they had in stock. It looked remarkably like the one she'd worn to Paris, and, while not a real Chanel like hers, its skin-tight red fabric looked fabulous clinging to her killer curves.

Wardrobe assistant Brad stood back in appreciation. Madeline, with her jet-black hair and flawless pearl-like skin was the fiercest woman who'd ever been in there, and that was saying something.

'Now I just need some heels,' Madeline said, completing her make-up with a slather of fire-engine-red Dior Addict lip gloss before scanning the vast shoe area. 'Those. There...' She pointed at some red stilettos high up on a shelf on their own.

'But—' Brad began.

Madeline held up a hand to silence him. 'I want those,' she said, climbing the stepladder herself to retrieve them.

Brad tried again to voice his objections, but Madeline cut

him off. 'You can go now. I'm sure you're needed somewhere,' she said.

As she sat down to put the shoes on, she noticed that a label inside them said 'Lucy Dean'.

'Perfect.' She smiled, then, in Lucy's heels, jumped in the buggy and zoomed along the corridor towards the set.

With the wind blowing her hair as she gathered speed towards the lot, she mused on how far she'd come in the years since she'd first travelled down these corridors. Even after last night's drama, it really did feel like she had it all, and yet in her gorgeous dress and Lucy Dean's high heels, she still wanted more.

56

Cameras followed as Lucy Dean paced at the edge of the waterside decking. Nearby, a couple of small boats were gently rocking on their moorings. Beyond her field of vision but on camera for the viewers at home, the shark's fin loomed ever closer, appearing to have singled out its prey without her having a clue as to its presence.

Earlier in the broadcast, Lucy Dean had received a text from an unknown number:

> Meet me at the dock for a very special
> Christmas present. T

Hoping that the 'T' was Tom, her estranged lover who hadn't been seen since the summer episodes but with whom she was still desperately in love, Lucy had fled the packed bar and all its Yuletide celebrations and rushed to the dockside.

As this was the last scene before the ad break that would

lead to the final part of the episode, Catherine knew that as soon as Farrah yelled 'Cut', she would learn of her fate.

The final scene was to open in the same way regardless of what the fans had decided. A boat would dock and Lucy Dean would come face to face with her long-lost daughter – the 'T' being for Tanya. There would be an exchange of harsh words as the estranged mother and daughter let rip with explosive dialogue that covered their difficult backstory, and this would culminate in Tanya slapping her mother, who would then plunge into the water. The shark would sense its prey and come for her.

If the audience voted to save her, Tyson, who'd followed her from the bar and wanted to rekindle their relationship, would dive into the sea to save her. He would sacrifice his life for Lucy's.

If the audience voted to kill Lucy Dean, there would be no heroic saviour. The shark would have his Christmas dinner and Lucy Dean would never leave the sea again.

As Catherine ran over both sets of dialogue in her head, she hoped Honey wouldn't hit her too hard; she'd only rehearsed with the stand-in and that was never the same. As she listened to the screaming of the gulls and the lapping of the waves and watched the shark's menacing fin circle the hidden tank, she knew there was nothing more she could do. Any second now the results would be in and whatever they were, she was determined to give her all to the fate the audience had chosen for her.

Farrah, who'd wanted to free up as much of the beach and sea as possible for drone shots, had moved the monitors and non-shooting crew into The Cove for the final scene, which meant she and Sheena were inside with Amanda when the results arrived on her phone. She opened the message, then turned the screen for them both to see.

Standing up, Sheena looked out at the forlorn figure of her client and friend standing hopefully on the water's edge.

'Let me tell her, please.'

57

In the press area overlooking the set, Helen and Ross both put down their phones as the voting figures flashed up on the monitors.

LUCY LIVES – 49.1 PER CENT
LUCY DIES – 50.9 PER CENT

A murmur of surprise rippled through the press pack. No one had really been expecting this.

Ross turned to Helen with an audio recorder in hand, wanting a quote, but she walked away, too shocked to speak.

Catherine was standing in the cold sea breeze on the dockside. When she spotted Sheena approaching, she called out.

'Is it good?'

As she continued the sad walk towards her friend, Sheena grimly shook her head.

'There was less than one per cent in the vote. I'm so sorry. No one can believe it.'

Deep down, Catherine had sensed this was coming, but

now the news had actually arrived, she couldn't quite take it in.

Sheena pulled her into a deep hug, being careful not to smudge any of her make-up, and spoke softly into her ear. 'Remember, we've planned for this,' she said with as much enthusiasm as she could muster. 'This is not the end, it's just a new beginning.' She pulled back and looked Catherine direct in the eyes to really make sure she understood the message.

With tears flooding, Catherine nodded.

Sheena squeezed her hand. 'It's time to end this chapter. Knock 'em dead, baby,' she said. Knowing she had to clear the shot as they were coming back from the ad break, she gave her the best smile she could manage.

Catherine nodded again, still unable to find any words.

Sheena raced back to the shadows of The Cove as Catherine returned to her mark. The vote was in, the decision made. Lucy Dean was all but dead. To think that it had been so close choked her, knowing that just a handful more votes would have saved her.

In a few minutes' time she'd be inside the reinforced inner tank in the cold sea, screaming as camera trickery made it look like the shark was eating her. Then, when titles rolled, Catherine Belle's forty years on *Falcon Bay* would come to an end, and Lucy Dean would be no more, consigned to soap opera history. Just like she would be.

'Action!' Farrah shouted solemnly from the beach bar door.

Almost on autopilot now, Catherine swayed gently on the dockside as she stared out to sea. The eyes of the world were on her, eagerly awaiting Lucy Dean's final moments.

In the distance the sound of a motorboat heading towards the bay began to get louder, and Catherine could just make out the shadow of the vessel she believed was bringing Honey Hunter to begin her reign as Tanya Dean. Lucy's long-lost daughter; the new leading lady of *Falcon Bay*.

Online chatter exploded as fans all over the world live-tweeted while they watched. WhatsApp, Facebook and Instagram were all on fire as audiences everywhere kept up a running commentary on Lucy's final showdown. Exact viewing figures would only be available after the broadcast, but up in the gallery Ross, who'd been told by his news desk that at least 160 million viewers were currently tuned in, had already started working on the front cover of tomorrow's *Herald*. 'She's Dead! *Falcon Bay* Becomes the Most Watched Soap in TV History' was to be his headline.

The motorboat was now near enough that the outline of a female figure could be seen standing on its deck. Catherine desperately tried to push her sense of rejection deep down and concentrate on giving Honey the best scene she had in her. It wasn't Honey's fault, she reasoned, and she was determined to give the new queen of *Falcon Bay* her blessing, even though it was breaking her heart.

In living rooms around the globe, fans were mesmerized by Catherine's shocked face as the shadowy figure on the boat finally reached the dockside.

For once, she wasn't acting.

As a familiar shoe stepped onto the dock beside her, her eyes widened in astonishment.

In the temporary control room in The Cove bar, Farrah called out, 'What the fuck?'

'Oh my God,' Helen gasped, 'she's cast herself.'

'Fucking hell!' Sheena breathed, beginning to suspect that Madeline's humiliation of Catherine was far from over.

'Madeline Kane is our new soap bitch?' cried Amanda in absolute horror.

'Shall I cut?' a frantic Farrah asked, looking around for other scenes to use but knowing she had none.

'There's nowhere to cut to. We're still live – we've got to finish this scene,' Amanda gabbled, pacing around the monitors.

'Cameras 3 and 4, pull back to a wide shot,' Farrah instructed down her radio, to buy them a few seconds more time.

'Will she even know the lines?' Amanda raged.

'Oh, she'll know them,' Helen said drily. 'She's done this before, remember.'

Sheena was watching intently as Madeline stepped resplendently towards Catherine. As much as she hated her, she could see the brilliance of what Madeline had done by taking the role herself. It was a horribly impressive move.

'She was pretty good, back in the day.' Helen placed a hand on a still-panicked Amanda's shoulder. 'And Catherine's a pro; she'll handle her.'

Amanda and Farrah looked at each other and after a tiny pause, Farrah radioed the cameras to change position. Both actresses would take this as the signal for them to begin the final scene's dialogue.

Sheena poured herself and the others glasses of champagne while they all watched Madeline's lip-glossed smirk on the monitor.

'We've got to hand it to her,' she said, with grudging admiration in her voice. 'We thought we'd won, when in fact Madeline had. And now, as the "star" of the show as well as the owner, there's no way to get rid of her.'

She looked Amanda and Helen in the eyes, raised her glass to her lips, and downed it. 'Good luck with your new leading lady, girls – you're gonna need it.' She set her glass down, ready to go and collect Catherine when the scene ended. 'Because that is one ruthless woman.'

58

The exhilaration that pumped through Madeline's veins as she stepped off the boat and into the world's gaze once more was off the scale. Like Norma Desmond, she thought to herself, *I've come home at last*. The sight of Catherine's horrified expression was an additional boost; it could have given Munch's *The Scream* a run for its money. Though to be fair, there was no way Catherine could have seen this coming; not even Madeline had imagined events would take this extraordinary turn.

Her thirst for revenge had been quenched the moment she'd arrived back on this lot as the new queen of her old show. She'd originally just intended to return *Falcon Bay* to its number one position, take the credit and conquer her demons by knowing that she now owned the very place that had cast her aside. Then she would sell the network on for a profit and return to Louisiana with Chad, where, having proved she knew what she was doing, she'd buy a bigger network and create her own soap from scratch. That was to have been her third and final fresh start, but everything had changed when she'd found out that it was Catherine Belle and not a gang of long-gone executives who was behind her being kicked to the kerb like an unwanted dog.

Once she'd discovered the truth, she knew she could not rest until Catherine had been made to understand exactly what that had felt like. She would put Catherine in that same position; she would make her feel similarly helpless, abandoned, discarded and lost. For that to happen, Lucy Dean had to die.

Although things hadn't gone *exactly* the way she'd planned, thanks to Sheena and her Columbo act, the result had still been the same. Even with the chance of an audience vote to save her, Catherine Belle was now just moments away from soap extinction. The unexpected cherry on top of Madeline's delicious revenge sundae had appeared out of the blue when boozy Honey Hunter had dropped off the radar at the last minute. The flash of Madeline's genius response had been immediate and blinding. She would cast herself as *Falcon Bay*'s new bitch. Where once she had played Lucy's son, she would now play her long-lost daughter, a daughter who would slap her to her death and usurp her place, making the circle of soap life complete.

It was so utterly brilliant that Madeline was struggling to keep the smile off her flawless face as the cameras rolled on her first scene, with the whole world watching.

TANYA DEAN: Hello, Mother. It's been a long time.

Madeline was line-perfect. Catherine stood open-mouthed.

From the moment that one of Lucy Dean's very own high heels, squeezed onto Madeline's foot, had touched the pier, it took only a few seconds for Catherine to realize just how clever her plan was. Lucy Dean would be dead, and with Madeline as the new star of the show – with the future of *Falcon Bay* in her hands both on screen and off – her secret would be safe.

Although Catherine was thrown, Madeline had clearly learned the script and was intending to go for it. So, as bizarre as this was, they were live on televisions around the world and Catherine knew that somehow she must carry on.

LUCY DEAN: Why are you here?

TANYA DEAN: Because you ruined my life and now I'm back to ruin yours. I'm the one behind Tate Holdings.

Madeline sneered, relishing every word.

Lucy Dean registered her shock as Tanya referenced a long-term storyline which involved a mysterious business owner buying up most of the bay, including the land beneath Lucy's beach bar. This was now revealed to be her own daughter's work.

As she acted, Catherine dramatically turned away from Madeline so that she could take one last look at the place she'd lived for so many years: this beautiful fictional bay that had been her only home. Suddenly, something in her shifted. Catherine wasn't ready to go. Yes, they were live and in the globe's gaze, but hanging on to all this was worth one last attempt to reach deep inside Madeline's scarred heart, like she'd tried last night when she'd discovered what she'd unwittingly done all those years ago.

LUCY DEAN: You're wrong, I always loved you.

Madeline was thrown. This wasn't the script. Catherine had gone rogue. Flustered, she continued with her next line as written.

TANYA DEAN: You can argue all you want, it won't change anything. I now own everything in this bay, including your beloved bar. Your time here is over.

Madeline postured like an evil goddess and prepared to unleash the slap in the script that would commence their tussle and culminate in Lucy falling into the water where the shark was waiting.

In the gallery, Farrah, Helen and Sheena all looked at each other helplessly as the two women hovered by the edge of the decking.

'Catherine's lost it. I think we should cut,' said a panicking Farrah.

Amanda looked to Sheena for help.

'Trust her,' Sheena said, her eyes glued to the monitors. 'She'll bring it home somehow. Stay on her.'

Reluctantly, Amanda gestured for Farrah to continue to

shoot. They all held their breath as the crew, the cast and the whole world waited for Lucy Dean's next words.

LUCY DEAN: I don't care about you owning everything. I understand why you wanted revenge on me, but please hear what I'm saying – from my heart, as the only mother you've ever known. I'm sorry. Please forgive me.

A shiver ran through Madeline's very core. These were the words she'd been longing to hear for years; words she'd always wanted to believe. She paused. The cameras zoomed in on her face, showing the uncertainty in her eyes.

Around the world, fans were on the edges of their seats. Even social media feeds, which had reacted very negatively to Honey Hunter having been replaced by this unknown actress, were now onside. People were raving about the chemistry between the two women to the point that there was now a surge of commenters saying they no longer wanted Lucy to die because they were desperate to see them on screen together again.

In the gallery, Sheena urged Amanda to update Madeline about this development via her earpiece. 'Appeal to her vanity,' she pleaded. 'Tell her how much the public are loving the two of them; tell her that they want Lucy to stay.'

Amanda spoke down the mic channel directly into Madeline's ear. 'She doesn't have to die,' she said slowly. 'The audience is going crazy for you on screen together; they don't want it to end. It's your network, Madeline – you can change this.'

The women scrutinized Madeline's face on the screen. As the words reached her, something flickered in her eyes.

Catherine took a step towards Madeline.

`LUCY DEAN:` Please, I am begging you, I want to make things right.

And Catherine was begging for real. Yes, she was begging for Lucy's life, but she was also begging for absolution for herself. She was begging Madeline to believe that if she'd known she was a victim of Ed Nichols, if she'd known she was born in the wrong body, she would have helped her and not had her fired.

Madeline continued to stare at her. Was it true – was Catherine really sorry? Had she really not known? Was Amanda right – should she change the ending and try to start afresh? So many conflicting emotions ran through her head as the cameras whizzed around the two of them, capturing the shark's fin circling in the water about a hundred feet from where they were standing.

Up in the gallery, all four women looked at the clock then back at the monitors.

'We're going to fall off air,' said Helen, manically running her hands through her hair.

'Call upstairs,' Amanda said. 'Tell them we might run over but they must keep us on.' Then she turned to Farrah and made a decision that she knew could affect her whole career.

'Keep rolling,' she said.

Out on the dock a storm appeared out of nowhere. Heavy clouds began to dump torrential rain onto the bay, soaking Madeline and Catherine, both of whom remained locked in position.

Catherine knew they were running out of airtime, and decided to prompt Madeline one last time.

LUCY DEAN: Make a decision before it's too late!

As the well-meaning words left Catherine's mouth, all Madeline's thoughts of reconciliation were replaced with rage. This was nothing more than Catherine trying to save her job. She clearly didn't mean those sorrys she'd uttered; she was just trying to cling onto the life she'd once robbed Madeline of. Well, it was too late. Catherine had shown her true hand and now Madeline was ready to deliver the fatal blow.

TANYA DEAN: Save your lies!

Madeline spat the words out as the rain continued to pelt them both, plastering their clothes to their skin and ruining their carefully styled hair. She readied herself to deliver the slap that would send Catherine into the protective tank and see the demise of Lucy Dean.

TANYA DEAN: This ends now!

As she lunged to hit Catherine, the heel of one of the

borrowed shoes broke, causing her to lose her balance. Madeline tried to steady herself with her other foot, but the drenched boardwalk caused it to slip, catapulting her whole body towards the water.

In the blink of an eye, before Catherine could even reach out to her, Madeline fell into not only the cold dark waters of the sea but into the actual shark tank, not the protective cage.

Both women shrieked as the waves crashed against the dock, the rain streamed down and Madeline sank into the water. Catherine threw herself to the ground and extended her hand.

In the control room, everyone screamed as the underwater cameras, deep beneath the surface, revealed that Madeline's long red dress was tangled on some rigging. The world watched in appalled fascination as she thrashed and struggled in a frantic attempt to free herself and return to the surface.

Catherine knelt at the dockside, arm stretched out. Alerted by the splashing, the shark turned in their direction. It streaked through the water with its fin looming, gathering pace as it closed in on its prey.

A terrified Madeline finally managed to tear her dress free. She resurfaced, reaching desperately for Catherine.

On screen, the two women's fingers appeared to touch, but it was too late – the shark had wrapped its massive teeth around Madeline's legs and ripped her in half.

A bloodcurdling wail echoed around the bay and down the earpieces of every member of the crew. Viewers around the world screamed as Madeline disappeared from view into the blood-red waters. Catherine fainted and everything went black.

59

Police and press helicopters descended on Falcon Bay within minutes of what would, as intended, go down as the most watched soap episode in history – unfortunately for the most gruesome of reasons.

In the back of an ambulance beside the set, a shivering Catherine Belle, wrapped in a blanket, was being checked over by paramedics. TV news crews were filming her through the open door as her body shook uncontrollably and tears streamed down her face.

'I was so close...' she stammered through chattering teeth. She stretched out her hand as if still reaching for Madeline in the water. 'But then... it had her. Oh my God, that scream...' Her voice was hoarse and barely audible, her words lost to gasping sobs.

Sheena raced over to the ambulance, pushed the news crews away, climbed in and wrapped an arm around Catherine. 'I've got you,' she said, gently guiding Catherine's face away from the prying cameras.

A police officer appeared, causing the press vultures to

disperse a little, and poked his head into the back. 'I'm sorry, Ms Belle, but we'll need to ask you—' he started kindly, but Sheena cut him off.

'Not until she's been to the hospital. Can't you see she's in shock and needs urgent medical treatment?' she said authoritatively, shooing everyone else away and turning to the paramedics. 'Can we please get going,' she said, keeping a tight grip on Catherine with one hand and slamming the door shut with the other.

Amanda stood staring after the ambulance, hugging herself to try and stop the shaking. The rain was still bucketing down, but she was barely aware of how soaked she was. The policeman splashed his way over to her just as a second ambulance drew up and more paramedics filled the set. Brad from wardrobe was sheltering under a gantry and breathing into a paper bag as Helen and Farrah held him upright.

'He became hysterical when Madeline fell into the water,' Amanda explained to the police officer, who was watching him intently. 'He says he tried to warn Madeline that the shoes she took from wardrobe had a faulty heel and were not safe to be worn, but she took them anyway.'

The officer cast a suspicious glance in the direction of Brad, Helen and Farrah. Amanda, sensing which way his mind was travelling, quickly intervened.

'We have CCTV with sound in wardrobe and I can assure you that it will confirm what he has said – this was nothing but a tragic accident,' she said. 'And of course we'll also make available all our footage from the underwater and dockside cameras.

'We need a statement from Ms Belle,' the officer said solemnly.

'I'll make sure all that happens first thing in the morning,' Amanda said.

As the policeman walked away, seemingly mollified, Amanda spotted Ross Owen filming a piece to camera and doing live links as two divers pulled the remains of Madeline Kane from the sea.

Her gut churned and she had to force herself to take several deep breaths to stop herself from vomiting. Cast and crew would be looking to her for leadership and support; she needed to focus on the practicalities and leave the soul-searching for later.

The shark had been steered towards the outer corner of the tank by its handlers and tranquilized, ready to be transported back to the aquarium it had come from.

If Amanda had had her way, the shark would never have been anywhere near Falcon Bay in the first place. But it hadn't been up to her. It was only now, after signing a contract which put her in sole charge if the network owner was absent, that Amanda had full control. *Falcon Bay*'s immediate future was in her hands – and she was determined to make sure nothing could ever put her beloved show in danger again.

As forensics sealed off the area where Madeline had been attacked, Amanda replayed on a continuous loop in her mind the image of a rain-lashed Catherine kneeling on the dock as Madeline's deafening screams filled the air. She'd witnessed the whole ghastly tragedy unfold in close-up on the monitors, had seen every desperate kick of Madeline's legs and grasping reach of her fingers, had watched every nuance in Catherine's face as she reacted to the plight of her nemesis. She had also seen how, at the very last moment, Catherine had very subtly withdrawn her hand from the woman whose revenge on her had veered so disastrously off script.

Suddenly another wailing sound pierced the air. Amanda turned to see a heartbroken Chad Kane being held back by police officers as he tried to reach what was left of his wife. It was distressing to watch, but Amanda had made her decision. There were a number of frames from that footage that would not be going to the police in the morning. Amanda could not bring Madeline Kane back to life, but she would do her damnedest to save Catherine Belle's.

This was going to be a long night.

The siren wailed as the ambulance sped towards St Augustine's tiny St George's Hospital. Both paramedics were in the front, leaving Sheena and Catherine alone in the back.

'Stupid question, but how are you feeling?' Sheena asked gently.

'I think I'm okay,' said Catherine cautiously. 'I just feel sorry for her.'

'Even after everything she did?' Sheena asked.

'Yes. It's tragic the way things had to end tonight,' she said, avoiding Sheena's eyes by looking away.

Sheena paused as Catherine's carefully worded answer percolated in her brain.

'Well,' she said, digging deep to find her old acting skills, trying to hide the shock that washed over her as the true meaning of Catherine's words sank in. 'She was a hell of woman, I'll give her that.'

'Yes, she was,' Catherine said, still looking away, as the ambulance sped onwards.

60

There were just thirty minutes of Christmas Day remaining and Amanda had one last thing to do before she could lock up the production office for the night. Dan was already on his way to collect her, with a sleeping Olivia in the back of his car.

She sat quietly at her desk and swivelled her chair so that she could stare out at the now tranquil moonlit bay. She began thinking about how Madeline's sheer determination to return *Falcon Bay* to the number one slot had worked. For all her faults, it was a shame she wasn't here to enjoy it. Her mind then drifted to Catherine, and the underwater footage. The show meant everything to them, so much so that they had both been willing to kill for it. Sitting here now in the production office, back where she belonged and in the position she'd always wanted, Amanda was troubled to realize that now she too understood why.

Within minutes, she'd typed out what she wanted to say to the world's media to ensure that *Falcon Bay*'s tragic heroine would never be forgotten. She timed it to be released at one minute past midnight on Boxing Day.

December 26th

Press statement from C.I.TV's new head of drama and acting controller, Amanda King. For immediate release.

Following the tragic events of Christmas Day, Falcon Bay will take a month's break.

When Falcon Bay returns, it will be to honour the late Madeline Kane.

It's what she would have wanted. She loved this show to death.

Acknowledgements

First up in the honours list are the actresses who without their trust in me, this book would definitely not exist.

Thank you to the wickedly wonderful Claire King for giving me a chance to slip behind the velvet ropes of the drama world that so few women like me ever get. Without you there is no doubt I'd never have 'made it' – thank you eternally, family forever.

To the darling Beverley Callard, what a privilege it's been to have had your trust in me to steer you through the choppy waters of the soap world and the walls beyond. You never cease to amaze me with your talent, resilience and true kind-heartedness.

To the indestructible Sherrie Hewson, Adele Silva and Gaynor Faye – soap queens who truly shaped my journey in the very early days and who still, almost two decades later, I am proud to call friends.

To the fabulous grand diva, Stephanie Beacham, simply for the honour.

To Patsy Kensit – for the experience.

Big love goes out to Stephanie Waring, Gillian Taylforth, Carol Harrison, Danniella Westbrook, Claire Sweeney, Samantha Giles and Jennie McAlpine for the fun we've had along the way, and the adventures ahead.

I am, if I say so myself, a very determined woman, but it truly took a huge midwifery team to get *Ruthless Women* birthed into the world and I needed stitches! Extra special thanks goes to my agent Jason Bartholomew, who believed in me and *Ruthless Women* way before anyone else did. Tory Lyne-Pirkis and the whole of Midas PR for, as ever, being incredible. The wonderful Laura Palmer, my editor, for understanding the way I write and encouraging me to 'be me' on every page and at my pace and in my style. This might not have been my first time at the rodeo, but with you holding my hand, it's certainly been my favourite. Thank you to the whole team at my wonderful publishing home, Head of Zeus, who have made *Ruthless Women* the best experience of my life. Thank you to Jessie Sullivan, Anna Nightingale and Dan Groenewald for putting your heart and souls into it as well as taking it around the world.

My fellow women in print and media who are always a constant support and inspiration to me, Caroline Waterston, Gemma Aldridge, Julia Davis, Charlotte Seligman, Karen Cross, Sally Morgan, Emma Jones and Alison Phillips – you ladies put the 'pow' into girl power. I am proud of how many years we've been on this journey together and am looking forward to our next chapters! I'd like to thank Gary Jones for being the first person to hire me as a national newspaper columnist, which was a game changer for me as it led me back towards my dream of writing full time, for which I am always grateful.

To my own personal co-stars in the drama that is 'my life', Amanda Beckman and Angela Squire – it's certainly never boring is it?! I couldn't do it without either of you and would never want to.

Let's hear it for the boys, with special thanks to Dermot McNamara, Nicky Johnston, Daniel Cocklin, Luke Smith and Paul Coates for all their hard work on 'Brand Blake'. Also to Dr Aamer Khan and Dr Daniel Wright for keeping my ship 'well-maintained and afloat' and my lovely driver Tony, well for everything really.

A woman like me is nothing without her glam squad, so please take a bow Lesley Reynolds, Moiya Saint, Amanda Bragnoli, Sally O'Neill, Carl Stanley, Cindy Weinert and Chantelle Sheehan – please never leave me – only you know where all the bits and pieces go!

To my friends Caroline & David, Marcy & Casey, Claire & Reece, Nick, Paul and Jon McEwan for being there. To Coleen Nolan & Saira Khan for the loyalty, understanding and love.

And last but definitely not least, a thank you to you – yes you – the person reading this book. Your choice to read *Ruthless Women* means the world to me – I hope you enjoyed it as much as I enjoyed writing it. I really did love creating this 'world'; find me on social media and let me know what you thought!

I'll round off with a final note to my vile English teachers at high school who told me that I 'couldn't write so I shouldn't waste my time trying because even if I did, no one would want to read anything that I'd create'. A career in print journalism, a bestseller and a hit box office play all say that I was right to ignore you. Ha ha!

Lastly, I'd like to add that I was forty years old by the time I started writing professionally, so never let anyone convince you that it's too late to chase your dreams. If you want something badly enough and are willing to put the work in, you will achieve it. So, whatever it is you've always wanted to do and no matter how 'late' in life it seems, please do go for it, we only get one ride on life's merry-go-round – make sure it's everything you want it to be!

Love,
Melanie Blake xxx

LOVED *RUTHLESS WOMEN*?
NOW MEET
THE THUNDER GIRLS!

'A pacy page-turner packed with twists and turns.'
Mail on Sunday

'A thrilling debut – don't miss it.'
Hello!

'A seductive thriller that will have you racing through its pages.'
Woman

Music brought them together.
Chrissie, Roxanne, Carly and Anita are best friends. They are also an eighties pop sensation outselling and out-classing their competition. Until it all comes to an abrupt end. When three of their careers are suddenly over, so is their friendship.

Betrayal tore them apart.
In their three decades apart, breakdowns, bankruptcy, addiction and divorce have plagued their lives. They've been to hell and back, and some are still there.

Thirty years later, can lightning strike twice?
Now their old record label wants the band back together for a huge money-making concert. But the wounds are deep and some need this gig more than others...

AVAILABLE NOW IN EBOOK AND PAPERBACK!

WWW.HEADOFZEUS.COM